# DIME
# A DEMON

## ORDINARY MAGIC – BOOK FIVE

# DIME
# A DEMON
## ORDINARY MAGIC - BOOK FIVE

# DEVON MONK

**Dime a Demon** Copyright © 2019 by Devon Monk

ISBN: 9781939853165

Publisher: Odd House Press
Cover Art: Lou Harper
Interior Design: Odd House Press
Print Design: Indigo Chick Designs

# DEDICATION

*To my family and all those who believe in ordinary magic...*

# CHAPTER 1

I ROLLED over, soft sheets slipping away from my shoulders as I snuggled into my pillow. A heat shifted behind me, the mattress bending beneath another body's weight. A heavy arm slipped around my waist.

"Morning, Myra," Bathin's sleepy grumble rumbled in my ear.

Bathin? No, that wasn't right.

I opened my eyes, blinked. Bathin leaned and kissed the back of my shoulder, his arm tightening to position me fully against him.

"What are you doing in my bed?" I couldn't have invited him. I didn't like him. As a matter of fact, I wanted him to leave Ordinary forever. He was the demon who had taken my sister, Delaney's, soul and wouldn't give it back.

He'd been using her soul to stay in town for over a year, and for over a year, I'd been trying to find a way to get her soul back and throw him out.

But the heat of him behind me, the strength of his body, was tempting, soothing. I might not have invited him here, but my untrustworthy heart didn't want him to leave.

"Bathin?"

He hummed as he placed a kiss in the curve of my shoulder and neck.

I moaned just a little.

"This is a dream, isn't it?" I tried to stop my body from reacting to him. Tried to stick with logic and facts, which had never let me down.

"It could be," he said.

"It must be."

"Must?" His lips pressed gently up my neck, beneath my jaw.

"I don't like you." My shiver betrayed my words, and he chuckled.

"No?"

"No."

He stopped, his mouth near my ear, his breath warm. I still hadn't turned to look at him. Didn't know if I'd be able to look away once I did.

My family gift meant I was always in the right place at the right time. It was handy for living in a town full of vacationing gods, and supernatural creatures, handy for being a police officer here. That gift had never let me down.

But my heart, well, that was another matter. I'd followed my heart instead of my head before. Fallen in love.

And unlike my gift, my heart had been wrong, and then it'd been broken. I knew better than to trust it now.

"This is a dream," I said again.

"Mmmm." His thumb rubbed a small stripe across my stomach.

"I'm dreaming. I know I'm dreaming. You're not really here."

"Good."

"Good?"

"If you're dreaming, and I'm not really here, then you can do anything you want. Anything at all. No one's going to know. This is just a dream."

He pressed another kiss at my temple, then bent to gently bite my earlobe. "It will be our little secret."

I pushed his arm off my waist, twisted quickly, and sat up. The covers didn't tangle with my pajama pants at all, so, yeah, this was a dream.

He was outlandishly handsome, this demon who could choose to look any way he wanted. Of course he'd gone with tall, dark, and devastating. He probably thought those good looks would make me forget what he was really made of: fire, brimstone, and treachery.

"Get out."

"But I'm just a dream," he said with fake innocence. "I'm here because you want me to be."

"This," I waved a hand to indicate the bedroom, fuzzy at the edges, the house that didn't have any lingering scent of the cinnamon rolls I'd baked last night in a gift-induced frenzy, and the blankets that had settled properly around me instead of knotting up my legs, "is a dream. But you're real."

"Real dreamy?" He propped his arms behind his head so his wide, muscled chest and washboard six-pack were on full display. Bathin was not a small individual. He was well over six feet tall, and the width of his shoulders took more than half of the space of my queen-size bed.

Too bad he was a lying jerk.

"Not in the least," I said. "You are invading my dream. Somehow. With your demon tricks."

"I see."

"And you need to stop it."

"My demon tricks?"

"Invading my dream. Go. Leave. Go away."

He smiled, the laugh lines crinkling at the corners of his eyes. He was gorgeous, spread half-naked in my bed. Even though I knew he had somehow found a way to get into my dream just to mess with me, there was a moment—a heartbeat or two—where I wished he wasn't really here. That I could have this dream, *my* dream.

No matter how much I knew it was wrong, I was attracted to him. To what he wanted me to think he was.

A warm breeze stirred the curtains, mixing the warm air with the salty scent of the nearby ocean.

It was September, and the beach-going swarms of tourists had been thinning even though the weather was still mild. A lot of the gods had returned from their forced exit a year ago, and still more were arriving at a fairly steady rate.

But this demon showed no signs of leaving.

I bit my bottom lip, wondering if there were any spells in the library Dad had left in my keeping that might solve my problem.

Bathin's gaze ticked down to my mouth and stayed there, focused. "I thought you said I was your dream."

"What?"

His gaze slipped up, held mine. "This is a dream, Myra. You've already decided it is, though I don't know why."

"No cinnamon."

One eyebrow twitched. "Cinnamon?"

"I baked last night. Cinnamon rolls for Roy's retirement party."

"And you...store them in your bedroom?"

"No, but I should be able to smell cinnamon."

"The door's closed."

"Still." I shrugged.

"I could make it smell like cinnamon."

"To prove this is real?"

"Or to prove it's a dream. Which would you prefer? To think you have invited me into your bedroom? Or to think this is a fantasy? Something secret, dark, forbidden?"

"I would prefer for you to get out of my bed."

"Happy to oblige." He grinned and threw back the covers.

He lay there naked. Very naked.

His chest and stomach I had already seen, hairless, and stone hard. But he stretched like a cat, slowly and languidly (the bastard), and every muscle of his thick thighs, stomach, chest, and arms contracted and flexed. My gaze traveled down and down, from the hard muscled V at his hips pointing down to his...

"Okay," I said. "Now I know this is a dream."

"Because I'm everything you've ever desired? Because my body is even better than your dirty, secret fantasies? Because you want what you see?"

"No."

"No?"

"No, it's none of those things."

"Then?"

"This is a dream, and you've found a way to get into it from the waking world because there is no way I would dream you so conceited, egotistical, or large."

His smile slipped to a scowl. "Large? You've seen me almost every day. I am exactly this large." He waved at his entire body.

I raised an eyebrow. "Uh-huh. No *padding* the truth a little here and," I tipped my gaze down, "there, since we're in dreamland?"

The most amazing thing happened: He blushed. Or

maybe it was anger that flushed his naturally olive skin darker.

"I am a prince of Hell! I don't *pad* anything!"

I waved my hand back and forth to cover the "anything" in question and pursed my lips as if I were unconvinced.

The scowl went hard, fury just pouring off of him. "You are the most *frustrating, maddening, infuriating* woman I have ever had the misfortune to meet!"

He stood and turned toward me, hands on his now-pants-clad hips.

"You should add *not gullible* to your list. Get out of my dream, demon. I don't have time or a care to spare you."

He inhaled, his nostrils flaring, then he smiled, all the anger melting away. "How do you feel about angry sex?"

"Opposed."

I shifted around, fluffing my pillow and shoving the one he had been using to the floor. I propped myself against the headboard. "You aren't gone yet?"

I plucked an imaginary fluff from my sleeve, ignoring him.

"Until next time," he said, "remember I can see you when you sleep, and I know what you're dreaming."

"Stalk me in my sleep again, and I'll find a spell that staples your tongue to your balls."

He laughed. Deep, loud, from-the-gut, making me think of barbarians and beer. It was a good sound, and it took some work to remind myself that he was not a good man.

"Fair enough," he chuckled.

"And Bathin?" I finally looked up. He cocked one eyebrow. "If you enter anyone else's dream, if you stalk them in a dream or outside a dream, if you stalk me, in a dream or outside a dream, I will throw you in a hole so deep, not even the gods will hear you scream."

He was still smiling when he raised his hand. "Promises, promises." He snapped his fingers and was gone.

I jerked and opened my eyes. I was in my bed—my real bed. The house smelled of cinnamon, vanilla, and warm butter. The bed beside me was cool and undisturbed, the sky beyond the curtained window still dark.

I was alone.

I exhaled through the flicker of disappointment deep in my chest.

Demons. We didn't make every supernatural creature sign a contract to live in Ordinary, but in the case of gods and demons, we absolutely had papers drawn up and signed.

Bathin had refused to sign a contract to stay in town.

Which meant he had to leave. Without my sister's soul.

Just like I knew my family gift would never fail me, I knew I'd be the one who figured out how to save Delaney's soul. And I'd be the one who kicked Bathin out of Ordinary for good.

Banned, as all his lying, cheating, double-crossing kind were banned.

He'd be furious.

I smiled. I couldn't wait.

# CHAPTER 2

I LEANED back on my heels, chewed on the end of the paint brush, and studied my handiwork. Not bad for my first demon trap. I hadn't been able to fall back asleep.

So I'd followed that instinctive tug in my chest, brewed some tea, and then ended up brewing a spell.

Juice of thistle, oil of sassafras, kosher salt, and beet root stewed in a silver spoon. The tug in my chest had led me here, on my knees in front of the fireplace, drawing out ancient symbols on the hardwood floor.

When the spell dried, becoming invisible against the wood, I waited for my family gift to tell me where I needed to be next.

Nothing. No tug. No tingle. No *need*.

Thank the gods. There was nothing else I should do with the trap. I could go about my own business.

I pushed up to my feet and stretched out the kink in my back, wondering why it was so important to draw the trap in front of my fireplace. Unfortunately, my gift didn't supply answers to my questions.

I followed the gift and did what I instinctively knew I should do, what I felt I had to do, without always knowing the cause or the results.

Which was why I preferred logic and facts when it came to the non-gift parts of my life. Logic and facts had never let me down.

I took a sip of tea that had gone cold hours ago and gathered up the spellwork items. It was six o'clock in the morning. I had to be at work in about an hour.

Lucky for me I had just enough time for a long shower and a quick stop at the drive-thru for a huge cup of strong, hot tea.

ROY HAD been a fixture at the police station for years. After he retired from being a cop in LA, he moved here and decided to put on the badge again for our little town and our "quaint" crimes.

Those crimes included monsters and ancient evils and yes, even murders, kidnappings, and shootings. So it wasn't exactly the quiet beat he'd expected.

But it wasn't anywhere near the violence level found in a big city, so he had remained and given us his level head, steady advice, and love of Rubik's Cubes for years.

I was going to miss him, the elder in our mix. The human who didn't stand for any kind of shenanigans on his shift, whether said shenanigans came from monster or god or us Reed sisters.

I parked the cruiser next to Jean's truck and strolled around to the trunk with my huge mug of tea. I retrieved the bag full of random things I'd felt the *need* to throw in there today: a turnip, a candy ring, a deck of cards, and a book I'd been hoping to take back to the library the next time I got out that way.

I slung the bag crossways over my shoulders and juggled the bulky carriers of cinnamon rolls and little chocolate-dipped, cheesecake strawberries I'd made for Roy's retirement party later today.

I tucked the tea between my arm and ribs, lifted a carrier in each hand and carefully, one hand balancing the carrier on top of the trunk, closed the trunk with a *thunk*.

Slow applause from the station made me turn.

Bathin stood up from a crouch, coming out of the shadows and into the pale morning light. A little black and white cat— one of the strays around town everyone fed—came out of the shadows with him.

Had he just been petting that cat?

Bathin leaned against the side of the building, green, green eyes bright, hair finger-combed back as if he'd just stepped out of a shower.

I scowled.

He smiled.

"My morning just got better." His voice was sex and sin and surrender.

"And mine just got worse," I replied cheerily.

He shouldered off the wall and strolled toward me. The cat

stopped licking its back and hurried to follow Bathin like he was a bag of treats. I lingered behind the car, waiting for a tug to tell me to *go, be, move* but nothing happened.

I sighed.

"Do I smell cinnamon?" He tried and failed to make that sound nonchalant. As if I didn't notice those laughing eyes, that wicked mouth.

"I know you were in my dream."

"What?" The surprise on his face was very good and very fake.

"And I told you I'd kick your ass if you do it again."

"I have no idea what you're talking about, but do go on. In your dreams, you say? Was I naked? Were you?"

"Get out of my way, Bathin. I have a job to get to unlike a certain demon drifter."

He snorted. "Let me help you with those cinnamon rolls."

"No."

"Let me carry your tea."

"No. What's up with the cat?"

"What cat?"

I made a point of staring at the cat rubbing along his calf.

"It's a stray. It's straying. Shoo," he said to the cat. "Be gone."

The cat wasn't paying any attention to him, rubbing on his other calf before becoming interested in a patch of sun in the middle of the sidewalk.

"Just a stray," Bathin shrugged. There was something more he wasn't saying, but my arms were getting tired of balancing the carriers and I wanted tea. I strode forward.

"Excuse me."

"Let me get the door." He was closer to the building and my hands were full of breakfast goodies so I didn't try to stop him.

He waited until I was right up next to him and then just stood there, arm across the doorway, hand on the latch so he could open the door. But he was not opening the door.

He was tall, this demon, and exactly as dreamy and tempting as he had been in my dream, kissing me, touching me.

Bathin watched me, silent, waiting. I was close enough to

smell his cologne, the scent of his skin warmer than cinnamon, almost bourbon, almost fire.

I wanted to draw in to him. Like a moth to flame. My heart wanted that, wanted the light, the heat, the wild spark. To ignore any tug of pre-ordained gifts. To just let go and be free.

Nope. No way I'd fall for that.

Demons tempted. It wasn't anything personal, it was just how they were made. People like me, logical people, reasonable people, always, always remembered that.

"What do we do now?" he practically crooned.

"You open the door. Or I barge through it without you." I stepped forward, ready to shoulder the door, but he twisted the handle. The door swung inward just before I hit it.

I miscalculated the size of his unnecessarily huge foot and tripped over his unnecessarily huge boot.

The floor rushed toward my face. I swung my hands forward to stop my fall, sending my travel mug of tea clattering to the ground.

I angled so I'd hit hip first, aiming to keep the carriers intact.

Two strong hands, one tight against my stomach, the other flat against my chest, caught me.

"Easy," Bathin breathed near my ear. "Easy now."

His body was pressed behind me, legs straddling mine. Just like in the dream, he was heat and strength, hard and demanding. And so, so fine.

I closed my eyes for a second, my heart racing from the almost fall and from more—from his touch, from his voice, from his presence.

Someone cleared their throat.

I looked up.

Everyone, and I mean *everyone* in the station was staring at us.

"Myra?" Delaney's long brown hair was pulled back in a pony tail, except for the little stray tendrils she couldn't ever tame. She had on jeans and her short-sleeve uniform shirt that looked good on her lean frame, the badge visible on her pocket. She held a steaming mug of coffee in one hand, a maple bar in the other, but she still looked like she was half a second from pulling her gun. "Everything okay there?"

"Oh, she's fine," Bathin said. "Tip-top shape."

"Let. Go." I got my feet under me and levered backward.

Bathin snatched his hands away like I'd just turned to ice. Good choice, because I wasn't above accidentally-on-purpose mule-kicking him if needed.

Over at her desk, Jean, who had pink hair this week, handed Hogan, her baker boyfriend, her donut. He slid off the edge of her desk to get out of her way.

Jean was taller than me, but not as tall as Delaney. She had a way of being friendly and non-confrontational that made people think she never got angry.

They were dead wrong.

"My intent was pure," Bathin lied like a liar-McDemon-face.

Both sisters walked toward me, eyes flicking over my shoulder from the demon to me, gauging my anger.

I shook my head. "I tripped over his stupid foot."

"Did he push you?" Delaney asked.

"No."

"You okay?" Jean asked.

"I'm fine."

She nodded, her loose, rose-colored hair shifting with the movement. "Do I smell cinnamon? Homemade, Myra? Really?"

"Made them last night. Dad's recipe."

"I was just thinking about these yesterday. It's been forever." She plucked the carrier out of my hand and set it down on the table in the middle of the room where other goodies were piling up. "Hogan, you gotta taste these."

He rambled over, all smooth grace and easy attitude. He was human and Jinn, which gave him the ability to see past a person's physical self to what they really were inside. It was a handy thing, especially when we had new creatures stroll into town who might not want to reveal their true nature.

"Better than mine?" he asked.

"Way." She held a soft, gooey bun up to his mouth.

"Bring it." He opened wide, and she shoved the whole thing in his mouth.

He made appreciative noises while he chewed and gave me

17

two thumbs up. "Think I can get that recipe off of you for the bakery, Myra?" I loved how his Jamaican accent kind of swooped through my name.

"I think you could."

"You sure Bathin's not bothering you?" Delaney asked.

"Bathin's standing right here," he rumbled.

"It was just a little trip. I'll get the mop."

"I got it," Jean said.

I handed the other carrier to Delaney. "Cheesecake strawberries."

Her pale blue eyes widened and she smiled. It transformed her from athletic and confident to little-girl-delighted. "You always know exactly what to bring." She leaned in and gave me a one-armed hug. "It's like a gift or something."

It was a gift. We all had one.

Jean's family gift was knowing when something bad— really bad—was going to happen. She tried to joke it off, but I knew it was a heavy burden.

Delaney's gift was being the only person who could allow the gods to vacation here. She was the bridge, the way in which they could put down their god power and try their hand at ordinary, mortal living.

"You doing okay?" I asked as we hugged.

"Same as always," she replied.

Which wasn't the same as good.

I didn't know how she put up with Bathin possessing her soul. If it had been me, I would have forced him to give it back, no matter the cost. But Delaney was patient and steady. She'd traded her soul so that Bathin would let go of Dad's. She wasn't complaining about the deal.

I was. I was doing everything I could to find a way to get her soul away from him.

Bathin was a ticking bomb. As soon as he got whatever he wanted out of owning Delaney's soul, I knew he'd explode. Then Ordinary, and all the people in it, would pay the price.

"Myra Reed," Roy called out. "Come on over here and sign my going-away cube."

Roy was a bear of a man, his hair tight and curly against his scalp, his cheeks wide, his eyes the softest brown in the world.

He wore casual clothes today, a sweater vest over a button-down in a nice coral that made his darker complexion look almost rosy.

"Where's your wife?" I asked as the big man gave me a hug.

"She's packing for the trip. We leave tomorrow morning. Up to Portland to catch our flight. She decided to buy five new pairs of shoes, and none of them have heels or cover her toes."

"Perks of retirement, right?"

He chuckled. "Still doesn't feel real. I'm going to miss this place. Miss you girls."

"Just the girls?" Ryder asked without looking up from the files he was scanning through.

Roy smiled. "Oh, I'll miss you too, Bailey. And those two chuckleheads." He jerked his thumb over his shoulder.

The chuckleheads in question were Hatter and Shoe. Hatter was tall, lanky, and liked to act like a laid-back cowboy. Shoe was built like a fireplug, terminally grumpy, and stole my secret stash of good chocolate on the regular.

I adored them both.

Roy wagged a pen at me then handed over his going-away card: a Rubik's Cube printed with all of our faces.

I turned it to the side with me in uniform, smiling. I was on the beach, it was a sunny day. I had Mrs. Yates's penguin in my hands. The little concrete statue was dressed up in swim trunks, sunglasses, and a flowing wig. It was a good memory, a beach picnic that had turned into a bonfire where friends and families gathered and mingled. I'd found the kidnapped penguin out on a rock before Mrs. Yates even called it in. I'd nabbed it up and out of danger of the big wave that would have washed it out to sea.

Right place. Right time.

Roy had taken the picture.

My stomach twisted. Things were changing. I didn't like change. I didn't like the mess it left behind, didn't like what it did to people, what it did to me.

Not that I would tell Roy he had to stay. He'd been waiting to retire until we Reed sisters got our feet back under us after Dad's death.

It had been two years now. We'd healed, maybe not smoothly or quickly or fully, but slowly and surely. And we had handled every challenge on the way.

Now was the best time, the right time for him to go.

"So much spice in your buns, Myra." Bathin strolled over, a stolen cinnamon roll in his hand.

Bathin was a challenge I still hadn't gotten a handle on.

Bad? Certainly. But he'd done good things too. He'd even helped us save people: Ryder from an accident in a snow storm, and Ben—a vampire—who'd been kidnapped and nearly killed.

He'd exchanged my father's soul for my sister's. And…well, the jury was still out on if that was good or bad. On the one hand, he'd let my dad go peacefully into death. But he'd taken Delaney in exchange.

"I didn't make them for you."

"And yet." He took another big bite and chewed. Nothing else, just that smirk, those eyes that told me he knew how much it bothered me to see him enjoying something I had made for others.

"Why are you even here?" I asked. "Roy's going-away party isn't until tonight. And last I checked, you're not part of the force."

"Technically."

"Yes, technically. And in every other way."

He nodded toward Delaney. "Her soul. My hands are tied…"

His head jerked up toward the door, as if he expected someone to blast through it with a gun.

"Uh…Delaney," he said, gaze still riveted on the door.

Delaney was laughing with Hatter, something about the last retirement-party-gone-wrong on the Tillamook police force. It involved live octopus, whipped cream, and a vat of Gummy Bears.

"What?" I asked.

"Hold on," Bathin said. "Hold on…it's—"

Delaney staggered and almost fell to her knees, but Hatter's quick reflexes eased her fall.

"Delaney?" Ryder rushed to her side.

"I'm fine, I'm fine." She pushed away Hatter's hands and got back on her feet, though she was pale as a sheet and had to lean against the desk.

Shoe, closest to the door, faced it, looking for an exterior threat that was not materializing.

Jean pushed Hogan behind her desk where the concrete wall would give him shelter. Roy put away his precious Rubik's Cube and pulled a nightstick out of his drawer.

Only seconds had passed.

I looked at Jean. Was this a bad thing? A *very* bad thing? She shook her head slightly, her eyes on the door.

Then I glanced back at Bathin.

He stood frozen in place as if his feet had been glued to the floor. Perfectly, perfectly still.

He wasn't even breathing.

"I'm fine," Delaney insisted. "Ryder, just. Let's figure out what happened." She gripped his hands and leaned on him instead of the desk.

"What the hell?" I asked Bathin. "What's happening?"

He didn't answer, although he finally breathed. The intensity on his face fell slowly into a frown. "That isn't...shouldn't...I don't know how..."

"How what?" Jean was trying to keep Hogan in place by holding her palm up like a traffic cop, but he rolled his eyes and came around her desk so he could take a drink of coffee.

"Go back there and stand by that wall," she ordered. "I don't know if it's safe yet."

He shrugged one shoulder. "Babe, it's Ordinary. It's always safe here, ya?"

She opened her mouth to argue, but he must have anticipated her move. With a flick of his wrist, he stuffed a donut hole between her lips.

She pointed at the desk and scowled.

"Fine," he said. "I'll stay here until the coast is clear."

"What's happening?" I asked Bathin again.

Delaney pulled out a chair and sat. Her pupils were pinpricks, and red smudged each cheek like she'd been slapped.

Ryder gave her a look then crossed his arms over his chest. "Start from the top," he instructed.

"I was just standing there and then, it was pain. But I don't think it was physical? It didn't feel like a god or god power."

"Where did you feel the pain?" he asked.

It wasn't Delaney who answered, it was Bathin.

"Solar plexus. Hot and sharp. Flash of light, red light. Laughter and bells. Butterscotch."

Delaney narrowed her eyes at him. "It was like burned rum, not butterscotch, but yeah," she said. "Yes. All of that. How did you know what I felt?"

Bathin finally thawed, his unfocused gaze sharpening, bringing with it the smirk, the confidence, the ego, but his pupils were pinpricks too.

"I do have a special connection to your soul."

"Stolen connection," I said.

"Old news," Delaney said, cutting the impending argument short. "What was that? What just happened?"

"I think…"

The door burst open, and Bertie, the town Valkyrie, strode into the station.

She was short, trim, and looked to be in her eighties. Her white hair was cropped close to her head, with jagged bangs. Her eyes and mind were as sharp as her gold-tipped nails. Today's outfit was a goldenrod tailored jacket and skirt, with a sparkly scarf wrapped around her throat.

"Delaney?" she called out, her voice commanding the room. "I will talk to you about two things. One of those things is the Slammin' Salmon Serenade."

I bit back a groan. So far, I'd gotten out of being conscripted into service for this month's community event. I'd done my time at the Skate and Cake, just like Delaney had done her time at the Rhubarb Rally. And Jean had…that's when it hit me.

Jean had not gotten roped into any of Bertie's schemes.

The little sneak.

"You little sneak," I said.

Jean blinked hard. "What? Me? I didn't do anything."

"No, you didn't, did you?"

"Myra," Delaney said in her boss voice.

"Jean's skipped out on all of Bertie's schemes."

"Schemes?" Bertie had a good set of lungs on her for a woman who looked like she was in her delicate years.

"Are you implying, Myra Reed, that the events tying our

community together, events bringing in tourists and therefore tourist dollars to support our community, are schemes I inflict upon you for my pleasure and entertainment?"

"No, Bertie," I said. Never argue with a Valkyrie. Never.

"Do you think I go through all of this trouble, all of this work to force people to do my bidding as if I were a queen?"

"Actually…" Jean started.

"No, Bertie." Delaney gave Jean a *shut-up* look. "What you do is important. *And* it's for the betterment of the town. It brings us all together, human, god, and supernatural. We know that. What did you want to talk about?"

Bertie paused, her head tilted slightly to the side as if testing the wind for the scent of rotten insincerity so she could swoop in for the kill.

We all held still. Even the demon. He might be a lying, cheating creature of the Underworld, but even he knew better than to talk back to a Valkyrie with ruffled feathers.

"I'll expect full participation from Ordinary's police department during the Serenade," she intoned.

"Of course," Delaney said. "We've already extended our hours to deal with all the tourists coming into town, and we'll be hiring on more reserve officers.

Jean was giving me big eyes while she mouthed, *"please don't."*

"Jean wants to help," I said. "She missed out on most of the events."

"No, I…" Jean said, but Bertie's attention swiveled to my cotton-candy-haired sister.

"You usually work the night shift, do you not?"

*Darn it.*

"Yes," Jean breathed. "I'm so busy. At night. Working. At night."

"Good news," Delaney said. "Jean's switching to days." Delaney sent me a wink.

Yes!

"Oh?" Bertie asked, scenting blood.

"Since Roy's retiring, we need someone on the early shift," Delaney said. "Jean volunteered."

"You did?" I asked at the same moment Hogan asked,

"You did?"

Jean went from annoyed to kind of shy in an instant. Hogan pulled the early shift at his bakery, and Jean worked nights. I knew it took a lot for them to find time to see each other. Jean didn't look at me, but when Hogan hooked her pinky with his, she grinned. "Worth a try, right?" she said. "Unless you'd like to open a nocturnal bakery?"

He shook his head. "People need carbs to face the day. But are you sure? You know we'll see a lot more of each other."

"I'm counting on it." And the sly little wink she gave him told me she and Hogan were doing just fine together.

"Excellent." Bertie clapped, snapping our attention back to her. "Since you'll no longer be working nights, I'll expect you to be a strong participant in all the activities."

Jean scrunched up her nose, but Delaney nodded. "Yes, Bertie. We can make that happen. Happy to help. Right, Jean?" Delaney nodded at Jean.

"Yes, Bertie," Jean finally said.

Bertie laced her hands together, her gold nails flashing. "Very well. Jean, I'll meet with you on Wednesday to assess exactly how you can assist. It will require quite a bit of your time. I hope you're prepared to give me your best effort."

"I promise I won't let you down," Jean said. When Bertie glanced away, Jean drew her finger across her throat and mouthed at me: "*You're dead.*"

I waggled my eyebrows at her.

"You said there were two things you wanted to talk about?" Delaney asked.

"Oh," Bertie said. "Yes. We seem to have developed a portal to Hell."

The pause in the room, the full moment of silence as we each absorbed that statement, was immense.

Bathin broke the silence with a little grunt. "Huh."

"A what?" Delaney asked. "No, just. Where?" She plucked up her jacket and shrugged into it as she strode across the room. "Where is the portal to Hell, Bertie?"

"Out by the lake, dear."

"Which side?"

"In the park. Near the dragon."

Delaney was all motion, already at the door, Ryder on her heels. "Bathin, with me," she said. "Jean, stay here."

"Yes, boss," she said.

"Hatter, Shoe, you're on patrol. We'll keep you in the loop. Ryder, stay here."

"Nope." He was moving behind her, with her. They had become more than just boyfriend, girlfriend over the last year or so. They had become a team: partners at work, partners at home. There was no chance Ryder was going to let her charge off to face a portal to Hell without him.

I didn't think Delaney realized it, but he had firmly planted himself in both her life and her career.

"Myra," Delaney said.

The tug in my chest was so strong I felt like someone had hooked me and was reeling me in. "Oh, I'm coming with you."

She nodded. "Be back as soon as we can, Roy."

"I'll save you a cinnamon roll," he replied.

# CHAPTER 3

DELANEY AND Ryder swung into his truck, and I marched over to my cruiser. As soon as I was behind the wheel, the passenger door opened and Bathin angled his way into the seat.

"No." I pointed at the door.

"Yes. Delaney wants me to come, and there is no room for me in the truck between those two love birds."

"Walk, transport, or find some other way to get there."

"There's a portal open to Hell. *Hell*, she said, Myra. And you don't want to keep an eye on the only demon in town? You want me to go off on my own, maybe show up at the portal before any of you? Left to my own devices?"

I scowled. I hated it when he was right. I wanted to keep a close eye on him.

Lucky for me, I could pass the time grilling the only demon in town about portals to Hell.

"What was I thinking?" I said. "How silly of me. Of course you can ride with me. Let's go."

He narrowed his eyes. "What are you going to do, Myra Reed? I hope you don't think crashing this car into a telephone pole would kill me."

Strange that he'd jumped to homicide, but I was more than happy to follow that line of thinking.

"No?" I started the engine and eased out of the parking lot, following Ryder's truck. He switched on his light bar, blue and red flashing, and I did the same.

No sirens yet, but if the road was too crowded—which it shouldn't be on a Wednesday morning in September—we'd go in sirens wailing.

"So tell me," I said, "what would kill you?"

He relaxed into the seat and flicked his blunt fingernail over the edge of the dash, as if there were a bug there.

There wasn't. I kept a clean and orderly car just like I kept a clean and orderly life.

"Nothing. There's a thing here and there which might damage me," he said, "but I haven't found anything that could kill me."

*Lie.*

"Not even vehicular accidents?"

"No."

"Beheading?"

"No. I am whichever shape I choose. I wouldn't construct such simple vulnerabilities."

Interesting.

"I don't suppose stabbing you in the heart would do anything?"

"Ah, Myra. It's sweet you think I have a heart."

"I don't."

He hummed like he didn't believe me.

"What about those scissors?" I asked.

"Which scissors?"

He knew exactly which scissors. "The ones your mother made that can somehow cut a soul out of your possession and will do you great harm?"

"Allegedly can cut a soul out of my possession. And will do the user great harm."

"Allegedly," I said.

"I'd need to see the scissors to know if they are the ones my mother made for my enemies to use against me."

Not happening.

"She sounds just terrific, by the way," I muttered, "your mother."

"Oh, I assure you, she's not. Where was it you were keeping those scissors, Myra? If you let me see them, I can tell you whether or not they could kill me."

"You're never going to see them until they're buried in your heart. If that's the way they kill you."

"Promises, promises. Shall we make a date of it? A good old-fashioned stabbing? A crime of passion? You provide the crime, I'll provide the passion?"

I bit my bottom lip so I didn't shout at him. Or smack him. Or laugh.

He was hard on my insides. I found him equally frustrating and darkly wonderful.

No, not wonderful. He was holding my sister's soul hostage. There was nothing wonderful about that.

"Tell me what to expect," I said.

"Of what? My passion? Well, when a demon likes an officer of the law, he—"

"What to expect at the portal to Hell." My heart was beating a little too fast. When he chuckled, it made me shiver and want to squirm in my seat.

*What about angry sex?* he had asked in the dream.

Oh, hell no.

"Your pulse, Myra," Bathin murmured. "Whatever has crossed your mind?"

"A portal to Hell," I lied. "What should we expect from it? Who opened it, and how did they do it? Is something coming into Ordinary or leaving?"

He waited a bit, about a block or so, staring out the window as our small, cloudy town zipped past.

"I don't know."

"You don't want to tell me," I corrected.

"No. There could be many answers to your question. I don't know which answers are the right ones."

"Give me your best guess. I've done the research, I know the basics."

He stared for a bit more, and when I snuck a peek at him, his eyes were narrow, that same look he'd had in the station, as if he were trying to read the head of a pin from miles away.

"I don't know what was used to open the portal. It's not a crossroads, it's not something laying quiescent beneath the earth. It could be a summoning, a spell. If so, then the portal was called into existence from inside Ordinary. And that...that would be interesting."

We had a lot of people with powers in town. It was possible someone from the inside had opened a portal to Hell. But it was against the rules to do so, and I didn't know anyone who would break that law.

"Do you know who or what could be coming through?" I asked.

"No. But I think the portal was opened to allow something into Ordinary, not out."

I worked to relax my grip on the wheel. Whatever we were about to face was coming out of Hell and straight into Ordinary.

I thought back to what I'd grabbed before I left the house today. Deck of cards, some tea bags. Extra socks. The bag I'd been carrying around for the last couple months had a rotating supply of oddities. So did the trunk of the cruiser.

Without really meaning to, I added and subtracted things out of the trunk and glove box with regularity. Delaney and Jean both gave me hell about it and liked to dig through the glove box to see what weird things I had stashed.

Jean called me the Swiss Army Reed, because she was a brat.

And yet, they never complained when I had exactly what we needed at hand.

"I think I know what's guarding the portal," he said.

"What?" I asked. "Basilisk? Sphinx? Devil?"

"No. Nothing like that. Nothing easy."

"Those are easy?"

"Each of those things has rules."

"The devil has rules?"

"Wouldn't you like to know?" He winked, and I refused to acknowledge what that did to my internal temperature.

"Okay, I'll bite. What thing without rules is guarding the portal?"

We'd made it to the park and turned onto the narrow road wending down the hill to the lake. Since it was early morning on a school day, the park was empty.

I followed Ryder's truck down the great rolling hill surrounded by tall fir trees to the parking lot at the bottom.

The big metal dragon statue stood watch at the top of the hill, a ramble of play structures stationed on two levels below. Behind us was a sandy stretch, the boat dock, and finally, the lake, bright and broad and waiting for swimmers, fishermen, jet skis, and boaters.

I'd seen the lake so many times—in sunlight, snow, rain—that it didn't always hit me how beautiful it was. I was born here, grew up here. I'd spent as much of my summers on the lake as I had on the beach.

It was home, familiar, common. But at moments like this, the lake polished into sapphire and milky opal by the wide blue arc of the sky and striated clouds, I realized what a lovely, special place Ordinary really was.

"Where's the portal, what's guarding it, why are you so quiet?" I parked and turned toward Bathin.

His eyes were wide, really wide. Like he had just seen something that scared the hell out of him.

"Bathin?" I almost reached for him, but course-corrected and reached for my firearm, checking to be sure it was at my side, in my holster.

Demons could be anything they wanted you to think they were. Fake any emotion, if it got them what they desired.

So Bathin might not really be afraid of the thing he was staring at. It might all be an act.

My gut said no. This man, this demon, was afraid.

The tug in my chest—sharp like salt in a wound—said it was time to get out of the car.

*Move, go, now.*

"It's worse than I thought," he whispered. He wasn't talking to me. Probably didn't even realize he was sitting in a car next to me.

Terrific.

I left him to it. It didn't matter what kind of monster we had on our doorstep. What mattered was, if the monster wanted to stay here, it had to wipe its feet on the mat and follow the rules of Ordinary.

*Move. Go. Now.*

I slipped my bag to one shoulder and got out of the car. I strolled over to Delaney who was next to Ryder.

Both of them stared up past the gray, brick retaining wall decorated by a school of metal fish, to the chain-link fence and the wooden maze of play equipment built and connected like a rambling castle.

Beyond that was a higher flat spot with brightly colored play equipment, and still farther, at the very top of the hill, and out of view from this angle, was the metal dragon statue.

Where was I supposed to be?

The tug in my chest became a warmth instead of a spike of pain. I was headed to the right place. To the right time.

Did I need to open the trunk? Pull out something I'd stashed there?

The tug didn't change, didn't pull that way. What I had on me—my weapon, my pockets, my bag—would be enough.

"You ready?" I asked Delaney.

"Oh, sure. So how do we handle that?" She pointed.

I followed her finger to the switchbacks, turrets, slides, and lookouts of the sprawling, castle climbing structure.

The wooden play equipment all seem to be where it should be. Swings, tunnel slides, monkey bars, cute little unicorn pony standing in front of a swirling vortex in the ground.

Hold on.

*Unicorn?*

"It's a unicorn," Bathin breathed, coming up beside me. "Holy shit, it's pink. Pink." He turned to me. "You see it, right? The unicorn? The pink unicorn?"

He didn't sound like himself. All the swagger, all the ego was gone. He looked like he'd just seen a ghost. Or, well, a pink unicorn in front of a swirling vortex to Hell in a playground.

"We see it," Delaney said. All calm, that girl. And obviously perplexed by Bathin's reaction. "I don't think it's evil, dude."

Bathin blinked. Several times. "It's a *unicorn*. Of course it's evil."

"Maybe to a demon," Ryder said.

Bathin laughed, one short, disbelieving bark. "Yes, to a demon. And to everyone. *Everyone*. It's *pink*."

We stared at the unicorn, which was about the size of a sheep and…well, posing was probably the best description. Its glossy, light-blue mane flowed down its neck, the light-blue tail arched elegantly, and four tiny, perfect, pearly-white hooves shone in the grass.

The rest of it was, indeed, pink. From the tip of its nose raised high and proud, to the bottom of its legs, one of which was lifted in a curl.

The wind, which wasn't stirring a thing around us, tossed the unicorn's mane so that it flowed hypnotically.

And the horn was a thing of beauty. It wasn't pearl like the delicate little hooves, no, it was diamond. Sharp and shining with fractal rainbows, clear as a star, glowing with power.

It was hard to look away from the horn. As a matter of fact, there was a palpable draw to the creature, or maybe the vortex swirling in the ground behind it.

Ryder had already taken several steps toward it, but Delaney reached out and grabbed his arm. "Me, first," she said. Then: "Myra?"

"I brought a turnip."

"Oh…kay?"

"It seemed like the right thing at the time." I dug it out of my bag and stood next to her. "I also brought a candy ring thing. So there's that."

"Do unicorns like turnips and candy ring things?"

"Nope. They like clear springs and virgins. We're basically screwed."

She snorted, and I grinned. Yeah, sometimes this job was just too ridiculous for words.

She opened her palm like a TV doctor asking for a scalpel. "Turnip," she intoned.

I slapped the turnip into her hand.

"Turnip."

"Candy ring thing."

I slapped it into her hand.

"Candy ring thing."

"Anything else I should know?" she asked.

"Other than demon boy is freaking out? No."

I thumbed through the massive library of data I carried around in my head. "I've never heard of evil unicorns. The old records don't say unicorns are evil. Or pink, for that matter. Or tiny. They have also never mentioned unicorns guarding portals to Hell, so…"

"Right. We're going in blind." She grinned. "Let's go figure this out."

Delaney, Ryder, and I strode up to the playground, shoulder to shoulder, to figure this out.

# CHAPTER 4

THERE WAS no wind, no matter how close we got to the unicorn. And yet its mane still waved, backlit by the swirling vortex on the ground radiating moonlight in the middle of the day. The moonlight made the vortex look like a clear puddle in the grass fraught with the same fractured rainbows, deep steel shadows, and star-sharpened brightness as the unicorn's horn.

The scent hit me next. Apple pie. It wasn't a fake apple smell like a candle or spray. It was the full, buttery, crusty combination of apples and spices and sugar and pie crust, melting and crisping together in an oven.

That delicious scent wafted up from the vortex. I felt a need to walk forward, to get closer, like a hungry kid spotting a candy-covered house. But the tug in my chest was a stone, stopping me, anchoring me right where I stood.

"You smell apple pie?" I asked Delaney.

"No."

"You feel the pull?"

"No?"

We stopped a good six yards away from the unicorn who still hadn't broken out of its pose, which was probably supposed to be majestic, but was starting to look a little staged.

I glanced at our surroundings, checking to make sure nothing was using this as a blind or a decoy.

We were out of the line of sight if a car approached, blocked by the bulk of the wooden castle structure. A set of monkey rings stood on our right, a swing set behind us, and a metal slide corkscrewed down from a stair stack of the castle's decks in front of us.

The park was empty except for three humans, a demon, and a unicorn.

"My name is Delaney Reed," she said. "This is Ordinary, Oregon. We welcome all kinds of supernaturals, humans, and gods here. But we do not allow portals to Hell. Do you want to explain why you're breaking Ordinary's law before I ask you to pack up that portal and leave?"

Reasonable, confident. Friendly even, considering she was staring at a hell mouth, and the unicorn it had spit out.

The unicorn didn't move. Ryder stood on Delaney's right, his body tense, as if he were having a hard time not walking forward, straight into the apple-pie-scented hell hole.

"Is that apple pie?" he whispered. "I smell apple pie."

"Ryder," Delaney warned.

"I just…I'll just take a quick look, all right?" He got exactly two strides forward before Delaney gripped his wrist and held him still.

"Not another step."

Delaney did not have the power of voice. She couldn't order someone to stop and make it stick, except…

…except she was the bridge of Ordinary. The earth of it. Her roots dug deep into this soil, into the stones beneath. She was a part of it in a way none of the rest of us could ever be.

And she used that, was using that right this moment. The whole of Ordinary, the dirt and trees and sand and sky, holding Ryder still, anchored there by her hand.

That urge to move forward hit me again—not my gift—and I cocked my head, considering the vortex shining moonlight reflections onto the metal slide.

It wanted my soul—the vortex, not the slide. But I was a Reed, so most supernatural things didn't affect me as much as they would a human.

Ryder was human, and even though he had been claimed by a god, it was clear the draw of the vortex was hard for him to resist.

Delaney was both a Reed and currently soulless, so that explained why the vortex didn't tempt her. Maybe that explained why she didn't smell the apple pie too.

Bathin was a demon so he didn't count.

But if any of our citizens, supernaturals or normals, came out here to enjoy the autumn day, they'd be jumping down that hole so fast, no one would be able to stop them.

Was the unicorn decoration? A lure to catch the eye and draw people close enough for the vortex to do its thing?

"Is it alive?" Delaney asked. I didn't know if she meant the unicorn or the vortex.

"Hello, Xtelle," Bathin said from behind me. Several yards behind me.

The unicorn blinked one of its huge, adorable eyes, and the wind ruffling its mane stopped. It tipped its head down stiffly as if it had been standing that way for an eternity. Its nostrils flared.

The hoof dropped, the waving mane and tail went flat, and the unicorn pranced in a little half circle to face us. "You."

Its voice had a fluting quality to it, like a wet finger running around the edge of a crystal glass. It was beautiful.

"You shit!"

Okay. Not beautiful. Loud. Definitely loud.

"You!" Louder still. I stuck one finger in my ear to stop the ringing.

The unicorn stomped in place and swung its horn, calling down the pale light of autumn to catch diamond fire.

Bathin walked up to my side, a huge hulking mountain of muscle and attitude. He planted his feet wide and crossed his arms over his chest. "There are rules here, were you listening?"

He sounded calm. Bored.

I was surprised. Last I knew he was terrified of this unicorn. But now...now he was smirking, enjoying the unicorn's angry—and adorable, the thing wasn't even as big as some dogs I knew—prancing.

"You!" it piped.

"Ah, ah, Xtelle, that's not very lady-like. Manners. Pay attention to the Reed sisters. This one's Delaney. You might have heard of her?"

The unicorn narrowed her innocent-kitten eyes and glared at Delaney as if just now seeing her. "You are *the* Delaney?"

"Yep. I'm the Delaney." Still calm. Still holding tight to Ryder's wrist.

Ryder was sweating, unable to look away from that vortex, but to his credit, he didn't try to break away.

"Which one are you?" Xtelle asked.

"This one's Myra." The way Bathin said it sent chills down my skin. He put an extra hard emphasis on the beginning, making my name sound possessive: MY-rah. As if I belonged to him. As if he belonged to me.

The unicorn did not appear to miss that particular detail either.

"I see." The unicorn snorted, and glitter puffed out of her nostrils in a little cloud. "Well, it's about time you Reed women got here. Someone opened a portal to Hell. Good thing I arrived to keep anyone from walking into it."

Bathin sucked in a soft breath, so slight a reaction, if I hadn't already been paying attention to him, I might not have noticed it.

Something wasn't right about what she was saying. It had surprised him.

I wasn't sure if that was a good thing or a bad thing.

"Someone opened a portal," Delaney repeated. "Is that what happened here? Because what I see is a vortex to Hell, and the only living thing anywhere near it is you."

The unicorn batted her eyes, trying to look cute and confused. Missed it by a mile.

"Did you open it?" Delaney asked. "This would be a really good time to tell me the truth."

The unicorn ducked her head and pawed at the grass. "I did. I opened it."

Bathin did that held-breath reaction again.

The unicorn's voice was quiet and small and apologetic. "It was...I didn't mean it to happen like this. But I've heard so much about Ordinary. I thought if I got your attention, if I saved you from something...bad?" She shot a sideways look toward Bathin.

He rolled his eyes.

"If I saved you from the bad, evil, terrible, dangerous vortex to heck..."

Bathin choked on a laugh. She ignored him.

"...if *I* saved you from Hell," she said, louder, "it would prove I should stay here. In Ordinary. Live here. Like all the other...unicorns."

Bathin grunted. But his stance hadn't changed. He was still a mountain, solid, strong. And he was standing with us, against the unicorn.

Didn't that say something about him? About his loyalty? About his—

—*heart*—

—determination to stay here, no matter what he had to do to make that happen?

"There aren't any other unicorns in Ordinary." Delaney wasn't buying the cute act for a minute.

"You wouldn't…" long, sparkling eyelashes blinked, blinked, "make me leave would you? Look, oh, look. I can help…"

She trotted in a little circle, then pranced—that showy hop I'd seen fancy Italian horses pull off—over to the vortex, and pranced/hopped around it counter clockwise, ducking so her horn didn't scrape one curve of the slide.

Because the day wasn't weird enough, she also started singing. At first I thought it was a spell, but no. No, it was not.

"Doo-dah, doo-dah! Camptown racetrack's five miles long…"

"What does that—" I asked.

Bathin held up one hand. "Shh. I'm enjoying this."

Delaney's eyebrows lifted, and even Ryder looked like the stage show had broken the thrall of the free-apple-pie-to-Hell.

"…dah daaaaay!" Xtelle landed back in front of the vortex and tossed her head hard enough, her mane jingled like silvery bells.

I stared at the vortex, hoping it had changed. Hoping it had closed.

Nope. Puddle. Moonlight. Pie.

"And?" Delaney asked.

"And?" the unicorn asked.

"What was that for? The song and dance?"

"For your enjoyment? Did you not enjoy watching me frolic? Did you not enjoy my singing? I am a legend among my kind."

Bathin coughed, and it sounded a lot like, "*Bullshit.*"

"A legend!" the unicorn went on, narrowing her kitten eyes into slits. "They call me Xtelle the Xtraordinary, and when I take the stage, every creature bows and sings my praises."

Bathin gave a begrudging shrug. "Not at all ironically, I'm sure."

"I will hoove you in the hatch so hard you'll spit glitter for a decade!"

I laughed.

"Try it, old woman," he said.

"Old!" She snorted again, and this time there was a little steam along with the glitter. "Hoove you," she snarled. "Hoove you so hard."

"No hooving," Delaney ordered. "Xtelle, the dance and song were nice."

Bathin grumbled something under his breath, but Xtelle turned so her ample ass was facing his way. She swished her tail, then twisted so she could see Delaney and ignore Bathin.

"Thank you, Delaney. Aren't you the sweetest?"

That tone reminded me of a Valkyrie swooping in to drag the dead off the battlefield and into a community event.

"You can only stay in Ordinary if you follow our rules. Can you do that?"

"Of course."

"You will not harm or kill any supernatural, god, or mortal while you are here. Nor will you reveal a supernatural's or a god's true self to any mortal.

"Use of power must be done without mortals seeing or suspecting you have said powers, and all mortal laws, whether local, state, federal, or global must be adhered to."

"Go on," she purred. "It's so…orderly."

"You can't let mortals see your real form."

"My—what do you mean, my real form?"

Even Bathin sent a quizzical look over to Delaney.

"You can't look like a unicorn. Do you have the ability to project a different image? If not, I'm sure we can ask a witch or a wizard to cast an illusion to cloak you."

"Cloak me? Cloak this? I am radiant! I am glorious! Witness my pinkness and tremble in awe!"

"Nope," Delaney said. "Pink talking unicorns don't exist as far as mortals know. I'm here to make sure it stays that way."

"I won't be stifled."

"This isn't about stifling. This is about following the laws of Ordinary, which my sisters and I, along with the officers in our department, enforce. It's about keeping mortals safe, supernaturals safe, and gods safe. If you can't follow the law, then you can't stay in Ordinary."

"B-But where would I go?" The kitten eyes were back. With sparkles. And tears.

"Anywhere else in the entire world. There are other safe places for supernaturals. This is the gods' vacation town, and therefore it follows strict, ancient rules the gods decreed. Rules of which I am the arbitrator."

"That's not fair." The unicorn pouted.

Bathin heaved a huge sigh. "By the love of—those are the rules, Xtelle. You're fond of rules when they work in your favor."

"I'm not listening to you."

"Yes, you are. In or out?"

She unwobbled her lower lip and canted one back foot, considering the offer. "Must I disguise my true self?"

Delaney nodded. "Yes."

"Something…drab?"

"Something that does not appear supernatural."

"Plain and boring, like the demon over there?"

All of us glanced at Bathin. His hands were curled into fists at his sides now, and his jaw was locked, nostrils flared.

"I. Am. Not. Plain. Or boring."

Okay, maybe I liked this unicorn. She obviously knew how to get under Bathin's skin, and anybody who could do that was a plus in my book. If she knew how to needle him, she just might know how to make him give back Delaney's soul.

"Which herd and meadow do you hail from?" I asked. I knew my unicorn lore. I might not know as much as my father, but I was getting there. Plus, I had a library full of books and scrolls and tablets. I could consult any one of them at any time and get the information I needed.

"My meadow," she hedged. "It is no more." Her eyes filled with tears again. "It is why I seek a new home meadow. This Ordinary meadow."

"And your herd?" I asked.

She tipped her nose in the air. "They have abandoned me."

Bathin rubbed at his forehead as if a headache had just hit him.

"Without your meadow and herd, will you be able to access enough magic to change your shape?"

The unicorn nodded, mane jangling like jingle bells. "Ordinary is just *full* of magic. Let me think a moment."

She shifted from hoof to hoof, one after the other, not lifting them all the way off the ground, but bending her knees in a little pop-diva wiggle. Any minute now I expected her to break into the Running Man or Moon Walk.

"Oh! Easy." She pulled on magic. I could see it gather around her, sparkling up out of the grass, gold and green, turquoise of the sea, orange of the sand. It spun around her slowly, and then there was no longer a unicorn standing in front of a vortex to Hell.

There was a horse. A very small horse. A horse no bigger than a medium-sized dog.

The horse was also pure white, except for the black mark right in the center of her forehead. Her mane and tail were a soft yellow, like straw shining with sunlight, and her hooves matched. Even her eyes, which had been an alluring sapphire, were now a warm, deep brown.

"Lemme guess," Bathin said. "Pony."

She lifted her head and gave a very sweet, horse-like whinny.

"Pony," he said again.

Xtelle stomped one tiny foot. "Miniature horse, you ass," she hissed.

I laughed, and Bathin cracked a smile. "If you say so."

"You are dead to me," she declared. The miniature horse once again turned her back on Bathin.

"I wish," he muttered.

Xtelle's pointed ears swiveled back, then forward, as she stared steadily at Delaney, ignoring him. "Will this do?"

"As long as you don't talk, I think it will work fine. We don't really have wild horses, miniature or otherwise, here on the coast, so I think it would be best if we found someone who would agree to own you."

There was nothing but complete silence.

Okay. Weird reaction.

"You know there's a vortex to Hell we still haven't addressed," I pointed out.

"I know," Delaney said. "I'm getting to that. Ryder, can you stand here without trying to run into that thing?"

"It's…" he said, "it's just…I'll just take a quick look inside. See what I can see." He sounded dazed, drugged.

Bathin nodded. "That's a great idea, buddy. Go tourist around in Hell. Pick up some tchotchkes, try the torture."

"Yeah," Ryder said. "I'll do that."

"No." Delaney tugged his wrist a little more firmly, and he stopped mid-step. "You are not going to vacation in Hell, Ryder. What's wrong with you?"

"It's a vortex," Bathin said.

"Which means?" Delaney looked at me first.

I had no idea. I shook my head. I hated that I didn't have the information because I knew who was going to open his big, fat mouth any minute to show me up.

"Well, since you asked," Bathin said grandly. "It means that it is more than just a portal or a doorway into Hell. It sucks. Both ways."

"You suck both ways," I muttered.

He heard me and wagged his eyebrows to let me know it.

"What kind of suck?" Delaney asked.

"Oh, let me count the ways," I said.

"Now, now, let's not bite the hand that leads, kitten."

"Kitten me one more time, and I'll shove you in a jar with a dead drunk poet until the end of time."

"But your sister's soul."

"In a jar, out of a jar, you'd still be in Ordinary, so I wouldn't be breaking any contracts. Right, Ryder?"

Ryder inhaled, exhaled. Asking him that question seemed to break the thrall of the vortex again. "Technically, true. She could shove you into a jar, Bathin."

"So the vortex pulls people in and pulls…whatever is on the other side out," I said.

"Yes," Bathin agreed.

"How do we close it?" I asked.

"Owned!" Xtelle yelled. And wow, that horse had a set of lungs on her. "No one owns a magical creature such as I! No one dare lay claim to a unicorn, pure and true! No one can put their...their *hands* on me and...and..."

"Feed you carrots?" Bathin suggested.

"Feed me *carrots!*" she repeated. "I will not stand for this. Xtelle will be no mortal's beast of burden!"

"How about a god's?" Bathin asked. "Because that's a possibility here too."

"I'd rather die."

"Also a possibility," he said with a huge grin.

"You wouldn't actually be owned," Delaney said. "But if you're going to be a part of Ordinary, you will need someone to host you. Someone who can explain the rules and act as a go-between with the humans of the town if you do something wrong."

"How would I do something wrong? I'm a unicorn, the very epitome of purity and temperance and perfection."

"You still need a host," Delaney said. "If you don't have one, we'll be happy to appoint one for you."

"Do all the creatures have to endure this degrading treatment?" she demanded, eyes narrow. "Did *he?*"

"Bathin appears human." I decided to jump in because we really needed to get this moving along. The weather was nice enough, we might have someone show up to play in the park.

If they saw their police force arguing with a talking horse, things might get dicey.

"If you could appear human, you would not need a host," I said.

The unicorn opened her mouth, closed it. Glared at Bathin like this was all his fault. He crossed his arms over his chest and shrugged.

A snort, a stomp, and finally, it appeared the fire went out of the little horse.

"I don't have anyone," she said, dejected. "May I choose a host?"

That was within the rules. It was also within the rules that the host could refuse.

"You can choose," Delaney said. "But first we need to handle the vortex."

She perked right up and batted those long horsey eyelashes. "I choose Myra Reed."

"What?" I said.

"Please? Will you please be my host while I learn the ways of Ordinary?"

"No." Bathin cut his hand in front of him like he was some kind of medieval royal declaring a beheading. "I forbid it."

And yeah, we all turned and looked at him. He glowered at the unicorn.

"Why not?" I asked. Before he could answer, I decided I didn't need to know why he didn't like the unicorn. It was enough that he didn't want the unicorn to be with me.

What a demon feared, then forbade me to do, was very interesting to me. Especially since I was the one tasked with finding the way to throw him out of town.

"Yes," I said. "Xtelle…"

"No," Bathin said. "Myra, you should not get wrapped up with this conniving little bitch."

"Whoa," Delaney said.

"Hoove you in the big, fat face!" the unicorn screamed.

"Enough." I said it loud enough, everyone shut up.

"Bathin, you have no say over what I do. Xtelle, yes, I'll be your host. I have a lovely back yard you can frolic in, if that suits your needs. I can make a place in my garage for you to sleep, if you need indoor space.

"Everything else, from what you need to eat, to how you prefer to spend your time, we can work out later. Because right now, we need to deal with those things crawling out of the vortex."

# CHAPTER 5

THE UNICORN glanced over her shoulder, let out an undignified "Eep!" and trotted over to stand between me and Bathin.

He pushed her to one side and wedged himself next to me instead. She snarled, which was a weird sound coming from a horse, but shut up as soon as the first tentacle wriggled out of the vortex to test out the playground bark dust.

"Okay, that's not right," Ryder said.

The thrall of the vortex didn't seem to be pulling on him anymore. I couldn't smell the apple pie, either. I didn't know if the lack of pie had broken the vortex's pull, or if it was because small, oozy blobs with eyes were staring up at us from within the swirl of moonlight and shadow.

"What is that?" Delaney asked.

"Demon spawn," Bathin said very quietly. "They're explosive. Don't spook them."

"They can be spooked?" Delaney asked just as I said, "Explosive?"

"Yes," he answered.

Three explosive, nervous spawns loitered there on the edge of the vortex, like blobby monsters peering up out of a manhole. The goo-boys were blobs of lava: red oozy heat and crackly black skin. They had two eyes each, and all of them glowed yellow.

Only one had popped its foot-like tentacle out of the swirl of light, but where it touched the ground, it left behind little lines of smoke and blue flames that quickly winked out.

One of them "*harrumphed*," another one gurgled, and then there were three tentacles barbequing the ground.

"How do we shut the vortex?" Delaney asked.

I had no time to reference the books.

"Bathin?" I asked.

"Oh, now you want my opinion?"

"Don't be an ass," I said.

"All right. You want the vortex closed, I want something in return."

Of course he did. He was a demon. It was all about devil's bargains with him. Getting more than he gave. Typical male from Hell.

"Name it," I said.

"Within reason," Delaney added.

"We shove the unicorn in the vortex and close it behind her."

The unicorn yelped in indignation, and all three of us—Delaney, Ryder, and I—chanted, "No."

Bathin's gaze tracked the demon spawn, but his voice was light. "Well, then, I don't think I can help you. Oh, look at that. Is that a nice mortal family coming to play at the park? I wonder how many seconds it will take the spawn to drag them to Hell. I bet five. Five seconds. Anyone want to throw in on this wager?"

"You're bluffing," I said.

He held up one finger just as the sound of an approaching engine reached me.

Dammit.

"Name something else you want," I said.

"Anything?" he asked.

"No possession of souls," I said. "No harming any person, creature, or god. Which, by the way, Xtelle now falls under the protection of Ordinary. So if you suggest that we do any harm to her, or if you try to do any harm to her, we will throw you out of Ordinary so fast, you'll break the sound barrier."

"I want you to date me," he said.

"No."

The car engine cut off. A door opened, and another. I heard children laughing, the sound of a mother getting a baby out of a seat.

Ooze One and Ooze Two seemed to have noticed the new arrivals too, which was kind of weird because the way the parking lot was situated, and how the vortex was level with the ground, made a clean sight line impossible. Maybe they smelled the humans.

Yeah, that was even worse.

Dammit.

DEVON MONK

"One date," I countered.

Ooze One and Ooze Two hefted more tentacles up out of the hole, their lava goo stretching across the ground like pulled Slinkys. The smell of burned dirt and wood chips and, weirdly, burnt pie, filled the air.

"One month," he countered.

Yeah, that wasn't happening. But time was running out.

The family was closing in and from the sounds of it, one of the kids was headed to the play equipment at a dead run.

I turned to Bathin and took hold of his arm.

A spark of something—not visible, but something real nonetheless—struck like a crack of lightning deep in my bones. It flipped my stomach, dried out my mouth, and suddenly all I could see was him.

He was warm, warmer than he had any right to be here in the cool, September air. I indulged in a moment to wonder what it would be like to touch his skin, to search out that warmth, to have him touching me.

Would his caress be gentle like the dream? Or would the fire in his eyes, the strength in his body overwhelm me, own me, swallow me whole?

He tipped his head just slightly, as if he could almost, but not quite, hear me thinking. Or maybe it was just the beat of my heart thundering so loudly he couldn't miss it.

"Yes, Myra?" His voice was hot poured chocolate.

The kid shouted at his mom to hurry up.

"Three dates." I had to clear my throat because that came out a little husky. "Tell me how to close the vortex to Hell, and you get three dates with me."

The unicorn scoffed. "Like he'd let you get away with such a shitty deal."

"Done." He pressed his hand over mine. I was still touching him. His hand, warm and wide, cradling the back of my own was more intimate than a handshake.

His unwavering gaze made it more intimate than a kiss.

Blood rushed to warm my cheeks, my chest, but I cocked an eyebrow at him.

He winked and pulled his hand away.

"We'll need a few things," he said, all business now. "I

46

don't think we'll find them before that family gets in range."

The blobs each had six tentacles out on the ground and were heaving the rest of their bulk up out of the vortex. They were larger than I expected, about the size of VW Bugs. They jiggled and cackled, a weird mutant language that I knew meant they were very pleased to have found a hole into our world, and were even more pleased dinner was running this way with a shovel and pail.

"Hey, there," Ryder called out from some distance behind me. "I'm Reserve Officer Ryder Bailey. Would you like to sit in a police car and try out the siren and lights? If that's okay with your mom."

I'd been caught up in negotiating the date with the demon and hadn't noticed Ryder going back to intercept the kid and mom.

Good move. That would buy us some time.

"What kind of things do we need?" Delaney asked Bathin.

"A ring of candy, a lump of turnip, and a demon kiss."

Delaney grinned and held up the turnip and ring. "Get over here and pucker up, Bathin, and tell me how to make this work."

"I think Myra should do it. She's the Reed who understands spellwork and arcane knowledge. You're more of a…traffic light."

"Traffic light." Delaney shook her head. "I don't even know what that means."

"That Mother-May-I thing you make all the gods do before you allow them into the vacation town *they* created?" he said. "All the Red Light/Green Light you pull on the supernaturals, making them hide what they really are just to make your job easier?" He *tsked*. "If the traffic light fits…"

Delaney scoffed. "You can't make me feel bad about doing the job my family has been entrusted with for centuries. Nice try, though, buddy. Now get your lips over here. Let's close this thing."

He frowned, glanced at me, glanced at the unicorn, then back at Delaney.

"I really think Myra would be more suited."

"Why?"

"The kiss?" He threw a look down to the parking lot where

Ryder was busy pouring on the small town charm for the mom and kids.

Delaney gave Bathin that stare that worked in the courtroom. "If you're kissing anyone here, it's me, not Myra."

He narrowed his eyes, and I had a fleeting moment of panic. When he'd first taken her soul, he'd robbed her of all emotion. I'd made it clear—hard and fast—that I would destroy him if he didn't reverse that part of the contract. That was when he'd only been in the town a couple of days, but even then, he'd listened to me.

I still didn't know why.

Delaney could feel, could laugh, could love. But sometimes, when she didn't think I was watching, I saw her stare off in the middle distance and go blank and still.

Long-term soul possession could do terrible things to a mortal. We Reed sisters were god-chosen to protect Ordinary, so that gave us certain strengths, certain advantages regular mortals did not possess.

Delaney was tough. But all the books I'd read pointed to the same thing. Go too long past a year of soul possession, and it permanently changed a person.

Those changes were never for the better.

Which meant I had a lot to do in a very little time to save her soul before permanent damage changed her.

Bathin heaved a sigh. "Fine. I'll kiss you, right here in front of your boyfriend, the unicorn, and your sister. Is that how you like it, Delaney? A little share-and-share-alike? I'm into that, if you swing that way. Is tongue on the table?"

I punched him in the arm because I was closest. "You'll kiss me."

"Ooooo," the unicorn said out of the side of her mouth. "Jealousy?"

"Myra," Delaney said.

"Nope. He's not coming anywhere near you with his lips or his tongue. It's off the table, by the way," I said to him.

Then I turned back to Delaney. "He already has your soul. I don't think a kiss is going to make it any easier to get it back. Demon kisses leave marks."

"And kissing you won't leave a mark?"

I was going to argue, but one of the oozes plopped out of the hole and chortled in victory, all its tentacles waving around like an over-caffeinated Kermit the Frog.

Then it wobbled to a halt. Yellow eyes surveyed the scene, the park, us standing there arguing. Delaney clutched the turnip and candy ring and glared at me, Bathin somehow lounged while standing, looking like he had all the time in the world to do all the nothing that crossed his mind.

The demon spawn stretched and spread, becoming more solid and less lava-blobby.

For a second, I thought it was going to take on a human shape, but no.

It became a merry-go-round, one of those flat disk, playground kinds with metal pipe humps welded into the base so it could be pushed.

It was pretty convincing too, except for the yellow eyes that peered hungrily from the center of the disk.

"Fine," Delaney said, considering our new problem. "I don't want anything else coming out of that hole, and I don't know how we're gonna shove that thing back in. Myra gets the kiss. I'll use the turnip and," she handed me the ring, "you use that. Now, let's get at it."

The three of us strode over to the vortex leaving the unicorn behind.

"Don't think this means anything," I said to Bathin as we approached the vortex.

The other two blobs were having a harder time getting out of the hole filled with light. There was background noise behind their chattering, something that sounded like a distant choir singing a beautiful lofting song. The smell of apple pie was back.

"What's the song?" Delaney asked.

"The Underworld," Bathin replied.

"Hell?"

"Hell's a part of the Underworld, sure," Bathin said.

"And this is a vortex to Hell?"

"This is. It's also a crossroads of sorts. It's loud, sparkly, and will drag anyone to their death given the chance. Just like a unicorn."

"Hey!" Xtelle shouted. "I heard you!"

We stopped so close to the vortex, I could feel the heat off of the blob that was half way out of it. The blob spotted us. No, it spotted Bathin. And it froze, absolutely stone still.

"Jib," Bathin said, "Draz. You boys couldn't find some other town to terrorize?"

"You know these demons?" I asked.

"They're not demons. They're demon spawn. Kind of like pets who enjoy devouring their owners." He bared his teeth, not a smile—definitely not a smile—and the blob in the hole wobbled happily.

"Draz here," he waved at the one furthest out of the hole, "has a sweet tooth. You like the shiny ring, Draz?"

I held up the ring. The blob focused on my movement.

"Throw it to him," Bathin said.

It could be a trick. The candy might just pour gas on the flame, bring more blobs into town. I hesitated.

"This would be a *good* time to trust me, Myra," Bathin said pleasantly, without looking my way. His gaze was locked on Draz, and Draz stared right back like it was trapped and couldn't look away.

I could feel it, couldn't I? If I focused on Bathin, if I focused on how he was standing, how his words were spoken, the air around him? There was a power to him that he didn't usually reveal so casually.

This was dangerous enough to warrant him stepping out of his billionaire-with-an-attitude-slumming-in-a-small-town act, to draw upon his power.

Bathin was showing just a small, a tiny, part of his real self. But that was enough to convince me he was not messing around.

I threw the ring at Draz.

Draz's eyes rolled upward, and Jib followed suit. Too many tentacles were flailing, stretching. Draz caught the ring out of mid-air like a hot rookie outfielder.

And then Draz tipped backward and collided with Jib, like it had just lost its footing on a very narrow ledge.

Draz tumbled over once, sending Jib down and down. Draz split in two, then oozed back together with an audible *snap*. For half a second, the candy ring glittered blue in the midst of the lava-red and black of the blobs and the white of the vortex.

Then two yellow eyes widened in what looked like absolute joy as the ring was stuffed into a mouth hole.

The vortex spun faster, shone brighter. Draz and Jib were gone.

"And the turnip?" Delaney asked, splitting her attention between the empty vortex and the merry-go-round.

"Should get Klex back in the hole," Bathin said.

"Klex is…" I asked.

"Scary-go-round over there."

"Okay." Delaney pulled her shoulders back. "Do I throw it?"

"No, you make it dance."

"The turnip?"

Bathin spread one hand in a "yes" motion.

"You know what?" she said, "I have a dragon pig that likes to hunt demons. Maybe I'll just go get him and have him shove this spawn thing back down that hole."

"You could try it."

"But?"

"Demon spawn are sticky. I don't think you'd like your dragon pig stuck to Klex for all of eternity."

They glared at each other for almost a minute before I got tired of it. "Give me the turnip."

She tossed it to me. I grabbed the tea in my bag.

It was a token I'd picked up from one of our town witches, Jule. She traded in magic spells and infused her tea with a little kick of the supernatural kind, usually just gentle blends for good luck, happiness, health, and comfort, which was in keeping with Ordinary's rules.

The tea was little dried flower petals and leaves all wrapped up in a delicate silk bag. I'd ordered the Awake and Aware tea before. It always had one side effect for me.

It made me want to dance.

Hopefully, it would do the same for Klex over there. But just to be sure, I incanted a little spell activator.

"Twinkle, twinkle, little spell," I whisper-sang, "send this demon back to Hell, with this turnip and this tea, make a magic lock and key. Twinkle, twinkle, little spell, please be strong and do not fail."

51

I tore open the tea and rubbed it on the turnip.

"Myra?" Delaney said. "Hurry."

There were more blobs in the vortex, dozens of them pushing and shoving to get up out of the hole.

"Come to think of it," Bathin mused as the pile of ooze fought to break into our world, "all demon spawn like candy."

"Delaney?" Ryder called out. "Could I see you, please? Now?"

From the tone of his voice, the kid was done playing with the friendly police officer. Also, there was another car turning into the park. And a school bus.

Time wasn't running out. It was gone.

# CHAPTER 6

THE UNICORN trotted up beside me and turned over her hoof like it was a hand. If she weren't a magical creature, that motion would have been impossible. She bent it in a "gimme" gesture. "Turnip."

"I'm not giving you the turnip," I said.

"Delaney?" Ryder called again, trying to sound casual and friendly, but not quite covering the panic straining his voice.

"Go," I told Delaney. "I got this."

She didn't even hesitate before jogging down the hill to the parking lot.

The rattle of the bus engine turned off, and the chatter of kids, a lot of kids, filled the air.

I heard Ryder raise his voice to tell them he was going to give them a quick rundown on the rules of the park.

I had seconds to take care of this.

"Give. It. To. Me," the unicorn said again.

"Don't," Bathin said. "You sang the spell, you used the tea. Just throw the turnip at Klex and let magic do the rest."

"Magic can't do everything," Xtelle argued.

"No, but you aren't compatible with the spell she cast."

"You know nothing about me." She shook her mane and stuck her nose in the air.

"*Unicorn* magic and demon magic don't mix," he ground out. "But go ahead. I'm happy to stand here and mock your efforts."

The unicorn stomped her foot. "You *dare*—"

"Both of you shut up and move."

Bathin gave me a slow-burn smile, as if I'd just told him I loved him rather than ordering him to get the hell out of my way. That smile did things to my stomach. And my breathing.

And my resolve.

He bent a half bow, his arm sweeping out as I marched to the merry-go-round.

"Look, Klex, is it?" I held up the turnip and drew my gun. "I have a turnip and a gun, and I'm not afraid to use them. So either you leave Ordinary peacefully, or I will destroy you, cut off your ties to the Underworld, and turn you into an *actual* piece of playground equipment for all eternity."

The yellow eyes narrowed and the merry-go-round spun lazily as if pushed by a gentle breeze. But it did not pack it up and blob back to the vortex.

Fine. Turnip first.

I snapped my fingers three times.

The turnip shivered and sprang out of my grip, landing squarely in the middle of the demon-go-round. There was a "*pop*," and the merry-go-round disappeared. Klex, the blob, wobbled in place, stunned on the singed dirt. The turnip bounced around it like a bobber in a stream.

That week-old root vegetable spun on its nubby end and danced a circle around the blob. As it did so, a wind began to blow.

The wind didn't feel all that strong to me, but Klex was not faring well. The blob looked like a weather reporter bracing against a hurricane. The breeze didn't even ruffle my hair, but it drove Klex end-over-blobby-end back to the edge of the vortex.

Klex teetered there on the edge, stretching and straining, before it plopped into the vortex and was sucked down on top of all the other blobs.

The turnip tumbled like it had also been caught by the wind, but it stopped right at the edge of the vortex. Then it dug itself down, turning and turning like a drill, rooting deep into the earth.

With each crank of the turnip, the vortex shrank smaller. A pond, a puddle, a cup of moonlight. When the turnip had drilled into the soil so only the tiny top of it, where a sprig of new green growth poked up, could be seen, the vortex sizzled like rain on a hot sidewalk…and was gone, leaving nothing but a circle of scorched dirt around the newly planted turnip.

The vortex was closed. The demon spawn was gone, yet the root vegetable remained, a plug between Ordinary and the Underworld.

Wow. That was easier than I thought.

"A turnip," the unicorn said from near my elbow. "Huh."

"People used to carve them on Halloween," Bathin said. "To ward off spirits from the other side."

"A pumpkin would have been cuter," Xtelle said. "And more modern."

"Wouldn't have worked," I told her.

The unicorn sniffed. "And how do you know this, Myra Reed?"

"I know the difference between gourd magic and good, old-fashioned root vegetable magic."

The babble of young voices grew louder, peppered with shouts and squeals.

"Brace yourself," Bathin said.

"Why?" I asked.

"Not you."

"What—?" But the miniature horse didn't have a chance.

A swarm of second-graders whooped as they ran up the hill and completely bypassed the play equipment. The tumble of messy hair, gap-tooth smiles, and untied shoes headed for one goal.

The miniature horse.

They descended upon her, sticky hands patting, short arms hugging, while they asked a million questions a minute.

Xtelle looked up in absolute terror and shock. Bathin cleared his throat and then laughed his head off.

The miniature horse narrowed her eyes and mouthed, "*Hoove you*," as the children clung to her in delight.

"That's, uh, maybe you kids should step back," Ryder said, as he and Delaney arrived with the children's teacher and several parents.

"Step away from the dog," Ms. Hen said. "Oh, sorry. Is that a pony?"

"C'mon, kids," Mrs. Ingrath, their teacher, instructed. "Everyone needs to take a giant step backward."

"Mother may I?" a billion little voices asked.

"Yes, you may," Mrs. Ingrath said.

All the kids took one largish step backward. Xtelle stood shivering in the hole they had made, surrounded by little people.

"Nicely done," Bathin murmured.

Mrs. Ingrath smiled and blushed just a little. He really was the thing dreams were made of. I mean, who wouldn't fall into that big ole pit of handsome and charming Bathin was projecting?

Me. That's who.

"We all know we're supposed to ask before we touch an animal," she parroted for the class. "Is the pony tame? Is it a pet?"

"Yep," he said.

Xtelle stomped her foot and neighed, except it sounded a lot like "kill you," instead of whatever a miniature horse was supposed to sound like.

"It's not a pet," I said. "But it won't hurt the children."

"It *loves* children." Bathin's eyes glittered with joy.

The mothers all looked up through their lashes at the demon like he was the first skinny-double-shot-extra-hot latte they'd seen in a year.

"Is it yours?" one of them asked.

I felt…well, not jealous that they wanted his attention. He was a demon after all, a trickster, and gorgeous.

But he was also someone who took things away from people for his own benefit, someone who delighted in doing harm.

I guess I was annoyed they couldn't see past his beauty to his inner scoundrel.

"It's mine," I said.

Bathin's eyebrows shot up, and his half smile spread into something wicked.

"It's not very tame or child-friendly," I added. "It would be best if the children gave it some room."

A collective "Awwww…" broke out, but that was it. That was enough to pull their attention away from the demon and the pony, and back to the park around them.

"*You want me*", Bathin mouthed as some of the children scattered to the play equipment and sand box.

I mouthed, "*Never*," and held my hand out for the miniature horse.

"She's skittish around too many people," I apologized to the kids and moms who lingered.

As if on cue, Xtelle lowered her head, snorted, and pawed at the ground, trying to look intimidating.

"Then we should give her some space," Mrs. Ingrath said. "Let's go, class. Time to play."

Most of the kids took off at a run, but a few dragged their feet in a pouty shuffle. Even so, Xtelle was finally free. She walked stiff-legged to stand next to me, her wide eyes trying to track all the kids at once like she'd never seen anything like them before.

Maybe she hadn't. Unicorns were highly reclusive.

"Thank you, um…Officer," the mom, a beautiful redhead who I knew had just broken up with her last boyfriend, said to me.

She stepped right up into Bathin's space. "And thank you too…"

"You're very welcome," he said, even though he had done nothing but stand there and smile at her.

She liked him looking at her. Liked it a lot. And he was not looking away.

Fine. Maybe he'd kiss her and that would be enough to do the final step of closing the vortex. Then I wouldn't have to. I'd prefer it, actually.

"All right," I said loud enough everyone started and stared at me. Delaney's eyebrows ticked down. She closed her eyes for a second, and when she opened them, amusement shone through.

I'd gotten that look from her a lot over the years. Usually when she thought I was being too stubborn.

She was always wrong, though, because I prided myself in being exactly as stubborn as the situation required.

"Have a nice day," I barked. "C'mon, Xtelle, let's go home."

I spun away from them all, ignoring Delaney's amusement, ignoring Bathin's heated gaze, ignoring the lovely redhead swaying closer to Bathin as if she were in a blizzard and he was a bonfire burning.

I tromped down the hill to my car. Let the demon kiss someone else. Then I wouldn't have to date him three times, either.

The tiny horse trotting along beside me nickered, something that sounded a lot like a laugh.

I strode to the cruiser. Stupid. This was all stupid. And what was up with my reaction to that woman flirting with Bathin?

I'd made it clear not only did I not want to be with him, I didn't want him to be anywhere near Ordinary. But it didn't stop my stupid heart from wanting what it wanted.

I groaned and leaned back on the trunk of the car, pinching the bridge of my nose and closing my eyes. "What is wrong with me?"

The tiny horse clopped around my cruiser as if getting a feel for the thing. She stopped next to me, leaning one hip on the side of the bumper. "Well, you're human."

"You're not supposed to be talking."

"No one is close enough to hear me."

"That doesn't matter. Horses don't talk in Ordinary."

"Well, I'm not a horse. I'm a unicorn. And unless you put the gag order on the other supernaturals who live in this town, I refuse to be silent."

I held her gaze, but I could tell from the stubborn thrust of her lip, that she was not backing down.

She had a point. We never told any man, woman, creature, or deity to remain silent. We just told them they couldn't reveal their true nature to the mortals in the town.

And yes, we'd had it backfire more than once. But we had enough powerful supernaturals in town to take care of anything that might cause an actual panic.

Ordinary was, for most people living here and for those coming here to vacation, a quiet, normal, possibly even boring, town.

If it weren't for the chronically kidnapped penguin and all of Bertie's community events, Ordinary wouldn't even be on the map.

"Ground rules." I held up my finger. "You live with me, you follow my rules."

"Harsh."

"You can pick a different host, but you'll have to follow the rules they set."

She glanced at Delaney, Ryder, and Bathin. "Fine. Rather

you than any of those. What are your rules? Bear in mind unicorns are not known for liking rules. At best I'll try to follow your top three."

"Top twenty."

"Two."

"Ten."

"One. Really, Myra, it's just not in my nature to behave. Two is stretching my limits."

"Three," I said since she'd offered that to begin with.

"Fine." The pout was back. "What are your rules?"

"If I ask you to do something, even if you don't understand why, you will do it. Without complaining."

"I—that's *very* presumptuous of you." Her eyes narrowed and little sparks of red flickered there. "To think you can order me around like a dog."

There was something more to her voice. Something deep and old and powerful. This thing was what had put so much fear into Bathin. This thing, this power churning behind that little horsey face, that little horsey mind, was something *dangerous*.

"I'm not ordering. I'm explaining that when I ask you to do something, I want you to do it. These things will involve your safety or the safety of others."

She held very still, and I waited for the dangerous crackle I felt, like heat over my skin, to subside.

"Understood."

"You agree?"

"I agree."

I'd never seen a horse snarl through clenched teeth. Her ears flicked back and she swished her tail hard enough it made a little whip crack sound. But the heat crackle was gone.

"Rule two, you do not reveal your true nature to anyone in Ordinary unless you clear it with me."

"Fine." Still ground out between clenched teeth. "And the third rule?"

"No magic of any kind." Bathin's voice startled me, and I jerked. He'd somehow come up behind me silently.

The unicorn scoffed. "It's amusing how you think I'd follow even one rule you set."

"You agreed to three rules," he went on like I wasn't even

there, like I wasn't standing so close to him, I could feel the warm puff of his breath on the back of my neck. "That's the third."

"It's not Myra's rule."

"It should be." He brushed his fingers across my bent elbow. I knew he was a demon. I knew he liked to manipulate me and my sisters more than most people. But there was something to the tone of his voice.

It sounded like he was warning me.

"Mind your own," the unicorn growled. "This doesn't concern you."

"Oh, Xtelle, we both know that's not true at all. Everything about you is concerning."

It would be easy to shrug it off. Or stick with anger and tell Bathin to butt out of my business. I didn't want a demon around the unicorn anyway. They were fire and napalm and getting in the middle of whatever rivalry they had would only leave me burned.

Bathin tightened his fingertips on my elbow. Asking me to trust him. Asking me to do what he said.

The tug in my chest was warm, solid. This was where I should be. This was what I should be doing.

His rule was that she couldn't use magic. It wasn't really all that unusual of a request.

Compromise seemed the best option.

"Rule three," I said, drawing the full attention of the little horse, "don't use magic unless you have cleared it with me first."

The horse stomped. "Not fair."

"Ordinary isn't fair, Xtelle," Bathin crooned behind me. "It's *safe*. For it to remain that way, we have all made exceptions. Do you understand now?"

"No." Xtelle shimmered a little, and I wondered if her hold on the horse illusion was about to fail.

"Not being able to use magic is cruel," she said. It looked like even the thought of it hurt her. "I'm made of magic," she whined. "I must be allowed to use it."

Bathin snorted, and it sounded callous and cruel. "You could go back to your *meadow*."

The horse gasped like he'd just clobbered her with a baby

seal. "Who made you so mean?"

"My mother."

The heat behind that was a slap.

Xtelle snapped her head back. "Not everything is meant to fall in your favor, Black Heart."

"That's abundantly clear."

"What does your mother have to do with—"

"Okay," I broke in. "We're done. Agree with the last rule. No magic unless it's approved by me."

"I don't trust you, Myra." The unicorn was still glaring at Bathin.

"You don't have to trust me. You have to follow the rules. If you want another host, tell me now."

She tossed her head and her mane shimmered with just a little too much sunlight. "Very well. Agreed. For the time that you are my host here in Ordinary, I will follow your silly rules. Now may we leave this park? I do not care for the damp. Or the children."

I opened the back door for her. "Hop in."

"I do not *hop*." She planted her front hooves onto the floor and sort of shimmied up into the car.

It was totally a hop. I shut the door behind her and headed to the driver's side.

Bathin put his hand on the passenger side and opened the door.

"No," I said.

"Hmmm?" He was already bent to duck into the vehicle.

"You ride home with Delaney."

"But I came with you."

"So?"

"You do remember the conditions of closing the vortex, don't you? The kiss?"

How could I forget it? It was all I'd been trying to ignore.

"And?" I was glad it came out cool, because I was burning up inside.

"There was a ring, a turnip, and a kiss involved," he went on patiently, as if he were trying to remember the details. "If I recall, we used the ring, and I remember using the turnip, but the kiss? No, I'm sure I would have remembered if that happened."

"Does it even matter now? That vortex has been closed all this time without anything happening."

"It matters. Life and death. Serve and protect. You wouldn't turn your back on Ordinary over a kiss, would you?"

"Fine." I shut the door and marched over to him. "Kiss me."

*Kiss me*, my heart said, softer, longingly.

Not that way. I couldn't let myself feel this kiss, want this kiss. The kiss he was only getting because he'd used a threat to manipulate his way into it.

I squared off to him, feet spread in a stance that would make it easy for me to sweep his feet. Not that it would do much since he was a demon and basically made out of granite.

His eyes didn't twinkle, they glittered like a river in sunlight, and his mouth curved up into a small, tolerant smile.

I wanted to wipe that smug smirk off his face. I wanted to kiss him. I wanted him to kiss me.

But what my heart wanted always led to disaster.

I crossed my arms and raised an eyebrow. "Don't wimp out on me now, Bathin. You wanted this. Come get it."

He half closed the door and sort of leaned on it. He looked amused. Maybe even intrigued. But he did not look like he was going to take the bait.

"Did we put a time limit on it?" he asked. "No, I'm sure that wasn't part of the deal."

"Don't push me, demon."

"Go out to coffee with me."

"No."

"Go out to tea with me."

"No."

"Go to Roy's retirement bonfire with me."

"No."

"You've agreed to three dates, I'll remind you."

"Not those three dates."

"All right." He didn't look one bit put off by my rejection. "We'll table it for later. Just so we're clear, this is a kiss which will hold that vortex closed."

"The turnip is doing fine."

He inhaled, exhaled. "I know you don't always trust me…"

"Ever. Don't ever trust you."

"…but sealing a vortex to Hell actually works toward my goals."

"Does it?"

"Do you think I want other demons here in this untouchable town, messing with souls?"

"I have no idea. Do you?"

"No."

"Why?"

"Because I care…" He seemed to catch himself and change tacks. "I care to be the only one who has that particular honor. You have no idea what kind of cred that gives me in the demon world."

"I thought you were hiding out here, not sending back postcards."

"You know the kiss doesn't have to mean anything. It's a simple *requirement* to seal the vortex. Very analytical. Very impersonal. You like those sorts of things, don't you, Myra? Logic, order. Nothing messy. Nothing with feelings attached."

"This is harassment."

He seemed proud of making me point that out. "Yes, I suppose it could be. Or you're going back on a deal you made because you don't want to face your feelings."

"I don't—." I swallowed and clenched my teeth around a smile. "I don't make deals to avoid my feelings. Try that on some other rube. You want more than a kiss. Which is manipulative and against the rules of our agreement. Therefore, I don't think the kiss is required after all. I think you made that up."

"All right. I see your line of reasoning." He shut the door and took the two steps. He was directly in front of me. "Let's not let a simple vortex to Hell—that will probably reopen since it hasn't been properly closed—get between us, Myra. We have too beautiful of a thing going here."

"We have nothing going here." That's what I said. And I meant it. But my heart? Oh, my heart had other ideas.

My heart liked that he pushed me, teased me, made me follow rules, or make up rules for everything between us. My heart liked how stubborn he was, liked that he wasn't cruel, and hadn't actually ever stepped over any of my personal boundaries.

If he were a man instead of a demon, he'd be just the type I'd date. Maybe even the type I could keep in my life for a long, long time.

I took a deep, slow breath, trying to clear my head with the cool, damp air, but instead got the warmth of his cologne spiced with the green of the park.

"We have nothing going here," he repeated. "So let's seal that vortex with a kiss. Nothing to it."

"No marking my soul."

"I wouldn't think of it." He extended one hand, caught my wrist lightly between his fingers, and squeezed gently. His long fingers were warm, calloused, and could completely wrap around my wrist. Then he transferred his hold, sliding his fingers sweetly down my palm and weaving them with mine.

Only one hand. He left the other free. He didn't step any closer to me. Just waited.

My heart was pounding, pounding, pounding. From just that touch. From just one hand.

This kiss was going to happen.

Nothing to it.

"No marking my…anything." It sounded lame, breathy, but it was hard to think beneath the full force of his attention, hard to do anything but give in to my need to fall into him and keep him.

No.

No. There would be no keeping a demon. Certainly not the demon who stole my sister's soul and wouldn't give it back.

"Give my sister back her soul," I said quietly as I stepped just that much closer to him and tipped up my chin.

"Ah, Myra. I can't. Not now." His other hand lifted, cupping my cheek, his thumb brushing below my lip.

"Why not?" I lifted on my toes, just a little. Because I liked the idea of him reaching down for me, bending for me.

"There are too many consequences."

"Which consequences?"

"I'd tell you, but it would cost more than a kiss."

And just like that, the mood—a mix of desire, blackmail, and challenge—evaporated. "You suck, Bathin."

"You have no idea how well."

To wipe the smile off his face, I finished the distance between us, gripped his face firmly and kissed him.

On his cheek.

He grunted, surprised.

He huffed out a breath. "I...that...really?"

I pulled back with a smack. "One kiss. As agreed. Now the vortex stays closed. Congratulations. You were right. Nothing to it."

I sauntered back to the driver's side and got in.

"What was that all about?" The unicorn had moved out of the back seat and made herself comfortable in the front, sitting upright like a dog, so she could see over the dashboard and out the window. She'd also found my sunglasses and perched them across her nose.

She looked ridiculous. And she was a little more glittery here in the lower light of the car than she had been out in the sunlight. I decided to let it pass. It would take her some time to adjust to living in Ordinary. That was normal.

"Just holding up my end of the bargain to shut the vortex for good." I started the car.

"Ah. The kiss. Is that what you think that was?"

"It was a kiss." I didn't know why I was so defensive.

"Not a demon kiss. Not exactly."

"There was a demon involved."

She made a little "*Mmmm*" sound and twisted to stare at Bathin, then looked over at me. "Ooooo. He's irritated. Very irritated. You do know how to shove a hot brand under his fleshy bits don't you? Oh, this is delightful."

"Gross. So glad you approve."

"Hoof bump." She held out a hoof still not looking away from the demon. The sunglasses had slipped down so she could look over the top of them.

I shook my head. She jiggled her hoof. "Bump me."

"You're very demanding for a reclusive magical creature." But she was also kind of cute and she obviously didn't like Bathin, so that gave her points in my book.

Yeah, I was in a good mood. Today had been a win. We'd just closed down a vortex to Hell with absolutely no repercussions.

That never happened in Ordinary.

So I reached over and fist-bumped her hoof.

She stuck her tongue out at Bathin and wiggled it.

He threw his hands up, his face like thunder.

"Boom," the unicorn sighed. "I am going to just *love* living here."

"Good." I drove out of the park toward home. "How do you feel about a fenced yard?"

"I suppose it depends on the yard. Is it yours?"

"Yes."

"Then I'm sure it will be entirely adequate." The unicorn wiggled her butt deeper into the seat and watched the town go by. She was alternately amused by how "quaint" and "backward" the town was, and irritated by how many supernaturals were "strolling around as if they owned the place."

I reminded her they belonged here, just like she belonged here, as long as they followed the rules, just like she was expected to. Also, if she broke the rules, it would earn her a one-way-ticket back to some other meadow.

"Of course I'll follow the rules," she demurred, eyelashes fluttering. "I'm a unicorn. Everyone knows unicorns are perfect."

# CHAPTER 7

XTELLE SNIFFED at the raised beds that lined the fence, took a second or two to glance at the rose bushes and wild honeysuckle, rhododendron and wildflowers that had taken over the south side of the yard.

She trotted up to me. "It's...nice."

"Nice." I liked gardening, which wasn't always easy here on the coast with the salt air and sandy soil.

"I'm just used to something more..." she waved her hoof at my gorgeous flowers and shrubs, "spectacular."

"Well, this is as good as it gets here," I said. "Not even Felix, who takes care of the heritage garden, has a nicer yard."

"Oh, I know you *tried*, dear. It's just you're so disappointingly human."

I decided to ignore the patronizing little jerk, and turned to the back door. "There's a door here to the garage. You can open it by pushing."

"The garage? Why would I want access to your vehicle?" Her eyes narrowed and became hard. "You don't think I'm a vehicle do you? A beast of burden?"

"No. I know what you are."

*A pain in the neck diva.*

"Look. I don't have a magical meadow for your frolicking needs. My garage is weatherproof, insulated, finished, and clean. It's the next best space."

"I—what about your house?"

"My house?"

"Surely it can't be any worse than your garage?"

"No, it's—"

"Then it shall suffice for the time being. Show me your master bedroom."

"No. Nope. That's mine."

"But I am your guest! Royalty. Should I not have the very best?"

"You're not my guest, you're my responsibility until you're more comfortable living in Ordinary on your own."

"Oh." She sniffed and lowered her head. "I see. I'll just stay out here like a common horse, a beast, a...a vermin of some sort, cold, shivering in the rain while my magnificent image rusts and decays, until I'm nothing but hooves and mushrooms not even fit for Felix's compost pile."

Drama. Queen.

No. Drama. Empress.

"Xtelle?"

"Yes?" she whimpered at the grass.

"Would you like to come inside my home and check out the guest room?"

"The master bedroom, you say?"

"No. The guest room. Since you're my guest. And I want you to be comfortable."

She swung her head side to side, her whole body rocking. "If that's the best you can do..."

"Oh, trust me. It is *everything* I can do."

"Well." She lifted her head and straightened, the wind stirring her horsey mane and setting a flickering of glittery lights free. "I'll humor you. Show me to the guest room."

"Wipe your hooves."

"What do you think I am? A lady keeps her hooves clean at all times." She scraped her hooves on the welcome mat then barged past me into the house trotting into the living room.

"Lace and frills? Really, Myra. Are you compensating for something? I didn't think you were the type to fall into stale female tropes."

"Judge me, and you're sleeping with the mushrooms."

She rolled her big eyes. "Fine."

"Fine."

"Don't you have such a nice home?" She spat that out through her teeth like a threat.

"Yes, I do, thank you. Guest room this way." I couldn't hide my smile as she huffed and trotted after me, muttering about humans and ruffles. I opened the door and stepped aside so she could get a good long look at the spare bedroom.

"It's...that's...I...is this the only guest room?"

I stuck my hands on my hips. "Yep."

"And the…uh…garage?"

"Still an option."

"How is the garage decorated?"

"It isn't. Just a concrete floor, walls with storage, and a nice dry area for straw bedding."

"Straw."

She hadn't walked into the guest room yet, but the straw comment got her moving.

"Rosebud quilt. My, it looks so…homemade, doesn't it? And matching curtains. So…sweet." She gave the shabby-chic dresser one look, rolled her eyes, then hopped up onto the bed and sort of sprawled on her side.

It was an unusual way to see a horse lie, almost as if she were a starlet posing for a silent movie.

Unicorns were oddballs. Which meant they fit right in with everyone else in Ordinary.

"This will suffice." She shifted, dragging the pillows to where she wanted them under her head and front legs. "Now leave. It's been a traumatizing day. What does he see in this town?"

"What?"

"What?" She closed her eyes and exhaled.

"Who, he?"

"Who, he…Myra, I'm exhausted. Leave me now. I need my beauty sleep."

"You said you didn't know what he sees in this town. Who are you talking about?"

"Bathin. I do not know why he is so fascinated with the place. It's all very…mundane."

"Ordinary," I said, not bothering to hide a smirk. "It's all very ordinary."

"Yes, it is. And yet, he refuses to leave." She yawned, then opened her eyes a slit. "I don't suppose you understand why he's staying here, do you?"

"Get some sleep, Xtelle. I'll leave out some oats for you."

"No need," she mumbled. "I'll make myself at home in whatever passes as a kitchen here."

I grunted. I was beginning to understand why Bathin didn't

like unicorns.

"Please," I suggested.

"You're welcome," she replied. "Now leave me alone."

I gave up. She wasn't listening to me. Agreeing to be her host was turning out to be a bad idea, even if I'd mostly done it to bother Bathin.

And why was I making life decisions just to spite a demon?

*You know*, my heart said.

Yeah, I wasn't listening to it either.

THE LATE afternoon sun hung over the ocean, only a thin beadwork of clouds streaking the sky. The wind was calm, the ocean the kind of blue you only saw in dreams, and the bonfire was crackling.

Roy's retirement party had drawn more than just those of us on the police force, his wife and kids, grandkids, and friends. It had drawn half the town.

We had a beach full of humans, supernaturals, and the few gods in town: Athena, Frigg, Hades. The only demigod, Piper, whose day job was waitressing at the Blue Owl diner, laughed over a beer with Chris Lagon, our local gill-man and award-winning craft brewery owner.

The guest of honor was enjoying the free beer and giving grilling tips to Jame Wolf, a werewolf and firefighter, and his brothers who were all manning the massive mobile barbecue they'd muscled down to the sand.

We even had a good showing of vampires, though Old Rossi, the head of them all, hadn't arrived yet.

He was still recovering from a very-near-death battle that had lost him one eye and almost put him in the grave, permanently. It had only been a year, but he hadn't even left his house for the first six months, and then only on moonless nights.

Jean and Delaney, along with Hogan and Ryder, were lounging on driftwood logs brought over to surround the bonfire. We didn't make a big deal about it, but since all of Ordinary's police were here instead of patrolling, drinking was at zero in case we got a call.

Of course, with half the citizens here, we weren't too concerned about the few hours we wouldn't be out on the street.

"Myra." Hera, owner of MOM'S BAR AND GRILL, strolled over and dropped down onto the sandy blanket beside me, pointing her bare feet toward the ocean just like me. "How are you?"

Herri, as she preferred to be called, was tall and graceful, her long, dark hair streaked with blood-red highlights. Her faded jeans were fashionably distressed, and her light jacket fell back off the white tank top embroidered with a peacock feather she had on beneath it. Her skin was that gorgeous all-year tan I envied.

"Good." I pointed my chin toward Roy, who had his head thrown back as he laughed at something the werewolves were saying. "A little sad. I'm going to miss him being a part of my every day, you know?"

She tipped back her beer, then pulled her hair off her neck with one hand before letting it fall again. "I think so. It's easy to get used to things being one way, isn't it? Easy to think life will continue in the same routine we like or are familiar with."

"Yeah." She was the goddess of women, marriage. I'd always thought she was really easy to talk to, which made her a great bar owner.

"What made you come back to Ordinary?" I asked.

"Are you asking for yourself, or is this going to be recorded in the Reed journals?"

I pushed the blanket to one side and dug my fingers in the soft sand. "Both. If you don't want me to record something, you know I'll honor that."

She curled her legs up, sitting with them crossed. "Well, one: I missed it here. There is peace in setting the power at rest. Two: I enjoy being among humans with predictable human wants. The rest of the townsfolk are pretty amusing too." She pointed her beer at the werewolves and vampires challenging each other to some kind of game that involved a football and several tennis rackets.

"It's a nice place to live," I agreed, feeling happy with my town and my people—all the people—here.

"The other reason has more to do with my day job."

"Bartending?"

"Godding." She rubbed at the wet beer label, rolling off a bit of the foil. "There are some events outside of Ordinary that I don't care to be a part of. Gods who are making a bid for...well, let's just say there are gods out in the universe who are pushing for changes. And supernaturals who want other outcomes. I don't care to take sides."

A cold shiver pulled goosebumps down the back of my neck. "Are you talking about a war of some kind?"

"I don't know what it will or won't be." She smiled. "But there is a certain amount of...jockeying between forces and powers out in the world right now."

"So you came here to hide?" I gave her a grin.

"I'm not hiding. I'm here to wait and see. Besides, Ordinary is one of my favorite places no matter what's happening on the outside."

The football-tennis-racket game was in full force, and a couple people—humans—had pulled up coolers as judging seats.

There seemed to be a constant argument as to what counted as a point. Also, some of the players insisted the rules allowed tackling their own teammates.

"Is Ordinary going to be affected by the jockeying between forces?"

She looked away from the game and reached over to squeeze my shoulder. "I didn't mean to make you worry, Myra. You already do enough of that."

"How bad is it going to be?"

She shook her head. "Your father wouldn't have pushed."

"I'm not him."

"No," she said, not unkindly, "you're not. I don't think Ordinary will be involved at all. But if it is, well, there are more than enough of us who will do our part to keep it safe."

I nodded, accepting that truth. The gods, the supernaturals, and the humans had all risen again and again in the town's time of need, whether it was devastating winter storms, petty territory battles, or murdered gods.

One of the werewolves dashed under the hastily constructed line strung between two sticks drilled into the wet sand, and body checked the vamp on the other side.

The two of them went down in a tangle, and someone passed them the ball. It didn't make any sense, but everyone was hooting and cheering and enjoying themselves.

I was impressed at the wolves and fangers carefully not revealing their supernatural strength or speed. That added a layer of challenge to the game the humans wouldn't pick up on, but the rest of us saw.

"So, Delaney's soul has been in the possession of a demon for over a year," I said.

She hummed.

"Some of the old texts say that when a person's soul has been in a demon's hands for over a year, it…fails."

She took a drink of beer, waiting for me to ask her what I really wanted to know.

"Do you think Delaney's soul has been damaged?"

"Yes." Quick. Without hesitation.

"Permanently?"

"I don't know. Reeds aren't exactly like other humans when it comes to power and powerful things. Your bloodline is bendy. But that doesn't make you invulnerable."

"She's the bridge for god power to cross into Ordinary and be stowed away." I chewed on my bottom lip. "Will a damaged soul change that?"

"Will it change her ability to do her job?" she asked.

I nodded.

"I can't speak for all the deities in creation, but for those of us who have been here? We're pretty comfortable with humans being flawed. That's part of what makes you all so interesting. And lovable."

She grinned, and I rolled my eyes at her. "I was trying to be serious."

"I know, Myra." She lifted her beer to encourage me to do the same with my iced tea. "You are always serious."

"It's my strong point," I grumbled as I took a swig of tea. It was something Chris was offering now. Non-alcoholic beverages including this tea with just a hint of bergamot and raspberry. I loved it.

"It might be one strong point, but it's not your real

strength."

"Oh? What's my real strength?"

"Balance."

I frowned. I had no idea what she meant, but didn't spend another second worrying about it. I was standing up, the tug in my chest telling me to move, to be on my feet, to be ready.

It wasn't hot or painful, just a nudge, so I didn't think wherever I was about to be was going to be dangerous.

Delaney shot up to her feet, handed Ryder her iced coffee, and took off walking down the beach. Toward a lone figure who waited.

A god.

I couldn't tell which god it was from here. But I wasn't going to let Delaney face whoever it was alone. I stopped by Jean, tapped her on the shoulder, and pointed at Delaney. She squinted against the light, then nodded.

"Let me know if you need me," she said.

"I will." I bent and dug a cold beer out of the cooler, then, on a whim, picked up a bag of chips. I started after Delaney, the shifting sand warm and dry beneath my bare feet, making every step a little slower and harder. That wouldn't stop me. Come to think of it, nothing would stop me from having my sister's back.

That included the demon I felt more than saw extract himself from the group of men around the barbecue and start up the beach behind me.

# CHAPTER 8

DELANEY WAITED for me to catch up to her. Neither of us waited for Bathin, who strolled behind as if he were just out for a walk and we happened to be in front of him.

"Who is it?" I asked as soon as I reached her.

"Raven."

Raven, or Crow as we called him when he vacationed here in town, was a trickster god.

"You going to let him back in?"

"If he can follow the rules this time. Why? Do you know something I don't know?"

"I doubt it."

We were close enough Crow could probably hear us over the waves. He leaned against one of the huge rocks that the tides had uncovered so that it stuck up out of the sand like a two-story haystack of black stone and bone-gray barnacles.

"Good evening, Raven," Delaney called out.

"De-laney! My baby girl. C'mere and give Uncle Crow a hug." He held his arms wide and made grabby motions with his cupped fingers.

I couldn't help but grin. Neither could Delaney.

She walked right up to him, stopped just long enough to look him over in the way that made her sort of glow if you looked at her from the corner of your eyes.

It was the bridge power she carried. Here, with a god in full possession of his power standing on the shore of Ordinary, she became more. Not just a woman with a bendy bloodline that stretched back and back, she was the earth of this place, the stone, the roots, the soul. Here, she *was* Ordinary, that remarkable place favored by gods and loved by the lucky.

Strong as the world. Strong enough to stand against the gods. Even this one whom we knew so well.

To me, Raven looked identical to how he looked when he was last in town as Crow. He was medium height, black hair cut in a messy style that only enhanced the handsome features given to him by his full-blood Siletz lineage. His eyes twinkled and his smile was warm and welcoming.

This trickster god had a swagger and love of mischief that turned both male and female heads wherever he went.

He flicked his gaze from Delaney, winked at me, then turned his attention back to her, his arms still wide and waiting.

"Well?" he asked. "You still love me, don't you, boo-boo?"

Delaney wrapped him in a hug, her head on his shoulder. He dropped his arms around her so he could pat her between her shoulder blades.

"It's good to see you," she said.

"It's good to see you too, little bit." He gave her one more gentle pat then released her. "Now, how formal is this going to be?"

"There are rules, Raven."

"Oh, do call me Crow."

"I will. When you put your power down. Until then, I will call you by the name that recognizes which god you are."

"The best god?"

"Raven."

"The god you love?"

"Raven."

"The god you trust and missed and would do anything for? Why, thank you, Delaney. I know I'm amazing. You're too kind."

"No," she said, the strength of Ordinary in that word, the stone of Ordinary, the power. "You are a trickster god, Raven. Of course, I love you. But I'm not letting you back into town until you agree to the rules."

"All right." He stuck his hands in his back pockets. "Shoot."

"You will follow all of Ordinary's rules while you are within Ordinary, especially the rules involving picking up or putting down your power."

It wasn't something that usually had to be told to a god once they had signed the contract upon their first entry into town. But Raven had broken that rule specifically.

"As if I'd ever do anything to break Ordinary's rules."

She held up one finger. "Stop. In case you forgot, I don't have to let you into Ordinary, Raven. You vacation here at the blessing of one person in the universe. And you're looking at her."

He gave her a hard look. "The demon has your soul, but you're still you, aren't you? Gotta love that Reed blood."

"That isn't a promise to follow the rules," she said. "Give me your word, Raven, that you will follow the laws of Ordinary."

Raven slapped his palm against his chest. "I, Raven, do solemnly swear to obey the laws of Ordinary, including that pesky power rule I broke last time I was here."

Delaney waited for a heartbeat, for two. Finally, she nodded. "See that you do." Then she took one big step backward.

Nothing changed.

Except somehow, everything changed. The day looked brighter, the air sweeter, the sounds of ocean and, in the distance, laughter and music, closer.

The barrier between gods and Ordinary was lifted, and Raven took three steps forward into Ordinary proper.

"Welcome back, Crow," Delaney said.

"Why, thank you, my sweet Myra. How about a hug for Uncle Crow?" He did that wide-armed "gimme" motion again.

I shook my head but came forward anyway, wrapping my arms around him. He was one of my favorite uncles growing up. Always willing to answer my endless questions, though not always with the direct truth. He was teasing and full of stories and puzzles. I'd always loved him for that.

"How's that demon thing going?"

"Fine."

He released me and his gaze zeroed in on Bathin. I didn't know what he saw in him, but he and the demon had some kind of history.

Crow had given Delaney her dragon. A dragon that preferred to look like a tiny pig and had the ability to find demons and move them.

"How's the dragon?" he asked, still focused on Bathin.

"Eating our house and home," Delaney said.

"Eating you *out* of house and home?"

"Nope. It's eating the house. We've lost a carpet, a side table, a loveseat, and the dishwasher. So thanks a lot for that. You owe us a household appliance."

Crow laughed. It was a glorious sound, wild and loud. Mixed with the crash of waves, the rumble of voices down the beach, and the sharp call of seagulls, it sounded like home.

"I'd apologize, but you know." He shrugged and draped his arm over her shoulders.

"You never apologize?" Delaney asked.

"No. Well, yes. But I think the dragon's usefulness beats losing a couple pieces of furniture."

"That dishwasher cost eight hundred dollars," she muttered.

"Serves Ryder right for installing something that expensive. I might be willing to replace it with something gently used in the four-hundred-dollar range. Now can we be friends?"

"We've always been friends," she said with a smile. "Let's get your power stored, and then you can join the party."

He opened his free arm for me, and I tucked under it, just as comfortable there as when I was a kid. I handed him the bottle of beer.

"You missed me didn't you?" he asked me.

"Nope."

"Better work on that lie, Myra. I can see right through you."

Yeah, then, he had always been able to do that.

We strolled toward the bonfire, Bathin walking ahead and to the side, as if he hadn't just been trying to follow us around. Delaney flagged Frigg out of the ball-and-racket game she was winning. Frigg took one look at Raven, gave him a chin tip, and then jogged up the beach to meet us.

"Hey, Bird. How's it shaking?" Frigg was tall and blonde, and had a set of strong shoulders and biceps courtesy of her very physical job owning the tow truck service in town. Her T-shirt advertised FRIGG'S RIGS and so did the baseball cap she had on backward.

Raven unhooked his arms from around us and shook her hand. "Not bad. Better now I'm here. You holding the goods?"

"Yep. My turn for a year." She swiped sweat and lose tendrils of hair off her face with the bend of her arm. "You want to ride with the girls or me?"

"He'll ride with you," Delaney said. "Myra and I will follow."

Crow raised one eyebrow. "I forgot how bossy you are."

"Oh, you haven't seen anything yet," she said sweetly. "I've had a full year of no gods in town. A full year. It's been eye-opening."

"You mean boring?" he said. "I know, poor thing. That's why I've returned. To put a little spice back into your life."

She stuck her hands in her back pockets. "You want a chance at getting some food and more beer before it's gone, you need to start flapping your wings instead of your mouth."

He waggled one finger at her, then turned and jogged a bit to catch up to Frigg who had already climbed up the rise of the shore to her truck parked nearby.

"So why do you want to drive there with me?" I asked Delaney as we trudged up through loose sand and rocks to the stairs to the parking area.

"I need to talk to you."

"About?"

She shook her head and pointed at the cruiser. I opened it up so we could get in. By the time we were settled, Frigg had already pointed her big diesel out onto the road, her blinker on.

I pulled up behind her.

"She's storing the powers out on her property," Delaney said. "Back in the wetlands."

"Hollow log?"

"No. She made a place for them. An altar of sorts. It's actually really pretty."

"Pretty enough to draw attention?"

"No, you have to know what you're looking for. It's secure."

"Sounds interesting. So talk. What's up?"

"About this morning. The whole vortex to Hell thing."

"What about it?"

"Are you okay?"

"Why wouldn't I be?"

"You agreed to host a unicorn, and I know how much you like your privacy. Also, Bathin kissed you." She glanced over.

"Nope. I kissed him. Smack on the cheek."

"Is that enough to seal the vortex?"

"It was a demon kiss. Why wouldn't that be enough to seal the vortex? Besides, he said a demon kiss was part of the ritual, but he's half a bag of bullshit and a half a sack of lies. Why? Did he say something?"

"No, but he's been...different."

Bathin liked to tell me he was connected to my sister and could feel her through that connection. Delaney was connected to him too, so I knew she had a good read on him.

"How different?"

She pressed her fingers to her eyes and talked through her palms. "I don't know. He just...he keeps looking at me funny when he doesn't think I notice. And he's been asking me questions."

"Keep going. Give me more details."

"He asked if he can stay in Ordinary. Permanently."

"No."

"Myra, that's not for you to decide."

"Like hell it isn't. He broke the rules to get here. He took our dad's soul, and now he's taken yours. He won't sign the contract to follow the rules..."

"We don't actually have a contract for demons."

"Because they've never agreed to sign anything! You know he'd find a way to wriggle out of the contract if we had one."

"No. I don't think that's true," she said.

"Who can write a contract that a demon can't break?"

"Ryder."

That was...well, it wasn't a bad idea. Since Ryder had pledged himself to Mithra, the god of contracts, and Mithra had made him a Warden over Ordinary, it did give Ryder some fire power.

"You think Mithra's going to have our best interests in mind?" I asked. "You think he would do something decent like allow Ryder to draw up a demon contract? That god hates us."

"We don't need Mithra's permission. We'd just need Ryder. He sees things differently now that he's chosen. He can build a watertight contract."

"Okay, so we get Bathin to sign a contract vowing to be a

good citizen of Ordinary who follows the laws, and gets a job—which, I can't even imagine what he would be good at—and then what? He still has your soul."

"I think, maybe we can use it as a bargaining chip. He gets to stay in Ordinary, I get my soul back."

"Have you floated this idea to him?"

She slumped in the seat a bit.

"You did, didn't you? And he told you no, didn't he?"

"He didn't say no. He said there would be conditions I wouldn't like."

"What conditions?"

"He didn't have a chance to tell me. Things got a little busy."

I mulled it over for a few minutes as Frigg took us out away from the main roads of town and into the forested areas with a lot of wetlands. Her house was tucked quite a ways off the bay. The road was a one-lane deal here, full of hairpin turns and snake-like curves.

"One other thing," Delaney said. "I'm starting to…I don't know. Maybe this is dumb."

"You can tell me," I said. "I'll just listen."

She picked at the door handle, then seemed to make a decision. "I think having my soul possessed is, um…sort of getting to me."

"How so?"

"I'm forgetting little things. My attention wanders. I don't think it's happened at work, and not often when I'm not working, but I just feel…drifty sometimes? Not lost, but…well. Lost."

"Is it worse when you're near Bathin?"

"No. He's…he's really not that bad of a guy, Myra."

I pulled back my shoulders. "He really is. He *took* a part of you and won't give it back. That is not something a good guy does."

"I gave it to him fair and square. You keep forgetting that. I *offered* it in exchange for letting Dad's soul free. I'd offer it again."

"I know. It was a stupid thing to do, but I understand your motivation. But it's been a year—more than. He needs to give your soul back, no strings attached, exactly as it was before he took it."

"Maybe if I gave—"

"No. You've done enough, given enough. If he wants to be a part of Ordinary, if he wants to follow the rules of doing no harm, he needs to step it up. Because he's doing harm right now. Has been doing harm since he got here."

She nodded. "Yeah, you're right. I think he might be able to understand that now."

"He's a demon, Delaney."

"Yeah. But we're no angels, Myra."

I couldn't argue with that. We turned off the twisty paved road to a just-as-twisty dirt road. Almost there.

"Do you really think demons can live in Ordinary?" I asked.

She thought on that for a bit. It was one of the things I loved about her. She made snap decisions all the time, but she was just as capable of looking at a problem from all angles.

"I think Ordinary is supposed to be a safe place for everyone," she said. "All those beings who don't fit the mold, all those who do. We're inclusive, even though we're only a tiny patch of dirt that the gods decided they liked way back in the beginning of things.

I parked the car and killed the engine. Frigg and Raven were already out of her truck, laughing like a couple of drunken friends heading home after a bender. Frigg stopped walking long enough to check on us. I waved her forward, and she gave me the thumbs up, knowing we would be right behind them.

And we would be. But I wanted, no, I *needed* to hear what Delaney thought about the demon who held her soul.

"What do you think?" she asked.

"Do I think he can live here? I asked you first."

"I know," she said. "I think…I think Bathin hasn't belonged anywhere for a long time. Maybe this is the place and the time to change that."

"You are way too close to the situation to see it clearly." I sighed.

"Not true. I'm exactly close enough. Don't you scowl at me," she admonished, and there was my sister who had scolded me for being too serious and stubborn for most of my life.

"Myra, do you like Bathin?"

I scoffed.

"Because he likes you," she went on like a steamroller with a fresh tank of steam. "He asks about you all the time, wants me to share stories, tell him what you like, where you are. All the time."

"That's none of his business!"

"I agree. And that's what I tell him. All. The. Time. But that doesn't stop him. He likes you, Myra. And the longer he's here, the more he's falling for you."

"He's not falling for me. He's just interested in the one thing that he can't have."

She rubbed at her eyes again. "I don't think so. I'm connected to him. There are times when I can tell he's thinking about you."

The blood hit my face hard enough to tingle. I knew I was blushing tomato red.

She chortled. The jerk.

"Not like *that*," she said. "I can't read his mind. I just…it's like knowing someone is drawn to a warm fire, or a blue sky, or clear water. He's drawn to you. Has been since he first showed up in town. And…" She held up her palm to stop me reiterating that when he first came to town it was because he'd just stolen her soul and used it as his very own key to break Ordinary's lock.

"It confuses the hell out of him," she finished. "He's not used to feeling things. Really feeling them."

"He only feels because he has your soul."

"Is that in the books?"

"No."

She gave my hand a little pat. "I think having my soul helps with the whole feeling thing, actually. But he's been feeling on his own. Trust me."

"I do trust you. I don't trust him. Not while he's holding you captive. You understand that, right?"

"Yes. Now how about the truth? Do you like him?"

"No." Even as I said it, my stupid heart knew otherwise. I did like him. Maybe too much. I winced and looked away.

"Just don't forget you're a part of this equation too, okay,

Myra?"

"My opinions?"

"Your feelings." She tipped her head down to catch my gaze. "You deserve to love someone too, you know."

"I don't—"

"Someone who challenges you mentally and keeps you on your toes emotionally. It might not be Bathin, as a matter of fact, maybe it shouldn't be Bathin, but it should be someone. You deserve love. And no matter my circumstances or Ordinary's or the job's or anything else that you're carrying like you're the only Atlas in the whole danged universe, you deserve to have love. To be loved. Okay?"

"Sure. Fine. Whatever."

She slapped my shoulder. "It's more than 'sure, fine.' It's yes. You deserve a yes. Also, how about: 'thank you for reminding me that life isn't all about work, big sister.'"

"Do you want that on a cake?" I asked.

"Yep. Red velvet, butter cream frosting." She opened the door and stood.

"I'm all outta frosting," I muttered. But she heard me.

"I'll just keep reminding you until you give in and believe it. Or bring me a cake."

"I got it. I deserve love."

"Say it like you mean it, sister. 'Cause even I can tell you don't." She crossed the yard to the path that wound around the back of the nice three-story house.

"Would it kill you to let it go?" I asked.

"Nope. But I'm not going to."

And that, right there, was what I was afraid of. But I didn't say anything, because we'd had enough honesty for the day.

# CHAPTER 9

"YOU CALL this an altar?" Raven asked.

Frigg slugged him in the arm. Hard. She was a deity and could pack a wallop.

"Didn't ask your opinion," she said. "And I never said it was an altar. That was Delaney."

He glanced over at Delaney and tipped his head. "How does this look like an altar?"

Delaney pointed to the five huge fir trees that surrounded us. "When you look around us, all you see is trees. But when you look to the sky?"

Raven did just that, and so did I. The tops of the trees carved a perfect five-point star out of the sunset sky, a whorl of orange and bubble-gum pink clouds swirling through the deepening blue.

"Not bad," Raven said.

Frigg made a noise of agreement. "It's old. And strong. It will hold the powers without the complication of them being in some small containment where they can be easily stolen. Like a water bottle." She raised an eyebrow and gave Raven the stink eye of all stink eyes.

Raven, well, Crow, had been stupid enough to leave the god powers he was supposed to be guarding in the old furnace of his glass-blowing studio. The powers had been stuffed in a water bottle and stolen.

It had been the beginning of a lot of trouble that had ended with the gods all leaving Ordinary.

He leered at her. "Like you didn't have a good time. Someone had to shake things up around here."

"If you're staying," Delaney said, "you need to release your power to me, Raven. And through me to this place of safe holding."

I didn't know why this was making me so nervous. Delaney had done this many times. She was made for it, chosen. But my stomach clenched when I thought about the family gift my sister possessed.

She, for a brief amount of time, was a conduit, a string, a road upon which the entire power of a god would travel.

She'd told me she didn't see power as much as she heard it. Dad had always perceived the god powers visually.

I did too, though my sight was not as keen as Dad's or Delaney's.

Jean wasn't here, which meant she hadn't had any bad premonitions about Delaney being soulless while handling god power.

"Settle down," Raven said to me. "I know what I'm doing." He could have made that mocking or light. Instead, he sounded exactly like my uncle. Sometimes when he was serious, no, always when he was serious, it settled me.

"I know," I said.

Delaney made a face at me. "For real? C'mon, you know we have this covered. It's not the first god power I've bridged since I gave away my soul. Unless you think someone else should be here?"

"Like who?" I was sincerely curious.

"A certain hunky demon."

"No! Why would I invite him to the secret place where all the secret god powers in town are being kept in secret?"

"Well, he has my soul. Maybe you think I could do this better if I had it nearby."

I snorted. "He can probably find this place because he has your soul, you know."

"Nope," Frigg said. "It's demon blocked. Untouchable."

"You can do that?" I asked.

She gave me a smile that was absolutely wicked. "Oh, sweet winter child. The things I can do."

"Hot," Raven noted. "Also, I'm starting to itch. Can we get on with this, ladies, before I hive up because I'm in Ordinary trying to vacation but am still carrying my power?"

Delaney shook out her hands. "Okay, bring it."

Raven laughed. "Things have gotten a little more casual since I've been gone, haven't they?"

She cleared her throat. "Raven, god of wings, black feather, trickster, storyteller, uncle, friend. Welcome to this place of rest. Welcome to Ordinary. To remain in this place, chosen by you, by power, by the stars, you must lay your power down.

"Do you agree to give it to the care of the goddess Frigg for the year in which she will be guarding the powers of all gods who rest here on this shore?"

"I agree," he said happily.

Delaney stepped over to stand right in front of him. They were in the exact center of the clearing, the sunset sky shifting colors above them. Frigg stood behind Delaney and put her hand on Delaney's shoulder, ready.

"Then rest your power upon this gentle earth," Delaney said.

And yeah, there was something about that, those soft words that embodied everything that she did for the gods, everything all our family had always done, that choked me up a little.

I was proud of us, who we were. I was proud of this town and all the people—whether mortal, supernatural, or deity—within it.

Right there, that moment, I was so proud of her.

"With great joy," Raven said. He winked at Delaney, then wrapped his arms around her and brought her into a hug.

The power transfer was different from god to god. Delaney had spent time talking about it, and I'd read all of Dad's accounts, and all of his Dad's, and those who had bridged before them.

Sometimes the process was very hard and painful. Sometimes it was so easy and gentle as to be nothing more than a handshake and a nod.

But this...this was something more. Because Raven—or Crow—was someone more to us. He had a bit of our hearts. And we, I liked to think, had a bit of his.

There in the falling twilight, his power glowed gold and black, flashes of silver, green, blue, and white shot through it like lightning hopping summer-fragrant air.

The glow surrounded him and flowed like slow honey to wrap Delaney. For a moment, several heartbeats, they were both surrounded by power. Then it drew away, almost reluctantly, from Raven until only Delaney was glowing.

Crow released her from the hug, and she turned to Frigg and held out both her hands.

Frigg took her hands, and the power drained away from Delaney.

I expected Frigg to glow, but she didn't change at all. It was her job to give the power a place to be kept safe and undisturbed. She didn't actually have to touch the power at all.

The ground at Delaney's feet pulsed with gold and all the colors of sky and night and earth and water. That pulse rushed out like a neon stream and flowed up the tree trunks.

Bark and limb glowed for a moment, briefly. I heard a sigh of voices singing, a song so old and sweet as to be impossible.

Then the glowing power, the distant song, the sweet fragrance of warm summer wheat was gone.

The dusk wind stirred the firs, a softer ocean song than the one that charged at our rocky shore.

"Good?" Delaney asked Frigg.

"Perfect. Almost like you've done this before."

They released their handclasp, and Crow sauntered over, kicking a couple pine cones like he'd forgotten what dirt felt like under his shoes.

"Nice job, Delaney. Now let's go get that beer and barbecue."

He patted her shoulder and walked out of the circle of trees. Frigg motioned for both of us to follow him, which we did, leaving her behind to secure the holding place.

"You okay?" Delaney asked.

"Me? Why wouldn't I be?"

"I don't know. You've been acting a little weird lately. I thought maybe you didn't believe I could do this anymore."

"Wait." I caught her arm before she could walk any farther. "I don't doubt you. I've never doubted you."

At her look, I amended, "Not when it comes to the job or your gift. You are the one and only. I know how good you are at this. It's just...I'm waiting for the other shoe to drop. We both know Bathin owning your soul isn't a good thing. I keep thinking, maybe this will be the moment we find out what kind of consequences we're going to have to pay for that deal."

"You could ease up on the worrying a little," she said. "It's making me jump at shadows. We both know if something really terrible is going to happen, Jean will give us advanced warning."

"I know," I said. "Sorry."

She smiled. "It's good. Let's go wish Roy a fond farewell before the party winds down or somebody calls in a report of Mrs. Yates's penguin being kidnapped again."

Since at least one of those things was a very real possibility, we got to the car and the party as quickly as possible.

WHAT HAD started as a going-away barbecue for Roy had turned into a town-wide, multiple-bonfire, food and drink thing.

Everyone was down on the beach. *Everyone.*

With weather this nice, I wasn't surprised. But as the sun sank into the ocean and the stars popped in a sky clear enough we'd be peering at the Milky Way soon, even more people arrived, laying out blankets, lanterns, candles, and starting fires for their family and friends to gather around.

It was one of those spontaneous, wonderful things that didn't happen very often.

I found a spot on a big rock up near the rise of the shoreline where I could keep an eye on the whole event. When the restaurants had realized where all their customers were headed, they'd brought out tables and awnings and food. All that delicious food was irresistible, and I'd filled my plate. Twice.

I was full, relaxed—well, as much as cop instincts would allow—and the laughter, crackle of fire, hushing waves and outbreak of singing, eased away the stress of the day.

Or maybe the stress of the year.

First, it had been Dad's death, then everything we'd had to deal with from murder to an ancient evil using our town for target practice.

Delaney had been shot—twice. Jean got hit by a car. Bathin had taken Delaney's soul.

And Death had been playing a long game. He'd come to Ordinary to vacation and take out an evil he'd been trying to get his hands on for years.

Things had calmed down for a bit while the deities were

out of town, but today's vortex was troubling.

"Always in the shadows," a voice said from behind me. "Brooding. I can appreciate that."

I hadn't heard him come up behind me, though that wasn't all that unusual. He was a vampire, after all.

"Hey, Rossi. Decided to leave the mausoleum to be seen among the living?"

He moved, and I could finally pick him out of the slabs of darkness impenetrable to my fire-blind eyes.

He was tall, with craggy features that were handsome even with the black patch over his left eye. His salt-and-pepper hair was long, brushed back and wavy, his prominent nose had a hook that only made him more interesting to look at.

"I heard there was a celebration."

"I think everyone's heard there's a celebration."

"Mind if I join you?"

"Sure you don't want to buddy up with Delaney?"

He unerringly found her in the crowd at the fireside, his one eye steady as a hawk in a dive, then looked back to me. "I prefer the sister in the quiet and shadows tonight."

I scooted over so he could sit. I watched him considering it, deciding if it was worth the effort to bend that far.

Old Rossi had very nearly been killed. He'd been shot in the head with a bullet made of the grave dirt from his making. Delaney had taken the same bullet in her chest, but she had healed much, much quicker than he had.

For the last decade or so as the owner of a yoga studio in town, he'd pulled off the easy-going-hippy vibe. He taught there, and was known for his grace and fluid movements, and Zen thoughts and comments.

Not so, now.

He closed the distance to the rock and eased himself down, holding one hand, long fingers spread out below him, to better gauge the distance to the rock. It was a slow, slightly shaky process before he finally made it down and sat.

He wore soft, dark-gray clothing, layers of shirts with a large, thick-collar sweater that covered his long throat and rested just beneath his chin.

From his clothing, which covered every inch of his skin

except for his hands and his face, I knew he was not up to full power, not fully healed. I wondered how many years it would take until he was.

"I haven't seen much of you, Myra," he said after he'd sat there a while, doing the vampire equivalent to catching his breath.

"That's because you haven't left your house. How are you?"

"Progressing. Did you notice the vortex to Hell?"

"Yes. You too?"

He inclined his head, his gaze drifting to the faces in the crowd. I watched as the vampires, all a part of Rossi's family, looked over to him as if they heard or felt him. Each acknowledged his presence in some way as he acknowledged theirs.

They weren't actually related by bloodlines, or at least not most of them. Rossi had a way of picking up lost vampires and bringing them into his fold. Since he also policed them and made sure they followed the rules of Ordinary or faced his wrath—which included killing them, if necessary—it all worked out for us too.

Ordinary had become a bit of a sanctuary for vampires who worked regular jobs and otherwise lived their unlives as happily as any other person here.

It didn't surprise me to see a couple familiar vamps, Leon and Evan, break off from the celebration and make their way up to where we sat.

They were coming to guard Rossi, to make sure he would be safe here among the people and supernaturals.

Old Rossi, however, had other ideas. He lifted his hand, a small motion even I could tell was a dismissal, to wave them off.

They hesitated, debating whether or not to follow his order.

"Wow," I said. "When did they get so dumb?"

He let out a sound very like a weary sigh. "My health has instilled doubt. It is, at the very least, irritating."

"And at the very most?"

"At the very most, someone will decide to challenge me."

I let that thought settle for a moment. "And how do you

think that's going to work out for them?"

"Poorly." His smile was all fang, and his entire body tightened with the readiness of a hunter who had been idle too long in a cave. A hungry predator.

"You're not supposed to enjoy confusing your family," I said.

"Oh? And you're going to give me advice on how to hold this clan of vampires together? What sorts of books have you been reading lately that make you an expert, Myra? Perhaps something I know? Perhaps something I've written?"

"Okay, fine, I get it. You're old enough you don't need my advice. Go ahead and ignore me. Everyone else does."

He let that comment fall into the evening air, and I wished I hadn't said anything. I really didn't have a close relationship with Rossi, or at least not as close as the one Delaney and he had. Delaney had taken him a stuffed, blue llama toy a few months back, and told him to stop being such a baby about his injuries.

A stuffed llama. For one of the most powerful supernatural beings in town.

From what I could get out of Ben, Rossi's actual blood son, Rossi sort of loved the little toy. Ben swore me to secrecy and told me Rossi had taken it into his private chambers where he kept all his favorite things.

So Delaney clearly knew him better than I did. The closest Rossi and I had been in recent years was when I ticketed him for streaking.

But still, he'd been a fixture in town, and I liked steady things. I liked it when the world remained the same, predictable. Safe.

My gaze roamed over to Bathin, who lounged among the werewolves like he was one of them. I was surprised they'd let him join them. I was also surprised he had a cat in his lap. Not the same stray, but maybe another one, that kneaded the fabric of his jeans as he ran his hand gently over her back.

Huh.

Delaney was curled up against Ryder at the fire. He was reenacting what appeared to be a very active chase scene, his arm snug around her, half-empty beer in his hand.

She laughed and shook her head, then took a drink of his beer. He didn't miss a beat, just kept telling the story to the people next to him, who were wiping tears from their faces.

"What do you know about souls, Rossi?" I stared at my smiling sister. Had her smile changed? Was it less bright? Were her eyes going distant, even there in the middle of all that life, all that laughter and camaraderie? Did she look tired? Worn down? Damaged?

Or was it just a long day and a retiring friend that made her look so sad?

"Is that the question you want to ask me, Myra?"

"What other question would help me get her soul back?"

"Ask me what I know about demons."

I shifted so I could look at him. He gazed placidly at the beach and bonfires, waiting.

"All right. What do you know about demons?"

"Demons do not lose."

I scoffed. "You're going to have to tell an awful lot of religions they got it wrong."

"Demons," he went on, even softer, which made me lean in to listen, "do not lose. Whatever they do, they win. No matter how many ages it takes, no matter how many stars rise, catch fire, and burn to ash."

"So they're competitive. Noted."

"Once they take a soul, they will forever possess it."

I rolled the beer bottle between my palms. That didn't sound good.

"If we take that as a known fact, which it is," he said, "then we must ask ourselves something about Bathin."

"Why he's such an ass?"

"Why he gave up your father's soul."

"He wanted into Ordinary."

"I agree. Why?"

"I have no idea. Do you?"

Rossi made another dismissive motion with his fingers, and the vampires who had been slowly creeping across the sand toward us stopped, hung their heads and went back to the party. They chose positions close enough they could reach Rossi in a split second. Vampires are fast. They were totally keeping an eye on him.

"They like you," I noted.

"They fear me."

"Fear for you, maybe," I said, calling his bluff. "You've made a family and they *like* you."

"Have I, now?"

I knew the vampires could hear him. Even over the roar of the ocean. Even over the crackle of the fire. Even over the laughter and singing and general pulse beat of the living.

I knew they were listening to my answer. Listening to him.

"Yes. There wouldn't be room for many vampires in Ordinary if you hadn't made a family here. Made peace here. I know you wouldn't offer this kind of shelter and community if you didn't like it. You're a good man, Rossi. Even when you're moping over old injuries."

He made a *tsking* sound. "Injuries. These are nothing but a scratch. I've had worse opening envelopes." He waved one hand toward his face and his chest.

"Those almost ended you," I said softly.

"You underestimate the danger of the envelopes I've opened, Myra."

I chuckled. "Just admit it."

"What?"

"You aren't going anywhere. You aren't going to let someone challenge you, and you aren't going to give up being the head of the clan."

The vampires on the beach seemed keenly interested in his answer, if their total faked lack of interest indicated anything.

"Of course I'm not going anywhere," he said so softly only the vampires and I could hear him. "If there is a challenge, I will meet it. And win. I am a very old vampire. I don't just stop existing so very easily."

If they could have breathed, every one of those fangers on the beach would have exhaled as one.

"I know." And I did. I had read everything there was to read about vampires. But more than that, I had known Rossi since I was a child. I knew what kind of vampire he was, what kind of man.

"Vampires and demons have one thing in common," he

said. "We don't lose well."

"So why did he give up Dad's soul?" I asked, bringing us back to that conversation.

"Because he saw something he wanted more."

"We went over that. He wanted to get into Ordinary."

Rossi turned his head, just a fraction. Enough that the shadows dug beneath his sharp cheek and jaw. Enough that I could see the unholy fire of the undead in his eye. "He didn't want Ordinary, Myra. Not exactly."

"All right. I give up. You tell me what he wanted when he traded my Dad's soul so he could possess Delaney's and become the only demon ever allowed in Ordinary."

"Love."

I laughed. "Of course! That's exactly what the demon was after. That's why he tricked my sister out of her soul and hasn't given it back while he makes her miserable and probably does irreversible damage to it. He decided he wanted to fall in love."

"How did you get so much more cynical than your sisters?"

"Practice."

"Bathin spent years with your father trapped as they were together between life and death."

"And?"

"Your father was a very convincing person. Strong. He had an almost unlimited capacity to love and forgive."

"I know how to forgive."

He smiled. It was the look someone who was very, very ancient might give a very young girl. "I know you do. I wouldn't be in this town if you and your sisters couldn't see beyond a person's flaws."

Delaney temporarily dying had been very much his fault, but he had been trapped in circumstances beyond his control. We knew that. I'd been angry at him for months, but Delaney had sought him out, stuffed the blue llama of penance in his hands and, with that, made it square between them.

"She's better at forgiving than I am," I said. "Delaney. Jean too. Delaney isn't even angry about Bathin taking her soul."

"And you are?"

"Furious."

"Ah. That's going to make what you have to do more

difficult."

"What do I have to do?"

"Maybe you should try yoga. I'm thinking of reopening the studio soon. Having a Reed there always attracts an interesting crowd."

"I have to do yoga?"

"No, I said you could try yoga. What you have to do is forgive the demon."

"I don't forgive assholes who hurt my family and break rules to get what they want."

He cleared his throat. "You might want to remember who you're sitting next to."

"You're…well, basically family. You've earned forgiveness. He hasn't."

"If he gave Delaney back her soul, would you forgive him?"

There it was. The question I didn't want to face. The possibility I was fighting for, with the outcome I didn't know how to navigate. What if Bathin gave her soul back? What if he apologized? What if he signed a contract and agreed to follow Ordinary's rules?

What if there was no reason for me to tell him to leave?

The wind shifted, bringing with it a lick of heat from the fire, followed by the cool exhalation of the ocean. I shivered, unmoored from the safety and order of the world.

"I hate change," I grumbled.

And Rossi, that ancient vampire, laughed.

# CHAPTER 10

THE UNICORN did not sleep in the garage because, "Really, Myra. I am not a beast of burden like you."

Instead, she took over my guest room, pulling the handmade doilies and lace curtains down with her teeth and trotting them into my laundry room where "they can be washed, but never improved."

When she complained about the color scheme being "too English-rose-meets-clown-school," I told her it was my guest room, and I'd be happy to consider her a responsibility instead of a guest and leave her out in the garage with the car and a pile of hay.

Since it was closing in on two in the morning, I pointed at the bed. Told her to use it or lose it.

I'd never seen a unicorn (because here, where no one could see her, she said she preferred to let her horn fly free) look so sullen. She slunk up onto the bed like she was made of liquid pout and ennui and sighed loud enough I could hear it from the hallway.

"Don't care," I called back.

I shut my door, decided at the last minute to lock it, just in case Miss Horn Flying Free decided to level a complaint in the middle of the hours I had left to grab some sleep.

I kicked off my shoes, shucked out of my pants, dragged my bra off from under my T-shirt, and fell into bed.

SOMETHING SOFT and fuzzy pressed down on my face, heavy as a cat sitting on my head.

I didn't own a cat.

I jerked awake, shoving away the intruder. A wide, fuzzy muzzle, round nostrils, and long horse face filled my vision.

"You're awake!" Xtelle declared. "Good. Make me breakfast."

"I'm not awake."

"Ah-ah. Lying isn't allowed here in Ordinary."

"I'm not lying," I rubbed at my eyes and scrubbed my face, "and of course lying is allowed."

"Oh? Well, isn't *that* interesting? Not that I would ever lie. A lying unicorn! Can you imagine such a thing? I can't imagine such a thing, no, not at all. But you shouldn't lie, Myra, because you're just so…so…*that*."

"That?"

She waved a hoof at me. "Reed-ish. It's…unavoidable."

I had no idea what she was talking about. "Go away."

"You said I'm your guest. I demand you make me feel welcome. I shall have breakfast!"

She jumped down off my bed, trotted across the room, hooves ringing like wind chimes in a hurricane as they struck the hardwood floor. "Hurry, Myra. I can't wait to try omelettes for the first time."

"I'm not making you omelettes!" I pulled the pillow over my head and locked it down with my arm.

"You can't expect me to eat a scramble. Peasant food."

I dragged the second pillow over my head and scrunched down deeper into the covers.

Something crashed in the kitchen, and the "Oops! Was that an heirloom?" was loud enough to stab through my down-enforced trenches.

I pushed the pillows off my head just in time for my alarm to go off.

Five o'clock. Time to get ready for work.

I groaned and slogged to the bathroom for a shower. Let the unicorn mess up my kitchen. Let her break my heirlooms (not that I had any). All I wanted was hot water, soft soap, and for the stupid unicorn to figure out how to start the coffee pot.

By the time I dressed and put on my makeup, I was in a slightly better mood.

I made my bed, straightened my room, and gave myself a little pep talk while staring in the mirror above my dresser. "Don't kill the unicorn."

"Myra, why aren't you making my meal?" Xtelle kicked at the frame of my door. "I am hungry and I've been waiting for you to…oh, what are you doing?"

"Getting ready for the day."

"By smothering your face in wax and dye?"

"It's called makeup."

"Well, it doesn't suit you at all."

"I like it, and I didn't ask for your opinion." I pushed past her, turning sideways to get through the door.

"Why are you even wearing it? Oh, I know! You're trying to attract a mate."

She sounded gleeful. And evil. Which was a weird mix on a pink unicorn.

"I'm not attracting a mate. I wear this for me."

"To signal you're available for a mate." She flounced into the kitchen and plopped down in the armchair she must have dragged in there, crossing all four of her legs neatly. "Who is it? I will help you."

"No, you very much won't help me." I opened the refrigerator, glanced at options for breakfast. I had eggs, and an omelette would not only be quick, it was actually what I was hungry for.

"Then why wear something to bring so much attention to your…well, I'm sure it's at least an *average* face."

"I'm not trying to attract people. I'm warning them." I retrieved the egg carton, located a bowl, and started cracking eggs into it.

"Warning them of what?"

"I'm ready to go to war."

She was silent as I cracked the rest of the eggs and whisked them. I heated the pan, added butter, poured in the eggs, and shot her a look over my shoulder. "Speechless?"

"No." Her eyes were suspicious little slits. "Who do you expect to go to war with?"

"Anyone who breaks Ordinary's laws. Including, but not limited to, pushy pink unicorns."

She made a short, offended noise. "Rude. But because I am a creature of magical pureness, I will not rise to your hateful, stupid comments. Even though that shade of lipstick makes your crooked teeth look like orange slices."

I stared at her a second, then burst out laughing. She was

just so put out and pouty and…I had a pink unicorn in the middle of my kitchen trying to domineer my dating life.

"Nice of you to hold yourself above petty insults." I went back to the omelette, adding the vegetables in the fridge I had pre-prepared two days ago, and sprinkling in some sharp cheddar. "Because if I thought you were being mean to me, I might not make you an omelette."

"Oh," she said. "Are you? Making me omelettes?"

"What does this look like?" I waved the spatula over the pan.

"Food."

"Omelettes. Enough for two and some left over for your lunch if you want."

"Why would I want leftover eggs for lunch? I'll be dining with you today. Out on the town, perhaps? Your finest establishment."

"Nope. I work."

"So will I. Right beside you. Learning the ways of Ordinary."

"Nope again." I cut the omelette cleanly in half then slid each half onto a plate. "You are not a part of the police force. Let's keep it that way."

"But how can I learn about Ordinary if I'm cooped up here in your house?"

"You aren't even supposed to be in my house."

I put the plate down on the kitchen table and pushed a chair out for her, then sat in front of my own plate. "The house is full of books you can read, a television you can watch, a computer to browse. There are some horse videos online you might want to check out so you can learn how to act like a horse. Or you can spend time in the yard watching the neighbors. You'll need to…" I waved one finger at her, "get back into horse form. You should probably do that now before you forget."

"As if I would."

She hopped out of the armchair and scrabbled up to sit across from me, her back legs stuck straight out under the table, her front legs bent on either side of the plate. "Is this an omelette? Just…eggs?"

"You don't know what an omelette is?"

"I'm a mythical creature. I don't do brunch."

"But you wanted me to cook...okay, right. Unicorns eat hay and oats and grass."

"I'm not a horse."

"Fine. What do unicorns eat?"

"We're about to find out, aren't we?"

She picked up the fork next to the plate and poked at the eggs. I stared at her, still thrown by her un-horselike movements. It must be her magic that allowed a hooved creature to manipulate an eating utensil. She neatly cut a bite of the pillowy eggs and forked them into her mouth.

"Nice trick with the fork," I said. "Subtle magic. Impressive."

She raised an eye ridge as she chewed once. "Unlike your breakfast skills." She opened her mouth and stuck out her tongue, dribbling the eggs back to the plate. "These are terrible. They taste like eggs and cheese and vegetables."

"Imagine that." I finished the last of mine and took both our plates to the sink.

"Here. Try this." I offered her a homemade oat and honey bar I'd made in the middle of the night about a week ago.

She sniffed it then took a tiny nibble. "That's...different." She shoved the entire thing in her mouth, chewed, and swallowed. "What is that called?"

"It's a breakfast bar. So now you can apologize about the omelette."

I handed her a second bar, then rinsed the dishes and loaded them into the dishwasher.

"Why would I apologize?" she asked with her mouth full. "I wasn't the one who made it."

"You are a terrible unicorn. Go be a horse."

Her mouth fell open and I waited, my arms crossed.

Then she laughed. It was a weird cross between a clown horn and a squeaky toy.

"Is that my laugh?" she asked wide-eyed. She giggled, all horn and squeak and ridiculousness. "That's my laugh! Listen, Myra, listen to me!"

I couldn't help it. I laughed too, because she was absurd. "You don't know what your own laugh sounds like?"

"Well, I do *now*!" She chortled, and it sounded like a rubber chicken shaken by the neck. She opened her eyes wider and pointed at her mouth.

I placed an extra bar on the table. "There's more in the cookie jar. You might want to try the carrots in the refrigerator, or the box of granola, which I'll leave out." I set the granola near the cookies. "I'll be back before dinner, we'll find something for you to eat then."

"No need. I'll go to work with you."

"We just went over this." I strode out of the kitchen to my home office down the hall. The door was locked because there were valuable books, spell items, and other magical things I didn't want to fall into the wrong hands. Or hooves.

I stepped into the comfortable, airy space, and followed the tug in my chest without focusing on it too much. I dragged my fingertips across the spines of the books, until I felt a tingle in my palm. I withdrew two identical books: COMMON AND UNCOMMON LAWS OF ORDINARY

"Huh," I said.

"I thought virgins were annoying."

"What?"

"What?" Xtelle paused just inside the room. "Are you listening to me?"

"You're not going to work with me." I tucked the training manuals for becoming a reserve officer into my bag. This wasn't just the human law stuff, though that was covered too. This was mostly the dos and don'ts of upholding supernatural and deity laws.

"Well, isn't it pretty?"

I glanced over. "No. No, no, no. Put it down."

"This?" Every drawer of my desk was open and it was obvious she'd rummaged through all the contents. I had no idea how she'd done that so quickly.

She was sitting in my chair, one pearly little hoof pointed at the carved wooden box she'd placed in the center of the desk.

The box contained the only weapon I had against Bathin. A pair of golden scissors with an ebony blade and a ruby blade. A crossroads demon had given them to me. They weren't enough to cut Delaney's soul away from Bathin's grasp—I'd need a certain page of a certain book to do that—but this was all I had to save her soul. A stick of dynamite without the fuse.

"That's private," I said.

"I'm a unicorn."

"What does that have to do with anything?"

"I thought we were just saying random things."

"This isn't yours." I picked up the box.

"There you go again. So random."

I slid the box onto the tallest shelf. "It contains things that are private and not for you to see. Promise me you'll leave it alone."

"Like I can reach it up there. Fine." She hopped off the chair and started digging in the drawers again. "What a strange assortment of junk. There's not even one disemboweling scoop."

"What?"

She looked over at me and batted her extra-long lashes. "Ice cream scoop?"

"No, you said—" The doorbell rang. It was followed by a brisk knock. "Wait here."

I strode to the front door and looked out the peephole.

Bathin had his hands in the front pockets of his slacks, his suit jacket unbuttoned, his crisp white shirt pulled back far enough to reveal the width of his chest and flat stomach. He stared straight at the peephole and smiled.

Back there on the sidewalk, in front of my house, a couple cats lingered. Strays again. Were they adopting him?

I opened the door. "What do you want?"

"Good morning to you, too, Myra. I'm here to collect on our deal."

"What deal?"

"Three dates. I'm here to claim the first."

"No."

"Have breakfast with me. We can take a long stroll on the beach, get to know each other. Find out if our star signs align."

"I already know your star sign."

"How studious of you." He leaned in, resting his arm on the doorjamb above my head. I rocked back on one foot and crossed my arms over my chest. "Want to share all the good stuff with the class?"

"Ass, you mean," Xtelle shouted from behind me. "You have some nerve coming here and trying to...what are you trying to do?"

"You like me," Bathin said, ignoring the unicorn. "I like you. Let's have breakfast."

"I already ate."

"Let's have coffee."

"No."

"Her? You're trying to date her?" the unicorn screeched. "That one? Why did you choose the most boring Reed?"

I raised my eyebrows and decided the demon had a good strategy. I ignored the unicorn.

"No breakfast," I said to Bathin.

"Then let's do lunch." His smile was almost fond. "I know you're trying to come up with an excuse for why you can't have lunch with me. I'm sure you have a dozen very good reasons. Here's my rebuttal: We made an agreement back at the Hell vortex. Let's not sully those memories by going back on our words. Lunch will be lunch. I'm not expecting anything else."

"Except two more dates."

"Except two more dates." His gaze flicked down to my mouth, then back to my eyes. "Let's do lunch today. Then you can choose our next date. How does that sound?"

"Weak," the unicorn muttered.

"Fair enough, considering you forced me into agreeing to this."

"There were other choices," he said. "There are always other choices."

Maybe I should just ignore him too. "What's up with the cats?"

He shrugged. "Strays."

"I know that. Why are they following you?"

He shrugged, but didn't say any more.

I frowned. "Are you feeding them? Are you...?" I tried to peer around him. Yep. Three stray cats. They looked healthier than the last time I'd seen them around town. And even though they were ignoring Bathin, it was obvious they were following him.

"You're taking care of them, aren't you?"

"I don't know what you're talking about. So," he said. "Lunch. I'll stop by around one."

"I'm working."

"I know. I'll find you. I will always find you." His gaze wandered from my eyes to my lips and back to my eyes. He winked.

"Knock off the stalker act, Bathin, or I'll have to throw you in jail. And then who's gonna feed your cats?"

I shut the door in his face. I waited for the chuckle and footsteps to fade, then went back to packing for the day.

# CHAPTER 11

DELANEY SHUT the door to the evidence room. Jean and I squished together a little closer between the shelves and stacks of boxes. It had been awhile since we cleaned out the little storage room and there wasn't a lot of open floor space left.

"Okay." She leaned back on the shelf behind her. "We have some volunteers for reserve officer. I want to run them past you two before we do the actual interviews."

"Is that how we do this?" Jean asked me.

"Since Ryder is the only reserve officer we've hired?" I shrugged. "We don't really have a procedure. Who've we got?"

"Half-a-dozen people are interested, but I've narrowed it down to two." She fished folders off the shelf behind her and handed one to me and one to Jean.

"No way," Jean said, flipping through the pages quickly.

I glanced at the first page.

Kelby, one of the local giants. She was level-headed, hard to ruffle, and physically in great shape. She'd be terrific at the job. Especially since she already knew about the supernaturals and deities in town.

I quickly scanned through the recommendation letters from her boss, her teammates on the volleyball team, the basketball team, and the golf team, then finally got to the second applicant.

"Oh." I read the applicant's name twice. No, three times just to make sure I was seeing it right. "Death? As in the deity? The god of? Thanatos?"

"That's him," Delaney said. "You've met him, remember? Sort of uptight and formal. Likes kites. Has terrible fashion sense?"

I would smack her, but there just wasn't any room. "When did he get back to town?"

"Around three o'clock this morning." As if just the memory of it made her tired, Delaney yawned and rubbed at her forehead. "I already took his powers out to Frigg. Ryder went with me. Than is once again, officially, a citizen of Ordinary."

"And he wants to do this?" I lifted his folder.

Jean handed her folder back to Delaney. "He didn't seem like the kind of guy who was all that interested in law enforcement when he was last here."

"I think he's the kind of guy who's interested in everything," Delaney said.

"How did he know we were looking for more people?" I asked.

"It came up when we gave him a lift back to his house."

"What about the kite shop?" Jean asked. "I thought he was all about selling those things."

"He said he wants to broaden his human experience. He thinks he should try being underemployed while working two part-time jobs."

I snorted, but he wasn't wrong. Crime really wasn't all that high in town, and we didn't have the budget to pay any more officers. Working for us meant volunteering. For free.

"So you're taking him seriously?" I asked.

"Yes," Delaney said. "I am taking death seriously."

"Shut up." I opened the file again and read it more carefully. "I'm not against the idea of getting some fresh resources, and I agree with Jean. I think Kelby will be a terrific fit."

"Plus, she's a supernatural, and all the rest of us cops are humans. We need better representation of our citizens in the department," Jean added.

"Right," I agreed. "And it makes sense we let a deity try out law enforcement if that's how they want to spend their vacation. But Death?"

Delaney shook her head. "Not Death. Just Than."

"Death, Than, I vote for the scary guy," Jean said.

"You think he'll be a good cop?" I asked. "Really?"

Jean unwrapped two sticks of gum, releasing the clean scent of mint into the air, and popped them in her mouth. "I don't know. Probably not. But it's gonna be hilarious watching him try."

I widened my eyes and shot Delaney a look.

"He can learn," Delaney said. "We all can learn. It's close-minded to underestimate someone. We all have the capacity for change. Let's give him a try. Just for a week or so. If it's not working out, I'll tell him."

"You're going to fire Death," I said.

She smiled. "You keep calling him that. While he's here, he's not really Death. He's Than, the kite shop owner. Just another quirky citizen in our quirky little town."

"I know. I get that," I said. "Do you understand my hesitation?"

"Yes. Noted. Do you have any other concerns?"

"Who's going to train him?" I asked.

Quick as a flash, both of my sisters pointed at their noses.

"Nose goes," they both chirped.

"No," I said. "I have too much on my plate as it is. Come on."

"All you have on your plate is a unicorn," Jean said. "Who I still haven't met."

"Trust me, you don't want to."

"I think a unicorn sounds fun."

"Oh, just buckets of rude, demanding, self-centered joy. She took over my guest room, complains about my cooking, and won't do as she's told."

Jean grinned. "No sympathy from me. You got me volunteered for the stupid Slammin' Salmon Serenade. Bertie is a task master. Every time I think I've slipped away, she shows up right in front of me. She tracked me down when I was hiding out over lunch yesterday."

"Where were you hiding?" Delaney asked.

"Here. Like, right here." She pointed at the room.

I laughed.

"The door was locked!" she said. "But she came in anyway."

"She's a Valkyrie," I said. "What did you expect?"

"Privacy. I expected to be able to eat lunch without her dumping a pile of paperwork on top of me."

"Aw, poor thing." Delaney cooed.

"There, there," I said.

"You both suck."

"Well, we both took our turn being Bertie's lackeys," Delaney said. "It is your turn, girl."

"But it's a salmon parade. It doesn't even involve costumes. It's just, like...dead fish walking."

"So don't care," I said. "I had to roller skate breakfast goods to people."

"And I had to judge a rhubarb contest," Delaney said. "*Rhubarb*."

"So you can march with the fishes, sister," I said.

She blew a bubble, popped it. "Fine. At least I don't have to train a rookie god."

"No," Delaney said. "You have to train a rookie giant. I want Kelby with you on the desk and ride alongs for the first week."

"That works," Jean said. "Except for when Bertie takes up all my time."

"I'll take Kelby if Bertie needs you," Delaney said. "Hatter and Shoe can help too. Sound like a plan?"

I reached into my bag and pulled out the rule books, handing one to Jean. "Let's do our part to make Ordinary safer."

Jean chuckled and Delaney shook her head. "Or at least keep it just as safe as it is now. Speaking of which, do you have any more info on the Hell vortex situation?"

Delaney opened the door, and we all headed into the fresher, non-minty air.

"I haven't had a chance to get to the library yet. I'll head up tonight, after my shift."

"Okay. Good. Let me know if I can do anything to help."

"You could tell Bathin to give back your soul."

We were both out in the hall now, Jean having moved past us to the front desk.

"I have asked him. He keeps giving me the same answer," Delaney said.

"No?"

"No. He keeps telling me he can't." She shrugged. "So until he can, or we find a way to make him, that's a no-go."

"Delaney," Ryder said, coming down the hall toward us. "You ready?"

"Just about. We're going to the casino to pick up god mail," she said to me. "You okay dealing with Than today?"

"I'll be fine."

"Okay, good." She pressed her hand on my arm. "Do you mind doing a drive-by on the vortex? I just want someone to keep an eye on it while I'm out of town."

"Leave the vortex to me. And Than."

"Tell me if you need help."

"I will."

She gave my arm one more squeeze, then moved out into the main part of the station.

Ryder tipped his head at me and moved to follow her, but I caught his sleeve.

"Can I talk to you a second?"

"Sure."

"Outside?"

"I have some books for you in my truck."

"Perfect."

We strolled through the station. Delaney and Jean were talking to Hatter and Shoe, giving them the rundown on the first week of training for our new recruits. Delaney held up her finger in the universal "be with you in a minute" sign as we walked by.

"So what's up?" Ryder asked as soon as we were out the door.

"How's Delaney? *Really*."

Ryder was over six feet tall, and his stride was naturally longer than mine, but he shortened it without me saying anything. We stopped at our vehicles, parked around the back of the station.

"She's good, most of the time," he said. "But other times...I don't know."

"The staring off into space thing?"

He nodded. "That, and she doesn't laugh like she used to. It could be because we've been together for a while. Maybe she's losing interest."

"Or maybe her soul has been in possession of a demon for over a year, and that is a lot of strain for anyone to bear."

He stared at the station as if he could see through the walls to his girlfriend inside.

"I need you to keep track of her, any changes," I said.

110

"All right. What should I be looking for?"

"Anything that isn't normal? Maybe you could keep a diary or journal and just note her behavior and moods? We can take a look after a week or two to see if any patterns emerge."

"You want me to spy on your sister."

"It's not technically spying."

"It's spying."

"It's observing. I want you to observe her so we can help her."

He hooked his thumbs in his jean pockets, pulling the flannel shirt away from the dark green Henley he wore beneath it. "Do you know how to get her soul back yet?"

"I have a date," I cringed, "with Bathin. Today. I'll knock some information out of his head."

"Sounds…violent."

"Oh, it will be if he thinks he can take my sister away from me."

Ryder's eyebrows went up, but the look in his eyes was respect. "I'd almost feel bad for the demon, thinking he can tangle with a Reed woman and come out on top, but that bastard is using my girlfriend's soul for leverage. That doesn't sit well with me."

"Or me." I pushed my bangs out of my eyes. "So, the books?"

"Yep." He lowered the tailgate and leaned in to drag a moving box toward him.

"Found them in the old house on Quay Avenue I'm remodeling. Thought you might be interested."

"I expected a book or two."

"Twenty."

"And you think they should be locked away in my library?"

"Well, half of them are in languages and symbols I can't read. They're old. A couple appear to be handwritten. All that is a pretty good indication I should hand them over to Ordinary's historian/librarian/knowledge-keeper."

I smiled because it was always nice when someone acknowledged my responsibilities weren't just policing and being at the right place at the right time.

"Thanks. I'll look up all the people who lived in the house

so we can get an idea of where the books came from."

I popped the lock on the cruiser's trunk, but before I could lift it, it was pushed open from inside.

"Freeze," I yelled, pulling my gun in one smooth motion. Ryder was half a second behind me, dropping the box with absolutely no hesitation, his weapon drawn.

The lid creaked open the rest of the way.

"Ta-da!" Xtelle threw her front legs up by her ears and jiggled them like jazz hooves.

"Jesus," Ryder said, holstering his gun.

"What are you doing in my trunk?" I didn't lower my weapon an inch.

"Exactly what you told me to do."

"I told you to stay at my house and watch videos about horses."

"I'm sorry? No speaka da being held prisoner in a town you *insist* is equally welcoming to all creatures."

"How long do you have to listen to that?" Ryder asked.

"Every minute her mouth is open."

"I never thought I'd be happy about the pig," he said.

"Pig!" She narrowed her eyes and tipped her head to ramming position. Good thing her horn wasn't visible. "What did you call me, human?"

"Simmer down," I said. "It's a dragon anyway. It just takes the shape of a baby pig."

She lowered her hooves and placed them neatly in front of her on the edge of the trunk so she could peer right and left. "It's a...a *dragon* do you say? Isn't that interesting? So interesting. Does it...uh...run wild in the town?" Her eyes were too big. She looked nervous.

Ryder gently pressed down on my gun arm. "We don't let it run wild."

I sighed and holstered my firearm.

"Dragon pig lives with Delaney and me." He nodded toward his truck. "And rides shotgun."

"So it's...here?" Her voice carried a small flutter. "Dragons and unicorns do not mix. I hope there's no reason we'd need to interact?"

"There's nothing written in stone about it," Ryder said.

Then the door to his truck flew open. Xtelle scrambled out of the trunk and quickly trotted around to hide behind me.

"Oh, come on," I groaned.

The pig seemed to get more adorable the longer it stayed in Ordinary. It tip-toe-trotted between the two vehicles, the pebble-on-rock sound of its hooves announcing its approach.

"Help me," Xtelle breathed into my knees. "It knows what I am!"

"Take it easy," Ryder started. "It's just a little…"

"Violence isn't allowed," I reminded Xtelle. And myself, because, really? The drama coming off of this unicorn could fuel a high school theater company.

"…dragon pig," Ryder continued. "Perfectly harmless. Hasn't done anything violent toward anyone. Unless you count that thing it did with the fire hydrant. And that was more a theft with intent to break my leg. Not actual violence."

"Just settle down," I said. "Laws of Ordinary apply to you too now, you know."

"I don't know the laws!" Xtelle moaned. "I haven't read them yet!"

"You would know them if you'd stayed home like I told you to."

"But that's boring, and unicorns cannot survive boredom. It's our one flaw."

One flaw? Oh, let me count the ways.

"Really? Boredom?" I asked, calling her bluff. "I've never read that fact before."

"We've never allowed it to be written down. Because it's our *weakness*," she stage-whispered.

"Uh-huh." I so didn't believe her.

"You so don't believe me!"

"Unicorns can die of boredom?"

"Yes! Why do you think we search out virgins?"

"Yeah, I don't want to know," Ryder mumbled. "C'mere, dragon buddy. Let's not eat any government property today."

"Virgins have nothing to do with their lives and are more likely to spend time keeping a unicorn company," Xtelle said.

"You have a weird idea about virginity," Ryder said.

"Keeping you company," I stated.

"So we don't get bored! And die. Of boredom."

I looked over at Ryder for some sympathy. He kept his expression blank, but there was a twinkle in his eyes.

"Yeah. Good luck with that, Myra. Keep your guest entertained. So she doesn't *die* of boredom."

"I will shoot you."

"Naw." He grinned. "That's just what you say to the guys you actually love."

I did?

He laughed. "The look on your face. Did you just realize that? When you like someone, you threaten them. It's how you show the love."

"I do not."

"You do. Pretty much constantly. Here we go." He bent and scooped the little pink bundle of piggy cute into his arms. "No eating a car today, buddy. There's not enough insurance in the world to take care of that again."

"He ate a car?" I asked.

"He is a dragon. Needs fuel for…whatever it is dragons do when they're not trying to chow their way through the town's infrastructure."

Xtelle behind me made a little "*eep*" noise.

"Oh, for all the…" I reached around to get a handful of her mane. "Come here, Xtelle. Let me introduce you to Ordinary's only dragon."

"No."

"This is a part of being a citizen of Ordinary. You have to get to know people. New kinds of people you might not have met before. This is a great first step, don't you think?"

She pressed her head against the back of my thigh and shook it side to side. "No, I do not. I do not need to meet a dragon."

Ryder rubbed the little piggy on the head right between its little pointy ears.

"Come on now, Xtelle," he said in a gentle tone that I thought might work on spooked horses. Too bad she wasn't a horse. "Dragons don't mean anyone any harm. The worst this one does is track down demons. We see that as a benefit, not a flaw. Since you're not a demon, this isn't going to be a problem at all. You might even make a friend."

"A unicorn does not cavort with those *things*."

I caught Ryder's gaze, tipped my chin at the unicorn behind me, nodded. He nodded back, shifting his hold on the dragon pig so its little piggy face was in his hands.

I mouthed: "*one, two, three.*"

Then I stepped to the side, exposing the unicorn at the same moment Ryder pivoted and bent so the dragon pig and the unicorn/mini-horse were eye to eye.

The pig rumbled, a very not-pig sound.

"This! I object!" Xtelle said.

The pig's eyes widened, going shiny with fire. Two puffs of smoke curled up from its little nostrils. The rumbling got louder.

"Huh," Ryder said. "That's weird. He's usually really good meeting new people."

"Unicorns and dragons do not mix," Xtelle whispered again.

"Hey," Delaney said as she approached. "What's going on?"

"Just doing a little community relations," Ryder said. "Did you know dragons and unicorns don't mix?"

Delaney reached over and tugged the dragon pig's ear. "I don't think dragons and most things mix. Isn't that right?" She scratched the little pig's eyebrow and the pig blinked, its eyes going back to more piggy and less dragon-y. "We're still a little fond of it."

"Our fondness is severely tested when the dragon eats his way through the junkyard," Ryder said.

"Again?" she asked, exasperated.

"Yep. Just a riding lawnmower this time."

"We said no eating vehicles, didn't we?"

"I think we mentioned no eating cars or trucks."

She lifted the pig's chin and stared it in the eyes. "No eating any kind of equipment. If you need metal to keep you going, we can get you some scrap buildings. Someone around here is almost always tearing down a shed or something. We can just say a strong wind destroyed it, okay?"

The pig wagged its little curly tail.

"No," she said sternly. "The cute will not work on me. I

need your word that you will not eat any vehicle or piece of equipment of any sort in this town unless you ask me or Ryder first. Yes?"

The dragon pig rumbled, and it sounded like laughter.

"That's not a yes," Ryder said. I had no idea he was picking up dragon-speak.

The dragon pig oinked once.

"Good." Delaney gave it one last tug on its other ear. The dragon pig looked inordinately pleased with itself.

"It's up to something," I said.

"Yeah," Delaney agreed. "It usually is. How's it going, Xtelle?"

"Better before I knew there was a dragon in town," she said.

"That makes two of us," Ryder said.

Delaney made a face at him. "Yeah, well, this dragon has been very handy. More than once. So. I'm glad it's here."

Ryder got that sappy look that meant my sister was the world, the stars, and the moon to him. She was looking right back at him with the same gooey bliss.

Last winter, the dragon had saved Ryder's life. He'd been coming back from a job and had been in a car accident in the middle of a snowstorm. Bathin, who is good at finding and moving people, hadn't wanted to bring him directly home.

It turned out the dragon was an amazing demon tracker.

Dragon pig had disappeared and reappeared with a very put-out Bathin and an injured Ryder in tow.

Knowing there wasn't any place in the world where Bathin could escape the dragon's reach was one of the only reasons I slept at night.

"All right," I said, breaking up the kissy-kissy looks. "Don't you two need to be going? God mail waits for no man. Or woman. Or pig."

"Hello, Reed Daughters," a mellifluous voice said from behind me.

I turned, and the unicorn trotted around with me so that she was once again hiding behind my legs. She stuck her head out to one side and watched the man stroll our way.

Well, not man. God. Death. Than.

He wore expensive gray slacks, shiny black shoes, and a light-brown leather jacket which was unzipped. Beneath that was an outrageously yellow T-shirt with 100% ORDINARY splashed in red across it.

Than was tall, lean, and carried himself with an unconscious authority that commanded attention. His hair was dark and trimmed to perfection, his skin pale, and unwrinkled. His eyes were deep and black as the night, cool and endless as the ages, older even than time.

He caught me staring and tipped one eyebrow up. There was amusement in those eyes now, but he didn't smile. I'd never seen him smile.

"Hey, Than," Delaney said. "Myra's going to handle your training for the day. Show you the ropes."

"As you wish." He turned his body to fully face me, and his attention carried weight. "The creature behind you?"

"Yes?" I asked.

"What is it?"

"What does it look like?"

"A unicorn!" Xtelle stomped out from behind me, head lifted high. "I, sir, am a unicorn."

Than notched his unsettling gaze downward to her. "I see."

His cool gaze drifted back to me. "You know what she is?"

"Yes. This tiny horse thing was her choice."

"Why?"

"Because if she were to run around Ordinary in her true form, it would cause havoc."

"Indeed, it would."

"All right," Delaney said. "Call me if you need anything or if anything weird happens."

"Weird in Ordinary," Than mused. "I do wonder what that would entail."

Delaney laughed and she and Ryder headed toward his truck.

They didn't catch the way Death directed his gaze back to the unicorn/not-unicorn.

They didn't catch the way his eyes went hard and bright.

# CHAPTER 12

THE UNICORN refused to ride in the trunk no matter how many times I told her to get back in there. She settled into the backseat and was not happy about it.

But hey, driver makes the rules, and Death rides shotgun.

I handed the other laws and rules book to Than. "Read through this and be ready for some pop quizzes. Later, you'll have to take a written test."

He held the book almost delicately between his long, thin fingers. "These are the laws I shall be required to learn?"

"All reserve officers must know not only the mortal laws, but also the supernatural laws."

"I'm sure it will be riveting."

I glanced over to see if he was giving me shit, but he already had the booklet open and was calmly scanning the page.

He was a hard guy to get a read on. Most of the time he seemed aloof to the world around him, but at the same time intensely focused, as if he were savoring every little detail. Like he didn't want anyone to see how much the mortal world, and being a part of it, fascinated him.

"If you have any questions about any of it, please ask me. We'll talk through it until it makes sense." I guided the cruiser out of the parking lot and onto the street.

The unicorn blew air through her lips and flopped her head on the window. "Boring."

"More boring than the trunk?" I asked with a sunny smile.

She met my eyes in the rearview mirror and flipped her ears back. "No."

"Good. I'm going to drop you off at my house. You can read some books, watch TV. About real horses. I'll be home later to check on you."

"Is that a threat?"

"Xtelle," Than said calmly.

"You can't boss me around," she snarled.

"Enough." Than snapped his fingers once.

Xtelle pressed her lips together, her nostrils flaring as she glared. Silently.

Blessedly silently.

"I don't know how you did that, the snap thing? But I want you to teach me," I said.

"First, you become Death. Is that a position you to aspire to attain, Reed Daughter?"

I grinned. "Nope. Not at all."

"Well, then. Perhaps there are other ways to install cooperation in those around you. Might I suggest coffee?"

"You want a cup?"

"Is it not the standard beverage for officers of the law, Reed Daughter?"

"First, you're a reserve officer. Second, please call me Myra. Third, this officer of the law prefers tea."

"Is that so?" He smoothed his fingers along the sharp edges of the book. "So do I."

I flicked on my turn signal and crossed traffic to head to the drive-thru tea shop—the first one in Ordinary. It carried a wide variety of specialty teas, because I'd basically promised I'd keep them in business by making sure I came there, and sent everyone else I knew too. They also carried homemade pastries and several coffee options.

Xtelle hadn't stopped breathing heavily through her nostrils, but her gaze slipped between the back of my head, which she looked like she wanted to punch, and the back of his, which she looked like she wanted to ignore. Finally she leaned her head sideways against the window with a defeated *clunk*.

"Still think that would be a really useful snap to learn. Does it work on anything other than unicorns?"

He looked away from the brochure and blinked. "I can only imagine it would."

I waited for a break in traffic, then pulled into the drive-thru behind two other cars.

"Can I ask you a question? Not about the snap," I said. He nodded. "What's going to happen to Delaney's soul?"

"Eventually?"

"No. If I don't find a way to force Bathin to give it back to

119

her. Will it kill her?"

He shifted in the seat, angling his shoulders so that he was more fully facing me. "Every creature eventually journeys through death."

"I'm not talking about eventually. I know we all die. I just want to know how much time I have left to save her."

The unicorn snorted and muttered to herself. Sounded like "martyr" and "ridiculous" and "boring" and "worst sibling ever."

But Than held my gaze, his own steady and solid. "I do not possess the ability to see the future, Myra Reed. I only know that she will die. As all living things are intended to."

"Pretty much what I expected you'd say."

"I see. Perhaps you could ask the unicorn's opinion."

"No!" Xtelle yelped. "She should *not* ask the unicorn about anyone's soul. Why would she ask the unicorn about souls? The unicorn is not a soul directory that can be dialed up at the whim of a derelict deity tramping about like a transient vagabond.

"The unicorn," Xtelle went on in a rush, "is a creature of purity and white light. I wouldn't know what happens to a human soul."

"A creature of light understands shadow more than any other," Than said. "Are you not well-versed in all things demonic?"

Xtelle shifted her eyes side to side, looking for an escape route. "You're saying I'm an expert on demons?" She jiggled the door handle. It didn't do anything.

"No."

"But you're inferring that, because I'm a unicorn, purest of all creatures, I would know about my very opposite, demons, the dirtiest of all creatures?"

Than lowered the visor and watched her in the mirror. "I advise you to tell Myra Reed the insight you may have on what happens when a soul is possessed by a demon such as Bathin."

"I don't have to listen to you. You're not even a god right now."

Than slipped two long fingers into the front of his jacket and removed a thin fold of leather. I knew exactly what he had in his hands. In that moment, I knew Delaney's instinct for our new hire was right on the money.

"This metal badge gives me a unique authority. I may not hold my power at this time, but my power resides in Ordinary. Therefore, as an officer of Ordinary's laws, I am still in possession of my power. In a sense, I am more powerful here than I could ever be outside of these gentle borders.

"If you wish to test my powers, whether of the supernatural or mundane, I would encourage that. I hunger to sate my curiosity as to which limits I might find no longer apply."

Let's hear it for the scary guy.

I wasn't even sure if he could do what he was implying— wield his power because he was more than just a vacationing human now that he was entrusted by us to uphold the laws here.

But the unicorn didn't have to know that.

"You like to threaten, don't you, Old One?" Xtelle asked.

"I value a word given and kept. You understand promises and bindings, don't you, *unicorn*?"

"Yes," she practically hissed.

I hadn't brought the car up to the order window yet. Luckily, there were no cars behind me, so I could sit there all day until she did what he wanted.

"Tell me what you know about demons," I said. "About Bathin."

The guy in the car in front of us handed his money to the barista behind the window and traded it for coffee cups and a bag.

"Bathin is different," she said, her voice as steady and flat as I'd ever heard it. "Very different, in some ways." She lifted her front hoof in a shrug.

"Why is Bathin different? How?"

"He's a prince."

"Yeah, I've heard. So?"

"He is the son of a king of the Underworld. That makes him something different than most demons. He's just very arrogant and insufferable and *princely* about everything. I'm sure you've noticed."

"What kind of king of the Underworld?" I asked. "A demon king?"

"*The* King. The king who is currently the *only* King of the

121

Underworld, because he is more vicious and powerful than any other demon who has ever lived."

"Why didn't I know that?" I asked.

"I have not a single idea," she said. "He speaks of himself *constantly*. Great Darkness this, Royal Darkness that. The All of the Null. So tiresome. I'd horn him in the brain if I thought that would shut him up for even three minutes."

"So Bathin is the son of a very powerful demon," I said.

Xtelle met my gaze in the rearview mirror. I'd only known this unicorn for a short time. Just over twenty-four hours. Most of that time she'd spent talking back and annoying the hell out of me. I'd seen outrage in her eyes, I'd seen curiosity, I'd seen scorn. But now, this moment, I saw a fatal sobriety.

"The most powerful demon who has ever existed. The King's power has grown beyond the souls he has feasted upon. It has grown beyond the minds he has broken and drunk dry. All those in the Underworld fear him. Fear that he has become the one thing that will destroy all demonkind."

"A tyrant?"

"Hunger that cannot be sated. Madness that obliterates all it touches. Teeth and claws and rage. A horror. The end of demonkind."

Than was very quiet. I was trying to process what it meant for us here in Ordinary.

"Are you telling me I have to wait for the king to kill Bathin before I can get my sister's soul back?"

"I am telling you that something has speared demonkind with a fear they have never known, a horror rising they have never imagined. They see their own end. Extinction."

"What does that have to do with Bathin and my sister's soul?"

Her big, watery eyes slipped to one side. She stared at Than, and I felt like I was missing out on a larger conversation going on between them.

I thought I saw Than nod just slightly.

"Think of it this way," Xtelle said. "Once the great hunger of the King of Darkness runs out of demons to feast upon, where will he turn?"

I ran through the ancient lore of demonology. We had

never had demons in Ordinary, and so our knowledge base showed real holes.

The next logical target after eating every demon within existence would be to find more demons. Or an alternate food source.

"He'll consume other supernatural creatures?"

"Eventually, yes. But supernatural creatures have defenses against demons. Why fight for a meal when you can simply sit back and let the meal come to you?"

"Who's going to go willingly to be eaten by a demon?" I asked but even as the words fell out of my mouth, I knew the answer. "Humans. He would lure them in with demon promises and then eat them."

"He wouldn't have to put in much effort," she said. "For the right price, and usually a very low one, he will be able to recruit humans, cater to their weaknesses and needs, and then...well, then the humans will be the sowers of their own strife. And destruction. And when they are screaming, one foot in the grave, the other in despair, he will crack their spines and slurp down soul after soul after soul."

A chill ran over my skin. Even though I wasn't the Reed with disaster precognition, I knew she was telling the truth. "Then there would be no humans."

"But there would still be Ordinary. Where the gods foolishly give up their powers to walk around like mortals. *Mortals*, Myra. Are you listening?"

I was more than listening, I was making huge intuitive leaps.

"Humans die, or are dying, eaten by demons, and the gods for some reason—maybe free will—don't put a stop to it," I said. "Then what? The king strolls into Ordinary and decides to eat up all the vacationing gods too?"

"No, that won't happen for two reasons," she said. "Tell me what would stop a demon from feasting on the souls of gods?"

"Gods don't have souls," I said. "Not like human or supernatural souls."

"That's one."

"Delaney, Jean, and I wouldn't let that happen."

"That's two."

She didn't say anything else, and I ran back through the information again. I felt like I was missing something. And it was big. And it was bad.

"What aren't I seeing?" I asked. "What am I missing?"

Then it hit me. Hard.

"Bathin has Delaney's soul. He's going to use it as a bargaining chip, isn't he?" I could feel my blood cooling, my guts knotting. "He's going to hand her—the bridge to Ordinary, a rare soul touched by many god powers—over to his father to save his own life."

"Or," Xtelle said, "he consumes her soul. And in doing so, becomes greater than his father, destroys the King, and saves Ordinary and all of humanity."

I heard her, I really did. Bathin could be a hero.

It was just that my mind was still slogging through the mud of betrayal, the huge swampy realization that Bathin had been hiding out from this confrontation with his father all the time he was holding our dad's soul hostage.

Now that he had Delaney's soul, he could still betray us. Could give her soul away to save his own hide.

Or he was going to eat her. *Eat her.*

A small part of me, very small, wondered if the unicorn was lying.

That small part of me didn't believe Bathin could do something so very deliberate, calculating, and cruel. The rest of me thought he was in the position to do exactly what the unicorn said.

But...

*His smile, his strength, his hands, steady and strong catching me so I didn't fall, didn't hurt myself. He'd saved Ben, saved Ryder. He'd fought with us against Lavius, helped us close the vortex.*

"How?" I breathed, though I didn't even know which question I was asking. My mind was spinning.

"If he consumed the soul of Ordinary's bridge, the one true doorway into Ordinary," Xtelle recited, as if this were already written down, in ink, in stone, in blood, "he would control Ordinary, and all the monsters, gods, and powers within it. It is possible he would use those powers to fight his father. He might even defeat him. But in the end…"

"In the end," I said, my voice a ghost of what it had once been, "he is still a demon. He would destroy. Ordinary, the world, and all the gods."

"It seems what a demon would do. Any demon. All of them. Given the chance," she said.

I inhaled, letting the shock wash through me. Letting the shuttering flashes of imagined horror chase lightning down my nerves.

Then a great calm, a great silence washed over me. My resolve was bone deep.

I had to stop Bathin.

And find a way to kill his father. The tug in my chest was pulling on me, this wasn't where I should be. Not here. Not how.

"We need to go home," I said.

Than was silent. The unicorn might have said something but I was too busy working out how to stop the one man—

— *no, demon*—

—I almost liked—

—*no, loved*—

—before everything and everyone I cared for were tortured and eaten.

# CHAPTER 13

IT BEGAN to rain, the lightest of drops, steady as a creeping fog. I made my way down roads as familiar to me as my own name.

When I pulled up in front of my house, the unicorn in the back seat sighed. "You're going to leave me behind because I told you the truth? That's not a very good way to make me want to tell it again."

"Just stay here for a few hours," I said. "I need to think."

"I thought you needed to train Detective Death over there."

"I'll do that too."

"Well, since you're such a good multitasker, let me come along. I promise I'll be as silent as the Grim Reaper's galoshes."

"Poor choice," Than said.

"Oh?" she asked.

"They squeak."

It was that, his attempt at a joke that drew me out of my mental fog.

"Your boots squeak?" I asked, trying to regain my footing in this new world of evil king demons, soul-swallowing almost-boyfriends, and unicorns who told a truth darker than any I'd ever known before.

"They were sold to me by the man at the grocery store. In the produce aisle. They were," he paused as if trying to remember the exact words, "a great deal."

"Wait. So you really have rubber boots?"

"I fail to see how this is beyond your comprehension, Myra Reed. I am aware of the need for appropriate outdoor gear."

"Are they black?"

"Mostly."

"And...green?" I guessed.

"No. Yellow."

"You have yellow galoshes?"

"Certainly not. The god of Death does not wear yellow

galoshes."

"What kind of galoshes does the god of Death wear?" I needled.

"Ladybug."

I laughed and choked. "You have…" I coughed, my throat full of a laugh that couldn't find its way out the right pipes, "…boots."

Than raised one eyebrow and watched me choke. "Yes?"

"Squeaky ladybugs?"

"I fail to see the humor in foot protection."

I sucked down some air, coughed again. "It's not about the boots. It's about the…boots."

"Enlightening."

"I need to see a picture of them. Oh, better. You need to wear them to work tomorrow."

"I wasn't aware galoshes were dress code for a reserve officer."

"Oh, I think they'll be just fine for the day. Perfect."

Just thinking about Than in those boots helped take the hardest edges off my mood. I didn't feel like I was shivering under cold water any more. Because I knew, somehow, I'd find a solution to our newest, gravest Bathin problem.

*His hands warm and roughened, stroking ever so gently down my arm, my hips, wrapping around the top of my thigh and burying there between my legs.*

The blush was back, heating me further. Stupid heart. No matter what I heard about Bathin, no matter what truth was handed to me on a platter, my heart still wanted to make excuses. He couldn't be that evil. There had to be something more to him, something kind and strong and good.

My heart might be a fool, but my mind was not. As for my body—

*—The flash of dream memory winged behind my eyes, lifting my heartbeat. His eyes curved as he laughed, his head thrown back, throat exposed.—*

—yeah, my body had it bad for him.

Two against one, I guessed. But my body and my heart were not going to win.

"I'm happy with my life just the way it is," I said, even

though it had nothing to do with Death and his boots, and everything to do with the demon I could not keep my mind off of.

Than had already tucked his badge into his jacket, and seemed nonplused by the sudden change of subject. "Of course."

He didn't believe me.

Problem was, I didn't believe me, either.

Being disastrously attracted to a man who was going to either devour my sister's soul and rule the earth, or sell my sister's soul to a different demon who would devour it and rule the earth, wasn't the makings of a happy life.

And in what way could that end? Would I have to kill Bathin to save my sister?

"I don't like killing people," I said.

"I find it relaxing," Than murmured.

"Me too," the unicorn sighed.

I'd almost forgotten she was still in the cruiser. What I needed right now was more information. Solid data. The tug in my chest was warming, and instinct whispered it was time to visit the library.

"All right," I said to the unicorn, "out."

"But I'll be bored!"

I threw the car into park, got out, and opened the door for her.

She hesitated.

"Nope." I pointed at the house.

"But…"

"Out."

She huffed, then lifted onto her dainty little hooves, and hopped out of the car. "I hate you."

"Yep. We'll find you another host who can entertain you. I think a couple of the Muses have room."

"I refuse to be downgraded to a mere Muse. I shall give you one final chance to do better by me, Myra Reed."

I opened the garage door and she sashayed inside, her tail swishing behind her. I waited until the garage door shut, then looked in the squad car's windows, popped the trunk, and checked in there too.

I was one hundred percent unicorn free.

Finally.

I swung back into the driver's seat and fastened my seatbelt. "You mind coming with me on an errand?"

"Will there be tea?"

I smiled. "My own private stash."

"Well, then. Do lead on."


THE LIBRARY was built on top of a hill on the eastern side of the main highway. It was squarely in Ordinary, but so out of the way, no one ever wandered up there.

The fact that it looked like an outbuilding or pump house helped keep the curious visitors to a minimum. Also, the powerful spells and guarding charms built into it and around it usually did the trick.

The clouds overhead raced and pushed, roiling in swirls of crisp white, slate gray, and charcoal. Hearty coastal pines threw mossy shadows over the road that unstrung like a child's scribbled line.

When I was younger, this drive with my dad always felt like trekking down some kind of mystical fairy highway, a road that would lead me to magic and trickery and dreams come true.

Death in the passenger seat was a comforting stillness. I felt like I'd been surrounded by a raging fire, and he was a cool cloak, an umbrella against the scorch of the world.

"You know Xtelle isn't what she appears to be?"

"I know," I said. "She says she has nothing to do with the Hell vortex, but she was there when it opened. I don't think it's a coincidence. Plus, she has a history with Bathin."

He made a small "*mmm*" sound.

The little structure came into view and Than leaned his long body forward, tipping his pale, pale face up into the wavering gray sunlight. "The library."

"The library," I agreed.

It *did* look more like a pump house than a library: four neat cedar shingle walls, a thin door, and a sharply peaked roof.

"I assume it is larger on the inside?"

"Well, it is magic." I parked the car and killed the engine.

"I don't usually bring people here. So…well, I just thought you should know that."

He sat back and unbuckled his seatbelt. "You have stoked my curiosity, Myra Reed. I shall be the soul of discretion."

We crunched over the gravel, and a crow called out from somewhere up in the tall pines. The air smelled cool and damp and green, earth with a tang of salt, wind whispering as it combed tough green needles as if the entire world was breathing, breathing.

I stopped at the curve of mossy stones ringing the little structure. Third stone to the left of the door wasn't anything special. It was about knee high, a common brown-gray rock found everywhere on the Oregon coast. I touched the top of it with my right palm, then whispered three secret words.

Than stood outside the stones, right in front of what would soon be the entrance to the place. I could feel his gaze on my back, and it was not unkind.

I walked backward, careful that my footsteps were even and fell exactly into my previous steps. When I was next to Than, I said, "Myra Reed."

There was the slightest sound of distant chimes, the scent of sweet honeysuckle, and the spells that kept the library hidden and safe released.

The little pump house stretched up and outward, fanning open like a book whose pages were flipped by a giant's thumb. It didn't build itself shingle by shingle, window by window, arch by arch, it simply wavered at the edges, out of focus, blurred. And then, from the center outward, it became sharp, clear, *real*.

"That is a very old spell, Myra Reed."

"It is," I said, happy he knew it. "This has been here since a Reed has been here. So, basically, from the beginning of Ordinary."

He tipped his head slightly to one side, taking in the sturdy log beams that poked out from beneath the roofing, the round chimney stones with bright flashes of quartz and glass nestled in the mortar, and the general stack and curve of architecture borrowed from a different age and a different world.

While all of Ordinary had been built by people who moved here, this one building had been built by the Reeds. And each

Reed who tended the library added to it in some way.

Dad finished his section before Jean had been born.

I hadn't started building mine yet. Every time I tried to do so, I walked away, thinking Dad could have done more, built more.

Lived longer.

The crow called out again, startling a jay's screeched response.

"Does everyone think about death when they're around you?" I walked up the path laid with stones in a swirling pattern that echoed growing things, clouds, the wind, the waves.

"I wouldn't know," he said archly.

"Okay. I have to say some things or the library will throw you out. So: This is the Reed library. I am the keeper of all which resides within. I welcome you inside on this day, for this day, Death who is Than." I lifted the latch. "Welcome aboard."

The door was locked to everyone but me. There was no key to the library, because I was the key.

Lights flickered to life with a soft series of *clicks*, and the voices in the room sighed.

"Myra," the voices said, a ghostly, ethereal chorus that was as familiar as a childhood lullaby. "Welcome back."

I nodded to the spirits of the books in the room. A poet lounged on the couch, one leg over the arm of it, tapping a bright blue peacock feather against his lip as he stared at the ceiling and mouthed the word *purple*.

A flight attendant who once posed as a soldier and saved her land, walked beside the shelves, running her finger along spines.

Two barefoot runners leaned in the corner, laughing. Birds that were not birds perched in the crooks and crannies of the huge open-beamed ceiling, eyes like pebbles. Creatures that had no names shimmered in the shadows.

A gaggle of old women playing cards argued in easy companionship, a brute in battle armor sharpened his sword, and a small boy and his dog napped on a footstool.

Than entered the room after me and went still. "Oh," he breathed.

I couldn't help but feel a little pride at the wonder in that one word.

The main room was the oldest portion of the building. It was lined with wooden shelves carved with animals, magical creatures, angels, devils. A staircase to the left led down, a staircase to the right lead up. The rooms above and below wouldn't appear until a person reached them.

Rules of time and space flexed here. New volumes, scrolls, tomes moved about as they wished, and their ghostly, pastel spirits appeared and disappeared along with them.

It was a very old, magical place. Built over one of the power nexuses the gods had impressed into this soil to preserve and protect the ancient knowledge.

It should have been inherited by the eldest Reed, Delaney. But Dad had left it to me. He knew how much I yearned for rules and order, information and conclusions.

Since the books liked to rearrange themselves, one volume was in charge of noting who was where at all times.

That volume was Harold. He was the spirit of a very old book which used to be part of the indexing system in the Library of Alexandria.

He'd managed to survive the fire and disaster due to several inaccurate entries made in his pages. He'd been tossed in the garbage and replaced by a new, cleaner index.

Someone had dug him out of the trash and he'd been passed from hand to hand, sometimes forgotten, other times bequeathed, until he eventually ended up with a priest who bequeathed him to a magician, who gifted him to a witch, who bargained him to a god, who gave him to a soldier, who brought him to Ordinary.

"Good to see you, Myra, my dear." Harold looked like Cary Grant in his glory days. He even had the same rhythm of speech as Cary, and wore a suit that fit him like a glove. "And you've brought us a god. Death, I presume?"

Than tipped his head. "The very same. Have we met?"

"I don't believe we have. Though you are spoken of often and, may I say, vividly."

"Than, this is Harold, the library's index. Harold, this is Death, though he prefers Than while he's on vacation."

"My pleasure." Harold thrust out his hand for a shake.

Than stared at his hand for a moment, then gravely placed his palm against Harold's.

"Indeed," Than said.

"Excellent," Harold said. "Myra, will you be having a hot cup of tea with me?"

"All three of us," I said.

Harold executed a smart half-bow and strode toward the narrow little kitchen tucked in the back. "I have drawn the curtains in the sitting room," he tossed over his shoulder.

"Thank you. This way," I said to Than.

"Why are your books alive, Myra Reed?" he asked as I sauntered off to the corner sitting room.

"Whatever do you mean?" I asked innocently. "All books are alive. Mine are just a little more obvious about it."

"Ah, Ordinary." He shook his head and said no more.

I stepped into the little room decorated somewhere between English cottage and French farmhouse, and plopped down on the big overstuffed chair that was covered in a fabric of purples and golds and blues and pinks that should not work together but did. The chair made me happy just because the big, clashing, ugly, beautiful thing existed.

Than chose the more sedate love seat. Behind him, record folders stacked flat and on edge in the slotted shelves, created a pattern that was almost modern art, it was so easy on the eyes.

This room held the loose leaf, handwritten records and tallies, little snippets and bits of forgotten passages orphaned from larger works.

It was always comforting hanging out with my fellow misfits.

"Do you know how to kill Bathin?" I asked.

"I know how to kill all things."

"Do you know how to kill his father?"

"Yes."

"If I asked you to do that, would you pick up your power and kill the king of the Underworld?"

He folded his long fingers together. "I rather enjoy dancing, what I have seen of it over the years. Did you know there is not a culture that has not discovered some form of it? Such a graceful thing, using one's body for nothing more than the desire to better experience music, movement, and perhaps another living being."

"Okay. Dancing. I like it too. Is that what kills the king? A dance off? Tell me it's not a dance off."

"It is not a dance off."

"I'm listening."

"Death is, in some ways, like a dance. Its partner is time. When one falls out of step with the other, the dance is broken, faltering. The partners fumble, trip, and the music stops."

He leaned forward slightly. "It is a metaphor. Death and time dancing."

"You're saying death happens when it's the right time, otherwise it screws up the natural order. Did I get it?"

"On the nose, I believe one might say."

"So I can't hire you out as my personal hitman. No big surprise there. Will you tell me how to kill Bathin?"

"Am I not an officer of the law?"

"Reserve officer, but yes."

"I read the table of contents in the book you gave me. I do not recall the section on carrying out a murder. There was, however, a section on catching and bringing to justice those who might commit it. Did I misread?"

"No." I puffed out a breath. For a being who never smiled, he sure looked happy with himself.

"Here we are." Harold strolled in with a tray holding three tea cups and two small teapots.

"Do you know how to kill Bathin, Harold?" I asked.

"I'm an index, my dear, not a dime-store novel." He smiled and set the tea on the side table. "But if anyone can do it, it will be you," he said heartily. "You are a Reed, after all."

I grinned. "I should buy you some pom-poms to wave."

"Yes, you should. I would be very good at varsity sports, were I alive. And human. And inclined to sports of any kind. Oolong?"

"Gods, yes," I practically groaned.

Harold made quick work of serving us, then sat and held the cup in his hands, bringing it up to his mouth now and then. He didn't drink, but had once told me he could taste the flavor and feel the heat in the steam.

Than and I sipped in silence for a moment while the library hushed and mumbled around us. I was waiting for the tug in my chest to tell me where I needed to be, but it was quiet. Content.

Maybe I just needed to be right where I was.

"All right, so I need the instruction page on how to use the scissors with one blade of ruby and one blade of black."

Than stilled. "Do you have those scissors?"

"Yes."

"Are they here?"

"Not in the library."

"But they are within Ordinary's borders?"

"Yes."

"You understand they are demon made?"

"Yep. Bathin said his mother made them."

Than nodded. "I believe that is true."

"But I can't use the scissors to cut Delaney's soul out of Bathin's possession without the book with the page. Or at least that's what a crossroads demon told me.

"That may or may not be true. But wielding a demon blade forged by the Queen of the Underworld is not without consequences."

"I know. They damage the user. Greatly and permanently, as far as I can tell. But I'm out of options. I've thought of offering him my soul in exchange…"

"I forbid it," Harold said gently, like we were haggling over which brand of crackers to stock in the pantry.

"…but I can't see how Bathin having another soul will do anything to fix the situation. So. Can you get me that book, Than?"

"The one with the page?" It came out as a simple question but the load of sarcasm he piled on top of those few words was staggering.

"The operating manual for the scissors. I think our best move is to get Delaney's soul back, and face the consequences before we're either attacked by the king of the Underworld or have that Hell vortex reopen."

"You live an interesting life, Myra Reed," Than said.

"Yay, for me." I finished my tea and had just set it down when my cell phone chimed.

"This is Myra."

"Where did you get off to, young lady?" Hatter's voice was low and slow like molasses. All of us were convinced he put on a southern accent to get the ladies. When he got drunk—really drunk—that accent sounded more like Brooklyn than Nashville.

"First, if you treat me like a child, you're pulling the shit shift until the end of time."

"What's the second thing?" Hatter asked, suitably sobered.

"I'm up at the library doing some research. What's wrong?"

"We got a rash of calls, and Shoe and I can't cover them all."

"Where's Jean?"

"She's been conscripted by Bertie for the next four hours. If I call Jean away, Bertie will, and I quote: 'Make you the acting president of January's Naked Seniors Pudding and Polar Bear Swim.'"

"Chicken."

"Guilty."

"Who's with Kelby?"

"Jean. She figured volunteering for Bertie would go over better if she had backup."

So much for locating the book today. "Okay. Lay it on me. We'll divvy the calls."

"Cat in a tree, penguin missing, Bigfoot sighting, drunk singing by the river, offensive graffiti at the restroom on 24th, abandoned car on the beach…"

"We'll take the penguin, Bigfoot, and graffiti. You take the cat, drunk, and car. Good?"

"Ten-four. Oh, and say…how's it going with our new recruit?"

"We're going to find out. Do the abandoned car first," I suggested.

"Tide's coming in," he said. "Got it."

He disconnected the call, but not before I heard him yell at Shoe to "put down the chocolate before she finds out you're in her good stash again."

"Son of a bitch." I stabbed at my phone. "If he eats all my good chocolate, I will put him on public restroom duty. In August. During the all-you-can-eat oyster and booze festival."

Harold chuckled. "No time for another cup?"

"No, we have to go."

We walked back into the main room. There, I pulled a small volume off the shelf. A very sad peasant girl watched me as I thumbed through the pages. When I found a small fold of thin cloth and pulled it out, she nodded and disappeared. Inside that cloth was a dried flower.

*This.*

And since I wasn't going to ignore my gift, I tucked the cloth and flower into my pocket.

The spirits called out goodbyes in their written language, those who were visible waved.

"Myra," Harold said just before I walked out the door.

"I'll be back soon, I promise," I said.

He rested his fingers on my shoulder. Harold wasn't a ghost, so his contact wasn't cold or spooky. Still, being touched by a spirit made of words, a book's soul and personality, was a heady experience.

I held my breath as a wild rush of knowledge, longing, hope, and determination shivered and rolled through me. For that one breath, I was connected to every author who had held quill to write on Harold's pages. More tenuously, I was connected to every volume and book they noted.

He was an index, connected to thousands of books, some of them lost forever. The sharp cut of sorrow—all those voices silenced—shuddered through me and then relief, as the new titles the Reeds had entered into Harold took over. We had written in his pages for years, making sure he was no longer filled with death and loss and sadness.

I exhaled, and all the voices, all the wordy thoughts and knowledge faded, faded, and were gone.

"Yes, Harold?"

"I think it is time you read your father's last journal. Perhaps over a cup of tea?"

I knew what he was offering. He would sit with me, up in our little room in the attic. He would listen to my questions, he would let me grieve my father. Then he would read me something ridiculous to remind me that somehow, even in sorrow, there was joy.

"I can't. Not...not right now."

"But soon." He bent just a bit and caught my gaze. "I think it's important, Myra."

"All right. Soon."

He nodded and stepped back.

I waved Death through the door, then pulled it shut. The latch clicked, locked until I touched it again.

"Shit. I forgot Ryder's books. Can you get them out of the trunk?" I tossed my keys to Than, and he caught them handily.

It only took us a second to get the box toted into the library. "Sorry," I told an amused Harold. "Some books Ryder found."

"Wonderful!" he said. "Welcome, all."

I popped open the lid of the box and scooted it next to the nearest shelf. "Is this good for now?"

The spirits in the room were appearing, one after another, to stare at the newcomers for a moment before disappearing. So many people and creatures and ideas and concepts popping in and out of visible existence, it was like watching raindrops turn into people who evaporated the moment they touched the ground, only to be replaced by more raindrops and people.

"We will all be just fine until you return. Thank you, Myra, my dear."

He leaned forward and pecked a very fatherly kiss to my forehead, then clapped his hands and bent over the box. "Now, who do we have here?"

I smiled and turned.

Than was staring at me, his endless black eyes glittering with curiosity.

"Let's get to work," I said, suddenly self-conscious. Maybe bringing Than out here, into my most private escape, had shown more vulnerability than I wanted.

Or maybe, my heart whispered, you wanted to see what death could do, wanted him to help you find a way not to kill Bathin, not to lose Delaney, and not to grieve like you are still grieving for your father.

I ignored my heart and left the library with Death on my heels.

# CHAPTER 14

CALL NUMBER one:

"It was huge!" Mrs. Kestner waved her hand straight up above her head. She was a local who worked at the bank. She also was an avid hiker.

"What were you doing out hiking at night, Mrs. Kestner?" I asked. "Alone?"

Her house was one of the many tiny cottages built in the thirties. This one had an addition off the back. The front room, which had once served as both the living and family room, was now a tidy home office and crafting space with a bright yellow couch, matching chairs, and some leafy plants in the corners.

Than stood at my side, observing.

"I got held up at work, and then Georgia needed me to pick up the kids and get them home because Paul was also working late. Georgia's pulling a double at the hospital, you know."

I didn't know her daughter's shifts, but I nodded and took notes in a little book. "Don't you think it might have been a bear?"

"It was carrying light bulbs."

I looked up from my notes and raised my eyebrows, giving her my patented I-don't-really-believe-you look. "Light bulbs."

"Yes. Look, I know how this sounds. But I saw Bigfoot. The real Bigfoot! Tall, hairy, ape-like...but with these eyes."

"Uh-huh. Do you want to describe Bigfoot's eyes?"

"They were round, and...soft. Gentle. I think Bigfoot is just a gentle misunderstood creature. Poor thing."

What Bigfoot was, was a kleptomaniac with a weird fascination with light bulbs.

"Well, I don't think Bigfoot is real, Mrs. Kestner. I think what you saw was a bear."

"No. It was much taller than a bear. And the light bulbs!"

"Don't you think those might have been marshmallows? We've had reports of campers who lost some food out of their coolers." That was a lie. I was covering for the big lug who was going to get an earful from me real soon.

"We thought it might be raccoons," I went on, "but I see we need to get the rangers out here to make sure the bears in the area are tagged."

"But...Bigfoot. I'm sure of it."

"Did he stink?"

"What?"

"Everyone knows that Bigfoot stinks worse than hot garbage."

This was actually a lie we'd sowed into the public myth of Bigfoot years ago. It helped throw people off the whole Bigfoot thing, because in truth, Bigfoot liked his cologne.

"Well, no, I didn't smell anything like that. There was a scent though. I've smelled it before." She frowned then snapped her fingers. "Axe cologne. I smelled Axe cologne. Tell me, Officer, what kind of bear wears Axe cologne?"

"The kind that breaks into a campsite and chews on everything, including the camper's toiletries," I covered smoothly. "That was part of the report from last night. Food missing, camp torn up. We checked it out, and the bear got into all their supplies. Frankly, destroying that cologne was an act of kindness on the part of the bear."

I grinned and invited her to join in.

But she just deflated. "You really don't think it was Bigfoot?"

"Do you have any pictures or video that could change my mind?"

"No. No, I was so startled. And by the time I got my phone out of my pocket, it was gone. Faded into the trees and shadows like nothing had even been there. It didn't make a sound. Don't you think a bear would have made a sound?"

"I think you were startled, it was late at night after a long day, and adrenalin does funny things."

"True. That's true. So, a bear?"

"They really are big when they're up on their back legs. And if we have a grizzly in the area, that's an even bigger fellow."

"So, should I avoid any particular area?"

"Just don't hike after sunset for a few days. Just to be safe.

I'll contact the rangers and they'll make sure any bears in the area are tagged and can be tracked. If we're lucky, this one's just wandering through to its home territory."

"Don't hike at night," she repeated.

"That's it. And if you happen to see anything like that again, even if it actually is Bigfoot," I paused to give her a tolerant smile, "don't approach it, don't take flash photography, don't do anything to startle it. Just call us again. Even if it's the middle of the night, okay?"

"I have a gun. I could hike with a gun."

"Handguns won't do much except make a bear angry. And while we don't know what a bullet would do to a Bigfoot," the smile again, "I'd rather not have you be the one who finds out, okay?"

"Yes. Of course. I could have really been hurt, couldn't I? A bear." She was going a little pale, so I helped her sit down on the couch.

"We've had them in the area before," I said. "Never had any deaths or maulings. So I think you're going to be fine as long as you stick to daylight."

"And if I see one again?"

"Stay very still and let it walk on by."

"Right. I can do that. I can do that."

"All right then. If you're feeling okay, Mrs. Kestner?"

"Yes. Yes, I'm fine, thank you. I'm sorry to bring you out here and ramble on about…well." She blushed.

I waved a hand. "No problem at all. That's what we're here for. Are you sure you don't want me to call someone to sit with you a bit? Georgia or Paul?"

"No, really. I'm good." Her color was warming up back to normal.

"All right then. We'll leave you to your day. I'm so glad you're okay, Mrs. Kestner."

"Thank you. Thank you both." She stood and walked us the short distance to the door. "Thank you for coming out."

"Any time."

We stepped into the bright afternoon sun and wind and she shut the door behind us.

"You lied," Than noted.

"Yes, I did. It's in the rules. Especially when it comes to keeping the supernaturals safe. If people knew that Bigfoot really lived here, swarms of people would come to try to find him, and eventually someone would, because he is a dumbass who can't resist a shiny glass bulb."

"Are you angry?"

"Not really." I started the car and waited until he had buckled, which he did with such a look on his face, before driving onto the street. "He's never been caught, not even spotted for long. So it's not like I'm going to have to squash hundreds of sightings."

"He is acting in his nature, and though it might be annoying, it isn't destructive," Than suggested.

"Exactly. We put up with a lot of this kind of behavior as cops. Although stealing the light bulbs isn't ideal."

"And the demon?"

"What about the demon?"

"Is he not acting in his nature by possessing Delaney's soul?"

"His nature is harmful."

"Do you truly think so?"

"It's obvious, isn't it?"

"Not at all."

I sighed. "You like Delaney, don't you? You have a...friendship?"

"Death is a friend to many."

"Vague."

He nodded in agreement.

"I need a solution, Than," I said. "To save Delaney's soul. To make sure Bathin doesn't make a terrible choice we'll all pay the price for."

"Perhaps the solution will reveal itself to you in time."

"You either have a lot of faith in me or time. I'm not sure which."

"I have known Time for all existence. I have never had faith in it."

I couldn't help myself. I smiled.

Call number two:

"When did you last see the penguin?" I asked Mrs. Yates. We were in her sunroom, which had become a large display space and museum for all things penguin.

Her concrete penguin statue was the unofficial star of the town. Framed newspaper and magazine articles filled the walls in neat rows, separated by photos of some of the more inventive penguin-nappings.

There was the little penguin stuffed in the barrel of a cannon. There was the little penguin dressed as an angel dangling above the main intersection in town. There was the little penguin strapped to the cross on the church steeple.

A few non-kidnapped pictures were sprinkled among the others. The little penguin out in Mrs. Yates's yard, in the snow, autumn foliage, spring flowers, and deep greens of summer.

Really, she'd gone all in on the famous penguin part of this gig, which had started as a high school prank and had turned into a national obsession.

Tour buses came by to see the penguin in her yard as part of winery tours, for heaven's sake.

"This morning. I was having coffee right here in the sunroom. It has the perfect view of the front yard." She pointed at the wall of windows. Than and I turned in tandem to stare at her yard. The marble podium she had commissioned for the penguin was noticeably empty of said penguin.

"I got up to get my toast, and when I returned, it was gone." She didn't sound upset. Not really. If anything, she seemed a little excited about this theft. It would, after all, be another picture on the wall if the kidnappers were creative enough.

"Did you see any suspicious cars?" I asked.

"Do you know who took it?" Than asked.

Mrs. Yates's gaze snapped up to his face, and she looked him up and down as if she had just noticed he was in the room. "What was your name again?"

"Than."

"Didn't you used to run the kite shop?"

"Yes."

"Why are you here?"

"He's a reserve officer. We're training up a few new people

143

over the autumn and winter months so we can better handle the influx of tourists next summer."

"Oh, of course. Like Mr. Bailey."

"Exactly, and it doesn't cost the taxpayers a thing."

"Well, isn't that wonderful! What a wonderful thing. How community minded of you, Mr. Than."

"Cars?" I prompted.

"No, nothing unusual. You know that house on the corner always has someone coming and going. I don't want to judge, but I think multiple families live there. I never see the same people for long."

It was a good guess on her part, and something that we allowed as a cover story for the family of shapeshifters who lived there. While they each had their preferred human shape, sometimes they took multiple shapes, especially the children who were still learning what it took to control their gift.

It could look like three different families lived there, but it was really two men, two women, and four kids.

"That property is zoned for multi-family use. There are two families living there, and they've let us know they sometimes have extended family stay for blocks of time. Being so close to the beach is a real draw."

I smiled, just like I always did when I was covering things up. Mrs. Yates took me at my word.

Than raised his eyebrows, but I stared back at him. Other than omitting the fact that they were shapeshifters, I'd been telling the truth. When other shapeshifters showed up in town, they always stayed with the Persons.

Yes, I got the humor in that last name.

"I don't know who may have taken my property, Mr. Than. That is why I called you here."

"All right, so no cars, no people you noticed walking by lately?"

"No one I haven't seen before. A lot of people stop by to see the penguin, you know."

I knew. Everyone knew.

"Were there any tour buses?"

"No. Although there was a couple who said they were driving Highway 101 from beginning to end, and they stopped by to take a selfie. They came up to the house to talk with me briefly."

"About what?"

"They asked permission for taking a picture in my yard. They were very polite."

"Did you get their names?"

"Troy and Trisha Smith. Cute couple. Young. Here, they sent me the photo."

She stepped over to the little dining table and retrieved her tablet. It only took her a moment to scroll through the pictures and find the one she wanted.

"This is them." She handed me the tablet. I studied the faces. Young couple. Cute. Their car was parked across the street at just the right angle, I could make out the plates. "We'll run their plates just in case."

"Oh, I don't really think it's them," she said hastily.

"No?"

She drew her hands together in front of her and picked at one of her thumbs. "I'm sure it's someone local."

"Why do you think that?"

Her eyes dashed to the side, back to me, then dashed away again. She was hiding something. She knew something.

"Who took the penguin?" I asked. "If you know, I can just go to them and retrieve it. It won't be a problem. If you want us to let them off with a warning, we're happy to do so."

"It's just that things have been quiet, with the summer season winding down."

"Yes," I encouraged.

"And there hasn't been an article for months now."

I scanned the framed clippings again, and noted they were in chronological order. The last was dated June. So it had been three months since there was any outside press.

"I thought stirring things up wouldn't be such a bad idea."

"Did you give someone the penguin?" But even as I said it, that didn't make any sense. Why would she call us in if she knew where it was?

"No. I…even I'm not that hungry for attention."

Jury was still out on that.

"But I might have seen who picked it up," she went on. "I

think…I don't think it was a normal kidnapping."

"Why?"

"It was that glassblower."

"Crow?" I asked.

She nodded. "He came by this morning. He seemed inebriated. Drunk. And loud. He was singing. And he waved. He knew I was right here in the sunroom."

"You watched him that long?"

She sighed. "When I saw he was taking the penguin I didn't want to interfere. He is an artist of a sort. I thought maybe he would dream up a delightful photo op. Maybe something that would renew interest? I mean, not for me, of course. I have all the attention I could possibly want. But it's good for our town. Brings in the tourists."

I didn't tell her that the nearby casinos, gorgeous open beaches, ample fishing, antiquing, wineries, craft breweries, and small town coziness was more than enough to bring in the tourists.

"Did you contact Crow and ask him to bring it back?"

"I tried. He wasn't answering his phone, so I drove to his shop."

"And?"

"It was closed."

Crow had just gotten back into town. It was possible he hadn't wanted to head straight back into the glass-blowing business. It was also possible he was still drunk from Roy's party.

"We'll look into it," I told her.

"You don't think he's going to…to harm it, do you?"

He was a trickster god. "I don't think that would be his goal, no. Have you thought about setting up your own photo shoots with it?"

She shook her head firmly. "I just wouldn't. Part of the fun is seeing other people get creative. If it were just me dressing up a concrete penguin. Well, my goodness, do you realize how much of an eccentric attention-seeker that would make me out to be?"

Than cleared his throat. I would have said he was choking back laughter, but I knew he never laughed.

"Right. Okay. We'll try to locate Crow and find out if he

still has the penguin in his possession."

"Do you think he might have given it away? Or might have *sold* it?" She was wringing her hands now.

"I don't think he sold it."

"But it is valuable. He could probably get a pretty penny for it on the dark web." She leaned forward as if sharing a secret. "I know what that is."

I nodded soberly. "Next time you see someone stealing your penguin, please just call us. We'll come out, stop the theft, and you won't have to imagine your penguin smashed into a million pieces and being sold, chunk by chunk, on dark ebay."

"There's a dark ebay?"

"There's a dark everything, Mrs. Yates," I said as seriously as possible.

She frowned, looked out the windows, and tugged on her fingers. "I hope you find Mr. Crow quickly. Tell him I will press charges if anything has happened to my property. I've insured it, you know. If it's harmed, I can sue. I will sue."

"I'll let you know the moment we have anything to report."

"Thank you, Myra. You have always taken this so much more seriously than either of your sisters. And don't get me started on Officers Hatter and Shoe. They make jokes when I call in my complaints."

"Yes, Ma'am."

"I am a taxpayer, you know. I pay your wages. Theirs too."

"Yes, Ma'am."

"And I pay your..." she pointed a finger at Death, then curled it back in on her palm. "No, you're a volunteer, that's right."

We let ourselves out, and I dialed Crow's number.

"Busy," he answered, and hung up.

I dialed him back.

"You hang up on me, I'll break your kneecaps."

"Myra? Is that you? What can I do for you, my darling?"

"Return the penguin."

"Penguin?"

"Crow."

"I...can't. Really. Not yet."

"Where are you? What are you doing with it?"

"What does anyone do with a concrete penguin in this town? No, don't answer that. I haven't been home in a bit and I'm afraid things may have veered into the X-rated zone since I've been gone. No kink shame, if that's your thing."

"Hand me the phone, Myra Reed," Than said.

I narrowed my eyes, but since I wasn't making any progress with Crow, I handed him the phone.

"Your excuses are no longer sufficient to ensure your further existence, Raven." He paused to listen to Crow's reply.

"I am an officer of Ordinary's law now." Than pulled the phone away from his face and lifted both eyebrows. He inhaled, exhaled, then placed the phone to his ear again. "I will uphold the law for mortals, supernaturals, and, more significantly perhaps in this regard, for deities. Bring the statue back to its proper placement within the hour, or I shall thoroughly enjoy interpreting Ordinary's laws as I see fit."

He swiped one thumb over the screen and handed it back to me.

"You...uh...I'm not sure that was exactly by the book."

"I clearly stated my rank, my intent, and my preferred outcome. As the book instructs. Also, it *is* Crow."

The look on his face, so long suffering, made me laugh. "Okay, fine. You know you can't kill him while you're here?"

"Yes. But then...accidents do happen."

That got me laughing again.

Call number three:

"I don't see the problem." I tipped my head to one side and back again. The restroom off of 24th was a nice, new, single building at the end of a small parking lot, which was at the end of a residential street.

The town had put in parking spaces, a restroom, a drinking fountain, and a picnic table, because 24th ended on an easily accessed rise above the beach. A new, steep, concrete staircase led down to the sand. A lot of tourists used it. So did the locals in the neighborhood.

"The yarn, perhaps?" Than suggested.

"Yeah, I see that."

It was pretty hard to miss. The picnic table was covered in

a patchwork of squares and each square featured some kind of creature, from little spiral snails to several patches in a row that made up a winged dragon.

The benches were also covered in squares of flower after flower after flower.

The trash can had been turned into a robot; the drinking fountain, a mushroom. I paced over to the stairway and noted the metal banister was now wrapped with a swirling pattern that arced like rainbows and clouds and birds swooping through them. I thought there, at the bottom of the stairs, it ended with butterflies.

It was actually very pretty. It also was not the work of one person. There was just too much of it.

"So who called this one in?" I wondered to myself.

Than glanced around at the houses. "Perhaps that man can tell us?"

He pointed to a man about four houses down on the left side of the block. He lifted a hand and started our way.

"Hello," he called out. "Hi there! Are you here to remove the…uh…graffiti?"

We walked toward him. "You called this in, sir?"

"Yes. I didn't think it was…sanitary."

I glanced back at the picnic table and garbage can. "Sanitary."

He followed my gaze, and his eyes widened. "No, oh, no. I don't mean the table and all this." He waved his hand in the general direction of the yarn bombing. "I think that's…well…my wife crochets, so I know what kind of work goes into something like that. It's more the inner stuff that I'm worried about."

"Inner stuff?"

"Inside the restroom? I told the officer, Hatter, I never call in stuff like this, harmless things. But the restroom is used by a lot of day visitors. I thought it a bit inappropriate."

I raised both eyebrows, far more curious than when I'd arrived. "Than, why don't you go take a look in the restroom."

He turned on his heel and strolled over to it, straight-arming open the door and disappearing inside.

I waited. Hoped whatever was in there was suitably

149

shocking. Got out my phone so I could take a picture of his expression just in case.

"Care to describe it?" I asked the guy next to me.

"I suppose it isn't the worst thing someone could knit around a toilet."

"It's on the toilet you say?" I rolled my hand in a keep-going gesture, my phone still held at the ready.

"Red lips with a tongue sticking out."

I snorted. "And where is it located, exactly?"

"On the toilet seat."

"Right. Anything else?"

"The tongue has something stitched on it."

"Go on."

"C.O.C.K. I don't know if it's a request, or a reference to the crochet club."

Than still hadn't come out of the restroom, darn it, so I headed his way. "I'll find out."

I strode over and knocked on the door. "You okay in there? Did you find what we're looking for?"

The door opened slowly, and there was Than, dangling a large, lurid pair of lips off of one fingertip, the tongue flapping gently in the coastal breeze. "Are we looking for toilet art?"

I snapped a photo. This was going on the bulletin board at the station. Maybe on my Christmas cards.

"Yep."

"Then I believe we have found it."

"Ain't police work grand?"

He raised one eyebrow. "Quite."

"Turn it so I can see the tongue."

He did so. Yep, right there. C.O.C. K.

"Looks like we need to visit our local crochet club. Put that in an evidence bag. They're in the trunk."

Than stepped out of the restroom, and I walked in, and took some pictures. The only other yarn bomb in the place was a frame around the mirror. It was golden with little dragonflies and a couple crabs in the corners and actually did a lot to brighten up the place.

I walked back to the table and stairs, taking more photos.

The neighbor guy watched me, his hands in his pockets.

"You wouldn't happen to know if the crochet club is meeting today?" I asked.

"Oh, I wouldn't know. My wife crochets, but isn't in that group."

"Why not?"

"She didn't want to get caught in another war. Just can't understand how knitters and crocheters are sworn enemies. Thinks both groups should just chill. Stitch and let stitch."

"She sounds like a lovely person."

"I think so." He gave me a grin. I'd seen that look before. I'd seen it on Ryder's face, I'd seen it on Delaney's. I'd seen it on Jean's and Hogan's faces too. It was fondness. It was love.

Like a mirage out of my dreams, Bathin came striding up the street, wearing dark jeans and a motorcycle jacket, his hands in black fingerless gloves, his black hair blowing in the wind.

He had on motorcycle boots too, and even from halfway down the block, I could see his eyes were locked on me and only me.

Before I could stop it, the dream from the other morning flooded through me. And I was there, could feel the cool silk of the dream sheets, could feel the heavy warmth of his dream hands touching me, his dream lips skimming my neck, his teeth biting gently before his tongue soothed the sting away.

My breath caught and my heartbeat drummed.

It had been a dream. It would only ever be a dream.

But what a dream.

Bathin kept striding toward me, a knowing smirk on his mouth.

"What do you want?" I asked when he was a house-distance away.

"We have a date."

"I'm busy. Working."

"I see that." He closed the distance, spared a glance at the guy next to me, who took a step back involuntarily. Yeah, Bathin had that way about him. That asshole way.

"Even officers of the law are allowed a lunch break. I know it's true. I checked it out with the union."

"We don't have a union."

"You should." He lifted a bag in his hand. "I had a feeling

151

you wouldn't want to go to a restaurant, so I planned ahead."

"And what, walked here?"

He lifted one eyebrow, that smirk in full go-mode now. "No, Officer Reed. I drove." He tipped his head to indicate the vehicle behind him.

"You have a motorcycle now? Wow, could you not fill out every square of the bad boy bingo sheet?"

"You think I'm a bad boy?"

"I think I should be going," the neighbor guy said.

"No, I'm not done getting your statement." I glared at Bathin. "You stay right here."

"I can give my statement to the other officer," the neighbor offered.

"Yeah, that's a great idea, buddy," Bathin said. "Give your statement to the other officer." He didn't look away from me. Nor did that smirk disappear. He liked it when I was angry.

Well, I could more than oblige.

I turned and made a grab for the neighbor guy, but he was fast-walking to the safety of Death over by the cruiser. Than had carefully sealed the toilet mouth into a plastic bag, holding it above the open trunk in his long, almost delicate fingers as if it were filled with dog poop.

"You can't just come here, barge into an investigation, and tell me what to do," I snapped.

"Which is why I came here, reminded you we had a date—a lunch date even though it is almost dinner time—and brought food so you don't have to stop the investigation."

"I have leads to follow."

He pulled something out of the bag and thrust it at me. "Do it while eating a sandwich, for Christ's sake."

I blinked, waited.

"What?" he asked.

"I was just wondering if lightning was going to strike you for using Christ's name in vain."

"Pffft," he said. "Those rules don't apply to me. If Christ wanted me dead by lightning, he'd do it in a face-to-face kind of way. Eat your food."

I glanced down to the brown wrapper in his hand.

My stomach rumbled. Other than tea, I hadn't eaten since

this morning, and from the low angle of the sun, it was headed toward four o'clock already.

"What is it?"

"It's a club with everything, extra peppers."

"Grilled?"

"Of course, grilled. What do you take me for, a heathen?"

"If the pentagram fits."

He grinned. It was all sharp teeth and wicked promises and my heart did that flip again, while all the blood in my body decided to heat up below my hips.

I knew I had to stop him or evict him or hurt him or kill him, but would it be such a bad thing if I slept with him at least once before all that? Angry sex? Goodbye sex?

Something that wouldn't mean anything in the morning sex?

"Oh, I like when you look at me like that," he crooned. "You should see your eyes, Myra." He leaned forward, just that extra inch. I felt cocooned in his space, in his warmth, in his need that echoed mine and made it more.

"Whatever makes your eyes look like that, let's do more of it."

I closed my eyes for a moment too long. Just long enough for my imagination to take off.

Bathin hummed, low in his chest, and I thought he might be bending toward me, his eyes searching my face, his breathing hitched as he angled his mouth toward mine.

Nope. All the nopes and then all the rest of the nopes. This was heart stuff. And I knew better than to fall for it.

I snapped my eyes open and quickly stepped backward. Away from him. Away from the things he did to me. The things he made me want.

He hadn't moved, hadn't shifted that smug little smile. He watched me with a calm expression. Then he lifted his hand with the bag.

"This spot is perfect," he said. "Let's sit at the table. Such a beautiful view."

He strolled toward the table, though it was more of a strut, then got busy setting up the sandwiches, the little bags of potato chips, and the cups that smelled like they were filled with hot coffee. Not what I would have chosen for lunch, but the aroma was rich and smelled wonderful mixed in with the cool sea breeze.

Suddenly a grilled club with extra peppers, chips, and a nice hot coffee sounded perfect.

"Sit," Bathin invited. "I'll even split my sandwich with tall pale and sickly over there."

I glanced at Than, who looked adorably ridiculous taking meticulous notes from the neighbor guy in a tiny notebook that seemed even tinier in his hands.

"It's a sandwich, Myra," Bathin said gently. "Everyone has to eat."

I finally gave in and took the bench opposite him. He'd sat so the beach was behind him, giving him the view of the street. That left me the view of the ocean, and he was right. It was beautiful today.

I unwrapped the sandwich paper, revealing two separately wrapped halves that were still warm enough to give off a little steam. It smelled heavenly, melted cheese and rich, salty meat, with the vinegar heat of the peppers.

I picked up half, moved the paper out of the way and took a big bite.

It was divine.

"Good?" Bathin asked, pointing his half sandwich toward mine.

"Good."

He was quiet after that and so was I. I hadn't realized how hungry I was. I polished off the first half and headed right into the second without a pause.

Than ambled over and folded down next to me at the table.

Bathin pushed his half sandwich over toward Than. "Half a Reuben."

Than glanced at the wrapped food, studied Bathin who was just now finishing up his portion, glanced at me, and then fastidiously unwrapped the sandwich and took a tentative bite.

Bathin watched him with an amused expression. "I take it you've never had a Reuben before?"

"I have not."

"Don't like it?"

"I don't have an opinion. It is hot flesh and spoiled cabbage?"

Bathin leaned on one elbow. "Pretty much. Also, there's a sauce made of pickles and sugar and tomatoes, so it has that going for it."

Than took another bite, placed just the fingertips of both hands on the edge of the table as he chewed. He stared out at the horizon, frowned, then took another bite and repeated the process.

"This is nice," Bathin said, staring at Than but talking to me. "Just you, me, and Death, sitting at a table someone decided to quilt? I'm assuming this is quilting. How cozy."

"Crochet," I said.

He raised an eyebrow but didn't look away from Than who was now halfway through the sandwich and still frowning between every bite as if he had no idea what he was eating or why.

"You don't have to eat it if you don't like it," I said.

Than nodded, frowned, took another bite.

Bathin hid a grin under his fingers as he rested his head in his hand.

"It is knitting," Than said.

"No, my friend," Bathin said. "It's a sandwich."

And oh, the *look* Than leveled at him. I was amazed Bathin didn't dissolve into dust.

Than turned toward me, ignoring Bathin as if he'd just been pushed off the cliff behind him. "It is knitting." He pressed his fingers into the colorful square on the table in front of him. It was crocheted, I mean, knitted, in the shape of a cross-eyed chicken.

"Okay?" I had no idea where he was going with this. Bathin was the one who had called it quilting.

"The neighbor, Curt, confirmed that the yarn bomb is knitting, not crochet, no matter what the tongue might suggest."

"Well, this just got interesting," Bathin said. "What tongue, and what did it suggest? Tell me it was something dirty, I've had an absolutely boring day."

"I thought you were following Delaney around all day." It came out as an accusation. Yeah, everything about him annoyed

155

DEVON MONK

me.

Bathin shifted upward out of his slouch and gave me a wary look. "She left to go to the casino to check on god mail. I don't leave Ordinary, remember?"

"Afraid your father might find you?"

He blinked, but other than that, was absolutely still. "Who told you about my father?"

"Does that matter?"

"It does. Very much. To me. Anyone who would have told you he's my father must also know where I am. That's a problem."

"That's not my problem."

"Was it you?" he asked Than.

"If it were?" Than asked.

"If it were, I'm not going to be worried about it. You happen to like Ordinary."

"What does that have to do with anything?" I asked.

"I like Ordinary too," Bathin said. "And some of the people and creatures in it. I wouldn't want anything to happen to any of them."

"Did you just threaten me? Us? The town? Is that what I just heard?"

"No. You heard the truth and interpreted it in the worst way possible, like you always do."

"You are a demon."

"That doesn't mean I'm evil."

"Uh, yeah. It does."

He winked. "Only if you want me to be. I'm not like the other demons."

"Really? How nice. Give my sister back her soul."

"No. But yes, really. I blame your father."

"What does my father have to do with anything? Oh, right. You stole his soul too!"

"Worst mistake in my life. Do you know how long we were together? And do you know what he did? He talked. And he reasoned, and he made sense, dammit. He made me something I've never wanted to be."

"A jackass? No, it can't be that, because you've always been a jackass, because you're a demon."

"Of course I'm a demon, and maybe I'm a jackass, but I am not evil."

"Using my sister's soul as a bargaining chip to save your life when your father comes here to try and kill you? What part of that isn't evil?"

He went deadly still. "Who told you that?"

But I was on a roll now, all the anger, frustration, grief, and yes, regret for not being able to act on my attraction to him, rolled through me so fast, I couldn't seem to stop the words falling out of my mouth.

"Maybe I just figured it out on my own."

"No, that's not something anyone would know. Except my mo…therfucker! It was the unicorn, wasn't it?"

"No."

"She told you about the king of the Underworld. And she painted him as a monster, didn't she? Myra, she's a unicorn. She hates all things demonic. She hates me. She'd like to see me kicked out of Ordinary. She's playing you so you'll get rid of me."

"I've been trying to get rid of you for a year." I was on my feet, braced between the concrete bench and concrete table. It was uncomfortable and bad footing. I snagged up his bag of chips he hadn't eaten and shoved them in my pocket.

"Those are mine," he said.

"No chips for liars."

His lips twisted. Almost a smile. "All right. So you're going to team up with my father? Do you really think that's smart? Use that big brain of yours, Myra."

"I'm not doing anything with your father. If he's anything like the unicorn says he is, I don't want him anywhere near Ordinary. Two demons," I jiggled my finger at him derogatorily, "isn't going to make anything better."

"We agree. I think my father coming to Ordinary is a terrible idea. You and I are on the same page. See how good we are for each other?"

"You're delusional."

"Now, now, Myra. You just said I was evil. Try to stay on message here."

This was serious. It really was. My sister's soul hung in the balance of his decisions, of my actions. But this back-and-forth, the heat and pull, was frustratingly enjoyable. Why did emotions have to be so confusing?

"I'm going back to work," I said archly. "Perhaps you should go to Hell." I lifted my feet over the bench and stomped across the grassy space toward the cruiser.

"See you for dinner then?" he called out.

I lifted one hand over my shoulder, middle finger in the air.

He laughed, a sudden, unexpected sound.

I hated how much I liked it.

# CHAPTER 15

THAN EASED into the passenger seat and handed me the coffee I'd left behind.

"I don't want it."

"You do."

I did. I took a sip. It was rich with just enough cream and a hint of sugar. Exactly how I liked it. "He's evil."

"It would seem so."

"Let me try that again. He is evil, isn't he?"

Than was quiet for a moment, then he steepled his fingers. "His demon nature would seem to be the strongest trait that defines him. He bargained for your father's soul, took it, then bargained with it again, and took Delaney's soul. That appears to align with the nature of evil."

"So he's evil."

"Is anything quite what it seems to be in Ordinary?"

"Yes. No. Sometimes."

"There you are."

"Not helpful."

"What does your heart tell you, Myra?"

"I'm not listening to my heart."

"Interesting."

I didn't like the sound of that. "Why is that interesting?"

"Is that not your gift? To follow your heart?"

I'd never heard it said like that before. "No. Not really, no. My heart isn't nearly as reliable as my family gift."

"Ah."

Then he was silent, waiting. Maybe he didn't know the answer, or maybe he did. Maybe he was just trying to get me to pay attention to what my heart already knew. That I wanted Bathin and I didn't want to want him.

"Is the unicorn lying?" I asked.

"About what?"

"About the king being Bathin's father?"

"No."

"About the king growing so evil and power hungry that he's going to come after Ordinary?"

"Not even I know the future, Myra Reed."

"Don't you?"

"Perhaps not every future."

"So this is salvageable. I can free Delaney's soul before it's used as a bargaining chip with the devil?"

"The king of demons is not the devil."

"Figure of speech."

"Every rose has its thorn."

"I wasn't asking for a figure of speech, I was just saying I was using one."

"Potato, potahto."

I shook my head.

"I do enjoy these talks, Myra. Shall we follow up on the stolen penguin, or dispose of the toilet art?"

"Toilet art. Then we'll call in on the penguin." I started the car and my phone rang.

"Myra Reed," I answered on speaker.

"Myra," Jean said, "We have a problem."

"Where?" I scanned the houses surrounding us and tuned in on the tug in my chest. Almost. Almost time to leave. Almost time to *go*. Almost time to be *there*.

Bathin walked up toward the cruiser with a determined stride.

*Almost, almost, almost.*

"Another vortex opened up."

"Where?"

"Out on the flats."

"I'll be there in four minutes. Close it down from the public."

"Do you know where Bathin is?"

"Yes. He's with me."

"Bring him. And hurry."

*Now.*

I rolled down the window and gave a short whistle. Bathin stopped and stared at me. "Get in. We have a problem."

For a minute, I didn't think he was going to do it. Then he

strode to the back door and jerked it open, dropping down inside. The car dipped under his weight. Even though he looked like he was hard muscled and lean, he was a massive mountain of a demon taking the shape of what he wanted to be. He was a lot heavier than he looked.

"You know, you say you don't want to be around me," he said, "but your actions make me think you might like me, Myra Reed."

"There's a vortex."

"I know. In the park. I was there."

"Not that one. A new one." I flipped on the lights and headed off at speed. "Do you know why this is happening? Another vortex?"

"No."

"Does it have something to do with your father?"

He frowned.

"Don't hold out on me, Bathin."

"I'm thinking. I haven't been around him for a millennium."

"Why?"

"Because he's evil, and I got tired of that a long time ago."

I glanced in the rearview mirror. It sounded like the truth, but demons weren't really known for swearing on Bibles.

He met my gaze. "I haven't been in contact with him, or anyone connected to him, for a very long time, Myra. That is the truth."

"Is this something he would do? Try to get into Ordinary?"

"No. He's more the blood-and-battle-and-raining-down-pestilence kind. This takes more finesse."

"Who can do something like this? Open a Hell vortex in Ordinary?"

"Before yesterday, I would have said no one."

"Okay, but now? Demons? A particular demon?"

He chewed on his bottom lip and scowled, thinking. I tried not to find it attractive.

"Crossroad demon?" I suggested.

"No. This tears the fabric between the Underworld and the land chosen by gods. Maybe it's not a demon. Maybe a god is behind it."

161

"Than, do you think a god is behind this?" I asked.

"Ordinary was formed by the combined will of a thousand deities. The universal truths and laws of that making cannot be breeched by a single god."

Yeah, that made sense. Mithra, the god of contracts, had wanted to take over the law in Ordinary, but since he wouldn't sign the contract all gods must sign to enter our town, he'd never stepped across the border. If Ryder hadn't offered to serve him, Mithra wouldn't have even the smallest say on anything that happened here.

Ordinary wasn't easily breeched, not even by gods.

I wracked my brain for other beings who could open up holes between realms. There were some interdimensional creatures, but most of them came to Ordinary like everyone else. They just walked or floated or appeared here and that was that. No tearing of the space time continuum.

"Demons," I said. "It has to be. Dammit, I don't have a turnip. Check in the glove box, will you?" I asked Than, "There might be a carrot in there."

He pressed the latch and rummaged through the small space. "Would a tube of lip gloss or a container of extra crunchy peanut butter suffice?"

The tug on my chest said no. I shook my head.

"Perhaps the toilet art?" Than offered.

The tug in my chest warmed. "Yes. Bring that."

I made a sharp turn, gunning down the side road that ran parallel to the sandy flat. This bay filled when the tide was high, and drained out to soggy sand flat when the tide was low. Several large rocks with stunted, twisted trees clinging to the tops poked up from the sand, looking like a Zen garden for giants.

The soggy sands were good clamming grounds, and when the bay was full, little flat skiffs puttered out to throw crab traps.

"Holy shit," I breathed as I came upon Jean's truck parked next to it. "What the hell is that?"

"It's a Hell vortex," Bathin said. "Demon. I'd say demons. Move." He was out of the car with a speed that was both shocking and impressive.

I flew out of the car, across the grassy knoll, and down through loose sand and washed up driftwood logs, over smooth stones and rough stones, then I was running full out, right behind Bathin who wasn't slacking his long stride for a second, his entire body—shoulders, chest, hips—tilted into the run.

The beat, beat, beat of his foot falls was loud in my ears, almost as loud as my own boots slapping into the soggy sand that threatened to trip me at every step.

For a second, my vision narrowed down to the man in front of me, and he was fine. Long, strong legs, inexhaustible pace, barreling full out into danger, the leather jacket open wide like leather wings, shoulders pumping.

A flash drew my attention ahead of Bathin.

This vortex wasn't a little moonlit puddle in the park. This vortex was a door, a gate, a yawning hole in the world.

This vortex was large and growing larger by the second. Much, much bigger than the one in the park. And it wasn't flat on the ground like a disk, it was vertical like a doorway. A doorway people were walking toward.

Every time a human hit that doorway, a burst of green light flashed and the human was gone, replaced by a...

...frog?

I blinked hard, but nothing in front of me changed. Shit. That vortex was turning people into frogs. Why would a demon want to turn people into frogs? Was the vortex a one-way portal from the other side *to* here, or was it a portal from here *to* there?

Jean wasn't bothering with the whys and hows. She was bending, scooping up as many frogs as she could carry before they hopped away and burrowed into the sand.

The frogs were a little stunned to find themselves suddenly of the amphibian persuasion, so they were easy to pluck up.

But her arms were full, and she was leaking frogs as fast as she could bend and replace them.

"Damn it!" she yelled. She shucked off her outer shirt, scooped up the edges of it and used it as a satchel in which to dump frogs.

"You okay?" I yelled.

"Yes! Go, go! Shut that damn thing down!" There were two more people just ahead of Bathin marching hypnotically toward the vortex.

Bathin put on speed to reach them before they entered the

163

light. He launched himself at the man and took him down in a tackle that would have made a line backer proud.

But the other person was a little girl, probably the man's daughter. Bathin rolled up from his dive and reached for the girl, trying and failing to catch her as she juked and jogged nimbly past him.

No little girl was going to turn into a frog on my watch.

I dug deep, wished I'd skipped the second half of the sandwich, and plowed toward the girl. I pushed hard and leaped, grabbing for her and tucking into a roll so that we would land with me on bottom and her on top.

It was not an easy move, but I'd been on the roller derby team long enough to know how to land safely, and how not to kill someone in the process.

We collided in a tangle, and I heard the surprised *woof* of air escaping her lungs as we hit the squishy sand.

"Shut it down!" I yelled, at Bathin, at Jean, at anyone. Only there wasn't anyone there who knew how to do that. Even I didn't know how to do that.

Then I heard it. A pattering gallop. Sharp, tiny hooves churning sand. And ragged on the wind, a battle cry like I'd never heard before.

"Aaaaaaaeeeeeeeeeeiiiiiii!" The hooves tapped out louder and louder, and the cry rose to a magnificent screech.

Then I saw it, a tiny pink unicorn, head down and extended at full gallop, horn shattering light into ribbons of rainbows, glossy mane and tail flowing in the wind. She was churning sand like a monster truck and picking up speed with every step.

I quickly checked the little girl in my arms. She was about ten, all legs and puffy, corkscrew ponytails. "You okay? Anything hurt?"

But she just stared at the sky like she could hear a song way up there she had to follow.

I eased up on my hold, and she wriggled, trying to get out of my arms, reaching for the vortex with one hand.

"Okay, nope, that's not gonna work." I grunted and got to my feet without letting go of her, pressing her back tight against my chest. "Don't let him up," I called to Bathin.

"Yeah, I got that." He had the man on his knees and was

keeping him there with a very neat half-Nelson. "What the hell is she doing?"

I followed his glare to the unicorn who had almost reached us.

"I'm saving the day, you dumbass!" the unicorn shrieked.

Then she pulled up to a hard stop, spraying the vortex like a hockey player snowing the goalie.

"We need a rope, a thread, a lasso," Xtelle said breathlessly, like she was calling out the instructions for how to disarm a bomb. "One of you must have bondage gear on you."

"I have cuffs," I said. I thought about cuffing the girl to keep her safe, but that wouldn't stop her from walking. I was working up a sweat trying to keep her still and not hurt her as she leaned and pushed toward the vortex.

"Cuffs won't work," the unicorn said. "Something longer, something loopy. Bathin, are you telling me you have nothing on you that can be used to tie up someone?"

"You don't know me, old woman."

"Old!" Xtelle stomped. "Old! I'll show you old."

"Perhaps I could be of assistance." Than strolled upon the scene. I had forgotten about him. He held up an evidence bag. "Toilet art."

"It's string," I told Xtelle, shifting my grip on the girl. "That's string. Bondage. It will work."

"Give it here," Xtelle demanded.

I glanced back at the man to see if he was paying attention to the unicorn, but he was just as oblivious to what was going on around him as the little girl. He gazed at the vortex, sweat running down the side of his face and neck, pushing hard to get free of Bathin's grip.

I followed Bathin's hands up to his arms, the bulge of his biceps under that jacket, the stretch of the shirt across his wide chest, sculpted muscles beneath carving ridges and valleys.

Gods, but I liked the look of him. Right there, on his knees, wrestling a suspect.

I swallowed, my throat suddenly dry, my face hot and prickling. I flicked my gaze to his face and a slow, sex-filled smile curved his mouth.

He squeezed his biceps to give me a show of all that rock-hard muscle, and then he winked.

It hit me like a fizzing bomb, deep in my belly, electric licks of lightning spreading down my arms, my legs, sizzling up my chest.

Who knew a man in a leather jacket physically restraining another man in public was my thing?

Or maybe it was just that knowing smile and the wink to let me know he was on for any fantasy I wanted to dream up.

"That's good. Now rub it on my horn," Xtelle said.

Bathin waggled his eyebrows.

I glared at the pink unicorn.

"You're not supposed to reveal yourself," I said. "And you're supposed to be locked up in my house."

"I got bored and followed you. As a horse. Mostly as a horse."

"I told you I'd throw you out of Ordinary if you broke the rules."

"Yes, Myra. Would you like me to leave right now and let you and that idiot deal with the vortex? Because, we wouldn't want someone who bends the rules—harmlessly, I might add—to actually close this gaping maw into the Underworld and save all those people from turning into frogs, would we?"

I considered the expanse of shore. About twenty people of various sizes, genders, and ages were getting out of cars, dismounting bicycles and hurrying toward us like it was Black Friday prices in the middle of summer break.

Jean was still chasing two frogs who knew exactly when to hop out of her reach while she juggled a shirt full of the little buggers kicking to get free.

Our options were limited. Our options were down to one thing.

The unicorn.

"Do it," I told Than.

He held the obscene lips out by the tongue and then rubbed the toilet seat cozy over Xtelle's horn. "Harder," she demanded.

Bathin snorted, Xtelle shot him a vicious glare.

"Just really give it to me, big boy," she said to Than. "I can take it."

Than raised his eyebrows, inhaled and then exhaled as if he were enduring the most tiresome request in his long, long, long life.

Instead of really giving it to the unicorn, he dipped his fingers into his front pocket and withdrew a pocket knife. He neatly sliced through the toilet mouth and tugged on a string.

"Well, if you want to be that way about it," Xtelle said. "Go ahead and use your little horn."

"Xtelle," Than warned. "I see what you are. Do not forget that."

Her eyes went large and she swallowed hard. "You can't."

"I can."

"Then why haven't you—"

"Myra!" Jean yelled. "People!"

The crowd on the shore stumbled our way, slowly, thank goodness, all of them aimed straight at the vortex. None of them took their eyes off it, didn't even see the unicorn which was still pink, her horn shooting off rainbows. Didn't see the man on his knees in a headlock, or that there were three police officers on the scene and far too many frogs.

All they saw was the vortex.

It called to them, just like the first, smaller vortex had called to Ryder.

"Stop," I shouted. "This is a crime scene. Turn around immediately and go back to your vehicles."

Nope. Nothing. The vortex filled their ears, their eyes, making them deaf and blind to everything else in the world.

Terrific.

The girl stretched, really pushing against my hold now.

"Faster," I told Than. "Whatever she wants, do it faster."

"Tie the end of the string to my horn," Xtelle said in a rush. "Now give it to Myra and Bathin. This is going to take all three of us."

"What is going to take all three of us?" I asked.

"Closing the vortex before a demon horde comes through," she said. "What do you think we're doing here?"

Than handed me the string, then unraveled the lurid red lips and handed that to Bathin.

"This is a closing?" Bathin asked, "Because it looks like—"

"Now you don't you trust me?" Xtelle said. "*Now?*"

"I have never trusted you."

"Why?" she moaned. "What have I ever done to you? Why do you hate me?"

"You told them about my father."

"Oh, boo-hoo. They would have found out eventually. No matter how ashamed you are of your parentage."

"This has nothing to do with being ashamed."

"So you admit you're ashamed?"

Bathin's nostrils flared and he shoved the struggling guy's face into the sand and put a knee in his back. "Not the time."

"Go!" I glanced at the shamblers headed toward us. "Close it. Close the vortex."

Xtelle seemed to remember we were in the middle of an emergency. "Do you remember the spell with the turnip?"

"Yes."

"Can you say it backwards?"

"Probably."

"Do it while I carry the string around the back of the vortex. Don't let go of the string and don't say the last word until I've reached your side."

"Wait," Bathin said.

"No," Xtelle hissed. "No more waiting. You've thrown your lot in with these people. So suck it up." She nodded at me, and I nodded at her, and for a fleeting moment it felt like she and I were on the same page.

She pranced, a hop from hoof to hoof, one hoof held crooked up against her body as she moved. Her head was high as she slowly hopped to one side of the vortex. "Da-doo, Da-doo, song this sing, ladies Camptown!"

I took a breath and began the rhyme: "Please be strong and do not fail, twinkle twinkle, little spell."

I paused, straining to hear Xtelle over the roll of the tide, the gusty racket of the wind, and the plod of people closing in on us.

"With this turnip fresh and spry..." I didn't have a turnip. I glanced at Bathin and he shook his head.

"You need a token," he said.

I patted my pockets and came up with the bag of chips.

"With potatoes crisp and fried." Bathin nodded. "Stick a needle in its eye. Close this vortex into Hellllll…"

I waited a few beats and then Xtelle rounded the vortex and prance-hopped double time, doo-dahing for all she was worth.

"Please be strong and do not fail," I sang.

"Night all sleep, gonna!" Xtelle warbled, "Day all sleep, gonna!"

"Twinkle, twinkle little spell!"

She came up between Bathin and me and finished her last, first line: "Song this sing, ladies Camptown!"

She tipped her horn, hooked the string in my hand, looped the string in Bathin's, and whispered, "By the binding of their hearts, let the fated never part."

"Wait!" Bathin shouted.

But it was too late.

I could feel magic zinging through the string, cut by Death's blade, wrapped in a unicorn's horn, released from a toilet (okay, that part probably didn't matter), looped between a Reed and a demon.

And I could feel Ordinary *shift*, as if the sand under my feet moved one *Mother May I? Yes, You May*, scissor-step to the left all at once.

The world snapped.

Thunder cracked the sky.

A blinding blast of light sliced the air and caught fire to the vortex.

I turned my back to the vortex, guarding the girl with my body, holding her head against my chest so she wouldn't look into that blaze.

A scream went up, and it was not from the people who had suddenly stopped their zombie march. That scream came from inside the vortex, the hole. It was an angry roar that was nothing like the demon spawn we had dealt with before.

I craned around to see if the vortex was actually closing or if we'd just unicorned ourselves into an even bigger mess.

A single pair of eyes stared back at me.

No, not at me. At Bathin. Yellow with hatred, shining with fire. There wasn't a drop of humanity in them, there was only fury.

"I. See. You." A voice roared from that portal to Hell.

Then the thin, simple string—super-charged with magic, with song—became a cleaver, a blade of lightning, that shattered the vortex into shards burning, burning into smoke and ash.

The vortex was gone.

I was breathing hard. Too hard. All the muscles in my back and legs were cramping. I groaned, unbent myself from shielding the girl, and loosened my hold on her. I felt like I'd run a marathon. I felt like I'd withstood a nuclear blast.

I was exhausted, but I still had a little piece of the string in my hand. I tucked it into my front pocket.

Whatever we had done to close that vortex, it hadn't been *just* magic. The taste of it in my mouth was red wine and honey.

"Daddy?" The girl in my arms looked up at me. "Where's my dad?"

"He's right here." Bathin hauled the man up and patted his shoulder, keeping one hand on the dad's arm while he spit sand and shook his head.

I let go of the girl and she rushed right over to her father, hugging him around his middle.

"Hey," he said. "It's okay. Are you okay?"

She nodded into his jacket and the man gazed blurrily around. "I thought…what happened?"

"What do you remember?" I asked.

"We came down here to look at the rocks. And then…I don't know." He brushed absently at his daughter's sandy back. "Did we get hit by a wave?"

"Micro burst," I said. "Sometimes the wind just picks a random spot and hits with almost tornado force. It knocked you and your daughter out. We were in the area and saw you go down. How are you feeling?"

"Oh, um. Good? Yeah, good. I don't think…do you think we hit our heads? I don't remember getting hit. Don't remember waking up either. Did someone lose a pony?"

I glanced over. Than was standing there, with what was left of the toilet mouth—really, mostly just the floppy tongue—looped over Xtelle's neck.

She did not look pleased about it.

Bathin coughed into his fist, and I could tell he was trying to keep from chortling over her predicament.

She held statue still, except for her tail that swished and her ears that swiveled back to lay almost flat against her head.

"No," Than said.

"Oh," the man answered. "I just thought. Okay."

"It's a miniature horse," I added, not sure quite where to go with this, still reeling from the *I see you* thing with yellow eyes in the vortex.

"My daughter likes horses, don't you, honey?" the dad said.

His daughter shook her head and clung to him even more tightly. I was beginning to worry that she might have some memories of what had happened.

"Can I ask your daughter a question?"

"Sure. Hailey, the officer wants to ask you something." He rubbed reassuring circles on her back and, after a second or two, she turned her head so her ear rested against his stomach. Her wide brown eyes fastened on me.

"Are you okay?"

She nodded.

"Do you remember falling?"

She shook her head.

"Do you remember anything else? Anything scary?"

"No." Soft, but getting stronger.

"Nothing noisy or bright?"

"No."

I searched her eyes. The fear was leaving, and she was already sneaking peeks at the pony. I think waking up with a police officer holding her and not knowing where her dad was, had been all that had scared her.

Which meant we didn't have to come up with a better cover story or do any actual memory manipulation. Every once in a while, we had to change someone's memory, and I never liked doing it. I was glad we wouldn't have to do that now.

"All right. If you and your dad want to get some ice cream, you can tell the parlor that Myra Reed said the treat's on her. You'll both get a single scoop for free."

"Oh, no, I really couldn't," he said.

"You'd be doing me a favor," I said, patting my stomach.

"Peggy over at the shop has a different special flavor every day, and she's always looking for people to try it."

"Well, then, thank you. Thanks, Officers." The guy nodded toward all of us, though he sort of avoided eye contact with Death and his pony.

Smart.

They started across the wet sand to the drier sand. The crowd was already disbanding, all of them coming to some personal conclusion as to why they were here on the sand.

Thank goodness for the human ability to ignore what was right in front of our eyes.

"Could have been worse," Jean said strolling up to me. She was covered in wet sand from head to toe, and the shirt she'd tied into a knot squirmed and croaked.

"They're still frogs?" I asked.

"Yep. Why did the vortex turn them into frogs?"

"I have no idea. Did you get them all?"

"Yes." She frowned. "I think."

We both scanned the sand. Nothing croaked or jumped.

"We're going to have to figure out how to turn them back into people," I said. "Not here, though."

"Maybe the frog thing will wear off?" Jean suggested hopefully.

I looked over at Bathin. He shook his head and stared at me as if he were absolutely fascinated. There was a slight crease between his eyebrows that hinted at a deep confusion. "Frogs were a side effect. Opening a vortex correctly isn't as easy as it looks."

"You know how to change them back?" I asked. And wasn't there something in his look? Something warm and inviting. Something that made me want to take a step just to be nearer him?

"No." He looked away from me and stared at Xtelle.

She snorted.

His eyes narrowed. "You." He inhaled, exhaled. "I'll take Xtelle back to your place and then meet you at the station, or wherever you're taking the frogs. We can compare notes."

"I don't think—" I said.

"Good talk." He patted my shoulder like he couldn't get

away from me fast enough and stormed toward the unicorn who was back to looking like a small brown horse again.

"I'll take this," Bathin plucked the bottom lip and tongue from Than, wrapped it around Xtelle in a makeshift bridle.

I stared at his hands for a little longer than I should.

"Soft but firm. I likey," Jean said.

I sniffed. "I don't know what you're talking about."

"No? You didn't totally drool over tall dark hunka-hunka whipping together some rather nice rope work on the spot?"

"Frogs," I said. "I noticed frogs."

She was grinning at me. With her face covered in sand, her hair all over the place, and the wet rucksack of a shirt over her shoulder, she looked so much like she did when we were kids, I couldn't help but grin back.

"You heard from Delaney yet?" I asked.

"No, but she should be back by now."

"Let's track her down and get her input on this. Where's Kelby?" I trudged across the sand, sinking almost to my ankle with each step. It was hard going. Funny how adrenaline and life and death made running through sand seem like an easy task.

"Bertie needed some heavy lifting for the parade float, and Kelby volunteered to stay and help get it done."

"She's supposed to be doing on-the-job training."

"Dealing with the only Valkyrie in town *is* on-the-job training."

"It's also you getting out of helping Bertie."

"Me?" She lifted her soggy shirt. "You may notice I am carrying around a wet slimy sack of wet slimy frogs?"

"And?"

"And do you really think I would choose this over working with Bertie?"

I took three more steps side by side with her before answering. "Yes."

She laughed and knocked her shoulder into mine. "It's good to have sisters."

I smiled, because I couldn't agree more.

# CHAPTER 16

THE FROGS were a conundrum. We'd taken them back to the station and quickly realized there wasn't room for them there. We didn't want to take them to Ryder and Delaney's place, both because of Ryder's dog and because of Delaney's dragon pig.

Jean's place was too tiny for all of us, and Hatter and Shoe declared "frogged-up people were a step above their pay grade."

So I offered my house.

The unicorn and demon were not there when we arrived. I knew I should go find them, but they would have to wait until after we un-frogged the good citizens of Ordinary.

Jean immediately headed back to the main bathroom with the frogs.

"Make yourself at home," I said, waving everyone toward the living room. "I'll put on coffee."

"Make it strong," Ryder said as he steered Delaney toward the comfortable couch.

I put on the kettle, started a pot of coffee—extra strong—and arranged the last batch of cookies I'd made a couple days ago on a platter. To the side, I added meat and cheeses and a bowl of grapes. I grabbed a box of crackers, tucked it under my arm, and carried out the food.

"You okay?" I asked Delaney.

She was tucked next to Ryder, his arm thrown over her shoulders to hold her there. They looked good together.

Ryder's eyes slid sideways and down, and I followed his line of sight. Delaney appeared to have checked out, an eerily blank expression smoothing her face.

He rubbed his palm on the outside of her shoulder, up and down, up and down. "Delaney," he said.

She blinked and seemed to surface and become aware of her surroundings again. "What?"

"How are you doing?" I asked. "I know you felt the first vortex, did you feel the second?"

I pushed a stack of paperbacks out of the way with the edge of the platter, making room for the food. I poured crackers into a bowl and waved at the snacks. "Eat. You look half asleep."

She rubbed her thumb over the bridge of her nose. "I'm not that tired, just thinking. And yeah, I felt the second vortex open."

"Painful?" The kettle whistled and I walked that way. "Keep talking," I threw over my shoulder. "I'm listening."

"We were on the way back from the casino." Delaney pitched her voice so I could hear her. We'd been doing that since we were kids.

"Did it hurt like last time?" I asked.

"Pretty much."

"No," Ryder said, pitching his voice too. "It was worse."

"I don't think that's true," Delaney said, loudly for me.

"I don't think you were in any state to compare how bad it was."

"Well, since it was happening to me, I think I am the only one who *could* say how bad it was."

It was funny how they were carrying on the argument loud enough for me to hear them.

"You were convulsing," Ryder said.

I had placed the coffee pot, all the fixings, a tea selection, hot water and mugs on a serving tray. But hearing that made me stop cold.

I inhaled, exhaled, pushing away the knot of frustration and fear. Something had to change. Before she could be hurt again. And I was going to have to be the one who changed things.

I calmly walked into the room.

"I'm okay, Mymy," Delaney said.

I placed the tray on the table. "Okay."

"You don't believe me."

"I believe you."

"She just believes me more this time." Ryder planted a kiss on her temple, and she smacked his stomach. "Hey."

"Don't forget I have a dragon on my side."

"Trust me. I can't forget that thing."

"Tea," I said, dropping down into the chair across from them, "coffee. Oh, and…" I dug in my bag which I'd left on the

175

floor by the coffee table. "Whiskey." I thunked it on the table next to the cookies. "Because I think we're going to need it by the end of the night."

"I love your family gift." Ryder bent forward, picked up a mug and the whiskey, and poured himself a finger or two.

"Why are we drinking?" Jean had changed out of her wet sandy clothes and had helped herself to a pair of my fuzzy pajama bottoms and a sweatshirt.

She'd also taken a quick shower to get the sand out of her hair.

"We drink because we live in Ordinary." Ryder lifted his mug and took a swallow. He passed it to Delaney and she did the same.

"Looks like you two are off duty for the night," Jean said as she eyed them.

"I'm not drinking any more than that one swallow," Delaney said. "I don't know about Officer Lush here."

"Officer Lush is keeping his options open. All right, Reeds. What are we going to do about the frogs?"

Jean plopped down onto my loveseat and draped the towel across the back of it so she could rest her wet, colorful head on it without staining the furniture. She stretched her legs straight out in front of her. "I put them in a nice shallow bath of cool water, closed the toilet seat and shut the bathroom door."

"Are they all okay?" Delaney asked.

"Hard to know, but since they all look like healthy frogs, I'm gonna say we're still in the clear."

"Any idea why they didn't turn back into humans when the vortex closed?" Ryder asked. "You said the thrall was broken as soon as it shut. The whole crowd shook it off and went about their day. And that dad and daughter…"

"The Carlbergs," I supplied.

"Right. They snapped out of it as soon as it shut, correct?"

"Yep," Jean said.

"So why not the frogs?"

"Good question," I said. "The only thing different is the frogs were people who touched the vortex. Right, Jean?"

"That's what I think happened."

"Think?" Delaney asked.

She nodded. "I was getting ice cream across the street when I saw the vortex form. I called Myra as soon as it started. By the time she got there, and she got there quick, every human who was in eyesight had taken off at a run toward it. I tried to stop people, call them back, but they wouldn't listen."

"Then what?" Delaney leaned forward, picked up a couple crackers and some grapes, then sat back and split them with Ryder.

"The vortex was black," Jean tipped her face toward the ceiling and closed her eyes. I knew she was trying to dredge up any detail that might make a difference. "There was movement inside it, like smoke, but thicker. More solid. And I saw eyes."

"Yellow?" I asked.

"Yeah, yellow. And those eyes weren't anything I've seen before. It felt evil, old school evil." She shrugged her shoulders and opened her eyes. "Those people threw themselves into that thing like…you know how koi go crazy at feeding time?"

We all nodded.

"Like that. It was a frenzy. They would have torn each other apart to get to the vortex." She rubbed her hands up and down the fuzzy pj pants on her thighs. "They ran at it and hit it. Hard. Like smacking into a brick wall. It sounded like that too. Soft flesh and bone crunching. Totally gross."

Ryder passed her the mug of whiskey. She drained what was left before passing it back to him.

"I ran down there, but instead of finding a bunch of concussed idiots bleeding on the sand, there were all these frogs jumping around."

"Did you actually see people turn into frogs?" I asked.

"I saw people jumping into the vortex, hitting it, and bouncing back as frogs."

"Is there a chance those frogs in the bathroom aren't the people? That maybe the frogs broke through the vortex at the same time people disappeared?"

"What are the odds on that?" she asked. "More likely those Kermits in the bathroom are people."

"We need to know for sure," Ryder said. "Who do we call?"

"Than?" I suggested. "He was there."

DEVON MONK

"Yeah." Delaney reached for the coffee. "He's one of those people who wouldn't bring something important to our attention because he'd just assume we already know it. Call him. Find out if he thinks the frogs are people. We don't have much time before their friends and family realize their loved ones are missing."

I pulled out my cell.

"Death has a phone?" Jean asked.

"Has to." Delaney slurped coffee. "It's required for the job."

Jean flipped her a thumbs up and helped herself to a stack of cookies and cheese.

"Myra Reed," Than intoned.

"Kind of an intense way to answer the phone," I said.

"And how would you expect me to answer a telephone?"

"Pretty much like that. Okay, I just need to know if the frogs are people."

"Yes."

"Are they the people who ran to the vortex?"

"Yes, they are the people who ran toward the vortex. As far as I can discern."

"As far? Do you have some kind of limit I don't know?"

"My power is currently in the root of a tree in what I believe Crow called a cosmic kumbaya circle. One could assume I'm allowed a margin of error."

I widened my eyes at Delaney, and she just nodded like, *yeah, he's all sass.*

"Do the frogs, I mean people, still have their souls?"

"Souls are not easy to harvest, no matter the shape a human may take."

"Is that a yes?"

He sighed. "Yes."

"Okay, that's all I needed to know. Wait! Do you know how to turn them back into their human selves?"

"That is not my expertise."

"So...no?"

"No."

I smiled at the distaste he packed into one word. "All right. Thank you. I'll see you tomorrow at the station. You'll be with me again."

"How my heart races at the thought."

And that was so much *more* sass, I laughed. "Good night, Than."

"Good night, Myra Reed."

"He's got nothing," I said. "Except he thinks the frogs are our people. So witch? Wizard?"

"Demons." Bathin strode into the room, the unicorn glaring daggers at his side.

"How did you get into my locked house?" I stood.

Bathin stopped where he was, smart man, and so did the unicorn. "Xtelle knew the lock code."

"Why didn't you knock?" Jean asked. She sounded relaxed and amused.

"*I* didn't even want to come here," Xtelle said. "But now that I am, I'd like to report a crime. He has bound me against my wishes. I am being kidnapped. He's breaking Ordinary's laws."

She hopped a little to show her front hooves. Around each was a loop of solid gold.

"You have gold handcuffs?" Jean asked. She gave Bathin a slow look up and down. "Respect the kink, dude."

He tipped his head like *you are not wrong*, but turned immediately to me. "I need to tell you something."

"If it isn't how to turn frogs into people, I don't want to hear it."

"It's important."

"What could be more important than un-frogging people?"

"Xtelle is my mother."

The silence in the room was like plunging into deep, cold water, dropping down, down, down to the bottom.

"What?" Delaney shot up to her feet and so did Ryder.

Jean, still in the chair, laughed. "Your mother is a unicorn, Bathin? Well, it might explain those eyes of yours."

"You like my eyes, huh?" he said with a smile.

She rocked her hand in a so-so motion.

This was the part where I was supposed to say something. Where I was supposed to take over the problem, figure out what was going on, and present the solution. But my brain refused to wrap around this new information. It was like all my wiring had shorted.

"I...I don't even..." I said.

Bathin nodded like that was the most cogent thing I'd ever said. "She took the form of a unicorn so she could trick you into staying in Ordinary. She opened the first vortex of Hell into Ordinary."

"I *told* you, I did no such thing," she snarled. "I found the vortex and stepped through it. I did not make it."

"I don't believe her," Bathin said, "and since I'm her son, you can trust my judgment of her character."

"What? Now I'm a terrible mother?"

"You've always been a terrible mother, but a fantastic demon. Which is why I don't trust you and have never trusted you."

"Oh, you can trust I'll make you pay! I'll tell your father you're upworld slumming with mortals and monsters and neutered gods. He will raise the fire of Hell and despair upon you."

"Xtelle," Bathin said, so cold, so unlike what I'd ever heard him say before, "if you put Ordinary at risk, I will break your bones apart, atom by atom, and leave your flesh for the crabs."

Bathin's delivery was so matter-of-fact, so certain, it shocked her into silence.

He had shown a glimpse, just a sliver, like the shine off the edge of a razor, of the power he possessed. It was massive. Destructive. Caught there just beneath his wicked smile and pretty eyes.

Jean was wrong. There was nothing so-so about his eyes. They were gorgeous. And dangerous.

And why was I thinking about his pretty eyes? I should be thinking about how to get rid of not one, but two demons who did not belong in Ordinary.

But first, it was time to get Delaney's soul back.

I walked out of the room and to my office. There was no tug in my chest, nothing that was driving me to do this. But I was done. Done being lied to by demons. Done with the tricks.

I wanted my town to go back to normal. I wanted my sister to go back to normal.

"Myra?" Bathin called.

"No." Delaney's voice carried the clean strength of the earth and stones that made Ordinary what it was. "Leave her alone. You're going to stay away from her until we get this worked out. Let's start with this: What the hell, Bathin?"

I pulled the keepsake box off the top shelf in my office, drew it against my chest for a moment, the edges of wood digging in, the faint, lingering magic embedded into it when Odin had carved it humming like an old tune.

"Your *mother* has been in Ordinary posing as a pink unicorn for two days, and you just now tell us?" Delaney asked.

"Yes," he gritted out.

"Do you want to give me an explanation that will make me change my mind about kicking you—both of you—out of town?"

"I won't make the lie worse by adding falsehoods to it. I didn't know what was coming through the first vortex until we got there. When I saw her like this…"

This would end him. These scissors in this little box. I would end him. And pay a great price for doing so.

But Delaney's soul would no longer be a pawn in a chess game we couldn't see.

I took a deep breath, pushed my heartache away, and strode into the room.

"Time's up, Bathin," I said.

He lifted his head as if I'd just come into the room with a gun. His gaze fixated on the box cradled against my chest. He knew what it contained, even though I had never told him.

But then, I would think the only weapon that could force him to release the soul that allowed him to stay in Ordinary might be something he would always sense.

"Bathin," Xtelle said. I heard it then, the motherly warning, protection for her son.

That was strange.

Or maybe it was just her saving her own neck. I wasn't sure what was going to happen to her when I banished Bathin. She had lied about her nature. We didn't allow that.

We had rules in Ordinary. Rules in place to keep not only the humans safe, but to also keep the supernaturals and deities safe. She had broken those rules by not only lying to us, but also by not signing a demon contract.

I was calm. Clearer headed than I had been in over a year. Since Delaney had traded her soul. Since Dad's death.

"No," Bathin said to his mother.

He stepped around the unicorn, closed the distance until he loomed in front of me. Everyone in the room shifted position.

"Myra," Delaney warned.

"You don't have the one book with the one page," he murmured as if it were just he and I in the room. As if this was our second date and he was still trying to show me I could trust him.

"I don't think I need it, do I?"

"You've been told you do."

"By a demon?" I laughed, and it sounded alien to me, as if it were not even my voice or my mouth.

I was sort of floating above myself, numb, aware, sharp. Waiting for this to happen. Finally. Finally.

"What makes you think I would ever trust what a demon says?"

"You wouldn't," he said.

"What makes you think I would trust anything a demon does?"

"You wouldn't," he said.

"What makes you think you can use my sister's soul, her *soul*, Bathin, and just walk around while it tears and rips and bleeds like it's nothing. Like it's *nothing*!" I was snarling by the end of it. Damn right I was snarling by the end of it.

"I can't. I shouldn't. I'm not."

"Myra," Delaney said. "Let's take this one step at a time."

"No."

I twisted the lock and lifted the top of the box. Since I'd put the velvet bag containing the scissors in it, I'd cleaned out all my other keepsakes. I had been afraid my childhood would be tainted by this dark weapon that demanded such a high price.

But now it was not fear I was feeling. It was power. I picked up the velvet bag, let the wooden box drop to the floor.

"Oh, shit," Jean said. "We need to lock this down. Holy

fuck, Delaney we need to stop this. Now, right now. Myra, don't!"

Then Jean was on her feet lunging toward me, and the tug on my chest was so hot it was like a knife stabbing bone. Stabbing right through my skin, my muscle, all the way through to the other side of me. The *wrong place*, the *wrong time* of this moment rang me like a gong the size of the moon.

"It's not worth it," Bathin whispered.

"It is."

I gripped the scissors and swung.

Bathin was fast. Supernaturally fast. He grabbed my wrist, stepped sideways into my body, and forced open my hand.

The scissors clattered to the floor.

*Wrongwrongwrong.*

A wave of vertigo washed over me. And then I felt nothing.

# CHAPTER 17

WE WERE no longer in my house. We were no longer in a room.

"This isn't ideal," Bathin said. He breathed hard like he'd just lifted a car one-handed. A big car. A bus. "And it isn't going to last long. I don't know what I can say to make this right, because you refuse to listen to me."

"You're a demon!"

"That's racial profiling, Myra. Just because I'm a demon doesn't mean I'm evil. I've been trying to tell you that since the first day I came to Ordinary."

"Where are we?" I asked.

"In a place."

"No. Where are we?"

Panic rolled under my skin. There was only blurry turquoise-silver where the sky should be, and other than Bathin, everything around me was a shade of tropical-ocean-blue and white—blurry and indistinct.

"Where are we? What are we inside?" There was no wind or air or growing things. Where was the air?

"There is air. Or what you need to survive in this state. You're not going to suffocate." He reached toward my shoulder.

I slapped his hand away and punched him in the solar plexus.

He *"oofed"* out air and bent, holding his hand over his gut.

"Keep your hands off me."

He nodded, spit, then slowly straightened.

"Take me home."

"No, you need to—"

I roundhouse-kicked him in the knee.

"Fuck," he grunted as he buckled to the ground. "You need to listen—"

I aimed another kick at his head. His hand snapped out, and he caught my ankle, holding my foot up high enough I had to balance on one foot.

"Let go!"

"Listen to me!"

I pulled on my foot, ready to use the leverage to hop and kick him in the head with my other foot, but he saw the move coming, shoved my foot away, and gained his feet so fast, he was a blur.

Both hands shot out, grabbed my wrists, and then his leg was around mine, our bodies locked together as he pressed my back against something smooth and hard and warm. It felt like sun-warmed marble.

"Just." He slapped my hands above my head, his incredible weight pinning the rest of me. His hands squeezed my wrists and the walls heated just at those points becoming liquid enough to flow up and over my skin, wrapping my wrists.

"Let me go."

"Not until you listen." He pressed my legs back and the wall heated there, flowed out and caught both of my ankles no matter how much I struggled.

"There," he said, breathless, still pressed against my body, his hands over the stone covering my wrists. "There." He swallowed, stared at my eyes, then let his gaze wander over my face.

I didn't know what he was looking for. I hoped it was anger because I had plenty of that to offer.

"Just, hold still long enough for me to get this out. Right?" He pressed down on my wrists one more time as if making sure the bindings were going to stay. "Right," he answered himself.

He paced away, limping heavily. "Balls, woman, you can kick."

"Come here, and I'll show you how I can break bones."

He paused with his back to me, and dragged his fingers through his hair, resting his hands on top of his head, fingers laced together, elbows out.

"It's not going to take your sisters long to find us. I'm sure they'll have some way to break this. If Delaney can do it once, I'm sure she can do it again."

I frowned, trying to figure out what he was talking about. Something Delaney had done before. Some place he'd been with her.

"We're inside a stone, aren't we?"

He turned, his hands still on top of his head, and there was a look of desperation in his eyes. "Yes. It's one of the things I control. Stone. One of the other things I control is moving a person from one place to another. You used to know that about me."

"I still know that about you."

"But for the last year the only thing you've seen about me, the *only* thing, is that I hold your sister's soul."

"Because you do."

He nodded. "That is true. She gave it to me. That's within the laws and rules of human-demon contract. But ever since I've had it...no, even before that...ever since I started listening to your father talk about humanity, about the laws of the universes, the worlds, about gods and monsters and blood and family—*family*, Myra—things changed."

He dropped his hands, but didn't move any closer.

"I changed." Here he shook he head and laughed softly. "You have no idea. I am not the creature I once was. Possessing a Reed soul for so long, your father's soul, was like being a candle in the sunlight.

"Wax melts, given enough time in the flame. Light reshapes it. I've been reshaped by light. At first by your father's words, then his soul, but then Delaney's..." He inhaled, exhaled, and it was as close to awe as I'd ever seen on him.

"Holding her soul—that light—has changed me. Taught me. Some days I don't even know what I am supposed to—" He shook his head again. "No, that doesn't matter. We're here for you and for Delaney. Here, where my mother won't hear me. Here, where my father can't hear me. But I don't have very much time. Because your sisters..."

"...will find us and break this cage."

He nodded. "I need you to hear me, Myra. I am giving you the truth as I know it. And if you hear me, you might find a way to save Delaney's soul. Because gods know, I don't know how to do it."

I waited. I had time on my side. Either he'd get close enough I'd be able to kick him again somehow, or Delaney and Jean would find us and break this stone.

He could talk all he wanted.

"You're right," he said. "I've been using her soul as a way to stay in Ordinary. I have never made a secret of that. But what I haven't told you was why I wanted to stay in Ordinary. Why I was in that stone to begin with. Why I caught your father's drifting soul like a feather in the wind and drew it into the safety of the stone with me.

"I am the demon king's son."

I just gave him a steely stare. I knew that already.

"He wants me dead, has wanted me dead for years. I am not his only son, but I am the only one of his offspring to defy him." He scrubbed at his face, then wrapped his hand at the nape of his neck.

"I've been running for a long time. Eons. He always finds me. Tortures…and lets me go. He likes the chase, my father. And the pain. And the blood. And the agony. Demons." He nodded once, his eyes locked with mine, as cold as a surgeon's knife. "There is no evil like them."

"So, what?" I wanted any excuse to look away from the raw honesty behind his gaze. I could almost feel his pain, his desperation, his hopelessness as if it were my own, scratching at the walls of my heart. "What do you want me to do about it?"

"Did you just feel that?" he asked.

"What?"

"My…my feelings?"

"No."

He nodded. "That's a lie. We can both tell when the other is lying here. This is an Amazonite. The stone of truth. Here, there is only truth and clarity. Try it out."

I pulled at my wrists and feet, but the Amazonite still held me strong. "Try what?"

"Ask me something and I'll lie. You'll be able to feel it."

"Just because of the stone?"

"Yes. You'll feel if I'm lying just because of the stone."

His expression was calm, his gaze steady. There was absolutely nothing about his body language showing any indication that he was lying. But I knew. I knew it as if I had uttered the words. As if his answer was a part of me that didn't fit.

187

"You're lying?"

"That was a partial lie, yes. I've been telling the truth since we've been here."

I waited for that wrong puzzle piece feeling to hit me again, but it didn't.

"Well, hell," I muttered.

He nodded. "I couldn't think of any other way for you to believe what I'm going to tell you. So here I am, putting it all out there and on the line in a way that you will know if I am telling any kind of untruth at all."

"So I can ask you anything, and you'll have to answer me?"

"No. I don't have to answer you."

That felt like a truth.

"But I will."

That felt like a truth too.

"Is Xtelle your mother?"

"Yes."

"Is your father as horrible as she says?"

"I don't know what she told you about him, but whatever she said, triple it, and you might be in the ballpark for his level of darkness and evil."

"Do you know where I can find the one book with the one page that will tell me how to use the scissors to cut Delaney's soul from you?"

"No."

And that didn't feel like a lie either, dammit.

"But I don't think there is a book," he said.

"Why?"

"Well, you got your information from a crossroad demon, and they are all about having backup plans. The small print always works in their favor."

"Explain that. And tell me the truth."

"The crossroad demon, Zjoon, is an old hand at getting what she wants and keeping it. She's had a crossroad so close to Ordinary that it might as well be inside of it."

"She can't run a crossroad in Ordinary."

"I know that. She knows that too. And yet…"

"…she found a way around it. Small print?"

"Small print," he agreed.

Truth.

"So," he went on, "Zjoon knows I wouldn't want her to tell anyone, much less someone who has an ax to grind, about the scissors. And before you ask, yes, they were made by my mother, and yes, they were fashioned to force me to release a soul."

"Zjoon knew you'd be angry."

"Furious," he agreed. "She padded her bet by giving you false information on how to use them. And, well, I wasn't happy about it. Her giving you the scissors. But not for the reason you think."

"Because it will force you to release Delaney's soul and leave Ordinary?"

"No."

That feeling hit me, the unfamiliar, unfitting piece. "You're lying."

He hummed. "Maybe to both of us a little, to you and to myself. I'd like to think the reason I'm keeping her soul isn't so selfish—staying here in Ordinary, hiding from my world, my father. But I can accept that's a part of it. It's not the main reason I don't want you to use the scissors."

I waited for that wrong feeling.

It didn't hit.

I sighed. "Just spit it out, Bathin. You've made your point. I can tell when you're lying, and you can tell when I'm lying. Let's get this over with. I'm not done kicking your ass."

His eyebrows went up in surprise. "Not a lie. Good to know. Okay, here's the truth, the whole truth, and nothing but. If you use the scissors, it will damage Delaney's soul. Possibly to a point beyond repair."

The feeling of wrongness never hit. He was not lying.

He was not lying.

Holy shit. He was not lying.

"Okay," I said, ready to listen for the first time since he'd dropped us in the middle of an Amazonite. "If I use the scissors, I'm going to hurt Delaney."

"Yes."

Truth and truth.

"Badly."

"Yes."

"Do you know who can use the scissors to cut her soul from you?"

"Probably. Yes, well, probably. It hasn't been tested, but I have a good guess."

There was a vague feeling of wrongness, but it passed as soon as he clarified his own doubt.

"Who?" I asked.

"Do I have to tell you?"

"Yes."

He looked pained. "All right. I said I'd be honest. You have no idea how difficult this is. It is completely against my nature. If your father hadn't...no, never mind. I'm deflecting. All right. Because of how the scissors were forged, I think the only person who can use them to free a soul from my keeping is another demon."

No lie.

"Well, we're screwed," I said.

He laughed, and it was a deep round sound that came from his gut and lit up his face, softening all the hardest, darkest edges of him into something lighter, brighter. Something good and real.

*Wax melts, given enough time with the flame. Light reshapes it.*

"We live complicated lives, you and I, Myra. And our courtship and love affair is going to be just as complicated."

"We're not in a courtship," I said. I shouldn't have. Because I knew it was a lie, and so did he.

"You did that on purpose," I whispered.

"Yes, I did. Habit. But that isn't what we need to address right now. We need to come to an understanding that you cannot use the scissors on me without hurting Delaney. Also, full disclosure, my mother bound us together, you and I."

Time ticked: one Mississippi, two Mississippi...

"She did what?" I almost yelled. "She bound us together?" I pushed against the stone cuffs.

"That's the other reason you can tell I'm lying."

"When? When did she bind us?"

"At the second vortex. With the yarn."

"You knew."

"Not until it was too late to stop her."

And that was the truth, dammit.

"Let me go."

"Not yet. You'll fight me again, and while I enjoy it…" he paused so I could feel the truth of that, "…we don't have time."

"It hurts you, doesn't it?" I asked. "When I hit you here?"

"Yes. I feel the physical hit as if we were equal—human and demon—and the power of your emotions lands with each contact like a second blow. I'd like to remain conscious until we make some decisions."

"What decisions?" My nose itched and I wanted to scratch it. I waved my fingers and turned my head, trying to get my tiptoes under me so my fingers and nose lined up.

"What are you doing?"

"My nose itches."

"Here, let me."

"No, I can…"

But he had already crossed the space and pressed his fingers gently beneath my jaw. He turned my face and held it still, peering down his nose at me like a nearsighted school teacher judging my handwriting.

"It's really…" I said, my mouth dry, "you don't have to…"

"Hush. I like doing things for you." He lifted his other hand and rubbed his pointer finger on the tip of my nose. "Here?"

I wasn't paying attention. He hadn't been lying when he'd said he liked doing things for me.

He liked doing things for me.

"Myra?"

"A little to the left." He moved his finger, rubbed. "My left," I said.

He nodded, moved his finger to the other side of my nose and gave it three little rubs. "How's that?"

"It's, uh…good enough."

"Good." He looked away from my nose and right into my eyes.

For a moment, for the longest moment in my life, he just stood there, breathing softly, holding my face, watching me.

I knew the second he made up his mind. I could feel it. Not

like a tug in my chest. No, it was a relief, a lightness. Like my heart had been tied down, weighed down by rocks and now, that look of his, that moment, it was feathers and sunlight.

A slight frown creased between his eyes, as if he knew what he was doing wasn't wise, but he had to do it anyway.

I didn't struggle, I didn't try to move away from him.

Because I didn't want to.

There were no lies here.

He bent, he had to, he was so much taller than me. I lifted as much as I could, angling my face up, wanting this. To know. Here, where there were no lies.

My eyes fluttered shut and I had to catch my breath to keep from making any sound. He paused, his lips only the barest distance from mine, so close I could taste the cinnamon of his breath.

"Are you sure?" he whispered.

"Yes." It was the only answer I had, because it was the truth.

He hummed, and it was acceptance and need and hope.

If I had ever imagined kissing a demon, which yes, lately I had, it was always a hot branding, a claiming, a fire-meets-kindling-and-add-some-gasoline kind of kiss.

But this, this kiss was something more. Something better.

Bathin shifted his thumb to stroke gently along the side of my mouth, and the gesture was so sweet, so intimate, I smiled.

He shifted closer with my exhale, his lips pressing, warm and soft—much softer than I'd imagined. He held me there, held us both, suspended in that connection, that first moment of being more than two.

I wondered how long he could endure the sweet ache of this gentleness, wondered how long I would let him hold us both in this moment, before doing my own claiming.

Just when it was too much, when he was drawing away slowly as if even the retreat of our lips was something to savor, he dipped his head again.

And this time the kiss caught fire.

A shiver ran through me—how could I be cold when I was burning, engulfed in flame—my nerves stretched and crackling, little *pop, pop, pops* of pleasure snapping hard under my skin.

I whimpered and he moaned, dipping his mouth to lick my lower lip and then bite very gently there before licking again.

I wasn't on fire, I was molten, a volcano.

I arched up into him, needing more, more touch, more. His fingers stroked along my throat, leaving mint-cool paths where his fingers had been, and he molded against me, one hand lowering so he could notch our hips together and move with me, a slow, circular motion.

My breath skipped like a stone over still water. And I still couldn't stop trembling. His tongue slicked my mouth, already too wet, too hot. I was hungry, but the more he touched, squeezed, stroked, tugged, the more I needed.

"I want," I gasped in between his onslaughts, the drugging nips and tastes, his tongue, teeth, mouth, the scratch of stubble on my tender skin that felt good, too good, but wasn't enough, not nearly enough, his hard grinding body. "More," I begged.

He groped blindly for the binds on my wrist, freed one, freed the other.

I threaded my fingers through his thick, soft hair and groped his back, the hard curve of his ass. I scrabbled to untuck his shirt from slacks that molded against his body like liquid sin.

*This. Now. Here.*

He twisted, skimmed his fingers under my shirt and then, gently, so damn gently, trailed the back of his fingertips across my lower belly.

"Myra," he whispered, his head bent into my shoulder, as if he would fall apart, fly apart. He didn't have to say anything more. I could hear the truth of his need, the truth of him, of us. Could feel it.

"Yes."

The cuffs on my ankles melted away, and he leaned back and rucked up his shirt exposing miles and miles of deeply tanned skin I wanted to lick, bite. Then his shirt was gone. He rocked forward again, his breath catching as if he'd been holding it for hours, for days, for years and years. I spread my fingers over his chest, then down, riding fingertips over the ridges and dips of his muscles.

His skin tightened, and goosebumps rippled under my feather-light touch as he shuddered.

I wanted more of him. To know what this—what we—could be, no lies between us.

His thumb rubbed the hard round button of my jeans, pushing it through the hole until the cloth parted and he could plunge his huge hand down, inside, questing for warmth.

I moaned his name, lost to that delicious friction.

"Beautiful," he breathed.

And then there was no time for slow, no time for thinking. There was only *here* and *now* and *more*, in our desperate quest to tear away clothing as quickly as possible.

And when, finally, he drew me down to where he lay, naked and stunning and hard, waiting for me, I followed him willingly, open and needing, until he filled my body, my mind, my world.

# CHAPTER 18

"TELL ME about the cats," I said.

"What cats?"

My head was on Bathin's shoulder. We were naked, but the stone around us was warm as firelight and silk.

"The three strays that are following you around?"

He sighed. "Five. Five strays. I just feed them sometimes. It's nothing permanent."

Lie. But a gentle one as if maybe he didn't even realize it was a lie.

He grunted softly.

"You feed them."

"Yes."

"Give them a place to sleep?"

"Not every night."

"They were wearing collars."

"The vet said—"

I laughed. "You *are* looking after them."

"Maybe," he conceded. "Maybe I am. Funny how these things sneak up on you."

"Things?"

"Life."

We were quiet a moment. Two.

"How do we go back to before?" I asked.

"Mmmm. To Ordinary?" His thumb stroked my ribs gently, running over the turtle tattoo I never showed anyone.

"To our lives."

"We don't have to."

I traced his chest, let my hand wander lower, along his tight stomach, pressing down the ridge of the V muscle of his groin and lower still.

"We could stay here." He gasped as I moved my hand, gently stroking him. "Or another stone. Every stone..." I twisted my wrist and he arched, his hips seeking more friction.

"Every stone in the universe is ours. Our private worlds."

My hand was warm, but I brought it up and made sure he was watching as I licked my palm, then laved my tongue between my fingers.

"Fuck." He rolled, settling his weight carefully on his strong arms, and holding a perfect plank position before he shifted his knees, urging me to open my legs. "Myra," he moaned.

I lost myself to him. Because I knew this couldn't last.

I wasn't made to run away for my own pleasure. I wasn't made to leave Ordinary behind, leave my sisters behind. I wasn't made to follow my heart.

He knew that. There was no future for us after this.

But oh, how my heart wanted one.

I dragged my fingers down his wide back, wanting him nearer, but lazy in my needs.

He dropped soft kisses up my shoulder, dipping to my throat. I rocked my head back to give him access, my mind a gentle buzz of sensation, my thoughts wandering to what we'd done here. What we'd said.

Wait. Hold on. Just a second.

I shoved at Bathin's shoulders. He lifted just enough to peer down at me, his eyelids heavy, his pupils blown from lust. His mouth was reddened, shiny, his hair a mess.

He looked ravaged, and sexy as hell.

"Yes?" he asked.

"What do you mean your mother bound us?"

He blinked. "You're…" He sighed and looked off over my head. "Wow. Is that a mood killer. Why are you talking about my mother?"

"Because you said. Back before…before…this…" He smiled at me and I frowned. "You said your mother bound us together."

"I did say that."

"Okay, that's it. Sex is off. Move." I shoved at his arms which were caging either side of my head.

"I'd plead and tempt, but you're not going to fall for that, are you?"

"No."

He let his head hang for a minute. "No lying. All right, but since we're being honest, I don't want to talk about it. I think more sex is our best play right now."

I slapped his arm again and he lifted up on one hand, moving his entire body to one side in some kind of power yoga move.

"Show off."

He grinned and flexed every muscle. I almost dragged him back down to me again.

Instead, I rolled out from under him, looked around for my clothes, and gathered them up. "Tell me. All of it. What did your mother do?"

"Many, many terrible things. But I'm guessing you want to know about the binding."

I rolled my hand in a hurry up move, hooked my bra and slipped the straps over my shoulders, then bent and unbunched my shirt, shaking it until it was right side out.

"I didn't catch it quickly enough to stop her."

Lie.

"Want to try that again?"

"I didn't want to stop her. It seemed like a reasonable decision at the time. However, I didn't know she was going to do it until it was done. And yes, I probably had just enough warning to stop her, but that would have meant the vortex remained open longer. We would have had to start the spell again. And we were about to be buried in frogs." He rolled to the balls of his feet and then stood.

"I thought one price was worth the other," he said.

"And that means?"

"Her binding us was worth all those people not turning into frogs. You'd be angry with me either way. Plus, this aligned with my desires, and I am a creature who follows his desires. All the way. You may have noticed."

"You are so annoying."

He smiled because he could feel the lie.

"How did she do it?" I asked.

"She used the string, cut by Death's blade, used to save the living. She bound the connection between the Underworld and above with the string you and I held. Poetry, really. She's particularly good at those things."

"Bindings?"

"Screwing with my life."

I laughed and he looked very pleased with himself.

"What kind of binding is it?"

"I'm not exactly sure. I haven't had time to explore it, though I did force her to agree to break it. With no strings attached, if you'll excuse the pun."

"Is that why she was hobbled?"

"No, I hobbled her because she was threatening to open another vortex and invite every demon from here to sunrise into Ordinary."

Dread hit my belly and suddenly the softness of this space, the quiet little hideaway safety of it felt stifling. "Can she do that?"

"I thought it was better to assume so."

"Are those cuffs going to hold her?"

"Yes. Until she talks one of your sisters into freeing her. And she will. Because she's a demon. And weirdly that pink unicorn thing is really working for her. It's amazing what being cute will get you."

"Yeah, you should try it sometime," I said.

He waggled his eyebrows. "Maybe I will."

"Forget I suggested it."

"Now, now. There is nothing I want to forget about you."

I blinked and stared at him because he meant that. It was the truth.

He rolled his eyes. "You'd think I'd get used to this place and keep my big mouth shut."

I decided to just let it go. We had a disaster to deal with. Several disasters.

"Let me see if I have everything straight," I said, shoving my feet in my shoes. I was fully dressed, and he was still standing there, completely comfortable in his nudity.

"Correct me if I'm wrong."

He nodded.

"You and I are bound because of how we closed the last vortex and because your mother can't keep her nose out of your business." I paused for confirmation. He nodded.

"We have a dozen or so people who turned into frogs when they hit the vortex."

"As far as we know. Your sisters might have found a way to turn them back by now."

"How long have we been in here?"

"Time runs at different speeds for stones. They are very old and durable. They aren't locked into time's gears like the living."

"Not helpful. An hour, a day, a week?"

He tipped his head up and put his hands on his hips. Gloriously naked, I found I wanted to go to him again, feel his arms around me, taste the sweat of his skin. I thought if I stared at him any longer, I'd do just that.

It had to be the binding between us, drawing me to him so powerfully. I was attracted to him, yes. But I'd been attracted to men before.

*He's not a man*, my heart whispered. *Not any man.*

I stared at the sky, wondering what he saw up there. All I saw was a soft turquoise-blue light that diffused around us like sunlight through morning mist.

"An hour? Two?" he finally said.

"All right. You need to take us back."

"Are you sure, Myra? This could be our life. A good life."

"This is just a dream."

"It doesn't have to be." And there was truth in that too. He was offering. He would give this to me, to us, if I asked.

"You're still holding my sister's soul hostage. I have people to de-frog and a unicorn to kick out of Ordinary. That's my life. My real life. And...and you. You're going to have to leave Ordinary, Bathin. You can't just break the rules for your own benefit."

"Myra..."

"No. You wanted me to listen to you? To really listen? Then listen to me. If you don't give her soul back. Today. I will use those scissors. I'll have to. No matter the cost.

"So I'm asking you. One last time. Please release Delaney's soul."

His expression was a broad brush of emotion: discomfort, embarrassment, and guilt. So much guilt. And when he spoke, it was a truth I did not want to hear.

"I can't."

# CHAPTER 19

HE WAS dressed, back in the jeans, T-shirt, and black leather motorcycle jacket I should not want to take off him again.

I had waited, for every minute it took him to locate his clothes, for every minute it took him to pull them on. Had waited for him to explain his answer.

"Can't," I finally said.

"Contracts…" He crossed his arms over his chest and frowned. "Contracts with demons are sacred. Once entered, never released. It isn't in our nature to give up something we've won."

"You didn't win it. She traded for Dad's soul."

"Even better."

"So you won't let go of her soul?"

"I can't. Not unless there is no other choice."

"There's no other choice right now."

"Not for me. There is nothing I want more than to keep her soul. To stay in Ordinary. That's…it's a demon thing." There was a blush on his cheeks, as if this were embarrassing to him, degrading to admit.

"I can't let go of it…*can't* until there is something…more."

That truth was a blade, a river, a mountain range between us. I could push it, I should. But the things I would tell him were too vulnerable.

That if he cared for me, he would let her go. If he cared more for me than he cared to be hiding from his father in Ordinary, he would let her go.

That if he loved me…

No. That wasn't what we were talking about. That couldn't be what we talked about.

"You could let her go," I said, voice even. "And you could leave Ordinary. We could find you a safe place to exist. We have supernatural connections, gods who owe us favors."

"But there is no other place I desire to be," he said softly.

"Ordinary has ruined me for every other place."

Something about that was not quite the truth. He smiled sadly. "Or perhaps it is just a Reed sister who has done so to me."

There was the truth.

"Oh."

It was sweet, and the soft fire in his eyes made me want to kiss him. But that was over now, that was done. This love affair, if that's what it was, this fling, couldn't continue.

Not in the real world. Not in my real life.

"You know I'm going to find a way to force you to let go of her soul," I said.

"Oh, I'm counting on it."

"I'll use the scissors. Her soul is already damaged in your keeping. What's another little tear?"

"Another little tear could kill her."

"Yeah, well. Favors, gods, and all that."

His smile tightened and his eyes narrowed. "I do love a challenge," he murmured.

I knew he wasn't talking about my sister's soul. Or at least that wasn't the only thing he was talking about.

I opened my mouth, and then...

...the world slipped, sweet as melted candy, the sky washing down in a tingling rush to pool at my feet. Everything was quiet, and in that silence, I felt Bathin's arms around me, felt his presence like a blanket cloaking me, holding me near and precious.

And then his voice, soft, low. "Easy now. This step can be jarring."

The world crashed and flashed and clattered. Too many sounds, too much color, so many scents coating my nose, my throat, my tongue, I felt like I was going to throw up.

"Myra, gods, are you all right?" That was color, candy, laughter and hope, with a ribbon of fear, dark and deep as hard licorice: Jean.

"Get the fuck away from her." That was water and earth and sky, clean, raging storm and the salt birds calling through the cracks of a forest fire: Delaney.

"Asshole." That was a paint stroke, a hard-ruled line, the

cut of a saw, the hot metal strike of hammer on nail: Ryder.

I knew them, could sense them, but couldn't see them. Until I could.

Jean and Delaney were both at my side, Jean pulling me out of Bathin's arms, Delaney spinning to face him, an unbreakable wall between me and him.

Ryder, surprisingly, shoved in front of Delaney and hit Bathin with a hard right I hadn't even seen coming.

Bathin hadn't seen it coming either. He took it square on the jaw and stumbled to the side. "You ever take one of these sisters out of this town or this reality without their permission again, and I will unstring your bones and feed you to the dragon like spaghetti noodles. Understand?"

It was. Wow. I didn't think I'd ever seen Ryder this angry unless it had something to do with Delaney's safety. Although this did. Bathin was in possession of her soul. If he left, so did her soul.

Holy shit. He must have been terrified.

"It's okay," I said.

"Shh. You don't have to defend that asshole," Jean said.

"I'm not. It's just. We're okay. I'm okay. He didn't do anything."

Bathin rubbed his jaw and glared at Ryder. "That's not entirely true."

"He didn't do anything to hurt me," I amended.

Delaney pulled at Ryder's arm. Probably a good thing because Ryder looked like he was just warming up and wanted to go another round. Maybe ten.

"Words, Bailey," she said. "Then dragon chow."

He looked like he didn't want to listen, but dropped his clenched fists and stepped back. I noted he remained angled so he could reach Bathin before any of the rest of us.

Protective Ryder was a good look on him, and I had a quick moment to be happy that he and Delaney had finally stopped dancing around each other and had settled into a life together.

They complemented each other, and I was pretty sure there'd be wedding bells any day now. Maybe when Delaney got her soul back.

Maybe when our lives went back to normal.

"Frogs," I said. "Where are we at with that?"

Everyone stared at me.

"You disappear out of thin air and out of Ordinary…" Delaney started.

"Not out of Ordinary," Bathin said.

"All right. Not technically out of Ordinary, and you want to talk about frogs?"

"Last I heard, that was still a problem. Did you already turn everyone back?"

"You've been gone three hours, Myra," Jean said. "We turned everyone back hours ago."

"Oh," I said. "Good. I'll make us some coffee, and you can tell me how that went down."

"Sit," Jean said. "You too, Delaney. And Ryder. And you," she pointed at Bathin as she strolled to the kitchen. "Better stick around, big boy, or you're not going to like the consequences."

"I wouldn't care to be anywhere else," he said blithely.

He strode to the fireplace and lowered himself to sit on the hearth. He looked tired, and that was not something I was used to seeing on him.

He must have felt me looking at him, or maybe he caught me thinking about him. Was that a part of the bonding his mother had done to us? Could we read each other's minds now? I thought about ice cream and roller coasters and little yappy dogs that people thought were adorable when they dressed them up.

Bathin gave me a quizzical look. "What?" he asked.

"Can you read my mind?"

"Not here." The smile he gave me, along with the slow lowering of his gaze as he took in every curve of my body, was absolutely scorching.

"Cool it, lover boy," Delaney said. "Talk to us. What happened?" That last was for me.

"I had the scissors." A sudden panic filled me. "You did retrieve the scissors? Tell me you didn't let Xtelle have them."

"We have them," Ryder assured me.

"You pulled the scissors," Delaney encouraged. "We saw that. Then from our perspective, you disappeared."

"Bathin took me into another place. A stone."

Delaney's breath caught and she nodded. "Right. I didn't think about that. Of course he did. One of the stones here?" she asked the demon.

"No. Not in her house. One that I have tucked away in Ordinary. Like I said," he nodded at Ryder, "I did not step outside of Ordinary. There are reasons why I won't do that."

"Oh?" Delaney asked. "Why?"

"Ask Myra. I'm sure she'll be happy to fill you in on every detail of our short escape from this madhouse."

I fought back a smile. I didn't know I would like broody and moody Bathin this much. Poor baby, all his evil plans thwarted by a girl.

He must have caught some of that because he slid me a very private smile.

"So?" Jean said, strolling back into the room with four mugs, a two-liter of soda, and my coffee carafe in her hands. "You were off getting stoned with Bathin."

"In a stone with Bathin," I corrected.

She winked. "Riiiight. In a stone with Bathin. That's why your cheeks are all pink and the rest of you looks all relaxed and healthy glow-a-fied. Why, if I didn't know better I'd say someone was getting a little possessed-by-a-demon on the side."

"Shut it," I said.

"Wait," Delaney frowned.

"Air five, you dog, you," Jean said.

Bathin just held his palm up over his head, and Jean did the same. They both slapped the empty space between them at the same time.

"But you know, if you hurt her, I will shove you into a hole you'll never dig out of and pour gasoline over your burning corpse for all of eternity," she added.

"You won't live for all of eternity," Bathin noted.

"I know people." She grinned.

"Point taken. Not that anyone wants to listen to me, but I give you my word I didn't take Myra from here to harm her. In fact, the only reason I left was to keep her from committing harm to herself and to Delaney. You're welcome," he added snidely to Ryder.

"Don't push me, Bathin. There are more ways to get rid of

you than reasons to keep you."

"And there's the trifecta. Everyone's had a chance to threaten me. Now can we get on with solving the problem?"

"Which one?" Delaney asked. "We took care of the frogs."

"Just curious," I said. "What was the solution?"

"Crow came up with it." Delaney didn't sound happy.

"Crow?"

"He showed up looking for you, looking for Bathin. You know how he has a knack for appearing whenever trouble is going down."

"Okay, so what did Crow tell you to do?"

"Kiss them," Delaney said.

She was staring right at me, and I knew she wasn't lying. "Kiss them," I repeated. "Like the fairytales?"

"Slimier," Ryder noted. "Smelled like mulch. And not a single prince in the bunch."

"All of you kissed them?" The idea of that, the image of that was something I was sorry I'd missed. "Tell me someone took pictures. I need photo evidence of this. Of the whole thing."

"No one took pictures," Ryder said.

"Crow took some." Jean handed me a cup of coffee with just the right amount of cream and sugar in it.

"Thank gods." I took the cup from her gratefully.

"That's what I said. I mean, we can't exactly publish it in the local paper, but still, it was a day for the Reed scrapbook for sure."

"Totally want to see them," I muttered to Jean over the top of my coffee.

"Got your back," she said with a wink.

"Anyway," Delaney said, dragging us back on track. "We took everyone to one of the rooms at the hospital, kissed frogs, then told them they'd been hit by a microburst and been knocked out, but that none of them had suffered concussions, so they were fine, and should go home."

"No lingering side effects? They still have their souls?"

"We had a witch—Jules—check them out. We asked a couple other people just to make sure. Turns out getting frogged by Hell doesn't really stick with you for long. But just in case, we're keeping an eye on them."

"Good. Really good. So why are you all in my house?"

"We were looking for you," Delaney said. "This seemed like the best place to begin."

"Where is the unicorn?"

"We locked her in the spare room."

There was a clatter from somewhere down the hall, a crash, and a muffled curse.

"Did you tie her up?"

Jean smiled. "It's amazing how useful duct tape can be. And those fancy golden cuffs? Bueno." She gave Bathin a thumbs up.

Funny how quickly she could forgive and forget. It was something I'd always admired about her.

I took another gulp of coffee, because I needed it if I was going to get through this conversation.

"So here's what I know." I cupped the mug between my hands and savored the warmth. "The unicorn is Bathin's mother, a demon who has taken the shape of a unicorn."

"We heard him when he said it. Is it true?" Ryder asked.

"It's true. And if she really can open a vortex into Ordinary, like Bathin thinks she can, it's only a matter of time before more demons do the same."

"Can we do anything to shore up our defenses?" Delaney asked Bathin.

"Against demons?"

"Against vortexes. People turning into frogs. Unicorns that aren't unicorns. And yes, demons."

"Ordinary is already nearly impossible for my kind to breach," Bathin said. "I can't imagine what else could be done to make it even more impenetrable."

Delaney took a deep breath and tucked her hair behind her ears. "Okay. So we have vortexes to think about, demons…"

"…with yellow eyes," Jean added.

"…with yellow eyes," she agreed. "We have the unicorn, and we have you, still holding my soul in trade…"

Ryder muttered something that I didn't catch, but which I would probably agree with.

"…plus, we have two new officers we're training and the

Slammin' Salmon Serenade coming up tomorrow."

"What does the parade have to do with anything?" Bathin asked.

"Busy tourist days. Everyone comes to town for the food and wine and beer and parade. A last hurrah before autumn really kicks in. So we're about to be up to our collective necks in people. How are we going to keep them safe if another vortex opens up? Or multiple vortexes?"

We were all silent, because, yeah, we might have more hands on the force now, but we couldn't be everywhere at once.

"We need more data," I said. "I say we grill the unicorn."

Bathin snorted. "Good luck."

"Oh, I didn't say I was going to do it. I think it's time you pulled your weight around here."

"I'm sure I'm going to love this idea."

"If she's really the one who opened the vortexes, I want to know why. And I want to know why she helped us close them." I headed toward the guest room. Bathin took a step, but Jean made a short sound.

"Nope," she said. "You stay here. Last time you got too close to Myra, you stone-napped her."

"You know I don't need your help," I said when she and I were in the hall.

"I don't know that. Plus, we watch each other's backs, right? We don't go off Lone Rangering any of this stuff, right?"

I paused with my hand on the door handle. "Do you have a bad feeling about this?"

"Not this, in particular. But when you pulled out those scissors." She bit her lip and shook her head. "Myra, there's something really wrong with those scissors. The idea of you using them scared the hell out of me."

"Doom twinges?" I asked.

She nodded. "Doom twinges."

"Where are the scissors now?"

"I used a pair of your gloves and put them in the bag and back in your box. I didn't know Odin gave you one of those."

"When I was little."

"Me too, but mine has moons and stars and butterflies on it instead of ocean stuff."

"He really should have stuck with boxes instead of going for the chainsaw art."

She chuckled. "Right? I miss him. I hope he comes back soon. I need some terrible art for my yard."

I smiled. "So where's the box?"

"Delaney stuffed it in your closet."

"Okay." I'd get them later. "Ready?"

"I don't think a hoof-cuffed, duct-taped mini-horse is going to be that much trouble."

I wasn't sure I agreed with her about that. Demons were tricky and underhanded.

They had a way of getting under your skin, making you change your mind about what they were, who they were.

I opened the door.

Xtelle was gone.

# CHAPTER 20

"CHECK THE room," I told Jean.

She gave it a quick glance. "No unicorn."

"She's a demon. She can take on the shape of anything she wants."

"Gotcha." Jean stepped into the room and started opening dresser drawers. "You better not be a spider, you bitch," she mumbled.

I stormed back out into the living room.

"Where is she?"

Bathin raised his eyebrows. "Xtelle?"

"She's gone?" Delaney asked.

"Jean's checking, but yes, she's gone." I strode over to Bathin. "Where is she?"

He held his hands out. "I don't know."

"I don't believe you."

He blinked, then narrowed his eyes. "I'm telling you the truth."

"Just like in the stone."

He stood up and towered over me. "Yes. Just like in the stone. I'm on your side here."

"I don't think you are. I don't think you have ever been on my side."

"You know that's not true."

"I know you're holding my sister's soul hostage."

"I've told you—"

"I heard you."

*There is nothing more I want than to keep her soul.*

Nothing more. Not even me.

I pushed the pain of that away.

"What we're going to do now is the smart thing. The thing we should have done a long time ago."

He shook his head. "I've been in Ordinary for over a year now. I have been a model citizen. I have saved lives—Ben's,

Ryder's, that family in front of the vortex. I have done everything you, or your sisters, have asked me to do, even when it was against my nature."

"Then release Delaney's soul," Ryder said.

Bathin didn't look his way. "I've told you, I can't."

Was that a lie? A demon lie? Maybe it didn't even matter anymore.

"Well, I can't let you keep it."

"Myra," Delaney said. "We don't have to do this right now."

"Then when?" I asked her.

She met my gaze. "I'm fine right now."

Same old story.

Jean jogged into the room. "I can't find her. Unless she's microscopic?"

"She's not microscopic," Bathin said.

"Then she's not here," Jean said.

"Do you know where she is?" Delaney asked.

"No," he said. "But I assume she'll stay in Ordinary."

"Why? What's the point?" I asked.

"Ordinary is the point, Myra. It's the whole point. The goal. The place the gods and Reeds forbid. It's unattainable, and therefore, irresistible."

"So she's going to stay here, hide here, until we find her. That works for us."

I reached into my pocket where I'd tucked away a little string. A string cut by Death's blade, bound by a unicorn/demon horn. A string that had closed a vortex and been used to bind together the above and below.

I pulled a lighter out of my other pocket, and set fire to the string.

It must have been wool—the knitting group used good quality fiber, even in their yarn bombings—it caught fast and burned hot.

"Myra," Bathin warned, startled. "What are you doing?"

"My job." I whispered a very short spell. It was not a binding. It was a trigger.

His eyes narrowed. "You don't want to do that."

I exhaled, blowing out the fire before it scorched my

fingertips, and at that moment, the spell I'd traced across my wooden floor flared to life.

Bathin threw his hands up in the air. "A demon trap? How…unoriginal. What good is that going to do?"

"It's going to keep you here while we find your mother."

"Then what?"

"Then we're going to make her use the scissors on you, get back Delaney's soul, and kick you both out of Ordinary."

The muscles in his jaw jumped as if he were itching to chew through stones. A mountain. An entire mountain range. Chew through a mountain range and spit out the gravel. Then he sat on the hearth. "She won't do what you want. Making her do anything you want is impossible."

"Yeah, well, this might be Ordinary, but that doesn't mean I am."

"Myra," Delaney said, "I need to talk to you in the kitchen."

That was her big sister voice. She was going to try to argue me out of my plan. Not that I had a plan.

"Don't let him out of the trap," I said.

"Like I'd know how." Jean flopped down on my couch and pulled out her phone.

"Don't give him anything that will break the line."

"Got it," she said.

"And don't listen to him."

"Myra," Jean looked up from her phone, "I know. I know how to handle a suspect in jail. I know how to handle a demon in a trap. Okay?"

I followed Delaney into the kitchen. She leaned on the counter in front of the sink, the window behind her. "Have you lost your mind?"

I stuck my hands in my pockets. "No. I'm thinking very clearly. How about you?"

"I think my sister is trying to deal with that demon out there on her own. Am I wrong?"

"Yes."

"So who have you talked to about whatever it is you started out there?"

"All of you. For the last year. But none of you have been listening to me. You're too stubborn. Jean thinks Bathin's a good guy. And Ryder wouldn't tell you you're wrong if his life depended on it."

"That's not true," she said, and yeah, she had a point. Ryder argued with Delaney probably more than any of us. "What's really going on with you?"

"I'm trying to get your soul back. From a demon who has somehow made everyone in town think he's a good guy."

"Myra. You like him."

"No, I don't. I…can't."

"That blush on your face and that look in your eyes tells me differently."

"The look is anger."

"The look is fear." She said that gently, and then walked across the kitchen, closing the distance between us. "I know you're angry with him. I am too." She held up a finger to keep me quiet. I crossed my arms and waited.

"I am angry that he hasn't given my soul back. And I know…I know I should be more than angry. I should be…more, just more than I have been. I know you and Ryder talk about me. You and Jean too. I see how you look at me. I might not have my soul, but I'm not dumb. I know I'm losing bits of myself. That it's getting worse. So, we agree on that, okay?"

I nodded, relieved to hear her say those words, and with that relief, even more worried.

She nodded too. "Okay. We agree we need to get my soul back."

"Yes. And we need to find Xtelle. So she can use the scissors."

"Xtelle? You really think letting her use the scissors on my soul is a good idea?"

"It's the best we've got. Only a demon can use the scissors without doing more damage to your soul."

She blinked, then blew out a breath. "Okay. That's. Well, that's not great. Do we agree that Bathin is holding onto my soul for a reason?"

"Yes. Because he's an asshole and he's hiding in Ordinary so his father won't kill him."

She blinked. "What?"

"I didn't tell you that?" I ran back over the last day. Had it only been a day?

"His father. The king demon of the Underworld. He wants into Ordinary. We—Than and I—think he's behind the vortex openings. Well, if Xtelle isn't behind them."

"Bathin's father." She tucked her long hair behind her ears again. "Okay. Crow said something about the King was looking for his son, but he didn't elaborate."

"Crow." I rolled my eyes.

"I know. But something doesn't make sense. If the king of the Underworld wanted into Ordinary, and is using the vortexes to do it, why was the first vortex filled with demon spawn? Why didn't he just march right through? Why was Xtelle there, posing as a unicorn? And why was the second vortex all about drawing people in and turning them into frogs?"

"I know who we can tie up and ask."

"Xtelle?"

"Xtelle."

"All right," she agreed. "Let's go get the dragon pig."


DELANEY AND Ryder's living room looked a little more sparsely decorated than the last time I'd been here.

"Where's that huge recliner?" I asked.

Delaney threw her coat down on the arm of the couch. "Eaten. I'll get dragon pig. You do your thing in the kitchen."

We'd left Jean at my place to keep an eye on Bathin. Ryder was catching a short nap there so he could relieve her in a couple hours. The Slammin' Salmon Serenade started tomorrow morning with a big parade. Jean had to show up early to help Bertie. It was going to be a crazy busy day.

Somehow we were going to take shifts watching Bathin, because he was not to be trusted, even in a trap in the middle of my house. I was beginning to think this non-plan stunk. But if we could find Xtelle tonight, talk to her, make her use the scissors, I was sure everything would work out.

Yeah…the plan stunk.

The dragon pig seemed very excited when Delaney told it there was a demon by the name of Xtelle somewhere in

Ordinary who needed to be found and brought to her. Dragon pig trotted around in a little circle, then sat at her feet, adorable head tipped up, flat piggy nose steaming.

While she explained exactly what she needed the dragon pig to do, I headed to the kitchen to draw a demon trap on the floor.

I heard the distinctive *pop* of disappearing dragon. Then Delaney strolled into the kitchen.

"So are you going to tell me what happened?" She poured herself a cup of coffee, then turned and handed me a mug of tea.

"When?"

"When you and Bathin left."

I sipped tea and shrugged. "We fought, then argued. He tried to tell me he was just misunderstood. He said he's on my side."

"And?"

"And we kissed."

"And?"

I didn't have to tell her. Just because we were sisters didn't mean everything we did had to be shared.

"You finally slept with him." She didn't ask. She told me. Like she already knew.

I had a sudden, horrible thought. "Tell me that was just a good guess and not because the connection from him holding your soul means you can feel…"

She snorted. "It was a good guess. Because now you're doing twice as much to push him away as you were before."

"You mean trying to save Ordinary and all the people inside of it?"

"I mean pushing him away just like you did to your last boyfriend."

"That's not fair."

"But it's not untrue."

Her voice went soft, and she put the coffee down. "You do this when you're scared."

"Do what?"

"Take on responsibility for everything and everyone."

"And you don't?"

She exhaled. "I think I do, though I've been trying to share the burden more. Trying to talk to you and Jean and Ryder when I'm confronted with really big challenges instead of just running off to do something stupid."

"Like giving your soul to a demon?"

"Like ignoring my feelings. Who I'm falling in love with. Those kinds of things."

"I don't know what you're talking about."

But I did.

"Yes, you do."

"He's a demon," I said over my tea.

"Is that enough of an excuse not to listen to your heart? Myra." She hopped up on the counter, her boots swinging gently, and for a moment we were just young girls again, sisters trying to navigate the adult world full of gods and monsters and supernatural powers we didn't understand.

"It's enough to make me cautious, more cautious," I said. "It might be different if he were willing to give your soul back. But no matter how many times I've asked him, no matter how many times I've told him that he's hurting you by keeping your soul, he refuses to do anything to change it.

"And I've heard his excuses. I know the scissors will change the one who uses them. I know that only another demon can use the scissors and not cause your soul more harm.

"So I have very limited room for what my heart wants. And I have very little patience for someone who is willingly doing my sister harm."

"Maybe him keeping my soul is for the better."

"You believe that?"

"Maybe a part of me being that close to the demon will help us figure out how to stop any more vortexes from opening."

"I don't think so."

She shrugged. "One of us has to look on the bright side."

"Naw," I said, "Jean does that enough for the both of us."

She grinned. "Then let me be the reasonable voice. Love doesn't just happen every day, Myra. It's worth following. It's worth fighting for."

*There is nothing more I want than to keep her soul.*

A burst of smoke and flame flashed in the middle of the kitchen. When the smoke lifted, a very irate pink unicorn stood in the center of the room, and a very satisfied dragon pig was curled on Delaney's lap.

"Hello, Xtelle," I said. "I have a deal for you."

# CHAPTER 21

"WHAT DO you think you're doing?" Xtelle demanded. "Deal? What deal?"

The dragon pig growled and wagged its curly tail.

"Nice job. Good dragon." Delaney reached behind her and offered the pig a metal napkin holder that must have come from the thrift shop.

The dragon pig's eyes lit up—and I mean literally glowed orange—and then the napkin holder was gone, eaten whole in one swift gulp.

Delaney scratched behind its perky little pink ears, and puffs of smoke floated up from its nostrils.

"How about you drop the unicorn thing and show us your real form?" I said.

"I have no idea what you're talking about." She took a step and stopped like she'd just run into a glass wall.

"That's a demon trap," I said. "If you were a unicorn, it wouldn't hold you. We know you're Bathin's mother. We know you're a demon."

She held very still. "You believe him? Bathin? The demon who lied and cheated to get into Ordinary? The demon who is hiding behind a Reed soul like a tattered old security blanket so his father won't find him?"

"I don't believe anything any demon tells me," I said. Except in that stone. That stone of truth.

She turned a circle in the confines of the trap. "What about you, Delaney? Aren't you the sister who says who can and can't be in Ordinary?"

"That's part of what I do, sure," she agreed easily. "But I need to know the truth of our supernatural citizens. And you've lied from the beginning."

"I don't know what you want me to do."

"For starters?" Delaney hopped down from the counter and, careful not to break the lines of the trap, walked around the edge of the room to stand shoulder to shoulder next to me. "It would be great if you'd show us your real form."

"This is my real form."

"Your demon form," I said.

"Oh, you would not want to see that."

"Try us," Delaney said.

Xtelle shrugged, and the pink unicorn was gone. In her place stood a creature built of fire and ash, a truly terrifying countenance. Her eyes were pink, but all the rest of her was the blaze of the inferno and blackness of the screaming void.

I blinked. Then a woman stood in the demon's place. She was tall and lean, but wide shouldered, her hair as dark as Bathin's, her eyes flat and black.

"If not a unicorn, I prefer this form." She crossed her arms over her ample chest. She was wearing a warm, soft-looking cashmere sweater and black leggings, her long hair drawn back in a simple braid that fell over one shoulder and was tied off with a pink ribbon. She was the epitome of casual wealth and understated, if a bit hard-edged, beauty.

"That'll do," Delaney said. "We need answers."

"And I need to be free of this tedious trap. So unoriginal." She leaned forward a bit. "That's your invitation to ask me whatever you want to know. So can we just move this along? Someone mentioned a deal."

"The deal is, we want the truth," I said.

"I can tell. You laced the trap with parsnip."

"People underestimate the power of root vegetables," I said.

"Will parsnips make you tell the truth?" Delaney asked.

"Yes." She smiled and it was impossible to trust.

"So this is going to be awesome," Delaney said.

I couldn't help it, I laughed. "We don't have to rely on parsnips alone," I said. "How good is your dragon for sniffing out lies?"

"Good question." Delaney crooked her finger at the little pig who was chewing on the dustpan it had dug out of the cupboard.

"Dragons aren't truth keepers," Xtelle said, a little too quickly.

"No," I said. "But this dragon is hungry. Like, constantly. Usually, we wouldn't allow him to eat another resident in Ordinary, but since you are here under false pretenses, and you haven't signed the demon contract or followed the rules, I think watching you try to lie your way out of a dragon gullet sounds entertaining."

"You wouldn't."

"I would."

She looked at Delaney. "You wouldn't let her."

"Yeah, I don't see why not. Dragon's gotta eat, and I'm all outta napkin holders."

"But you're the reasonable sister."

"Is that what they told you? Huh." Delaney just smiled and continued scratching behind the dragon pig's ears.

"First question," I announced. "Did you open the vortex in the park?"

"That's not exactly how it happened, no."

I glanced at the dragon pig. Its head cocked to one side and an ear flopped over, as if it were considering that statement. It grunted.

"All right, I'm going to take that as true."

The dragon pig grunted again. Delaney nodded.

"Why were you at the vortex when it opened?"

"I've been...interested in Ordinary for some time. When the vortex opened, I was in the right place at the right time. I stepped through."

"You shouldn't be able to do that," Delaney said. "Demons aren't allowed."

Xtelle didn't appear to have anything to say about that.

"Did you open the second vortex?" I asked.

"No."

"You just happened to be there?" I didn't buy that for a second.

"I was following you. I happened to be there because you happened to be there."

"And you knew how to close it?"

"It's a vortex to the Underworld. The only thing that makes it different than any other vortex is it opened in Ordinary." She rolled her eyes at my look. "Yes. I know how to close it because

I have been a demon for all of my existence. I'm very good at what I do, and one vortex is like another. Happy?"

I glanced at the dragon pig. It grunted again.

"Next question," I said.

"Boring," Xtelle muttered.

I ignored her. "Is another vortex going to open in Ordinary?"

She paused, rocked her head to one side. I thought she was going to lie, but then her gaze slid to the dragon pig in Delaney's arms and she frowned. "You don't know, do you?"

I waited.

She glanced at Delaney, then back at me. "One of you must know."

"Know what?" Delaney asked.

"You don't!" She laughed, and there was nothing comforting in it. "Yes. There will be another vortex."

"When? Where?"

She spread her hands. "I am not the one in possession of that knowledge."

"Who is?" I asked.

She just shook her head.

"Go back to before," Delaney said. "What were you surprised about? The thing you thought we knew, but don't?"

She didn't say anything.

"What does it have to do with the vortexes?" I asked, putting two and two together.

"I'm not sure what you mean," she said blithely.

The dragon pig rumbled, a deep dragon growl I could feel in the soles of my feet.

"False," I said. "I think I'll find something else to contain you. Something smaller. Luckily, I have a warehouse full of things that will keep you bottled up for eons."

"You won't do that."

"Why? Because I'm the nice sister?" I scoffed.

"No. Because you love him."

The splash of heat across my face was fifty percent anger and fifty percent embarrassment. Okay, more like eighty-twenty.

"You're talking about Bathin, right?" I asked. "The demon I just locked in a trap so that I could find you and get information out of you for how to *stab* him and throw him out of Ordinary?"

"Is that what this is about? Then I'm not sure why you're talking about vortexes."

"I know you made the scissors that will cut a soul away from his possession."

There was no more smirk, no more smug. Her eyes were bright. Sharp.

"Yes."

"I have them."

"I know."

"Is there a book and a page that must be used with them to release a soul?"

She watched me for a moment. "That is a very specific question."

"I expect a very specific answer."

"No."

I raised an eyebrow.

"No, there is neither a book nor a page needed. Just the scissors. Snip. Snip." She mimicked the motion with her fingers.

"What happens if a human uses them on a demon?"

"It doesn't end well for the human."

So, Bathin had told the truth. Okay, next question.

"Can a demon use the scissors on a demon to free the soul?"

She gave me a look of respect. "Yes."

"Will you use the scissors to remove Delaney's soul from Bathin?"

"It depends on what you would give me for that."

"How about we let you leave Ordinary?"

"I don't want to leave Ordinary."

"Let me put it another way," I said. "The only way you're staying here is if you're locked in a box."

"Or an easily digestible napkin holder," Delaney said.

The dragon pig oinked. Yep. We were telling the truth.

"You wouldn't break the rules of Ordinary to imprison me."

"We're police officers. We imprison people all the time. Natural, supernatural, deities. All of 'em," I said.

She looked off over my shoulder as if she'd heard a sudden sound. Then: "I'll take my chances."

"What—"

Delaney clutched the dragon pig closer to her chest and stumbled backward.

"Delaney?"

She groaned and I dashed over to catch her by the arms as she crumpled to the floor.

"Hey, hey." I tapped her face. "Come on. Delaney. Wake up."

"You might want to strap her down," Xtelle said. "A vortex is going to open. And oh, this one's going to hurt."

I pulled Delaney up against me, my arms around her. The dragon pig hopped up on Delaney's legs and stretched its small body, as if it wanted to cover as much of her as possible.

I fumbled for my phone.

"You could let me out."

"No." I dialed with my thumb. "Ryder, I need you at your house now."

"Is it Delaney?" I could tell by how he was breathing he was already on his feet, running.

"She passed out. I've got her. A vortex is going to open."

"If it hits as hard as last time, she's going to go through convulsions," he said. "Call 911."

"On it."

I disconnected and dialed.

Xtelle just stood there watching me calmly, maybe even enjoying this. "She's not moving."

"She's breathing. Her pulse is steady," I said as the phone rang. How many times had it rung?

"You really should let me out of the trap."

"No."

"I can help you."

The dragon pig growled, and Xtelle held her hands up and chuckled. "Fine. I'm happy to stand here and watch."

The call finally connected. "911," Hatter's warm voice said. "What do you need, Myra?"

"Get an ambulance to Ryder and Delaney's place."

"On the way. What happened?"

I had barely finished going through Delaney's symptoms when the approaching siren was loud enough. I knew they were almost here.

Ryder beat them to it.

"How long?" He came to a skidding halt beside me, already out of his coat and putting it under her head. I could smell the cold salt air and sweat on his skin as if he'd run the whole way.

"Seconds before I called you."

He ran his hands carefully and quickly over her body, checking her pulse, her breathing. "What happened?" He asked once he had ensured she was still breathing, still alive.

His eyes flicked from mine to Xtelle's. "What did you do to her?"

"I had nothing to do with this."

Ryder's hands clenched into fists and his thigh muscles bunch under his jeans. He was a coil, a spring, a bomb ready to go off.

"She passed out," I said. "Xtelle said another vortex is going to open."

"Xtelle?" He wasn't tracking details.

"Right there in the demon trap."

She waved.

"Don't break the line," I said.

The EMTs pushed through the front door with their equipment.

"Back here!" Ryder yelled.

"All right," Mykal, a vampire who was one of our best EMTs, said. "Go ahead and move to one side so we can get a look."

I stood and pulled Ryder up with me. I forced both of us back one step.

"Does she have anything to do with this?" asked the other EMT, Steven, who was a human and well-versed in the secrets of Ordinary's citizens. He tipped his head toward Xtelle while Mykal quickly took Delaney's vitals.

"We don't think so," I said.

"She's a demon, right?" Mykal asked.

"Yes. We have her contained."

"I see that." He nudged the dragon pig. The dragon pig

growled.

"You can come with her to the hospital, okay?" Mykal patted its little head. The dragon pig oinked and hopped up off her legs so they could move her onto the gurney.

"One of you riding with us?" Steven asked. The dragon pig jumped up onto the foot of the stretcher and settled in, eyes glowing. "Other than this guy?"

"I am," Ryder said, just as I said, "He is."

"Where will you be?" Ryder asked me.

"Here. I'll take care of Xtelle. Keep me in the loop with Delaney."

"What about the vortex?"

"We'll handle that when—if," I clarified, "it happens."

The EMTs were already halfway to the door.

He glared at Xtelle, then turned his searching gaze on me. "If you want—"

"Go. She needs you."

He frowned, but gave in and jogged after them.

As soon as the door closed, I turned on Xtelle. "Tell me everything you know about Delaney being tied to the vortexes. Now. Or all those promises of letting you leave Ordinary alive are off the table."

I pulled the fold of very thin cloth out of my front pocket. The flower inside those folds was dried, having been pressed for a century or more in the center of an old poetry book from a long dead, very sad, peasant girl who had also been a demon killer.

I'd found the book months ago, looking for anything that would free Delaney's soul.

"That is a very rare flower," she said. Her voice tightened, each word clipped, as if she were facing down a viper that would strike if she so much as breathed too loudly.

"It is. A very rare flower that can kill you. As long as I use the right words. Words I've memorized. So, once again. Tell me everything you know about the vortexes in Ordinary, and why they're hurting Delaney. And then tell me how to stop them."

She licked her lips, and I saw what might have been the first open and honest expression on her face: fear.

Good.

225

"Very well," she said, softly, eyes riveted on the flower. "The vortexes are triggered by demons. From the Underworld. There is a knowledge, that Bathin, the Lost Prince," and she didn't say that like it was a good title, "can be found in Ordinary. There are many demons who would like to find him."

I ignored the flip of my stomach and the kick of my pulse. More demons hunting for Bathin scared me. I could brush my fear off as being frightened for Ordinary, but that wasn't true.

It wasn't Ordinary I instantly feared for. It was Bathin.

Stupid heart.

"Does he have a price on his head?" I asked.

Xtelle shrugged. "As much as, yes."

"He's been here a year, and we haven't had any vortexes. Why now?"

"It could be many things. You did tell the crossroad demon that he was here."

"I didn't have to tell her, she knew. And he stood right in front of her and threatened her. So it's not like he was hiding out."

Xtelle didn't look impressed.

"Why now?" I lifted the flower which I held by the stem. If I snapped my fingers and incanted the spell, I'd find out if the fear on her face was real.

"You said it yourself. Bathin has been here a year. Inside Ordinary."

I waited. There was something more I wasn't piecing together. "His presence is drawing demons?"

"Yes."

Yes, but that wasn't all. "Him being here for a full year is drawing demons?"

"Yes."

That wasn't all of it either. I tipped my head back and stared at the ceiling for a second. What was I missing?

Then it hit me. "He's had Delaney's soul for a year."

"Yes." This, in a whisper, her gaze locked on mine.

"Now her soul is damaged. She's the bridge to Ordinary. It's made…holes. The damage to her soul is…punching holes into Ordinary. So vortexes can open. So demons can walk through. She's a broken bridge."

She didn't say anything, and I almost snapped my fingers. Almost.

"The longer Bathin holds her soul, the more vortexes will open because Delaney will become more vulnerable," I said.

She didn't agree or disagree, but I knew I was right. I had to be.

"Those scissors," she said casually, "do you still have them?"

"You know I do."

She nodded. "Let me give you some advice. No, don't look so surprised. I am a very old being. I have seen this world rise and fall and rise and fall again. Cultures, civilizations, peoples. While you might be more than human, you are still very human, Myra."

"And?"

She clasped her hands behind her back. The gold cuffs were gone, which meant they'd never really held her in the first place. More lies. She gave me a soft smile.

For a second, she appeared to be a wise and patient woman who understood my pain. Who understood my life had just taken a corner I'd been barreling toward and trying to escape in equal measures.

"You are going to have to make the choice so many have before you. The choice that changes history. Are you willing to hurt someone you love to save someone you love?"

I didn't know what to say. I knew the answer, what it had to be, what it should be, no matter how hard my heart was beating. "No one hurts my sister."

She nodded, her eyes still soft, almost kind. "Are you willing to pay the price for her? To sacrifice for her?"

Was I willing to use the scissors to possibly hurt her soul while saving her? Even if it meant I would also hurt myself? I think I'd always known the answer to that. But I'd promised Delaney I wouldn't use them.

No Lone Rangering.

"I need a demon," I said.

"To use the scissors?"

I nodded.

She tipped her head. "To spare yourself and your sister, yes.

227

You need a demon. Are you going to ask me to do it?"

"Not now, no."

"No?"

"You're his mother. I'd never make you harm your own child."

That surprised her. She blinked once, then just stared at me, expressionless. I'd never seen her so still. "You wouldn't, would you? Not even for your sister's soul." She sounded incredulous.

"It's not like I could trust you to follow through, anyway," I said.

"You'd have to trust me."

"And I don't," I said.

"And you don't," she agreed.

We stood there in silence for a full minute. Then she spoke. "So what will you do, Myra Reed?"

"I'm going to save my sister."

She exhaled, and it was a mix of acceptance and maybe regret. "I have never doubted you would."

# CHAPTER 22

THE PROBLEM was three fold.

One: How to keep Xtelle locked down, but close, in case I needed to use her. She was my Plan B, and killing or banishing her would mean I couldn't use her if I needed her.

Two: How to summon a demon to use the scissors so I didn't have to use my Plan B.

Three: How to stop caring if Bathin lived or died.

The easiest thing would be summoning a demon. I had the books. I had the incantations. I had the ingredients. All I had to do was go to the library, summon a minor demon I could bribe and control, then take it to stab Bathin, who was trapped in my living room.

But I couldn't leave Xtelle in Ryder and Delaney's kitchen.

I called Jean.

"Just checked on Delaney," she said. "Doctors say it's a coma." Her voice shook a little, but then it steadied. "I left Shoe at your place to keep an eye on Bathin, and I'm going to head out on patrol. See if I can spot the vortex when it opens."

"I don't think you need to do that. I'm going to the root of this problem and am digging it up."

"And where is that?"

"In the middle of my living room."

"Bathin. The scissors." She didn't ask. She knew. "You promised Delaney you wouldn't use them."

"I'm not going to. Do you get any doom twinges when I say that?"

She shifted, and murmured something to someone, maybe Ryder, then I heard a door open and close.

"No," she said a little quieter. She must have found a private spot to talk to me. "When you say you're going to confront Bathin, it's not doom twinges. But…something is going to happen. And I think it has to do with the vortexes."

"Can you tell where the next one is going to open?"

"I'm pretty good at being drawn to disasters, so maybe? But I think…"

"Tell me, Jean."

She inhaled, exhaled, a steadying of her nerves. "I keep feeling like something is going to go wrong at the parade tomorrow morning."

"You mean this morning? In a few hours?"

"Gods, it's late. Yeah. I mean this morning."

"You know something probably will go wrong at the parade, none of these events ever go to plan. The town's stuffed with tourists, and a lot more will be driving in for the day."

"I know."

"But you feel like something is going to go *really* wrong?"

"I can't pin it down," she said, frustrated. "Part of me thinks the parade is going to be fine, like, no actual threats. But part of me feels like…like it hasn't been decided yet. Maybe something might go terribly wrong. Maybe it won't."

"So no immediate disaster," I said.

"I don't think so?"

We had precautions in place if any of the run-of-the-mill disasters turned up. This wasn't the first time we'd held this event. We knew how to handle the influx of people and the chaos it brought.

None of the gods in town carried their powers any longer, so unless it came down to life and death, I wasn't going to ask them to use their powers because then they'd have to leave town for a year.

We had plenty of vampires, werewolves, giants, muses, sirens, and humans who would be more than happy to lend us a helping hand if things went sideways.

"Let's keep the event going as is. If you feel any warnings about it at all, we'll take care of it as it happens. For now, I want you to get some sleep if you can—"

She made a little sound of protest.

"—or stay there with Delaney until you need to go help Bertie. Ryder's still with her, right?"

"I'd like to see anyone or anything make him move."

"Good," I said. "I'll lock up Xtelle, then deal with Bathin. After that, I'll be by to see Delaney."

"You're going to do all that by yourself?"

"Not by myself."

"Before the parade starts in a few hours?"

I grinned. It wasn't a challenge, but I was naturally competitive. "Time me."


STEP ONE: Call Death. "I need you to do something for me," I said.

"Are these not the hours in which most humans require sleep?" He didn't sound like I'd woken him up, which I probably hadn't. He did sound faintly amused.

"I'm pulling an all-nighter, all-morninger."

"How, then, am I involved in this endeavor?"

"I need you to help me with a demon."

There was the slightest pause. "Shall I inquire as to which demon?"

"Do you care?"

"Not in the least."

I grinned despite myself and finished pouring the strongest cup of coffee I could tolerate into one of Delaney's giant mugs.

I found Spud, Ryder's dog, who had gotten left out in Ryder's truck for a half-hour in all the chaos. He'd taken up a post at my feet, following me like a hairy shadow as I moved around the kitchen and the very annoyed Xtelle.

He trotted beside me as I stepped into the living room where I could finish my plans in relative privacy.

"Meet me at Ryder and Delaney's house as soon as you can."


THAN ARRIVED promptly. He had on a dark plum T-shirt with ORDINARILY GIFTED written across the chest. He'd paired that with a smart silver-tipped walking cane and a gray fedora.

"I need a demon."

He glanced toward the kitchen then back at me. "Perhaps you should explore the kitchen area?"

"Not her. She's…I need her trapped and out of the way. I can't use her."

"And the demon known as Bathin?"

I was pacing now, which he watched for a minute before settling himself into the straight-backed chair I knew Ryder must have picked because Delaney was all about comfort and lounging when it came to furniture.

"He's the worst."

"I see."

"He won't let go of her soul, so now I have to trap Xtelle, then raise another demon, then bargain with it or blackmail it and make it use the scissors to cut Delaney's soul away from Bathin. Why are you scowling?"

"What do you suggest would be the proper response? You are planning to trap the kitchen demon, then raise a minor demon to do surgery upon your sister's soul. Shall I frown thoughtfully? Grimace?"

I blew out a hard breath and threw my hands up.

Spud was giving Than all his attention, but hadn't left my side. Than snapped his fingers softly, and Spud hustled over to sit at his feet.

"What else can I do?" I asked. "He has her soul, and it has holes in it now. That means there're holes in Ordinary, so now the vortexes to Hell…"

"The Underworld," he corrected gently.

"…which might as well *be* Hell, for all the demons and demon spawn coming through those vortexes—which also try to suck people into them, by the way."

"And turn them into frogs." He nodded. "I was there." Was he amused? Was there something funny about this?

I planted my fists on my hips and glared at him. "You have a better idea?"

"Oh, I wouldn't assume so. But I am curious as to what you think will happen when you summon a minor creature of darkness."

Spud was absolutely fascinated by him, tail wagging slowly, stopping, then wagging again as he listened to every word that fell out of Than's mouth.

"For one thing," I said. "I'd expect it to be less judgmental than the current creature of darkness in front of me."

His eyes glittered. He didn't smile, but he did narrow his eyes in something like glee.

"You will order the minor demon to wield the scissors against Bathin. The Prince."

"Yes. I'm going use a demon to cut Delaney's soul away from Bathin."

"Who is a creature you harbor feelings for."

"I harbor feelings for a lot of creatures," I said evenly.

Than *tsked*. I ignored him.

"Listen. My sister is in a coma. I'm done waiting for a better solution. This isn't ideal, but I don't care. Waiting for perfect isn't going to work anymore."

He was silent, dark eyes intense as if there were nothing else in the universe as interesting as me. It was disconcerting and welcome. If I was going to pull this off, I'd need him engaged and on my side.

"Delaney Reed is in a coma?" It was said softly, but there was enough power behind it, I fought not to step back, turn, run.

"Just happened. Ryder and Jean are with her. She's stable."

"But unconscious."

I nodded, not trusting that I could get the words out. My throat was closing up. It was fear, it was instinct. Survival instinct.

He blinked, once, and the terror pushing at the back of my throat eased.

"I see."

"So I'm going to get her soul back," I said. "Now. Before the next vortex opens."

He stroked his palm over Spud's head, once. Spud leaned his whole body into Than's knee.

Than tipped his head downward, the slightest of movements. It made him look like a predator catching the scent of its prey.

"You will not entrust Delaney's soul to some low-level demon, Myra Reed." The words were soft, but they were deep and sonorous, and a shiver feathered down my spine.

"I'll do anything I have to and you can't stop me. Not here in this town where I'm the law."

Than lifted one eyebrow. Right. He was also sort of the law. But he was a god on vacation who had to follow the rules.

"Let me clarify," he said. "It would be foolish to summon an unknown demon to do your bidding when you have other options."

"What options? I can't use the scissors, I can't trust Xtelle to use the scissors. Who else do I have?"

"Me."

Spud wagged his tail while I tried to get my brain around that. "You can use the scissors?"

"Perhaps. Could I see them?"

"Sure. Yes. Hold on." I had taken them from my closet and brought them with me when I left my house. There was no way I was leaving Bathin at my house with the scissors if I wasn't there to keep him away from them.

I jogged out to the car and after gathering up the wooden box, I stuffed an extra bag with a clay pot, some random boxes and bags, until the *this, this, this* tug in my chest settled down and went silent.

Spud was in doggy heaven as Than's long fingers rhythmically scratched and smoothed along his ears.

I opened the box and pulled the bag out of it. Than leaned forward just an inch and his hand rested on the arm of the chair.

I tugged the cuff of my sleeve down over my palm and fingers, then tipped the scissors out onto my sleeve-covered hand.

They didn't fall out of the bag so much as slide onto my hand like poured silk. Gold and deadly, the metal glinted as if it were fashioned around a fiery core that still burned.

"May I?" Than extended his hand. I nodded.

He plucked the scissors off my palm using only a finger and thumb. If it were possible, his eyes went even darker.

I waited. I wasn't sure what he would decide. Maybe that he wouldn't do it, maybe that he couldn't. Maybe that the scissors were a fake, a fraud, and I would have to go back to square one to save Delaney's soul.

"Can you?" I asked. "Can you use the scissors to save Delaney's soul?"

His gaze finally shifted to meet mine. "There will be consequences."

"For Delaney?"

"That is yet to be seen."

"To her soul?"

"No."

"But you can do it? You can cut her soul away from Bathin?"

He stood, tall that man, tall that god, and held his other hand out for the spell bag.

"Myra Reed," he said as he dripped the scissors into the velvet, "I am the god of Death. Even on vacation, there is very little that I cannot do better than a creature of the Underworld."

"Okay." This was it. This was our chance to get Delaney's soul back.

A part of me was crowing with the victory almost in our hands. Another part of me knew this would mean saying good-bye to Bathin.

Forever.

There was no place in Ordinary for demons. No matter what my heart wanted.

I exhaled through my mouth. Calming. Preparing. "Don't interfere, okay? I want to lock Xtelle away on my terms."

He tipped his head in a nod.

"Good," I said to Than, to myself, to that little part of me shattering into a million pieces. "Let's do this."


STEP TWO: Contain the demon in the kitchen.

I marched into the kitchen, Than silent behind me, Spud on his heels.

Xtelle's gaze flicked to me, then stopped on Death.

Than just strolled past her, ignoring her as if she weren't worth his attention. "Is there tea?" he asked.

"Upper right in that last cupboard," I said.

"Thank you. I believe I am going to enjoy this." That was when he looked at Xtelle. It was amazing to see her eyes widen, her nostrils flare, and every muscle in her body go hard.

Afraid. She was afraid of him. Good.

But he wasn't the one she should be worried about.

I was.

I opened my bag and began taking out the items.

A heart-shaped ruby on a pure gold chain, a bumble bee's wings in a tiny glass box, a few drops of red ink, the very rare, very dangerous dried flower from my pocket, and lastly, a chipped terra cotta teapot from the local thrift shop.

As soon as I placed the teapot on the countertop, Xtelle broke her silence.

"I will not be crammed into that grimy little thing."

I turned the teapot in my hands so she could get a good look at it. It was just your basic orange-brown, with a perfect surface for the glyphs and symbols I had written across it in thick, black Sharpie a month ago.

"I am not some common demon spawn you can defeat with a turnip."

"Yeah, I got that. You're a demon who forced her way into Ordinary, passing herself off as a unicorn—a creature of purity—who then lied about who she was, what she was, and why she was here."

"You never asked me why I came here."

That was true. But it was also a diversion. Words were a demon's sharpest weapon. Best way to disarm her? Ignore her.

Than put the kettle on and selected two mugs and two tea strainers.

There was something soothing about his long, pale fingers delicately tamping tea leaves into place as if he had all the time in the world. As if we all did. It was calming. Ritualistic.

The last thing I pulled out of my bag was a piece of chalk that I kept on the windowsill during the full moon.

"Xtelle, you are no longer welcome in Ordinary." I used the chalk to draw a triangle on the counter, placed the teapot in the center of it, then opened the pot. Next, I placed the ruby heart and bee's wings into it, then tipped out three drops of red ink and added the flower.

So far so good.

"It won't work," she said. But her arms were crossed and her lips were wet. Her gaze kept skipping between Than and the teapot, and there was a heavy dose of fear in her eyes. Anxiety.

It would work. It was just going to take some time.

"Tea?" Than offered. He placed the mug of tea on the counter a good distance away from the teapot, but still in my reach.

"Thank you." I picked up the mug, inhaled the woodsy green scent, blew across the liquid and, for a moment, just centered myself. I sipped the tea, savoring.

Then I began the spell.

It wasn't something that could be done quickly. It wasn't one or two lines of Latin, like they did in the movies, and call it good. This had to be strong enough to hold her and keep her until I found a way to send her back to the Underworld and make sure she would stay there.

I got the spell wrong three times.

After the last attempt, which had ended with a small puff of smoke rising from the chalk triangle that surrounded the teapot, I groaned and slumped down onto a kitchen stool.

"What am I doing wrong?" I growled at the ceiling.

Xtelle snorted. "For one thing, you didn't summon me. That's an uphill battle right there."

"You could just agree to get in the vessel," I said.

"It's not even fine china. Really, Myra. What are you thinking? Do I look like a woman who is going to willingly occupy a cramped kitchen vessel? "

She sounded so much like the unicorn version of herself that I fought back a smile. "No, you do not."

"You bet your ass, no I do not." She gave me a smile and a wink, and it reminded me so much of Bathin, it made my chest hurt.

"I need tea."

Than handed me another cup, perfectly brewed.

"You're good at this," I told him.

"Perhaps I shall pursue a barista career if the life of a law officer and kite enthusiast longer suits," he intoned.

Imagining him working a drive-thru coffee kiosk was hilarious. I could just imagine what kind of apron he'd pick out.

"There is an easier way," Xtelle said.

"Yeah, no."

"You could let me go."

DEVON MONK

"No."

"You could tell me to leave Ordinary."

"Would that even work?"

She shrugged. "The Reed family has always had ultimate say over who can and can't be here. It seems like it would work."

"If Delaney told you to leave and forbade you from coming back, *that* would work. She's the bridge. I'm not that sister."

"You aren't a demon hunter, Myra. You aren't a witch. You aren't even a magic worker. You're out of your depth here."

"And?" Listing off my faults wasn't going to stop me from doing what I knew had to be done.

"Despite what your eyes tell you," she swiped her hands down her curves, "I'm a lot older than I look."

I rolled my eyes. "Wow. I am so surprised you aren't what you seem to be."

"I am tired of playing this game." She threw her arms wide. "You can't hold me. You could never hold me." She snapped her fingers.

I hit her in a full tackle just as the spell around her evaporated into steam and ashes that flew in a whirlwind of black-winged moths.

"No! You can't—"

Her words cut short as I wrestled her to the ground.

If I didn't know she wasn't human, that would have been when I found out.

She was heavier than she looked, much heavier than she should be, built of rocks instead of bones. Her skin was so hot, I expected to hear my hand sizzle as I yanked both her wrists behind her back.

"I refuse to allow" she sputtered.

I flicked the cuffs from the back of my belt opening them around her wrists—which were no longer there. Neither was Xtelle.

I was flat on the floor, no Xtelle to be found.

I scrambled up, scanned the kitchen. Still no demon. Just Death, sipping tea.

"Is she gone?"

He placed his cup carefully on the countertop. "Define 'gone'."

238

"Not in this house."

"That is true."

"You couldn't stop her?"

He raised one eyebrow. "I didn't interfere. As you asked."

Right. Right. I'd wanted to lock her up by myself. Wanted the satisfaction of being the one who closed the lid on her smug face so I could look Bathin in the eyes and tell him I'd defeated his mother.

That was dumb.

I rolled my shoulders and suddenly felt too tired for any of this. I hadn't slept for over twenty-four hours and obviously wasn't thinking things through. I should have just snapped my fingers and said the spell for the dried flower.

I should have killed her when I had the chance.

The parade would be starting in a couple hours and I'd need to be on crowd control.

Delaney was in a coma.

Any minute a new vortex might open.

Xtelle was gone.

But Bathin was still trapped at my house.

Than was right that summoning a minor demon was a bad idea. I was too tired to do it now anyway.

"This isn't how I wanted any of this to go," I said, rubbing at the headache creeping up the back of my skull. "But hey, I have a pair of evil scissors, a vacationing god of death, and a kiss-my-ass attitude."

I picked up my bag and swept my spell supplies back into it, erasing the chalk triangle on the counter. "I say it's time I do what I should have done over a year ago."


STEP THREE: Break up with my evil not-boyfriend.

Than was silent on the drive, taking in the calmness of the town, the gray and damp. In moments like this, I thought I could see Ordinary as it had once been, dirt roads and foot paths between the sea and shore, little cozy cabins and bungalows built from the wood harvested from the forested hills. Peaceful, beautiful, hidden.

Moments like this, I knew what the gods saw in the place, the breathing of life in the rivers and streams, the churning ocean breaking itself against the rocky cliffs, the high, open sky calling eyes and dreams up and up.

It was like living inside of a beautiful pearly marble.

Or a beautiful stone. My mind flashed back to Bathin, to his hands, his eyes, his body. We had been there, in that beautiful stone, and he had promised we could live that way, together, safe and tucked away from everyone and everything.

But I couldn't leave this town. This life. My family. No matter how much my stupid heart wanted to.

"Myra Reed," Than said quietly. "Why are you crying?"

"It's the salt in the air." I quickly brushed away the tears I hadn't felt falling and parked the car.

I killed the engine and turned to him. "I need you to use the scissors on him. And I need you to be gentle. For Delaney. I need you to be gentle and careful for Delaney. I don't want her hurt. I don't want her to die. If anyone's going to an early grave, it has to be Bathin."

He waited to see if I would say anything else, then nodded solemnly. "I will be gentle in my *undertaking*."

I blinked. Blinked again. "Was that a joke? Did you just make a joke?"

"Did you enjoy it?" He looked terribly pleased with himself.

"I…uh…it was good."

"Excellent. Shall we?"

We strolled into my house, and I smelled cinnamon. I wondered if Jean had found the leftover cinnamon buns I'd tucked in the freezer.

I dreaded every step into the living room. I half hoped Bathin wouldn't be there. If he had found a way to break the trap like his mother, then I wouldn't have to do this, see this, watch as Death shoved a weapon of demonic origin into his heart.

But then I pictured Delaney unconscious, strapped to the gurney, and loaded into the ambulance. All the soft, worried thoughts about the demon disappeared.

He had cheated his way into this town, he had used my sister, and he had done it with no regret or remorse. He couldn't be trusted. Not really. If I forgot that, if I let him make me forget that, there would be no one to blame but myself.

Bathin raised his head as I entered the room.

"Myra."

He stood right where I'd seen him last, at the fireplace, his back leaning against it, arms crossed over his wide chest.

"Than," he added.

Bathin was power controlled, a fire burning in silence, steady as the heart of a distant star. When his gaze took me in, slowly, from head to foot, and then back, lingering on my face, my lips, my eyes, I could not look away.

Didn't want to be away from him.

Didn't want to be alone.

*Here. This. This.*

"Hey, boss." Hatter strolled in from the kitchen.

I looked away from the questions in Bathin's eyes and heard him sigh.

I'd forgotten we'd left someone here to keep an eye on the prisoner. "How long have you been here?"

"Just relieved Shoe." He held up the cinnamon bun from the plate in his hand. "Hope you don't mind. Jean said to raid the freezer."

"I don't mind. I'm here now, so you can go."

"You sure?" he asked through a mouthful. He nodded at Than, who walked across the room to stand directly in front of Bathin. "Parade's coming up, and I'm pretty sure you haven't gotten any sleep. I could stay a little longer. Say an hour?"

"No," I said, "I'm good. I got this."

"All right. Good. Good. Just leave you and Death alone with the demon, that right?"

"That is correct," Than said, never once looking away from Bathin.

To Bathin's credit, he didn't back down, didn't move, didn't stir under Death's gaze. He just stood there, every line of his body radiating a mix of confidence and ease. Like he could escape at any moment if he wanted to. Like this was a picnic. A cakewalk. A breeze.

241

"Really," I said to Hatter. "We have it covered, thanks."

He nodded, then ambled out of the room, shutting the door behind him.

I stepped right up next to Than.

"You're done here," I told the demon.

"Is that so?" Bathin still stared at Than, and yeah, I didn't blame him, because: death.

"I'm done, Bathin. With this. With…us."

And it was that, the words that came out too softly, his name catching before it fell out of my mouth, that made him look at me.

And *see* me.

Understanding hit him, hard enough he opened his mouth and his pupils dilated. This was it. The end of the road. The end of him in Ordinary. The end of whatever we'd almost had, before we'd even had a chance to really begin.

That tug in my chest went hot. Burning.

"You can't keep her soul." I wanted the words to come out with the anger I'd been building over the last year or more, but all I had was sorrow and regret. "She's hurting, *you're* hurting her. And those holes in her soul…that's how the vortexes are opening. You've broken her. You've broken Ordinary. And I can't let you do that anymore."

"Myra," he whispered. But he didn't move, didn't plead. He just waited, as if he'd accepted his fate, had seen it coming from miles away.

Maybe he had. I'd been after him to let go of her soul ever since we met. If he had compromised, if he had met me halfway—hell, I would have been happy if he'd met me a quarter of the way—this could have been different.

Maybe it could have been a happy ending.

Maybe.

"You had to be such an ass," I said.

He blinked in surprise before a small smile softened his expression. "I'm a fan of putting my best self forward."

"You know I have to do this," I whispered as if it were just he and I. As if our sky and air was a safe, turquoise stone.

He shifted slightly, tilting toward me. But his arms remained crossed, his hands clenched. He knew what was coming. From the anger I could feel burning off him beneath that calm exterior, he was fighting not to lash out.

I wouldn't blame him if he did. He was a demon, and a demon's nature is to keep what they claim.

"There is always another choice," he said.

"Not anymore."

I stepped back, not trusting myself this near him. It would be too easy to reach out, touch him, hold him, or shake him until sense finally rattled into place in that head of his. "You didn't give me any choice. Because you never trusted me. You never really wanted to be a part of Ordinary."

He opened his mouth, but I plowed right on over the top of him. "If you wanted to be here, you would follow the rules. Sign a contract. Let her soul free. You don't. If you wanted me, you would follow my rules. You don't."

The last came out rough, like my voice had picked up gravel, dragged on the bottom of the river.

"So, no. You didn't give me a choice. But all your choices added up to this. This choice, this now."

He was silent, eyes steady on me, only the muscle in his jaw ticking.

"Than?" I asked. "Do you have the scissors?"

Than produced the velvet bag stitched with spell-soaked threads and withdrew the scissors, holding them between his finger and thumb.

Bathin didn't even look at him. "You don't know everything," he said to me. "But know this. I have never lied to you. Never about what I feel for you. And this…this is more than it seems."

Yeah, he wasn't going to long-suffering-hero his way out of this. I felt no pity. I didn't dare risk pity.

Than slipped the scissors, gold and bright, over his boney knuckles, opened them once, exposing the flash of ruby and obsidian.

Bathin jerked and took a step back. "Wait!" He held up his hands as if that would be enough to stop Than from doing the deed. "Wait."

But Death did not wait. He crossed the spell's barrier, the scissors dripping with light and heat.

Bathin's gaze cut to me. "It's opening."

Than pressed his palm down on Bathin's shoulder and, demon or not, Bathin shivered under that hold.

"The vortex," Bathin said. "You need to stop it. Myra. Now. Now."

And wasn't my chest tugging, hard, hot, echoing Bathin's words: *Now, now, now.*

Than paused. I paused too. This could be a trick.

Oh, who was I kidding? Of course it was a trick.

But didn't I feel the need to go? Didn't I feel the heat in my chest that tugged and twisted, painful because in a moment I would need to be *not here* and instead be *there* wherever *there* might be? Be *there* now, now, *now.*

I had seconds before I'd be grabbing my bag and running out the door, no matter what was happening with Bathin.

I let out a groan. "Are you kidding me? Did you trigger it? Did you make this happen?"

"No." Bathin scowled. "I don't care if you don't believe me, that's the truth. It was coming. Ever since Delaney fell. Now it's here."

The ground trembled, shook. "Earthquake?" I asked.

"Vortex," Bathin said. "You'll need Xtelle. She'll know how to close it. But for the love of Hell, keep Delaney away from it. The closer she is, the more pain she'll be in."

"If I take her soul back now? Will that close the vortex?"

Bathin shook his head, hard. "You do not want a soul floating free, not even for a second when a vortex is open to the Underworld. We already know the vortex lures humans to it. A human soul, even Delaney's soul, would be gone in an instant."

"But Than can—" I said.

"No," Than interrupted. "He is correct in this, Myra Reed."

"Which part? The vortex thing or the soul thing?"

"Both."

The little tremble got a lot bigger. It sounded like a huge, monstrous train speeding past my house, close enough the windows rattled and the dishes in the cupboards clattered.

I met Bathin's eyes. He was waiting. Letting me make the call. But he was worried. If I didn't know him better, I'd say he was very close to panicking.

244

"Can you close it?" I asked.

He frowned. "Xtelle will do it faster than I can, cleaner. And she'll do it. She doesn't want more demons pouring into town any more than I do. I'm not the only one running and hiding. I promise I'll be here when you're done. We can pick this up right where we left off."

I scuffed my boot over the spell line, breaking it with a bubble-wrap *pop*.

"Xtelle is gone. You're the only demon I have left."

# CHAPTER 23

THAN RETURNED the scissors to their bag, which he handed to me with a sniff.

"Can you close it?" I asked Bathin again. I was already at the front door. I had to go, drive, be *there now, now. Now.*

"Yes," he said.

Something in my chest warmed and solidified. I liked how certain he was. I liked the illusion that he was on my side, that he had my back. A brief, insane image of him beside me, always right where he needed to be just like I was always right where I needed to be, flashed through my mind before I shoved it away.

*This.*

I didn't have time for fairytales. I had a demon gate to close.

Thunder rolled, and the lights in the house sputtered and died.

"Do you know where it is?" I was out the door and in the garage. Sirens wailed in the distance. The power outage was widespread. All the houses on the block were dark, and the streetlights were out too.

The garage door wouldn't rise with the electric motor. I started toward the override cord, but Bathin jogged past me. "I got it. Get in the car."

I corrected course and slid into the driver's seat, starting the car almost before I got the door closed.

Death was in the passenger seat, looking wholly unconcerned.

"You know this is part of your job now," I said.

"And that is?"

"Protecting Ordinary."

"Yes, Myra Reed," he said patiently. "I am aware. Shall I turn on the lights and siren?" He studied the instrument panel in the dash, looking like a starving kid who had just been given keys to the bakery.

Sometimes I forgot how much all the details of living—the little ordinary things—were still new and exciting to him.

"Not until we hit the main road. We don't want to scare the neighbors to dea…"

"Death?" he suggested when my voice faded. "No, we wouldn't want that, would we?"

The humor was so dry, it could have soaked up the Nile in a nanosecond.

Bathin opened the back door and dropped down into place behind Than.

"Go," he said. "It's south."

The radio filled with Jean, Hatter, Shoe, and Kelby checking in. So far we had a car accident—the lights were out and someone had slammed into oncoming traffic—but no fatalities.

I gunned it out of the garage and onto the street, headed toward the main road. It was still early enough there shouldn't be too much traffic, but with so many people in town, and the parade almost ready to go, I decided to use a side street instead of the main drag to swing south.

"Tell Jean I'm headed south," I said to Than. He operated the radio as if he'd been doing it for years. But still, his other fingers poised over the siren and light buttons, at the ready.

The moment I turned onto the side street instead of onto the main road, he made a little moue of disappointment and folded his hands on his lap again.

"Don't pout," I said. "There's plenty of time for flash and bang. River?" I threw over my shoulder to Bathin.

"I think so." He had planted one hand on the door to counter-balance the turns I was whipping through. The other hand gripped at his chest like he was in pain.

Come to think of it, his color was off.

"Are you having a heart attack?" I asked, too loud in the confines of the car. That was the last thing I needed to deal with. If a demon *died* and still possessed my sister's soul, what happened to her then?

"I don't have a heart, remember?" He tried to deliver that with his usual smirk, but did not stick the landing. "When we get there, to the vortex, I need you to let me handle it. Handle whatever we find."

"No."

He shook his head and stared out the window.

And that was strange, him not pushing back, not fighting me. All my internal alarms went off. "How bad is it?"

"Bring your gun. And any other weapon you have."

"I brought Death," I said.

"Who is on vacation," Than reminded me, "and would prefer to remain so."

Which meant he didn't want to pick up his powers and do the big, Death things that would make him have to leave Ordinary for a year.

If push came to shove, I hoped he'd change his mind.

"This is it," Bathin said.

"What are we facing?" I asked.

"Something worse than we've ever seen."

"Details, Bathin."

"A demon. A very powerful demon."

"You know which demon is opening the vortex?"

"Yes." He sounded like it pained him to admit that.

"Who is it?"

"My uncle."

I didn't even have a second to process that because a crowd of pirates was blocking the road.

Yes, pirates.

The road was filled with human beings of every size dressed as pirates. A few wore other costumes—I spotted a couple princesses, an astronaut, and that hockey mascot who looked like a psychotic Muppet—but mostly it was pirates.

"What is this?" Bathin asked.

"I don't know."

"It is the Slammin' Salmon Pparade," Than said. "Costumes encouraged. Nautical theme."

And, yeah, as soon as he said it, I remembered hearing Jean say something about contributing to the event to make it more fun, and gods knew she loved a Halloween party.

I swore. There would be no getting through this crowd with the cruiser.

The street wasn't even one full lane, and it was uneven, with no sidewalks or shoulders. Houses rose on one side stacked up on a rise, and hotels closely packed the other side between us and the beach. This was one of the older roads that had originally been used by horse or bicycle. There was barely room for one car when the street was clear.

The street ended at the beach, where the short river from the lake wandered out to meet the sea.

"Shall I turn on the sirens and lights now?" Than asked politely.

"No, we'll go on foot." I muscled the car onto the edge of someone's yard, blocking the mailbox and half the driveway.

I scanned the crowd for Bertie, but couldn't spot her in the throng. What I did see was a weird green light coming from the beach where the river met the ocean.

"Vortex?" I asked. We were all jogging now, pressing through the crowd. I shouted in my Police Voice for people to step aside, but the crowd was mesmerized by the light.

They thought it was part of the show.

Or maybe it was actually hypnotizing them.

Than stepped in front of me and extended his hand, long fingers relaxed, palm forward.

"To one side," he instructed. "This is your police."

And just like that, every person took a unified, jerky step to one side, leaving a perfect, narrow passageway.

"Creepy," I said. "But good."

I turned the jog into a run, Bathin and Than keeping pace.

The crowd was still talking, not worried, not afraid. Not even aware that they had all done half a hokey-pokey for the god of Death.

They were excited about the day, the event, the light in the sky.

I swung my bag across my body and it bumped against my hip as I ran. I wanted it at the ready as soon as we reached the vortex. Not that I knew what to do or how to close it.

"Myra?" Jean's voice came through my shoulder radio loud and clear.

"Copy. Where are you?"

"South side of the river, just hit the parking lot. Headed to the beach."

"I'm north side, almost to the river. It's a vortex."

"I know."

"I have Bathin with me. And Than."

"Good."

There were no more questions because there wasn't any time left. I burst out of the crowd and into the soft sand. The river was one of the smallest in the world, running from the freshwater lake just four hundred yards away until it spilled into the ocean.

Between the river and the ocean, about three hundred yards away, stood the vortex.

"Holy shit." That was the last thing I spared a breath to say. I needed all the oxygen I could get to fuel my headlong sprint down to the mammoth gate.

The vortex was a huge, gothic doorway carved out of twisted iron and polished silver, simultaneously sucking in all light, and reflecting it back in painful, eye-stabbing shafts of light.

It was vertical, a doorway, a gate, tall enough I could drive a semi-truck through it if I wanted, wide enough, two city buses could rumble through side by side.

It was positioned so I should be able to see the ocean behind it, but instead all I saw was swirling darkness sparking with gold and shattered-green lightning.

Bathin's long legs outpaced mine, and just like the frog situation, he was going to reach the gate before me.

Dammit.

I put on all the speed I had, soft sand slowing me, kicking out from under my boots, rocks and bits of broken driftwood littering the way, hard sand making a crust that only slowed me more before it became harder and wetter so I could run faster, surer.

I dug in and got it going. Jean plowed across the knee-deep water of the river to my left, splashing out on my side of the river in quick order. She had something clutched in her left hand, not a gun, but something that looked like a long knife.

I didn't know why all the people just stood back there near the river and weren't coming toward the gate. The other two gates, both much smaller, had drawn people in like bees to buttercups.

This one was bigger, more powerful. It radiated energy like a storm ready to break.

It wasn't fear that held the crowd back, though it should have been. It was more like thrall.

They weren't rushing the vortex because they were waiting.

Waiting for whatever was on the other side to show itself.

"Oh, shit!" Jean shouted.

The swirling mass of lightning and fire inside the vortex drew together, funneling into something solid and tall. Much taller than Bathin who had come to a stop just feet away from the vortex, every line of his body poised to fight, to strike, to attack.

"Myra, stop!" Jean lunged for me, caught my arm, and had enough momentum to knock me sideways and slow my pace. She collided into my side, spinning to get her shoulder in front of mine.

"What are you—" I said, but I saw her eyes. Wide. Panicked.

"Doom twinge! Doom twinge! This is bad. Big bad. We need to back the fuck up. Now."

She didn't wait for my response. She tightened her grip and muscled me back several steps before my brain kicked into gear and I dug in my heels. Literally.

"Talk," I instructed.

"We need to get back, more back, way back." She was pushing again, and even my dug in heels weren't stopping her.

"Out of the blast zone?"

"Dead zone." She was breathing too hard. She was in shape, we all were. Being a police officer in this town meant we kept in shape. It wasn't the run that had knocked her lungs out of whack, it was fear.

I stopped fighting her, and we ran.

Than was strolling our way, having decided not to run toward the danger on the edge of the waves.

I stopped in front of him, and Jean didn't push me to move. "How are we going to shut that down from here?"

Than glanced at the vortex. "I don't believe that is possible."

The gold and green in the vortex had become a man shape, ten feet tall, condensing, thickening, sharpening into a body as if that gold and darkness were being pressed into an empty body mold.

"What is it?" I asked.

"A demon?" Jean said.

"A demon knight," Than clarified. "Bathin's uncle."

My chest was tight, but it wasn't fear. It was need. Everything in me was screaming that I needed to *leave here* and be *there*, now, now, *now*.

Right *there* at the gate, right *there* beside Bathin, right *there* facing that demon knight.

"Stay here," I told Jean.

"No."

"Yes. I have to be there with him. I think I know how to shut it down."

"Think?" She was angry. She was scared. "You expect me to let you run up there with a think-you-have-a-solution?"

"Will I die?" I asked.

That was unfair, asking that of Jean. She shook her head. "That's a shitty question."

Yeah, it was. So I decided to ask someone else.

"Will I die?" I asked Than.

He raised his eyebrows as if surprised by being consulted.

"Everyone dies, Myra Reed."

I rolled my eyes so hard, I thought I pulled a muscle. "Out there. In front of that. Stopping that." I pointed.

Than shrugged. "That is yet to be seen."

If that wasn't the least helpful thing he'd said among all the least helpful things he'd ever said, I didn't know what was.

"Keep the crowd back." I dug in my bag, in the little terra cotta teapot, fingers brushing a very rare dried flower. A flower that could kill a demon.

I took a step. Jean grabbed my elbow, stopping me.

"Don't—"

I pulled out the velvet bag with the scissors. "I have a plan."

"You can't use those."

"That's what they all say, but I don't think they're right." I held the bag up toward her. "You get any doom twinges off these?"

"All I get off those is evil stank."

"But no bad feelings."

"Yes. Bad feelings. Bad evil stank feelings. "

"How bad? Honestly, Jean. How bad?"

She scowled. "Not…not as bad as whatever is in that damn vortex."

"Good enough."

"No," she said.

I put my hand over hers. "Trust me. I really do have a plan." She was going to say no again. I could see it all over her.

But then the vortex exploded.

# CHAPTER 24

IT WAS the lack of sound that worried me. The world was fine one second, I could hear the ocean hushing and churning. I could hear the mutterings and other conversations of the crowd behind me. I could hear traffic on the highway, the lap of river water, the call of seagulls and crows.

Then there was a blast—strident and painful like ground zero in a head-on collision—horns blaring, voices screaming, metal grinding.

And silence.

Jean still held my arm. Hadn't budged an inch. As a matter of fact, she wasn't moving at all. My heart clenched, fear so sharp I gasped. Then the details of the world around me pressed through that fear, parting it like fingers in Venetian blinds.

Jean wasn't moving because no one was moving. The entire world had frozen.

For a heartbeat, I wondered if all of Ordinary had been transported into a bubble, into a stone where time, and all living things, stopped.

Correction. All living things that belonged in Ordinary.

Things, other things—including the *thing* coming through the vortex—were moving into Ordinary and moving fast.

I pulled my arm away from Jean. She was still frozen in place. I glanced at Than, who nodded once, his eyebrow rising.

I supposed I should have expected a god—even a vacationing god—wouldn't be affected by whatever was happening. Good. That meant I had back up.

"With me," I said. My mouth felt numb, slow. No sound came out of it.

Than nodded once again. Maybe he could understand me. Maybe he was just planning on following my lead like we were in the middle of an on-the-job training simulation and it didn't matter if I were actually speaking words.

I ran toward the vortex. Or at least I tried to. Instead, the tug in my chest flared hot at my first step, and a mind-blurring rush of *there* dropped me in front of the vortex, right next to Bathin.

Than was not with me. I glanced back, and he was walking this way, but with every step, the world seemed to pull away backward, as if he were trying to walk up a down escalator. He was making progress, but it was slow. Very, very slow.

Bathin was braced in a stance that made it look like he was holding up an invisible wall with his palms. One leg locked behind him, one leg bent, every muscle in his heavy, strong body straining, sweat slicking his thick, black hair, running down his face.

"Run," he said. I heard it, in my head, clearly, and with my ears as a buzzy, distant thing. "He…he'll kill you, Myra. He'll kill everyone."

I wasn't going to run. But I did look into that vortex.

And immediately wished I hadn't.

The man—no, creature—in that swirling mass of blackness was now easily twelve feet tall. Made of whips of gold lighting and squirming flesh, he was in human form, but warped, stretched, and burning. Screaming mouths opened and closed, bubbling up to the surface of his flesh before drowning in flames. Hands reached out of his chest, his arms, fingers eaten down to bare bone scrabbling against the fleshy prison.

It would have been horrifying, I supposed, to someone who hadn't grown up in Ordinary and teethed on bedtime stories read out of Necronomicons.

I'd seen all sorts of horrors in my life, and some of them even made pretty good neighbors.

What was on the outside did not always match what was on the inside. Ordinary had taught me that young. But this thing, this demon creature, was either showing me his true form, or was just trying to scare me.

"I will chew your bones and burn your soul on a spit," the uncle demon intoned.

Yawn.

"This is god-chosen land," I said, planting myself right beside Bathin, one hand on my hip, the other in my bag. If this plan was going to work, Bathin couldn't see it coming. Couldn't guess I would have brought the scissors here. Now. "You will not enter."

I was close enough to stab the scissors in Bathin's back, close enough to release Delaney's soul.

Than wouldn't let Delaney's soul be taken by another demon, I was betting on that. Banking on it. He might act cool and removed, but he had a thing for my sister.

He wasn't going to let her soul get sucked into the vortex. He wouldn't allow her soul to be destroyed.

As soon as I released her soul, I'd shove Bathin through that vortex. A snap of my fingers while crumbling one very rare flower, would finish the job.

With any luck, it would blow up the vortex. And everything in it.

"You are not welcome here, demon." I drew the scissors out of my bag, and held them in my palm, a knife ready for stabbing. "Leave. Now."

"Myra," Bathin shouted. "Run! I can't hold him back for long."

The demon tipped his horned head toward me. Two yellow eyes stared back, caught like hooks in my brain.

"Your weapon is useless," he rumbled.

That was when Bathin noticed what was in my hands. His eyes widened and he straightened, drawing his palms away from whatever invisible force he had been fighting.

I braced for something to explode now that he had stepped back, but if anything, the vortex appeared less violent.

"You dare—" the demon inside the vortex said.

Bathin held his hand over his shoulder. Dismissive. Nonchalant. Except I knew him. He was tight under all that swagger. A wire stretched and thin. A trigger squeezed tight.

"Hold," he commanded.

Uncle demon crossed his massive arms over his chest, the screaming mouths nothing more than black-hearted flames now. "This Reed sister? Really? She is…"

"Fire," Bathin agreed. "Myra, what are you doing with those scissors?"

"I've been thinking," I said, my mouth dry, my heart pounding, but my words steady. "An awful lot of people have told me I can't use them to free Delaney's soul. All of those people have been demons."

"Who else would know the truth of it?" He was watching my hand, or really, he was watching the scissors.

"No one. So I think there is only one way to find out if the scissors have been the solution to our problem all along."

I held up the scissors.

The demon in the vortex made a sound that was so close to laughter, it almost broke my concentration. "Yes! Kill him!" the demon bellowed.

But it was Bathin's voice that caught me. His one, gasped, "No," so quiet I almost didn't hear it.

He moved. Fast. His hands, massive, warm, strong, closing over mine. "Don't do this, Myra. Don't do this. The price—"

"Mine to pay. Say good-bye to my sister's soul, Bathin." I shifted my weight, not forward like he might expect, but backward, breaking his hold on my hands and the scissors.

I pivoted, faster than humanly possible, as quick as a thought, demon laughter pummeling the air around me.

"Love..." Bathin reached for me again, his hands on mine raised in an arc meant to bury the scissors square in his chest. His fingers tightened, inhumanly strong as he twisted the scissors out of my grip.

"No!" I yelled, battling for the weapon. Knowing it was the only chance to save Delaney. To close the vortex. To keep Ordinary safe.

"...you," Bathin breathed. He plunged the scissors into his chest.

We were bound in some way. His mother had made sure of that. Right then. Right—

—*there*—

—I could feel it, the pain that lashed through him, the fire that spread out from the deep, brutal puncture, burning like a poison through his body.

Like a flame held against a spider's web.

He was standing there, both hands around the scissors buried to the hilt in his chest.

Then he flew into a thousand thousand burning embers, specks of dust gone star-hot, a volcanic eruption that flashed into ashy-white snow and was carried away on the salted wind.

Something in me broke too. A soft, thump deep in my chest.

The world roared back. Colors, sound, movement clashed and crashed, rose in a huge wave bent on destruction, too big, too strong, to survive. I yelled, one hand over my eyes, the other over my heart.

Bathin was gone.

I couldn't breathe.

I couldn't breathe.

The churning gears of time and reality collided, cogs smashing to rubble.

I was lost.

"Myra," Jean's voice, clear and strong. "You're okay. You're okay. What did you do? Myra, what did you do?"

I didn't know. I couldn't think. I couldn't breathe.

A hand fell on my shoulder, heavy and so very cold. "Myra Reed."

Than's voice, his touch, settled the world, organized reality, and my place in it.

"Hey, there you are," Jean smiled.

I was sitting on the sand. She was crouched in front of me, the ocean behind her.

I glanced around wildly.

No vortex. No demons. There was just a beach filled with pirates, Jean in front of me, and Than standing at our side, staring pensively off to the north. His hand was closed, and tucked in his pocket. I'd never seen him stand like that before.

"The vortex?" I asked.

"Whoa, cowboy," Jean pressed harder on my shoulder to stop me from getting up. Probably a good idea. I was a little dizzy from just trying. "You are going to sit here until we have the paramedics check you out." She glanced up. "Look at that, they're almost here."

I did look, and saw Mykal and Steven trotting over with a stretcher and a medical case.

"What happened?" I asked.

"I have business to attend," Than said. He turned abruptly and strode away down the sand toward the north, toward the hospital.

I watched him go. Even though there was a crowd of happy pirates who didn't appear to think anything was amiss, he sort of blended right into the bunch of them and was gone.

"What part do you remember?" Jean asked.

"The vortex, the demon...Bathin. Holy shit. He stabbed himself."

Jean shook her head slightly. "No, I'm pretty sure you did that."

"Did you see it? Were you close enough to see whose hand was on the scissors?"

"No. You disappeared so fast, I couldn't track anything."

"Fast?"

"You were next to me, then popped up by Bathin. Before I could even yell, there was a flash of fire, and he was gone and you were here. Kneeling in the sand. "

"The vortex?"

"It disappeared with Bathin. I'm pretty sure no one even remembers it."

She tipped her chin toward the crowd. Families laughed and talked, hands wrapped around coffee, children bundled against the cool morning winds as they milled about waiting for the parade to start.

Everything was normal. Ordinary.

Except Bathin was gone.

He had used the scissors—his own hand, a demon hand— to free Delaney's soul.

—*Love you*—

I felt my eyes fill with tears, was too tired to fight them.

"Mymy?" Jean said. "Are you okay?"

I dashed at my damp face and used the leverage of her shoulder to try my feet again.

"We usually tell our concussion patients to stay sitting while we examine them," Mykal said as he and Steven finally reached us.

"I'm fine."

"Yeah, considering you were ground zero in the blast zone of a vortex to Hell exploding, you're just going to have to let us make that decision." Mykal gave me a stern look and Steven caught my elbow and helped me sit.

"You saw that?"

"Nope," Steven said. "But he saw something."

Mykal gave me a funny look. "I'm a vampire, so yes. I saw the supernatural portal to Hell disappear."

"Vortex," I said. "Underworld, not Hell."

"Whatever you say, Officer. Now, let's get a look at those eyes."

I knew I wasn't getting out of this, so I sat back down and let them do their thing.

I watched in a daze as the Salmon Queen—who looked a lot like Kelby in a costume—came down the river in her flowing dress and hip waders throwing gummi salmon and clam chowder coupons to her adoring pirate crowd.

I realized music was playing, but it skipped forward raggedly, like a scratched record, a flickering movie, as if I were blacking out for small stretches of time, only to tune back in again.

Pirates followed the Salmon Queen giant, singing, skipping, swaying up to the main road. There, if everything went as planned, she would mount the huge salmon-shaped float and take up the reins. The fish would wave its tail as it rolled at the head of the procession, its mouth flapping to sing songs where the lyrics had been changed to rhyme with salmon.

I should be happy, even if I wasn't quite sure I was steady enough to walk.

Ordinary was safe. The vortex was closed. No one who wasn't a supernatural or a Reed had any memory of seeing it.

But all I could see was Bathin's face, his eyes.

—*Love you*—

Yeah, well, if he'd really loved me, he wouldn't have possessed my sister's soul for a year. He wouldn't have worn it down so thin that it had allowed demons to open vortexes to Ordinary.

He would have...

*... Not taken the scissors away from me. Used them on himself to save me...*

...been honest with me.

I shivered, though I couldn't feel the wind. Steven wrapped a blanket over my shoulders, and after a few more questions, I was told I could go home.

"I'll drive you," Jean said, helping me to my feet, blanket and all.

I let her lead me. By the time we got to her truck, I decided I was probably in shock.

"Stupid," I said as she started the engine.

"What is?"

"All of it." I pushed the blanket off my lap and readjusted the seatbelt. "We should check on Delaney."

"We should get you home."

"We need to see if she's awake. If her soul is back. Oh, gods! What if her soul went in the vortex?"

"Her soul didn't go in the vortex."

"How do you know?"

"Than. And the hospital already called."

"And?"

"She's awake. Ryder's there with her."

"Tell me we're driving to the hospital."

She flashed me a grin, and something inside me untied a little, like I could breathe. "Of course we are. I want first row seats when Delaney chews you out for taking on a Hell vortex single handed."

"You were there."

"No. I was getting us out of there. You ran back in."

"Bathin was..." My throat closed up a little, my heart threatening tears again.

"Yeah," Jean said gently. "He was. Do you know what happened to him?"

I shook my head. "He had the scissors."

"We looked for them. They weren't on the beach."

"Are you sure?" Sand had a way of swallowing up all sorts of things that never surfaced again.

"Yeah, those scissors are gone."

"Okay." I wasn't sure how I felt about that.

Not excited, since they were a very rare and specific weapon. I was sorry to lose them from a purely historical perspective.

But on the other hand, I was glad I didn't have them anymore, that I didn't have to make the decision of whether or not I should use them anymore.

"What about the parade?" I asked.

"Hatter and Shoe have it covered. Bertie pulled together some citizens who are trained for security and peace-keeping. So, they're available."

"Who did she get on such short notice?"

Jean gave me a funny look. "She started it weeks ago."

"Okay." So maybe I'd been a little distracted with my own problems. Maybe I'd been a little single-minded. "Who did she train?"

"The knitters and crocheters."

I snorted a laugh and rubbed my eyes. The members of the K.I.N.Ks and C.O.C.K.s had been rivals for years. We got called out to break up their insult matches and arguments weekly. If anyone could make them work together, it would be Bertie.

"And it just so happened that you got out of helping Bertie. Again," I said.

"I don't know what you're getting at." She batted her eyes at me, wide and innocent.

Liar.

"I could have driven myself to see Delaney."

She chewed on the corner of her lip. "I know. But you just single-handedly took down a vortex and you were going to use those scissors on Bathin, and might have actually used them—"

"—I didn't use them. He didn't let me."

"Still. That was intense, Myra. I want to check on Delaney. I want to keep an eye on you. And let's be honest. Bertie could handle the parade by herself with both wings tied behind her back. She just likes bossing us around. I'll volunteer for the next thing to make it up to her."

"I'll remind you of that."

"I know."

# CHAPTER 25

DELANEY WAS laughing. I paused, just outside her hospital room, stunned. I hadn't heard her laugh, really laugh like that for...well, since her soul had been taken by a demon.

Ryder's voice carried through the wood of the door, but I couldn't make out the words. I could make out the tone, though. He sounded happy.

"You don't have to knock." Jean straight-armed the door, shoving it open, and sauntered past me into the room. "Hey!" she said. "You look better."

I followed her in, bracing for...I didn't know what. A part of me worried I'd pushed too hard, because that was something I did a lot.

A part of me worried I'd botched the entire soul thing. That letting Bathin take the scissors and use them on himself had done even more damage to her.

"Myra, are you okay?" Delaney sat on the bed in comfy leggings and one of Ryder's old sweatshirts. Her hair was pulled back in an easy pony tail, and her skin was flushed like she'd just gotten out of a shower.

Ryder sat in the bed with her, leaning back against the headboard, arm thrown across the bed like she'd just been lying there, her head on his arm before we came in.

"Me?" I said with a smile. "I wasn't the one in a coma."

She frowned and shook her head. "Still really weird to hear that. I hate that I've lost so much time. Just. Ugh." She rubbed at her arm that had a small cotton square taped down, but no IV lines.

Ryder's hand stroked her back, soothing circles. His gaze locked on me. "What happened?" His voice was easy and low, but it carried a little bit of the power from the god who had claimed him as a follower. I was immune to said power, but I found it interesting that he was projecting it.

He'd been through a lot in the last twenty-four hours. I didn't blame him for still being a little on edge.

"Bathin's gone," I said. "So is Xtelle. The vortex is closed. Yes, there was another vortex. Down on the beach at the river, practically in the middle of the parade."

"Today's the parade, isn't it?" Delaney said.

"Yes. You're not getting out of bed," I said. "You don't need to. Bertie has it covered."

"C.O.C.K.s and K.I.N.K.s for the win!" Jean declared. She waved me toward the single chair and even though I was trying to prove to them that I was fine, I decided sitting down sounded okay too.

Delaney rolled her eyes at Jean. "I figured you'd find a way to get out of helping Bertie."

"Me?" Jean gave her a cheeky grin. "I'll make it up on the next crazy thing Bertie has planned. That's in what, a week?"

"Two," Delaney said. "Yoga and Yodel-in."

Jean winced. "Yay."

"All of it," Delaney leveled her boss glare my way. "Tell me everything."

I sighed, rubbed at my forehead for a second and wished I'd thought about making Jean stop for tea.

Yeah, I was wishing I'd done a lot of things differently.

"My?" Delaney asked. The concern just dripped off that word.

"It's good. It's fine. Okay. We're going to start with Xtelle trapped in your kitchen and how Than and I didn't shove her into the teapot like I'd planned."

"Sure," Delaney said, settling back into Ryder as he made himself a comfortable leaning structure. "Let's start with the demon in the teapot."

"Not in the teapot," I said.

"Right. Go."

So I told her. Everything that had happened. Everything I remembered. I left out the last words Bathin said. I should have just told her. I was used to relating every last detail of an event. Police work relied on accurate recall of details.

But that was too personal. It wasn't something I could share with anyone yet. Might not be something I'd ever share.

"Okay." Delaney tucked invisible hair behind her ears, a familiar, self-soothing habit. "So the parade is fine?" She glanced at Jean.

Jean lifted her phone. "Hatter and Shoe say everything's smooth as salmon pâté. They both send their congrats on you being awake, but note that you did it at the moment when it would pull both me and Myra away, and leave them at Bertie's mercy."

"I can feel the love," Delaney said. Ryder snorted. "Parade's good, vortexes are good. Both demons are gone. Right? Both?"

"I think so?" I said. "You have a better feel for that than me. I mean, there's probably something back in the library that would tell me how I can sweep the town to make sure they're both gone. Or you could just send your dragon pig to find out."

Delaney was watching me very closely. Too closely. Had I said something wrong?

"I don't think we should just assume they're gone," I added. "Demons don't play by the rules. They say things and do things to make you think, to make you feel, to make you do what they want."

"Myra," she said softly.

"Enough of that," I interrupted with false cheer. "What *I* want to know is if you have your soul back."

Ryder chuckled. "Oh, she has it back."

Delaney slapped him gently on the leg. "Yes. I do have it back. Than was here. He helped make sure it settled back correctly."

"He can do that without using his power?" Jean asked.

Delaney nodded. "Yeah. He was just observing."

"He made her open her mouth and say 'Ah' and used a tongue depressor to stare down her throat," Ryder said. "Then he used that little light cone thing to look in her ears."

"So he could see her soul?" I asked.

"No," Delaney scowled. "He said he's just always wanted to do that."

Jean barked out a laugh, and I couldn't help but chuckle too. That was a ridiculous enough image, I could push the snarl of emotions I had no hope of untangling away. "He said you're all right?"

"He didn't have to," Delaney said. "I can feel it. Not like it's a physical thing, just…colors are more colorful, and smiling feels more normal, and…it's hard to explain. But I feel right. I feel good. I feel my soul. And now that I know what it's like to give it away…" Her voice faded, and she sort of stared into the middle distance.

Ryder rubbed his hand on her arm, comfort, connection, an anchor to this now.

"Well," she said, shaking off whatever had taken her attention. "I don't want anyone to ever make a deal like that again."

"No one but you is dumb enough to do that," Jean said.

Delaney just shook her head.

"What about Bathin?" Ryder asked.

My skin tightened at the sound of his name. "What about him?"

"Think we should send the dragon pig after him? Find out if he's in Ordinary? Xtelle too?"

"Yes," Delaney said. "As soon as they release me, we can get the dragon pig from Crow."

"Are you sure you should go home so soon?" I asked.

"I wasn't out that long, and really, we know it wasn't a medical thing that caused the coma."

"Finally!" Jean said. "We can call this one a win. I thought we'd never find a way to get your soul back. Nice job, My," she added. "Let me see if I can speed up your check out." She stepped out of the room.

"I'm fine," I told Delaney before she could say anything. "I really am." I didn't try smiling because she wouldn't believe it. "I'm still processing everything, though. This was a long fight, and having it over so quickly has me a little off balance."

"Why don't you stay with us tonight?" she offered. "I'm going to stay in and make sure Ryder sleeps." He grunted. "You and I could watch some Netflix."

"I'm good," I said again. "I should get out there on the street, keep an eye on things." I pushed up onto my feet.

"No, Myra, don't." Delaney got out of bed and walked over to me. Her eyes, stormier blue than mine, searched for something in my expression. I just raised one eyebrow.

"You giving me the day off, boss?"

"Yeah," she said. "I am. And I don't think you should be alone."

I reached out and gave her a hug. "I'm good," I said again. "I really am. I just need some alone time."

She hugged me back, and I could tell from the tension in her body that she was trying to intuit the truth of my words.

"Just. Give me a day or so, okay?"

She drew back, her hands still on my arms, and searched my face again. "Okay," she agreed.

"Look who I found!" Jean walked into the room, the dragon pig curled up happily in her arms, enjoying the scratching behind the ears it was getting.

"What was it eating?" Ryder asked.

"Nothing. Because who's a cute little piggy dragon? You's a cute little piggy dragon," Jean cooed.

The dragon pig soaked up the praise like a little pink sponge.

"Okay, buddy," Delaney said, scooping the beast out of Jean's arms. "We need you to find any demon who is inside Ordinary's boundaries. Specifically, Bathin and Xtelle. If they're inside Ordinary, I want you to bring them here. Got it?"

The piggy wagged his curly little tail and squeaked, a puff of smoke drifting from his nostrils.

He disappeared with a *pop* and a whoosh of wind, as if massive wings had suddenly beat upward.

"Well, that was—" Jean said.

And just like that, the dragon pig was back, sitting in front of Delaney and staring up at her adoringly.

"No demons inside Ordinary?" she asked.

The dragon pig oinked.

"Nice job." She looked around the room, spotted the kidney-shaped barf bucket that all hospitals seemed to include with every stay, and offered it to the dragon pig as a treat.

The dragon pig opened its sweet little mouth and…yeah, I don't know exactly how, but it swallowed the bucket down in one go.

It sneezed, which would have been adorable, but two little spouts of flame shot out its nose.

"You okay there?" Delaney bent and the dragon pig jumped up into her arms, wriggling around until its ears were in position for her to scratch. It grumbled, a deep, contented growl that almost sounded like a possessive purr.

"No demons," I said.

"Yeah, if they were here, this little beast would have found them."

My shoulders relaxed but the tangle of emotions I was ignoring rolled around inside me like tumbleweed made of barbed wire. "You're headed home with Ryder. And Jean?"

"Present," she said as she tapped something on her phone screen.

"You're back on parade duty."

She glanced up, and slowly nodded. "Yeah. That makes sense. All of you are going home, right? If I drive by just to make sure, you're all going to be there?"

"Yep." Ryder dropped his feet to the floor and stood, stretching and yawning. "I can be on call, if you need me."

"So can I," I added, "but not Delaney."

Delaney rolled her eyes. "Yes, I'll take a full twenty-four hours off. But I'll be at work tomorrow."

We'd need her. The parade was just the start of a full weekend of clam-karaoke and salmon feasts.

"All right," Jean motioned toward the door. "I'll drop you off at your house."

"Just take me to the cruiser," I said. "It's down near the river."

I DID not drive home. Instead, I stopped off at the store and bought a box of tissues, extra soft with Aloe, vitamin E and lotion. Then I made my way slowly through the tourist-crowded roads to the library.

The afternoon had been forecasted to be sunny, and for once, the weather guessers got it right. Blue sky arced from the edge of the ocean's horizon to the ragged tops of the trees and hills to the east. The air smelled of salt and that honey-sweet pine scent lifting from the warmed forest floor.

Birds sang. Ocean rolled, wind blew, people went about their happy lives.

I couldn't wait to get away from it all.

I stepped into the library, and Harold was right there, the only spirit in the room.

"I've set out the tea," he said kindly.

I shut the door behind me, walked forward, and kept walking until I reached him. I wrapped my arms around him, pressed my face against his tenuously solid form, and cried.

I didn't know how long I stood there, how long ghostly hands gently patted my back, ghostly voice gently crooned and hushed and hummed. But finally, I drew myself away, standing fully on my own and wiped my sleeves over my eyes.

"I'm sorry."

"We'll have none of that. Apologies." He tutted, then put his arm behind my back, and guided me up and up to the little tea room.

I went quietly, still trying to get my breathing under control as I sniffed. New tears were falling, but I couldn't even feel them anymore.

"There now," he said. "Comfortable?"

I nodded, then burrowed into the comfy couch, pulling the quilt my grandmother had made up over me, adjusting pillows so I could turn my face into the back of the couch.

I wanted the world to go away, just for a minute. Just for an hour.

Light footsteps climbed the stairs. The soft clink of china chimed. Then there was a *thunk* and the shuffle of a tea tray being settled on the oversized ottoman.

"Myra, dearest. I've brought you tea," Harold said.

"I don't want tea." My words were muffled and stuttered between my sniffing and choppy breathing.

"Now, now. You'll feel better."

He was probably right. I needed to blow my nose anyway. So I sat up, drawing the quilt with me.

"Tissue?" Harold offered the extra large, extra soft box I'd brought with me. He was putting a lot of energy into being solid, but I knew he, of all the tome spirits, was the most experienced at it. The library supplied the magic, he supplied the intent.

He wiggled the tissue box making the plume of paper wave like a pink feather in a fancy hat.

I plucked out three tissues, blew, plucked out some more, wiped my face, more tissues, wiped my eyes, and finally settled back.

"Thanks." I pulled a few more tissues, and settled the box in my lap. "I don't know why I'm crying." I mopped at the new tears tracking over my cheeks.

"I do." He handed me the tea. My favorite cup, a delicate soft green with honeysuckle blooms painted across it. I took a sip. Oolong. My favorite.

Harold lifted his own cup—he preferred a strong English Breakfast—and blew across the top.

We sat there, each enjoying tea and silence. It was how we always started these visits, allowing the quiet and tea to soothe and settle. I needed it more than ever today.

"Shall I tell you now?" he asked.

"Tell me what?"

"Why you are crying."

I took another sip of tea. "Okay. Hit me. Why am I crying?"

"Your heart is broken."

He said it calmly, matter-of-fact. Like this was something one commonly diagnosed when one was a very old spirit of a very old book.

I pulled my feet up so I sat cross-legged. "I just forced my not-boyfriend-demon-enemy to kill himself with a pair of scissors. So. That happened."

"Are you sure?"

"That he stabbed himself? Yes."

"Are you sure he was not your boyfriend?"

I sniffed and stared at the tea. "I wish he weren't."

"Why would you wish that, my dear?"

"Would be nice to skip the heartbreak." I rubbed at my eyes. "Why did I do this? I know better. It never works out for me. Love isn't made for me. And a demon? What was I even thinking? I didn't want to fall in love. I tried really hard not to."

I sat there feeling miserable while Harold sipped tea. Finally, he set his cup down and clasped his hands in his lap.

Harold concentrated for a moment, then leaned forward with Dad's last journal in his hand. Nice trick, plucking it off of a random shelf in the library.

"I know you don't want to read it yet, and I trust your instincts. But there is one entry I've marked with a ribbon, I feel might help you."

I took the book, the weight of it familiar in my hands. All of Dad's journals were about the same size and had the same bindings. But more than the physicality of the book, it somehow still carried some of Dad's energy. I knew, as soon as I saw his handwriting, that I would be reading every word in his voice.

"I don't think I'm ready."

"Well, then. Let me find some cookies for this tea. And maybe a new read? We have some delightful additions I'd like you to meet."

"Just the tea, I think. Thank you, Harold."

He patted my hand, then settled back in the chair and positioned his cup in his left hand, like he always did.

I finished my tea, the silence of the room, the soft sigh and shuffle of the books all around me the only conversation I needed.

I didn't mean to fall asleep, but I had been awake for over twenty-four hours and it had been a hell of a day.

Harold moved Dad's journal out of my hands. I would have helped, but my eyes were too heavy to open, my limbs impossible to move. He pressed his hand gently on my shoulder before the soft light clicked off, and all the spirits of words and thoughts and long-forgotten histories sighed and swayed into dreams.

# CHAPTER 26

"A BROKEN-down teapot. Really?" Xtelle pushed the offending vessel off to one side and sat down at the table across from me.

We were at the Blue Owl, the only twenty-four hour restaurant in town. I'd stopped by for lunch and was waiting on my soup and salad. Instead I got a demon.

"You can't be here," I said.

"True." She smiled, and her eyes twinkled. "Can you guess how I am?"

I couldn't smell the tea in my cup, nor the pies and bread the Blue Owl always baked fresh every day. The sound of people around us was unnaturally muted and the music playing over the system was wind chimes instead of country and rock.

"I'm dreaming."

"Bravo." She sat back. "You do catch on quickly, don't you?"

"Apparently not. I thought you were a unicorn for days."

She laughed, a full-body thing, with her head tipped back. It was a wholly delighted sound, and I found I couldn't be angry with her.

This was a dream after all. There wasn't anything she could do to me here, and there wasn't anything I could do to her. It was the most neutral ground between a human and a demon.

"That was so much fun! The look on Bathin's face when he first saw me." She chuckled again and wiped fingertips under her eyes. "I would have paid a much higher price for that alone."

"What do you want, Xtelle?"

"I'm not here to make things worse." The laughter was gone and she was as sincere as I'd ever seen her.

"Of course not," I said.

One eyebrow rose. Apparently my sarcasm had not been missed.

"You asked me why I made the scissors. I didn't tell you the whole story."

"What? A demon lying? This is so shocking."

"Don't be tedious, Myra. You are the Reed best at finding information and using it. I am bringing you information. Since you are also the Reed who is always in the right place at the right time, then may I suggest you trust your own abilities and believe that being here, in this dream, listening to me give you information that no other creature knows, is in your best interest?"

"Excuse me for not trusting a demon."

"You're excused." She held up one finger. "You understand that when a demon possesses a soul, it is vital we keep that soul."

"So you can torture and feed off of it."

"Don't be ugly, darling. But yes. So we can draw from it that which we desire. Not every soul is the same. Really, no two souls are the same. And some souls will never catch a demon's interest. Others do."

"Why?"

She shrugged gracefully. "Which souls we want is a very personal thing for demons. A vulnerable thing. I would no sooner share those details with you than you would explain to me exactly how to best manipulate your sisters. But what I came here to talk to you about is my son."

"Is he—" I stopped before I asked what I really wanted to know. "Is he behind you being here? Doing this? Talking to me?"

"No. Bathin has no say in what I do or don't do. You should know that."

I did know that. So I nodded.

"Is he here?" Demons could take any shape, even in dreams.

She drew her fingers back through her long, luxurious dark hair. "No. I haven't spoken to him since he used the scissors to free your sister's soul."

"You knew about that?"

"I made the scissors. I know if they have been used. Do you know why I made them?"

"So his enemies could cut a soul away from his control."

"Well, yes, that's what I told him. But that isn't the truth."

I picked up my dream tea and took a dream drink. It was the perfect strength and heat and I savored it.

I sighed. "This is where you tell me you were lying all along and now you're going to tell me the real truth, honest this time, and I should trust you, right?"

"You don't have to trust me. I'd be surprised if you did. You aren't like that, Myra. Your heart is not made so softly. But your mind is logical and clear. Which is why I know you know I'm telling you the truth.

"I made those scissors as a test. A proof. Bathin knew they would do great damage to the one who used them. But the truth is they would not have worked for anyone but him."

"Because he's a demon," I said.

"No. Listen to me. Only his own hand could use those scissors to remove the soul he had possessed. *Only* his hand."

"But you said…" At her look, I nodded. "Lies. Got it."

"I made the scissors to know one thing: If my son would ever value someone, something over his own wants. Whether he could be unselfish."

There in the dream diner, the wind chimes turned to music, something soft and far away.

"That's not the truth," I whispered.

She reached across the table and placed her hand carefully on my wrist. It was warm, solid, real.

"It is the truth. I give you my word on that. A demon never gives up a soul without receiving something greater in return. Bathin could have given up Delaney's soul at any time he wished. Except there was nothing valuable enough to exchange it with. He wanted to stay in Ordinary. He needed to stay in Ordinary. His life depended on it.

"But when the choice was allowing you to use the scissors, knowing it would harm you, change you, hurt you, he took them away. He used them instead.

"He freed Delaney's soul by his own hand and bore the consequences, not knowing how brutal they might be."

"He didn't do it to protect me…"

"Yes. He did." She waited a moment, then went on. "One might even assume he did it because he loves you. He willingly sacrificed his own needs, comfort, desires, and life to save yours."

"He can't love me. He's a demon."

"It is not hard for a demon to love. You might not understand that, but we love easily. It is, however, difficult for us to learn how to care for someone, how to give to someone before we satisfy our own wants."

She drew her hand away. "Sharing and compromise and honesty are difficult concepts for a demon, but not impossible. Still, the only things that can teach us those concepts are sacrifice and community and love."

"Family," I said.

"That too. It is, I think, why he was so curious about Ordinary for so long. Why he and your father met and spoke for so many years. Bathin was looking for family. When he finally found a way to enter Ordinary, when he found you...well.

"He was totally out of his depth, so he acted like an asshole." She straightened the cuff of her sleek blouse, which did not need straightening. "Typical demon. Assholery is the number one go-to."

"You don't say," I said.

That earned me an eyebrow quirk. "So what are you going to do about this?"

"About what?"

"I just told you my son loves you."

"I heard you." Even though this was a dream, I believed her.

That didn't mean I knew what to do about it.

"Now you know," she said. "I thought that was important. Even now."

She sipped out of her cup. I wasn't sure what was in there, but it squirmed and squeaked.

I knew she was baiting me, but curiosity won out. "Even now?"

"I made those scissors as more than one kind of test. To see if he could learn sacrifice, selflessness, love." She blew on her squeaky liquid, sipped again.

"And?"

"And if he could endure the price it demanded."

"What price? Where is he? Is he hurt? Angry? Do we need to brace for an attack?"

She chuckled. "Any chance to ignore your own feelings, you take it, don't you? Not a single second admitting you're worried for him. Instead you jump to the conclusion that you must protect Ordinary from him. Maybe I should have designed a pair of scissors to determine your worth."

"Harsh."

"It's not Ordinary you're trying to protect. It's your heart."

Here, in this dream, I didn't have the energy to argue that truth.

"I am very curious as to which truth you will follow—love or fear." She lifted her hand to get the waitress's attention. "Humans are so easily misled by both." She snapped her fingers.

I woke with a jerk. The old wooden beams of the library tea room came into focus at the same moment the scent of warm cookies reached me.

I was still on the couch, covered with the quilt. A little stiff, which meant I'd slept for hours. I wondered why Jean or Delaney hadn't called, but remembered Delaney and I were taking the night and day off, and Jean wouldn't bother us unless there was an emergency.

Harold still sat in the chair, reading a large leather-bound book. I had the feeling it was way past morning. My stomach rumbled.

"I warmed the cookies," Harold said. "And brewed fresh tea."

I sat, stretched, and rubbed my eyes. "Tea sounds great."

He put the cup in my reach, the saucer holding two little chocolate-dipped raspberry sugar cookies. I'd picked them up from Hogan's bakery the other day and stashed them here, partly to keep them out of Shoe's reach, and partly because I liked a little cookie fortitude when I did research.

Harold knew how to use a mean microwave.

I ate the cookies and finished the tea, thinking over my dream which was not a dream.

"How much would you believe a demon who says she's telling the truth?"

"That would depend on the demon, the subject, and the situation. Why do you ask?"

I went over my dream. He didn't ask questions, but made encouraging sounds as I related everything I could remember.

"Would you believe her?" I asked.

"This is a bit beside the question, isn't it? Let's take it in steps. Do you believe her?"

"I shouldn't."

He *hmmm*ed.

"I think I do. But that could just be wanting to believe her. Wanting *this* lie out of all the others to be true."

"We know he took the scissors from you and used them to free Delaney's soul."

"Yes."

"We know that in doing so he closed the vortex to the Underworld."

"Yes." It would be hard for that to have been a trick. I'd been there, and even if my heart or mind wanted to misinterpret the events, I'd seen it with my own eyes.

"He is no longer in Ordinary."

"Yes. Dragon pig confirmed. But is that enough to trust everything she said?"

"It wouldn't seem so. Your father did meet with Bathin when he was alive."

"That's true?"

He nodded and pointed with his cup. "It's in the journal."

"How long did they meet?"

He tipped his eyes to the ceiling. I knew he was accessing the collective data of all the books and works in the library. Which meant he was checking the facts in Dad's journals too. "I'd say two years at least."

"Did they meet here?" That didn't make sense. Demons wouldn't have been invited into Ordinary unless they signed the contract and vowed to follow the rules. "No, it couldn't be. Somewhere else? Outside of Ordinary?"

"Yes. He discussed it with me on several occasions."

"And...what did he think about Bathin? What did they talk about?"

"He thought highly of him. Why the surprised look? Your father was a very good judge of character. He had to be since he was the bridge before Delaney."

"He liked Bathin?"

"I believe he did. He thought Bathin was following a path most of his kind never attempt. To truly understand humans and souls in a way alien to him. To understand emotions and caring and love."

"Dad said all that?" My words came out stilted. My fingers were stiff from holding my cup too hard.

It was a lot to take in. That Bathin had done more than steal my Dad's soul. That maybe it had been part of their agreement, him keeping Dad's soul from passing into death.

That maybe Bathin didn't have all the manners and norms of being human figured out, but that he'd been trying to do so for years.

"Why wouldn't Dad tell me any of this?" I asked.

Harold pressed a finger to his lips. "I can only guess, of course. He hoped Bathin would come to an understanding of the human world. He wanted him to understand why there was a contract he must sign to enter Ordinary, and why he must follow the laws and rules while here."

"But he wasn't going to tell any of us a demon wanted to live in Ordinary?"

"He may not have thought it worth mentioning until Bathin made his decision. Perhaps now you'd like to read the marked section?"

The journal. It was right there on the oversized ottoman.

"I'll get us both some more tea." He gathered our cups and quietly left the room.

I drew the journal into my lap and brushed my palm over the cover. If there were answers, they'd be here.

I opened the book to the yellow silk ribbon tucked between two pages.

I had to blink several times to get my eyes to focus on the page. Every time I saw his handwriting, it was like a string in my heart plucked and sang out that one, sweet lonely note, echoing away and never answered.

*I'll be meeting with Bathin this evening at sunset. I can tell he thinks that makes him more mysterious, but, yeah. No. Mysterious is why my Tupperware never has matching lids, and how come the massaging chair is always too strong on my ass and not strong enough on my shoulders. If I wanted an ass massage, I could drive any coastal road after spring wash out. Demons have nothing on the mystery of why Bertie can't just leave me out of one—just one—of her community events. I swore to give my life and soul for my community, but if I have to judge one more soggy rhubarb pie...*

I grinned. I'd forgotten how much he liked to complain in his journals. He never did it in person, not around us girls. But I imagined he and his friends, mostly gods, but some humans like Hatter and Shoe, got into epic bitch sessions when they went out for beers every now and then.

*I think he's finally going to admit he wants to be a part of Ordinary. He's risking a lot to come here. The learning curve on rules and law will be steep, but I think he'll manage. It will be the beginning—the first demon to come into this land set aside and blessed by the gods. Monumental, really. I can't think of a better demon, or man, to take this plunge. Bathin is reaching for something that's been out of the grasp of demons: empathy, compassion, hope, love.*

*I think he'll find it. Faster here in Ordinary than any other place in the universe.*

*Honestly, I'm looking forward to him taking this step. I think he'll fit in just fine. I think he'll find his legs. I think he'll find his heart.*

*That's one of my favorite parts of being the one who can say yes or no to the creatures and gods who want to come here: Saying yes.*

*So, let's do this, Bathin. Let's get you to that yes. Let's get you to this new life.*

*I have a feeling once you taste it, you'll never turn back.*

*I have a feeling once you learn love, feel love, you'll do anything to keep it. Do anything to protect it.*

*I expect you to eventually become one of my most loyal friends.*

*You might even turn out to be perfect for Ordinary...especially if you take over judging that damn rhubarb contest.*

He didn't sign it with his name, he never did. He just drew a circle with two curving lines hashed across it and a star in the middle. O for Ordinary, the lines for his job as the bridge, the star for his place as Chief of Police.

I closed the journal, leaving the yellow ribbon marking the place.

Harold arrived with more tea. "I brought a few more cookies."

I took three. "Thank you. Do you know where Dad met with Bathin?"

I could thumb through the journal until I found whichever entry Dad had recorded that information into, but Harold would find it much faster.

"Down at Cape Perpetua. Cook's Chasm."

South of Ordinary by several miles, it was one of my favorite places Dad used to take us. The coastline of rugged basalt showcased three natural attractions that drew in curious sightseers.

To the north was Cook's Chasm—a deep fissure where waves bashed violently against the stones to spray upward hundreds of feet in a booming *whoosh* of salt water. To the south, Spouting Horn—a hole in the stone—blasted like a geyser at every pounding wave. In between those two sights was Thor's Well, a weird sinkhole that swallowed up incoming water and appeared to drain the ocean dry.

Thor's Well was sometimes called Hell's Gate.

So, yeah. It was a fitting place to meet a demon.

I stood and handed Harold the journal. "Thank you."

He smiled. "My pleasure, Myra. Always."

I gave him a hug, and he hugged me back, his hand a comforting weight between my shoulders.

"What will you do now?" he asked, as I stepped away and looked around for my things.

"I'm going to go talk to a friend."


THE VAMPIRE was sitting in his living room sipping a very small cup of a very dark coffee.

The lighting in the room was warm and yellow—cozy—and from the big dresser-sized record player against one wall

Ethel Waters crooned about bread and gravy and goodnight kisses.

If there were vampires in the large, sprawling house other than Leon who had answered the door and made himself scarce, they were giving Old Rossi his space.

"Myra. Come on in, have a seat." Rossi gestured to the very formal, uncomfortable-looking chair across from the curved love seat he was lounging in.

I glanced at the chair, decided it looked too much like a job interview, and took the couch next to him instead.

A smile flitted over his lips. "So this is personal business then?"

I sighed. "I'm thinking about doing something really foolish."

"You?"

Yeah, I couldn't believe it either.

"I could use someone at my side who can give me an unbiased, unvarnished opinion."

"Why me? Why not your sisters?"

"I know Jean and Delaney's opinion. They've been on me about this for over a year."

"And the gods?"

"No. This is outside of Ordinary. Gods don't leave unless they pick up their power."

"Have you no other friends?"

"I do. But I have you. And right now, I could use a vampire's—a very old vampire's—opinion."

"We aren't talking about a new tattoo are we?"

"No. We're talking about a demon."

Rossi's eye lit up, and he lifted the tiny cup, drained the dark contents, then licked the corner of his lip, erasing a stray drop that was too red to be just coffee. "I'll get my coat."

# CHAPTER 27

THE DRIVE to Cook's Chasm usually took about an hour. But it was good weather, Ordinary wasn't the only coastal town throwing some kind of shindig for tourists, and it was a Sunday evening. That meant traffic was heavier than usual.

I didn't worry though. We made it to Yachats before sunset, so I stopped off at my favorite fish and chips joint and got a snack. Then I drove to the short road that ended in a wide parking lot facing the ocean.

Rossi seemed content to sit in the car with me and watch the sun go down. Since we were outside of Ordinary, he'd donned his vampire fashion statements: a peacoat, an expensive-looking beanie, leather gloves, light scarf, and sunglasses.

He should have looked ridiculous, instead he looked like a model from a magazine explaining how to vacation in the Swiss Alps for only millions a day.

Vampires didn't burn up in sunlight, I knew that. But it wasn't exactly comfortable for them to be in full sun for long, either. Except for inside Ordinary. It was one of the reasons Rossi had come to town, stayed, and built his family.

"So." Rossi lowered his sunglasses, his shocking-blue eye gazing out over the top of them, the black patch a harsh reminder of his injuries. "How long are we going to stay here and not see Bathin?"

"We're going." I watched the cloudless sky blush bright and hard—that bright, angry slap of color slowly bruising toward purple and deep blue. "I'm just giving the tourists a little time to thin out."

He hummed and didn't call me on my lie.

Another few minutes ticked by. Maybe a half-hour. The stars were popping out above us, the lights of the little town glowing through windows behind us.

"What's the worst that can happen?" I asked.

"You could be wrong."

I nodded, chewing on my lip. "What's the best that can happen?"

"You could be wrong."

I sighed and rubbed at my eyes. "I hope you're going to give me clearer opinions once we're there."

"You want my opinion on everything I see?"

I knew better than to fall into that trap. "No. Just if I ask you something, give me two loaded barrels of truth, okay?"

"That was always the plan."

I started the car. Fiddled with the heater, turned the radio to a different station, messed with the volume.

"Maybe I should drive?" he suggested.

"No, you don't get to drive the police cruiser. I'm going. We're going."

Rossi pressed his sunglasses back up his nose and waited.

I finally shifted the car into reverse and made my way slowly, maybe a little too slowly, through the neighborhood, and back onto the highway.

It was a short drive to the pullout. A very short drive. And no matter how slowly I drove, no matter how much my palms sweated, or my heart beat like I was running instead of sitting perfectly still in a car, we were there all too quickly.

We were the only car in the long, curved pullout. The two-lane highway hissed with cars heading through the deepening night. Even with the windows closed, the sound of the ocean was everywhere.

"I'll see you down there." Rossi opened the door and strolled in front of the car to the narrow concrete sidewalk that paralleled the shore. One more step and he hopped up to stand on top of the four-foot concrete wall that was there for people to lean their elbows on while they stared at the three notable geologic sights down, down, down below.

He should not be standing there, his hands in his pockets, the last, dim, blurry light of dusk carving him a shadow against shadow.

He tipped his head, as if scenting something. I was reminded that vampires were predators, always, but here, outside Ordinary, where the idea of live-and-let-live wasn't subscribed to, even more so.

I got out of the car. If there was trouble, vampire trouble, I was going to make sure both of us got home in one piece.

"Problem?" My hand dropped to my gun.

"No vampires, if that's what you're asking." His words were teasing, but carried reproach. I knew Rossi could take care of himself. He was one of the oldest, strongest vampires on Earth.

But his injuries weren't healed yet.

Of course I worried. "How about demons?"

He shook his head. "Not that I can sense. One way to find out."

Then he jumped.

*Jumped.*

The road was built into the side of the hill, and a very nice, very easy switchback path allowed people to walk down the one-hundred-and-fifty-foot drop to the rocky outcropping where the ocean pounded and rolled.

Did Rossi walk that path? No. No he did not. He had to jump off the wall like a jerk and make me gasp before my brain kicked in.

Vampires could fly. This was nothing. This was easy. This was second nature. He wasn't a broken bloody splatter of bones and fancy winter wear down on the basalt shore.

He was, however, an asshole.

"You, sir," I called out into the blackness, "are a jerk!"

Low, infectious laughter drifted up with the crash of waves and slick of salt in the air.

Then there were no more excuses, no more waiting, no more reasons not to walk down to the shore.

"Just walk," I said quietly. "Just go down the path and settle this."

The unlit path was officially closed at dusk, but I made my way through the thin stand of trees, north, south, north, south, following the zigzag down, out of the trees, the ocean a wild thing at one side, the cliff green and wet and silent on my other. I watched my boots and took my time. The path was smooth, but it was wet from the spray.

Rossi leaned against the railed staircase that led down to the southernmost rocky flat. Walk down those steps, ramble and climb over the huge black basalt stones, teeter there on the edge, and I'd be staring straight down into a crack in the land, a canyon the ocean snarled and chewed and banged its way into, while the Cook's Chasm bridge, a lovely open-spandrel, arched above me.

Instead, I faced the ocean, the vampire to my left, Thor's Well down and out ahead of me another fifty yards of humping hillock, craggy basalt and sand, the chasm to the north of me growling away.

It was dark enough, starry enough, I couldn't make out the waves except for the luminous white of foam spraying upward, great winged owl feathers fanning the night.

The wind was steady here, not hard, just a shifting, constant movement.

I wanted to turn around and go home.

What if I was wrong?

What if I was right?

The tug in my chest was quiet. Calm. Waiting.

A line from Dad's journal flashed in my mind's eye: *Let's get you that yes.*

Maybe that was all I needed. A yes. Did he love me? Did I love him? Was this all a lie?

*Let's get you that yes.*

"Ready?" Rossi's voice was steady. Familiar as my history, my childhood. An uncle, an ally. He would be my eyes if I was lost and staring at the world through heart-colored glasses.

He had my back.

He draped his arm across my shoulder. "Do you know how to summon him?"

I shook my head. "I think he'll hear me." I stepped forward, just one, two, three steps so that I was off of the concrete pad and on the little span of grass-covered dirt and sand.

Ahead of me was another drop, this one a hill I could walk straight down, and beyond that the flat wide reach of raw basalt shelf jutting out into the ocean waves that rolled over it.

I knelt and ran my fingertips across the dirt by my boots, peering through the darkness for what I needed. My hand finally brushed a little rock, and I tucked it into my palm, and stood. I placed the stone near my heart, hoping Bathin would feel me, know I was here, waiting on the edge of this stormy dark sea.

"Bathin," I said quietly to the stone, loudly in my mind, in my heart. "We need to talk. About the scissors. About Delaney's soul. About you and me. I need to know...know you're okay. Please come here. Come talk to me."

The edges of the stone bit into the soft flesh of my palm, but I couldn't seem to stop squeezing it. There was no guarantee this would work. I wasn't going by logic or tradition or rules. There wasn't a lot of logic in this at all, just a trembling, nervous hope.

I was just a speck of light holding a microscopic stone on a tiny planet spinning through a vast and endless dark.

There was no reason for him to hear me. There was no reason for him to answer if he did. There was no reason for him to meet me here, at the edge of the world.

Minutes ticked and ticked and ticked. He did not answer.

My heartbeat, which had been fast, nervous, excited, slowed. I closed my eyes and tipped my face to the stars.

I knew what this felt like—being left behind. I understood loneliness, had become comfortable with silence. So I breathed in, and breathed out, letting the wind whisk away my hope like sifted sand.

I would be okay. I *was* okay. Whatever I felt about Bathin, that complicated mix of emotions, that love I'd fought and reasoned into submission, was not to be.

It was time to let go. I'd had my answer and it was yes.

*Yes, you should be alone.*

I stood there for an hour. I knew that because Rossi finally came up behind me and draped his arm across my shoulder again. "He's an asshole. Let's get you home. You deserve more than he can give."

I huffed out a short laugh and nodded. I was not going to cry. The tears were there, waiting, but I was scrubbed clean, empty. Free. The wind, the water, the salt, the stars, had soaked into me, scoured the tangles of my heart until the strings unwound.

I was unknotted, floating, lifted by starlight and wind.

There, above myself, in the stars, in the blackness, alone, alone, alone, I felt safe. I felt whole.

"Myra."

My heart jumped and the spell was broken. I wasn't floating, not up in that wide black sky. But I still felt clean, scrubbed, settled.

I felt new.

I tipped my head down and opened my eyes.

Bathin strode up out of the darkness of the sea like some kind of a hero of old. His dark hair was longer, his eyes wilder, and instead of an expensive suit he wore black. Black leather pants and black tunic with burnished armor flowing over the width of his shoulders and chest.

The ocean raged behind him, but that man was rage embodied.

His eyes glowed red, embers burning iron hot. He didn't stop until he was a few feet away from me, just out of reach. As if we needed that space to maneuver in case I had a knife. Or in case he did.

"Bathin," I said through lips that tingled from the cold. My breath felt too warm. My skin too hot, too tight. A shiver ran deep, deep inside me. Deeper than my muscles, deeper than my blood. Deeper than my bones.

I couldn't stop shaking.

"You're here," I said.

Those red eyes did not waver as he stared at me, his hands in loose fists at his side as if he had recently put away a weapon, his stance squared and looming.

"What are you doing outside Ordinary, Officer Reed? You know the rules of your little town don't apply here."

Old Rossi shifted behind me, and I could feel the cold burning strength of him, the promise of violence coiled and ready to strike.

I held up one hand, so Rossi would stay where he was, then I closed the distance between Bathin and me.

"I asked you to be honest with me, but you never once asked me to be honest with you. Why not?"

He blinked, and the coal-red simmered to a deep-cinnamon burn. "This is what you want to talk about?"

"Why didn't you ask me to be honest with you?"

His mouth jerked a couple times at the corner, like there were too many words and he was trying to keep back the worst of them. "Because I could see you, Myra Reed. I could always see you."

"My soul?"

"Yes. And more."

"My mind?"

"Some of it."

"My heart?"

He paused, swallowed, and said nothing.

"Could you see my heart? See how I felt?"

Still the silence.

"Can you see inside human hearts? Other hearts?" I asked.

"Yes."

"Did you look inside mine?"

"No."

That answer surprised me. "Why not?"

"It's not...Your father...No...I don't..." He seemed to realize he had said too much, even though he hadn't finished a single sentence. He shut his mouth and glowered at me again, eyes burning in the black, black night. "I am done here."

*Nownownow...*

"I'm sorry." It was out of my mouth so suddenly, so unexpectedly, even Rossi made a sound.

Bathin stilled.

I'd seen dead people, corpses, ghosts. I'd seen the undead, vampires, ghouls. So I knew stillness.

But if I weren't looking right at Bathin, if I couldn't feel the heat radiating off of his body, I wouldn't have known he was there. I would have thought I was standing next to empty air. Cold, cold wind.

"Why?" he asked, slow and low, that gaze snapping to my face.

I puzzled through his chopped off sentences and knew why he'd stopped talking so quickly.

He could see everything in me if he wanted, but my dad had taught him why that was an invasion, why that would never be allowed. And so he didn't. He hadn't. He wouldn't.

My secrets would remain mine, had remained mine the entire time he had been in Ordinary.

Because he wanted to do what was right. Wanted to do what my father had taught him. Wanted to get that yes.

"I didn't trust you," I said. "At the beginning, that made sense. But you were changing, and I kept holding up your past and seeing you as that. Only that."

He wasn't breathing. His expression was so intense, I felt my overheated skin heat even more. Could I scorch from his attention? Be burned down to cinder and ash by the sun in his eyes?

"I'm sorry I didn't see you changing. Not even when you were standing right in front of me."

He exhaled, his whole chest moving, his shoulders shifting. "And now?" He took a step toward me, just one. But it felt like he spanned a mile, a hundred miles, and was there now, right there in front of me. In my space. In my world.

*Now.*

I'd run out of air. I'd run out of words.

*Now.*

For a moment, I was lost to him. It would be easy to begin here, to start new promises.

He leaned over me. Just as I tipped my head back, my neck exposed, my pulse blowing apart at even the idea of being kissed, I said, "Why didn't you just give Delaney back her soul in the first place?"

He paused. It felt like the entire world paused. The wind, the stars, even the vampire behind me, who I thought might have snorted a short laugh, paused.

"What?" Bathin was so close his breath was hot on my mouth. The scent of him—fire and cinnamon and hot stones burning—made my knees weak.

"Delaney's soul. You could have just given it back. Then you wouldn't have had to use the scissors to stab yourself."

"We're...here. And you're still..." He grunted and rocked back on his heels. "You couldn't just let it be? We were having a moment!"

"Why are you yelling at me?"

"I'm not yelling!" he yelled.

I planted my fists on my hips and gave him an incredulous look.

The strangled sound that came out of his mouth turned into a growl, and he ran his fingers back through his hair over and over again. Then he wiped one hand down his face, and the scowl was a little less severe.

"I knew." He paused, shook his head. "Look. I was...afraid. Afraid if I released her soul, you would make me leave. You would force me out of Ordinary. You had every right to do so. Her soul was—*is*—strong. And she did give it to me willingly. In the world in which I was raised, that acceptance is everything. Means everything.

"I knew if I gave it back to her before you...before we had a chance to..." He sighed. "I was afraid. Afraid I'd lose you."

That last bit came out thick and chopped off. As if they were the hardest words he'd ever had to say.

"Was I wrong about that?" he asked.

No. He was not wrong. Forgiveness was not my strength.

"But if you'd just let her soul go..."

"Would you have seen me? Would you have spoken to me? Would you have let me get this close to you, to your life? Would you have forgiven me?"

I wanted to say yes. But he deserved more. He deserved honesty.

"I don't know. I've been angry for a long time. For how you tricked her. For how you tricked Dad. For how you tricked your way into Ordinary."

Even as I said it, I knew Dad wouldn't have been tricked by Bathin. He knew the demon, knew what he was like, what he was made of. Maybe Dad had hoped Bathin would catch his soul before he died. Maybe Dad had hoped in doing so, Bathin could finally step into Ordinary and live that new life he'd been circling for so long.

"No," I said. "I would have washed my hands of you."

He spread his hands, accepting my answer.

We stood watching each other, letting that truth settle between us. Letting that truth shape our way forward.

Was I happy he had taken my sister's soul and held it long enough he'd damaged it?

Hell, no.

Could I forgive him for that mistake? For trying to navigate the human world with limited understanding? For doing the wrong thing while he strived to be something better?

That—making a mistake while hoping to learn how not to make a mistake—was a very human failing.

And forgiveness was a very human strength.

"I know I fucked up," he said. "I should have given her soul back months ago. But I couldn't seem to find the right way, and you were always fighting with me—which I liked, so that was confusing, but nice—and I didn't want that to change.

"I was wrong to take her soul. I know that now. Holding your father's soul changed me. Holding Delaney's?" He blew out air. "Nail in the coffin."

"And the scissors?" I asked.

"Taking them away from you meant you could never be harmed by them. It would keep Ordinary safe. It would release Delaney's soul. I had to."

"We always have choices. There is always a choice," I said.

"I chose. I chose you. Myra, I will always choose you."

I leaned up and caught his mouth in a kiss.

He grunted, surprised. For a moment, he was back to that stillness, that totality of silence.

Had I made a mistake? Had I misunderstood what we were doing here?

Then he groaned and his arms locked against my back, one hand cupping my head because he was a big guy and I was not all that tall. One massive leg shifted so that I was pulled even tighter against his body, balancing on my tiptoes, straining and tight with delicious stretch, while safe and solid against his chest, between his legs, with his hands holding, searching, needing.

And the kiss. He may have been the first to groan, but I wasn't far behind him, lost in the zinging fire that licked luxurious waves through my body.

*This, this, this. Here. Now. Now.*

My mind chanted while my heart thrummed just one word: *Yes.*

When we pulled back, it was barely an inch, as if neither of us were ready to break this connection, to shatter the perfection and wonder of the moment.

The slow-clapping vampire behind us did it instead.

"You two kids are just adorable," he crooned.

I freed one hand and flipped him off behind my back.

"You'll have to sign a contract," I said to Bathin, searching his face, his eyes. "That you'll follow the rules of Ordinary."

"I will. I will follow the rules of Ordinary."

"You can't possess souls."

He nodded. His thumb stroked the side of my face as if he were amazed I was standing here. Offering him this. Offering him us.

"I won't possess souls."

"Your mother is not allowed to visit unless she signs the contract too."

"Yeah, she can go to Hell. And stay there this time." He leaned, kissed me again, a nibble, a bite, and then another kiss, deeper, warmer.

There were more things I needed to tell him. More rules he would need to follow. Promises he would have to make. But suddenly none of them seemed important.

All that mattered was him, me, here, now. All that mattered was…

*Yes.*

# ACKNOWLEDGMENT

ORDINARY, OREGON has a special place in my heart, even if it is (mostly) an imaginary town. Each time I write a story set in Ordinary, it's like a strange little treasure hunt. But instead of digging for gold and jewels, I uncover weird, ridiculous things about the people, monsters, and gods wandering about the place. Not gonna lie. I laughed a lot writing this one.

However, Ordinary wouldn't be nearly as fun without the wonderful people who help make it shine. Thank you to artist Lou Harper at Cover Affairs for making Myra so sassy. That pink unicorn? Mwah! Thank you also to Dejsha Knight for her resoundingly quick beta read and fantastic suggestions. You're the best! I am eternally grateful to Sharon Elaine Thompson for her speedy, thorough editing, and to Eileen Hicks, for her eagle eyed proofreading, and Skyla Dawn Cameron for her fabulous formatting.

To my husband, Russ Monk, and my sons, Kameron Monk and Konner Monk, thank you for being the best part of my life, even when I do talk your ears off about taglines and logo designs. I love you.

And to you, dear reader. Thank you for taking one more trip to this sleepy little beach town. I hope you come back soon to put your toes in the waves, fly a kite on the breeze, or go for a long, sandy walk with a god or two. Just remember to ignore that "bear". Because it is absolutely, positively not Bigfoot.

# ABOUT THE AUTHOR

DEVON MONK is a national bestselling writer of urban fantasy. Her series include West Hell Magic, Ordinary Magic, House Immortal, Allie Beckstrom, Broken Magic, and Shame and Terric. She also writes the Age of Steam steampunk series, and the occasional short story which can be found in her collection: A Cup of Normal, and in various anthologies. She has one husband, two sons, and lives in lovely, rainy Oregon. When not writing, Devon is drinking too much coffee, watching hockey, or knitting silly things.

**Want to read more from Devon?**
Follow her online or sign up for her newsletter at:
www.devonmonk.com

# ALSO BY DEVON MONK

Age of Steam:
*Dead Iron*
*Tin Swift*
*Cold Copper*
*Hang Fire (short story)*

Short Fiction:
*A Cup of Normal (collection)*
*Yarrow, Sturdy and Bright  (Once Upon a Curse anthology)*
*A Small Magic (Once Upon a Kiss)*

CPSIA information can be obtained
at www.ICGtesting.com
Printed in the USA
LVHW031522260919
632369LV00003B/564/P

9 781939 853172